Praise for
THE FINAL PROCEDURE

"A lethal prescription for a stay-up-all-night read."
—*Publishers Weekly*

"By the time you've finished reading, you'll be convinced this isn't just great suspense, but a kind of mind terror you can't forget." —*New York Times* bestselling author Nelson DeMille

"An unstoppable ride with hairpin twists and turns. This is the best book yet from a master who truly knows how to thrill."
—*New York Times* bestselling author Tess Gerritsen

"Pottinger mixes a healthy brew of science, suspense, and just plain menace in this, his third novel. A former district attorney in Washington, he combines a feel for how federal law enforcement works with a powerful style of storytelling."
—*Houston Chronicle*

"Settle in where you like to read, throw a blanket over your lap, and prepare for a sleepless night. Adalwolf is a villain for the ages. There are moments when he makes Hannibal Lecter look like the Easter Bunny."
—*New York Times* bestselling author Michael Palmer

"The disturbing thing about this novel is its chilling demonstration of how future advances that will save us from many genetic and infectious diseases have the inevitable potential to be used by 'bad' scientists. To me, it's the possible reality of schemes like Adalwolf's that is scarier than the fiction." —C.J. Peters, M.D., Director for Biodefense, University of Texas Medical Branch

MORE…

A SLOW BURNING

"Ingenious." —*Time*

"A new generation of cutting-edge thriller."
—*Entertainment Weekly*

"Pottinger proves he is a master of the art of the medical thriller and a formidable voice in examining American race relations. . . . this kaleidoscopic thriller is marvelously complex, charged with emotional impact and resounding ethical questions." —*Publishers Weekly*

"*A Slow Burning* is a shake, rattle, and roll dance with danger. The plot is a lightning jolt of tension."
—Lorenzo Carcaterra

"Steadily build[s] tension in every subplot. That means once you're fifty pages in, don't expect to put this one down… a quickly burning fire of a story that you won't be able to extinguish until the last page." —*New York Post*

THE FOURTH PROCEDURE

"Harrowing." —*New York Newsday*

"The breakneck momentum will keep the pages turning."
—*Elle*

"A chilling medical thriller." —*Vanity Fair*

"Impossible to put down." —*Chicago Tribune*

"A mind-boggling medical thriller." —*Kirkus Reviews*

Also by
STAN POTTINGER

The Last Nazi
(in paperback as *The Final Procedure*)

A Slow Burning

The Fourth Procedure

THE BOSS

STAN POTTINGER

St. Martin's Paperbacks

This is a work of fiction. All of the characters, organizations, and events portrayed in this novel are either products of the author's imagination or are used fictitiously.

First published in Great Britain by Hodder and Stoughton, a division of Hodder Headline.

THE BOSS

Cover photography by Getty Images.

For information address St. Martin's Press, 175 Fifth Avenue, New York, NY 10010.

Library of Congress Catalog Card Number 2006050614

ISBN: 0-312-94534-5
EAN: 978-0-312-94534-3

Printed in the United States of America

St. Martin's Press hardcover edition / December 2006
St. Martin's Paperbacks edition / November 2008

St. Martin's Paperbacks are published by St. Martin's Press, 175 Fifth Avenue, New York, NY 10010.

10 9 8 7 6 5 4 3 2 1

For Matthew, a gift to the family

SIXTEEN YEARS AGO

THE SMELL OF WATERMELON, dead fish, and oil told me we were getting close to the Galveston harbor. I'd been up since five, pulled on my jeans and boots, fed the dog, downed a quick bowl of cereal, and was ready to go before Dad and my older brother, Will, even got to the kitchen. It was the end of June, school was out, and I was driving us to a boat that would take us to a drilling platform out in the Gulf of Mexico.

Crossing the bridge to the docks, I saw seagulls flying around huge cranes, rusty barges, and enormous jack-up rigs that looked like giant Erector sets poking out of the sea. This is Texas, where oil, money, and egos are as big as they say they are, at least in the oal'n-gaz bidness.

"Turn right at the stop sign," my dad said.

My name is Max McLennon, and I turned sixteen last week and got my driver's license yesterday. My family's been working for oil companies for three generations, all the way back to the days of Henry Ford. When I graduate from high school, I plan to go into the business myself.

I pulled up to the stop sign, looked both ways, and turned left. "Hey, little brother," Will said, and didn't need to say more. I stopped the car, made a U-turn, and headed back to the right, where Dad had told me to go. Right, left—sometimes I get them confused.

I pulled into a parking lot, locked up the car, and followed Dad and Will onto a service boat that would take us out to sea. Three hours later, a drilling platform called Wild Stallion—a semisubmersible sitting in two thousand feet of water—loomed on the horizon like a city in the middle of the ocean. It had a main deck over a hundred feet high, and above that, towering cranes and stacks of drill pipe. No matter how many times you saw one of these things, their size still knocked you out.

The ocean swells were too big for us tie up, so we used a "swing line"—a rope like Tarzan's vine—to get from the boat to the platform. From there we took an elevator twelve stories up to the main deck where some roughnecks welcomed us aboard. I like the name "roughneck." I like putting on boots, leather gloves, and a hard hat and spending a day working with the guys who do the tough, dirty job of drilling for oil.

I get to do this because my dad's a drilling rig supervisor for Gulf-Tex Oil and Gas. He's a cool head in the middle of a dangerous business, and the men rely on him to keep them out of trouble.

My brother Will is a rookie roughneck everybody says will someday be as good as Dad. He's a nice guy with a good attitude, washboard abs, and a handsome, tan face that makes him popular with the girls. I'd say Dad's my hero because he takes care of the family, but I'd say Will is cool. I take the same courses in school he took, play the same sports, lift the same weights, and listen to the same Bruce Springsteen albums. I make no bones about wanting to be like him.

After giving us their how-dos, the men went back to work "turning right," which means drilling into the ground at the bottom of the sea. In the on-deck control room—a rebuilt construction trailer called a doghouse—you could see the charts and computerized pictures of the oil field they were aiming for, a deposit about ten thousand feet below seabed.

At least, that's what they hoped was there. According to Dad, there's a small glitch in the oil industry that has never really been solved: how to find oil. Engineers and drillers have various ways of trying, but none of them's foolproof. The best of the bunch—sound waves—can tell you where to find liquid, but can't always tell you whether it's oil or water. Until somebody invents a pair of eyes that can "see" under the ground, drilling for oil will always be a Las Vegas–sized gamble. But that's another thing I like about this business. It's sink or swim. Make it big or not at all. You have to have the stomach for it or you won't survive. For some reason, that works for me.

I stood on a raised metal grating coiling up the heavy chains they use to set drill pipe. Even with noise protectors on my ears, the decibel level of the diesel engines was shouting-loud. It didn't seem to bother the roughnecks though. They communicated with hand signals when they had to. Some of the signals were easy to figure, like a circle to rev it up, and some weren't, but the roughnecks knew them all. They had to. Their lives depended on it.

I looked up and saw a helicopter settling onto a landing pad above my head, its high-pitched engine screaming like trumpets introducing the boss himself.

THE CHOPPER'S SKIDS HADN'T hardly touched down when out stepped Jack Patterson, better known as Spin, the thirty-eight-year-old CEO of Gulf-Tex Oil. With him was Joe Wright, his chief engineer, and Bud Hightower, the sixty-five-year-old founder of Gulf-Tex, who was chairman of the company and its biggest shareholder. He also happened to be Spin's father-in-law, considering Spin had married Audrey Hightower when they'd graduated from college.

Mr. Hightower was lean and tall with a gray buzz cut and weathered skin and a cigarette that never fell out of his mouth. If he'd had a cowboy hat on, he would have been the Marlboro man. Joe Wright, the chief engineer, wore glasses and a baggy jumpsuit, a bit of a geek but smart as a fox.

Spin was another story. He was rich, powerful, and good-looking, the kind of big dog all the other dogs wanted to run with. He had on this dark suit and a silver hard hat with the Gulf-Tex logo on it, but underneath the glitz he was a regular guy who was comfortable shooting the breeze with the roughnecks and getting a feel for what was really going on. According to Dad, Spin's biggest problem is trimming the company's fat by getting rid of old rigs, obsolete machinery, and things they don't need.

Even though Spin was young and married to the boss's daughter, everybody respected him because he'd come up the hard way. First he was a roughneck, then a wildcatter, then he was head of a drilling service company in Corpus. Dad said he'd taken over Gulf-Tex when it was about to go bankrupt and in only three years turned it around. Will said he was a man with vision who understood that the only way to find oil was with modern technology. Apparently that's why he'd hired Joe Wright, this genius engineer from the University of Texas.

Spin led the way down the metal steps to the landing where I was standing. When his helicopter shut down the engines, I lifted off my ear protectors and waited for him to come by. The minute he saw me, he smiled and stuck out his hand.

"Hey, Max, what brings you out here?" he shouted.

"It's June, Mr. Patterson, school's out," I yelled. "It's my chance to be a roughneck."

He pulled the strap under my hard hat and hit the top. "Keep that thing on tight, OK?" He started to leave, then stopped and looked at me. "You know what?" he said after thinking it over. "Why don't you climb up to the crane cab and watch from up there? You'll get a view of everything and Puck can explain what's going on."

He lifted his walkie-talkie, hit the transmit button, and told the crane operator, Puck Tarver, I was coming up. I don't think Puck liked the idea at first, because Spin turned away to talk to him in private, but after that, he smiled at me and pointed at the steel ladder leading six stories up to the control cab. I waved at him, grabbed my ear protectors, and went for the ladder while Spin and Mr. Hightower walked down the metal steps to the main deck.

By the time I'd reached the cab it felt like I'd climbed up a circus ladder to a high-wire platform. I opened the door, entered, and sat in the chair behind Puck, who got his nickname because he'd played semipro hockey. He was wearing a hard hat, earphones with a microphone curled in front of his mouth, and dark sunglasses, and he was busy raising a heavy, new Caterpillar diesel engine from a seagoing barge up to the main deck of the platform. I watched him operate the crane controls—the joysticks, foot pedals, and buttons—while he talked to the guys on the deck below. I was curious about which levers took the crane hook in which direction, but I didn't interrupt to ask.

There was an extra headset on the control panel, so I picked it up and put it over my head and listened as Puck and a roughneck guiding the payload into position talked to each other. I recognized the other voice instantly: It was my brother Will's. I looked down and saw him standing next to an empty mud pit—a shallow well on the deck where they were going to store the engine—waiting for the crane to bring the engine to him.

Looking at the other side of the deck, I saw Spin, Joe, and Mr. Hightower greet my dad with handshakes and shouts over the noise, then I saw Spin and Mr. Hightower walk to the railing on the far side of the platform and look down at a fuel-boat delivery hose that was being lifted by a small crane. When it got up to the deck, a couple of roughnecks with goggles and gloves grabbed it and guided its nozzle into a metal coupling, and a few minutes later the hose swelled up with diesel fuel that was being pumped into a huge tank on the deck. Diesel oil's critical on a drilling platform because it runs all the engines, generators, and pumps you need to produce a field. It seemed kind of ironic to me, all that oil being burned to find more oil.

Back on the near side of the platform, the Caterpillar engine dangled a few feet above the deck. Puck talked into his mike—didn't get an answer from Will—asked Will if he could hear him—then repeated himself but still got no answer.

He tapped the mike with his finger, cussed when it didn't work, and pulled a plastic pill case out of his breast pocket. He opened it and fished out a couple of white pills and said, "Excedrin?" to me, holding three in his hand. When I shook my head no, he put the case back into his pocket and held on to the pills.

I could hear him talking into the mike, but I heard no answer in my headset from Will or anyone else on the deck. Evidently the intercom was busted. How they could put a man on the moon but couldn't get an intercom to work was a mystery to me, but it happened all the time.

I saw Puck change channels from number two to number three on his headset and say, "My reception's out, Spin. Can't hear Will on channel two, and I can't hear you on channel three. Can you hear me? If you can, give me a hand signal!"

I saw Spin wave to Puck saying yes, he could hear.

Puck cupped his hand around his mike and talked into it so he didn't have to yell at Spin over the cab noise. I couldn't hear what he said, but apparently he and Spin got their hand signals worked out. Puck popped the three Excedrin pills into his mouth, chewed them up without water, and worked the joystick. A second later, the Caterpillar engine began moving across the deck toward the mud pit.

That's when it happened.

PUCK LOOKED OVER AT ME with his mouth open in surprise.

"What's wrong?" I said.

His face turned red like he was doing sit-ups—his hands rose to his throat—and he pitched forward against the glass window, knocking his hard hat to the floor.

"Puck!"

I got out of my chair and leaned over him. His cheek was pushed up against the glass, his eyes were half-open, and his skin was sweaty.

I looked down and saw the diesel engine swinging across the deck a few feet above the surface. I hit the transmit button on my mike. "Puck's passed out!" I yelled. Channel two: "Will?" No answer. Channel three: "Can anybody hear me down there? Puck's passed out!" I tried talking on "All Channels," but nobody answered. As I found out later, they could hear me but I couldn't hear them.

Will and the roughnecks looked up at me. I pointed at Puck collapsed against the window—yelled into my mike again—"Puck's out!"—and threw my hands high into the air—*What should I do?*

The two-ton diesel engine was approaching the mud pit, but when the roughnecks raised their hands to stop it, its weight was too much and it sailed by. They looked up at me: *What's happening up there?*

I looked at the control panel. The joystick had arrows pointing in four directions—north, east, south, and west—but

I couldn't tell what they meant when it came to understanding the direction of the swinging payload.

I started talking to myself. "If I push it forward, which way will it go?" I could see an arrow pointing forward but I didn't know if that meant "up" or "down." Same for right and left. Fuckin' dyslexia. When I played quarterback, my center had to touch his right or left knee just to make sure I knew which way the play was going.

I wiped away the sweat dripping off the end of my nose and looked down at the deck. Everything was happening fast: The diesel engine was headed for the edge of the platform—Will was drawing his hand across his neck telling me to cut the engine—I looked for the ignition switch but couldn't find it—the payload kept moving.

It was headed right at Mr. Hightower, who was leaning over the railing looking down at the fuel boat.

I saw men cup their hands at their mouths and yell at him.

I grabbed the joystick and pushed it to the side, hoping for the best. The engine started moving left.

Too late.

It hit Mr. Hightower just as he was turning to see what they were yelling about, lifted him off his feet, and knocked him over the railing.

Oh, Jesus.

The engine continued swinging out over the sea. I saw my dad run over to see where Mr. Hightower had fallen and look down. The engine swung out over the water as far as it could go, like a kid on swing, and started back. Men were pointing and running everywhere.

The Caterpillar engine picked up speed and headed back across the deck toward the mud pit. I stared at the arrows and told myself to figure it out, but I couldn't. I looked out the window and saw the engine heading toward the fuel tank next to the mud pit.

That would be a disaster.

Blinking away sweat, I grabbed the joystick and started to

pull it back—would that lift it or drop it?—I wanted to lift it—get it to clear the fuel tank—pulling back would drop it, right?—so pushing it forward would lift it!

I pushed the stick forward but it didn't lift. Instead, the engine dropped to the deck, hit a steel bin that held drill pipes, spilling them like Pick Up sticks, then spun around and dropped onto the deck and rolled, cutting the diesel fuel hose in two and knocking one of the roughnecks and some equipment into the mud pit.

The engine fell into the mud pit on top of the roughneck.

The severed fuel hose rose up in the air like a cobra and lashed back and forth spewing diesel fuel, then flopped onto the deck and continued gushing. Some of the men were running toward the roughneck in the pit.

The door to the cab opened and a roughneck came running in, pushed me aside, and worked the joystick and some other controls.

I felt like I'd left my own body. It was all my fault.

I pushed open the cab door, swung around a metal pole, found the top rung of the ladder beneath my foot, and started climbing down. When I got to the deck, I ran toward the mud pit, which was the size of a living room sunk five feet into the deck. I could see the roughneck pinned against the wall by the engine. Was he dead? No, but his face was red with pain.

It was my brother, Will.

Good God, what have I done?

SIXTEEN YEARS LATER

THE PRESENT

I SHOULD HAVE BEEN PAYING attention to what was going on in the meeting, but I couldn't take my eyes off her neck.

Tacoma and I were an audience of two sitting in club chairs listening to our boss, Spin Patterson, practice a speech he'd be giving in a couple of weeks to a group at the United Nations. At the moment, his shirtsleeves were rolled up, his bow tie was loosened, and a Jack-and-water was within reach, but come the day of the speech he'd be the elegant, dynamic, highly respected CEO of Gulf-Tex Oil who'd have everyone's undivided attention. Which was good, because what he had to say stood a good chance of turning the oil industry into a world-class engine of peace, win him a Nobel Prize, and make all of us very rich. Everything was riding on his words, including my career, and yet here I was staring at Tacoma's neck.

The object of my affection was thirty-one-year-old Tacoma Reed, a colleague of mine here at Gulf-Tex who serves as Spin's in-house counsel while I serve as his thirty-two-year-old vice president for special projects. That's a fancy title for right-hand man and chief bottle-washer, but it's not the title that matters, it's what I do. My proximity to the throne gives me the opportunity of a lifetime.

I love this job. And I love my boss. For better or worse—and it's usually worse—I also love Tacoma. Her neck would have been beautiful enough as a piece of Michelangelo's marble, but in real life it was more than that. You can see her breathing there. Imagine her pulse. See it as the bridge between her face and her body. She was wearing a beautiful white dress—after practicing the speech, we were all going to the company Christmas party at one of Houston's finer country clubs—and it revealed just enough of her elegant figure to fuel a not-so-elegant lust in my heart. I wanted her so much I would have taken her to the opera.

I got up from my chair while Spin spoke about changing the world with the biggest invention since the steam engine, then I walked over to Tacoma, ran my fingers up the nape of her neck into her coal black hair, pulled her head back, and kissed the hollow of her neck . . .

"Max? Hello?" Spin's voice snapped me out of my fantasy.

"Yes, boss," I said. "I'm listening."

"If this speech is boring you," he said, "keep in mind that you wrote it."

Tacoma flashed a gotcha smile at me from across the coffee table. She knew I was daydreaming about her, I have a bad poker face. I gave her eye daggers in return. She and I have this friendly—well, mostly friendly—professional competition that is complicated by tormented personal feelings. Mine, not hers. We're sort of like Romeo and Juliet except she refuses to be Juliet. If I were Romeo with any brains, I'd remember how that story ends, but love isn't just blind, it's stupid.

"Speaking as an American," Spin read from his speech, "I find it outrageous that every time I fill up my gas tank I'm helping the terrorists who want to destroy my family and country."

"Give it more from the gut, Spin," I said. "You're gonna be a rock star up there, don't be afraid to act like one."

He took a sip of bourbon, mumbled something about Mick Jagger, and read the draft in silence. At fifty-three he was as charismatic as anybody you could find—handsome without being pretty, intelligent but with a common touch—a sophisticated Texan as prime as a perfectly aged sirloin steak.

"Yadda, yadda, yadda," he said, turning pages to the end. "When I'm done, the lights dim and the screen behind me gives them the video show, right?"

"Right," I said. "After that, it's Q and A with the press and members of the audience." The room at the UN would be filled with oil company executives, petroleum explorers, ambassadors, and reporters from all over the world.

"I think the speech should be shorter," Tacoma said.

"I've already cut it twice," I said.

"Maybe you should cut it again."

"Maybe he should stand there and say nothing?"

She gave me her Mona Lisa smile—*Maybe he should*—then turned to Spin and said, "What are you planning to wear?"

"What do you suggest?" he said.

"A midnight blue Armani with a blue silk tie," she said.

"Not too bright," I said. "It shouldn't compete with the message."

"But it shouldn't be funereal," Tacoma said.

"Did I say funereal?"

"In so many words." Delivered with another sultry, half-lidded smile.

They say people have bad dreams about the people they love because of a deep-seated fear they'll lose them. Me, I get wide-awake, flirtatious insults from someone unattainable. I know, I know. I can't help myself any more than Romeo could.

Spin gathered up the draft and sat on the sofa next to our chairs. His black tie hung loosely around his unbuttoned collar and the studs on his French cuffs sparkled. Tacoma lifted a remote control from the glass coffee table, lowered the room's lights, and opened the vertical blinds, giving us the Houston skyline.

Spin said, "If everything goes right, two weeks from now nothing will be the same—not for Gulf-Tex, the three of us, or the rest of the world. Here's to Black Eyes."

Black Eyes was the code name of the company's new deep-earth sonar technology Spin had spent years developing and would soon unveil to the world. If it worked as advertised, it would be able to find oil and hydrocarbons in new places all over the globe, far beneath countries that, possessing no petroleum of their own, were hostages to the few that did.

We drank to Black Eyes, then Spin checked his Rolex and

said, "Time to go, Audrey will be downstairs in the car and I don't want to keep her waiting." He stood and pulled on his tux jacket, then reached out and grabbed my arm and squeezed. "It's a good speech, Max. I only wish he could have been here to hear it."

He didn't have to say who "he" was. We both knew. There was a picture of him right there on the wall.

Spin let go and patted me once. "Can we give you guys a lift?" he said, walking to a mirror on the back of a closet door to tie his bow tie.

"We've got a car, thanks," I said. I escort Tacoma to this party each year. Notice I didn't say "date" her, just "escort" her.

Tacoma said to Spin, "We'll see you at the party," then to me, "I'm going to the ladies' room, be right back," and went out the door.

Sitting there alone, toying with my glass of Scotch, I looked at that picture hanging on Spin's wall. It was a black-and-white photograph of the four of us—my brother Will, my dad, Spin, and me—standing on Wild Stallion, hard hats off, goggles down, leather gloves in hand, squinting into the sun and smiling as if we owned the future. It was a year before the accident, at a time when we were fearless and full of life and the thought of disaster never entered our minds.

"I only wish he could have been here to hear it."

It came rushing back like it was yesterday.

WILL'S LEG WAS PINNED AGAINST the wall of the pit by a broken steel rod on the diesel engine. The men had thrown off their noise protectors and were kneeling around the edge of the crater to help get him out. The engines on the rig began shutting down and the deck turned quiet enough you could hear people talk. The hook on the crane line was still trapped under the engine, which was on its side.

My dad yelled at Will to hold on.

Out on the deck, a bunch of roughnecks tried to get control of the spewing fuel hose. One of them ran to the edge of the platform and signaled down to the boat captain to stop pumping, but for some reason, the fuel kept shooting out.

My father jumped into the hole to check on Will. Spin and Joe Wright joined the roughnecks ringing the pit. After a few minutes, Spin received a message on his headset and his face went kind of white. He looked at my dad and shook his head. They'd found Mr. Hightower's body floating face-down in the sea.

I told myself none of this was my fault, but of course I didn't believe it.

Will was propped up on his elbows looking at his foot. As I positioned myself to see him better, I saw something else that spelled trouble.

"Mr. Patterson!" I yelled at Spin. "Look!"

He looked and his face froze. Diesel fuel was rolling across the deck toward us. The surface wasn't exactly level, and I guess we were on the downhill side. Spin ran toward the men who were fighting the severed hose.

"Dad!" I said. "Fuel's coming!"

His eyes turned to the platform as the first trickle spilled over the edge and dropped onto the floor at his feet. He gave me a worried look I'd never seen before, then said to one of the men, "Get a pneumatic jack," and went back to work on Will's foot. I couldn't believe how calm he was. The rest of us were pretty much terrified.

So was Will. At the first smell of fuel he backed up against the wall like a bird in a cage. A moment later the fluid oozed against his waist and elbows. A second later a roughneck appeared with two fire extinguishers, pulled the safety pins, and laid a blanket of foam on the floor around Will's body. But the fuel kept spilling in, and it wasn't a dribble.

Spin was on his headset talking to the man who'd climbed up to the crane cab to help Puck and operate the hoist. He told two of the men to get down in the pit and try to free the hook from under the Caterpillar engine and told the man in the cab to get ready to lift it off with the crane.

The men on deck were trying to stop the flow of fuel using boards and pipes and anything they could find to make a dam. I ran over and helped them, but it was like telling the Mississippi to go back. One of the men yelled at me to take another fire extinguisher to the pit, so I did.

Lying in a pool about three inches deep, Will tried to yank his foot loose but it held fast and his hands slipped in the goo. Dad leaned over to him, put his hand behind his neck, and said something that calmed him down. After that, Dad straightened up and yelled, "Where's that jack?"

Somebody came over with it and lowered it into the well and tried to position it against the steel rod, but they couldn't fit it in right.

Come on, Will, pull your leg free or you're gonna drown.

The sound of the crane engine revved up. I looked up and saw Spin motioning to the operator to raise the hook and lift the Caterpillar engine off Will's shin. The cable line went taught, and there was the sound of metal against metal, but the instant the Caterpillar engine started moving, Will yelled out in pain.

"Stop!" Dad yelled. "We're crushing his leg!"

Spin made some hand gestures and the crane operator stopped and eased the line.

I set down the extinguisher and licked my lips. I remembered seeing a gas-driven chain saw they used to cut timber with, so I ran over to the equipment room, picked it up, and brought it back.

"Cut the rod!" I said holding it out to Dad.

"Can't," he yelled. "Sparks." Even with the protective foam, he was afraid they'd ignite the diesel fuel like a pan of hot grease.

There was blood running down Will's leg into his torn pants. Dad and another guy were using a huge crowbar to force the rod away from the wall without smashing Will's leg.

"It's moving!" one of the men yelled.

That was the good news.

Then came the bad.

It was a single word yelled by one of the roughnecks, the worst word you could possibly imagine.

He yelled, "Fire!"

"FIRE! FIRE! FIRE!"

I looked over and saw yellow flames and black smoke spreading in our direction.

Some of the men helping Dad got up and ran toward it. More extinguishers roared out white foam. The flames stopped for a minute, then kept coming. Men beat at the licks with jackets and canvas tool bags, but it didn't help. Burning metal stank up the air with the smell of a shorted-out light socket.

I lay on my stomach at the edge of the pit, took off my gloves, and reached down for Will's hand. Spin looked at the fire and yelled at my Dad.

Dad heard him but didn't even look up. He calmly tore Will's pant leg up to his knee.

Spin looked at the approaching flames and said, "Sam, for God's sake!"

The flames were about a front yard away.

Spin got on his knees and joined the men who were pushing back the fuel with boards and shovels trying to keep it out of the pit.

I couldn't see how my brother was going to get out of this. I felt trapped myself. My heart was pounding out of my chest.

Dad picked up the chain saw and pulled the starter cord, and I thought, what the hell is he doing? The second it touches steel the fuel's gonna ignite.

I didn't get it, but Will did. He reached up, gave his hands to Spin and the roughnecks on the edge of the pit, and closed his eyes. The chain saw revved up the way it does when it's about to cut a tree limb, and that's when I realized Dad wasn't going to cut the metal rod.

"No!" I yelled, and jumped down into the pit next to Will.

Dad reached out and slapped my face to bring me to my senses. He'd never hit me before and it felt unreal. Two roughnecks grabbed my arms and yanked me out of the pit.

Then Dad lowered the saw.

Will screamed as a pink mist rose in the air. My face was tingling from what I saw.

The flames crept over the side.

Spin and the roughnecks yanked Will out of the hole.

The flames whooshed up from the floor of the pit.

After that, my memory gets a little fuzzy. I remember men yelling and shooting tons of white foam on Dad and throwing a canvas tarpaulin over him before pulling him out. I remember voices talking to him, and I remember Will lying on his back yelling for Dad and trying to crawl over to him. I remember pushing my way through the guys to get to Dad. I remember wanting to make sure he was going to be OK, and wanting to tell him I was sorry I'd tried to stop him from cutting Will loose, I knew why he'd slapped me, it was a good thing he did, I could have screwed everything up even more than I had.

After that, I don't remember much at all. I know I was too stunned to cry, and so was Will.

I guess we were saving that for the funeral.

Over time, Spin had become the hero I'd lost with my dad and the idol I'd lost with my brother. With his foot amputated, Will never worked as a roughneck again. He lost the swagger that had made him everybody's favorite and put on weight, drank too much, and turned kinda bitter. He was the family's chief provider, which he managed with his disability insurance, dad's wrongful-death insurance, and a private settlement with Gulf-Tex that remains confidential to this day. Once I got to law school, I assumed Spin had engineered an unusually large settlement from Gulf-Tex and didn't want people with a jealous streak to know. Anyway, there was no reason for me to get nosy about it.

For a while, Spin kept Will on the company payroll to do odd jobs here and there—he walked with his prosthesis so well you wouldn't know he had one—but in time he stopped working altogether. Photography, a solitary endeavor, suited him fine and became his only interest. The girls who'd once melted in his arms now simply melted away. He never married.

The door opened and Tacoma came back into the room. "Ready?" she said.

"Ready."

I took a last sip of Scotch, got up, and walked to Spin's mirror where I fixed my tie, combed my hair, and practiced my smile. The accident at Wild Stallion had been sixteen years ago, but when it appeared on my mental horizon, my bravado and self-confidence dropped away like a mask off a trick-or-treater. And I didn't like what I saw.

LONG BEFORE MAX AND TACOMA arrived at the country club, the band had been playing and people were dancing and having a good time, but Audrey Hightower Patterson, the party's hostess, didn't notice. She was watching her husband, Spin—as trim and handsome as a movie star—regale friends with one of his oil-patch war stories.

It was only five days to Christmas, but more important, it was their twenty-fifth wedding anniversary, and that was an occasion for reflection. Standing there, she summed him up with the clarity of the six-carat diamond he'd put on her finger: He was powerful and respected, inventive and rich, a loving father and good in bed. If she was honest about it—and Audrey was honest about everything—she was as smitten by him now as she'd been the day they'd met.

She turned away and crossed the dance floor, smiling at guests the way a seasoned hostess does, making everyone feel comfortable and welcome. The ballroom was studded with Valentinos and Armanis, beautiful smiles, sparkling champagne, and more diamonds than Harry Winston had in his showcase. She was a Texas redhead born into wealth and power, a sophisticated, headstrong woman who'd always lived by the first rule of public life: never explain and never complain. She showed no sign of the trouble that was brewing beneath the surface, but she knew that before the night was over, everything would change and never be the same again.

Looking at the faces of the older men in the crowd, she thought about the company's first Christmas party years before. Like all the others, it had been held here at Houston's Oak Creek Country Club and had included everyone who was anyone in the oil patch: CEOs, corporate lawyers, investment bankers, executives. Those were in the days before the Enron scandal, when their top executives were still acceptable company. No more. The last time one of them had showed up, a shareholder had threatened to lay a bottle of merlot on his head.

Like all oil companies, Gulf-Tex suffered from a highly volatile market, but at least the company didn't have fraud and bankruptcy to contend with. With Spin Patterson in charge, it was in the hands of a brilliant CEO who was respected by oilmen, politicians, the press, and Wall Street. And now he stood on the brink of announcing one of the most dramatic developments in the world of energy since the gusher at Spindletop.

That first company party had been held forty-four years earlier when Audrey was six years old and wore crinolines and danced on her father's shoes. She'd sipped her first Shirley Temple from a champagne glass that night, compliments of her dad.

Tonight it was straight bourbon and she wasn't anyone's daughter.

She walked through the crowd smiling and thinking she'd gladly trade in her Manolo Blahniks for a pair of Mary Janes and one more turn in her father's arms. She missed him, and never more than tonight.

Spin had grown up dirt-poor and fatherless with a religious mother who'd made ends meet working in a church basement in Corpus Christi. When Audrey had decided to marry him, she'd worried that her dad wouldn't approve, but he'd said Spin's hardscrabble background was a plus in the oil business, executives with financial brilliance were easy to find but men with street smarts and a common touch were rare. It had been twenty-five years of a good marriage ever since.

They'd met at the University of Texas, where he'd had a reputation as a lady-killer, but that didn't bother her because she had certain assets of her own: intelligence and charm, a big Texas name, a sizable chunk of Gulf-Tex stock, and a great pair of legs. With her father looking for a candidate to succeed him as CEO of Gulf-Tex, she thought she and Spin would make an unbeatable pair. And she was right. Before long, she was enjoying his kisses and breakfasts of huevos rancheros.

Spin joined the company before they got married and quickly established himself as a rising star. When her father had a heart attack on a land rig near Anadarko, Spin drove him to the hospital at ninety miles an hour, which probably saved his life. Soon after, she and Spin were married and Bud Hightower had big plans for his new son-in-law. At the ripe old age of thirty-five, Spin became the company's new CEO while Hightower remained chairman of the board and its controlling shareholder. He and Spin didn't always see eye to eye, but they wrote it off to young ambition clashing with experience. They'd learned how to live with it and work together until the accident on Wild Stallion took Bud's life.

Spin had proposed to her at a Christmas party in this very room, big and boldly, which was his style. Not that there was any risk she would have said no. He knew that long before he asked.

Audrey saw Max coming toward her before he saw her. He was walking with a handsome smile, strong cheekbones, and hair that fell boyishly over his forehead. She thought he looked dashing in his tux—a chip off the old block, if the block had been her husband.

Max reminded her of Spin quite a lot, actually. They were both well-liked, had lots of energy, and were driven by a big streak of ambition. Calling Max their son wasn't that much of a stretch. Spin had sent him to law school, where he did well, then introduced him to the company's law firm, where he made junior partner quickly. Soon after that he became Spin's vice president because he knew how to get things done. It put him as close to the throne as a natural son would have been.

Max's mother had died after a long illness when Max was in his twenties. It was only a matter of time, Audrey assumed, before he'd inherit the crown and succeed Spin as CEO.

The band played "Long Tall Sally" and everyone started dancing madly.

I SAW AUDREY IN THE CROWD and went for her as straight as a cowboy goes for ham and eggs. She was standing with her hip cocked slightly to one side, looking me over, her red hair a little wild like her personality. She was the kind of woman you'd pick to be first in any contest she entered, whether it was captain of the softball team, winner of the Miss Texas beauty contest, or the chief suspect in a police lineup—all of which she'd been at one time or another. In her Dolce & Gabbana dress, she had that magnetism that only Texas women had. It made me happy to see her.

"Evening, Audrey," I said, and gave her a kiss on the cheek.

She patted mine and took a step back and looked me over.

"My, my," she said, "you scrub up pretty good. You working out these days?"

"Twice a week."

"Who for?"

"Why's it have to be for anybody?"

"Mm," she said. "I was hoping it was for someone new. You can have anyone you want, you know—why pick the one person you can't?" Looking over my shoulder, she said, "So where *is* that date of yours?"

"Over there," I said, nodding.

Across the room, talking to Joe Wright and his wife, Jenny, was Tacoma in her white crepe sheath. A Narciso Rodriguez, she'd said in the car on the way over, but that didn't mean much to me. All I knew was that it seemed to float over her buttery skin and make her look great. Actually, she looked great in anything, and even better in nothing. That I knew from our first year in law school.

As if she sensed I was watching her, she turned toward me and smiled. Her movement was graceful and her face slightly enigmatic, and her eyes—those supernova black eyes—were so dense nothing escaped them, not even light. Sometimes a woman captures your imagination so completely she ruins you for the rest of your life.

Tacoma and I had met at the University of Texas law school and fallen in love, but by the time the second semester ended, I was behaving as if law school meant more to me than she did. I don't know why. Well, yes, I do. Whenever I got too close to her, I felt as if I didn't measure up, that sooner or later I'd disappoint her or be discovered as a fraud or a felon, although I didn't know what crime I'd committed. Except down there where the ghosts dwell, of course I knew. The accident at Wild Stallion would haunt me forever.

When the first year of law school ended, we agreed to split up for the summer, clear our heads, and try to make things work when we came back to school in the fall. Only problem was, she didn't come back. While lobbying for the Native-American Council in Washington, D.C., she met some guy with a tan face and a fast car and transferred to Georgetown Law School. I was sorry about it for a long time afterward. Guess I still am.

Tacoma was a complex woman, which is one of her many attractions. Her grandmother, who was half-Indian and half-Scottish, raised her after her mother and father died in an automobile accident. Being part Indian, Tacoma set her sights on a career helping Native Americans, although she was also interested in things like money and success. Stereotypes simply don't work with her: She's neither an "earnest Indian" nor a "ambitious white woman," which is fine with me. I like a good poker game.

Despite my unsuccessful efforts to make contact with her, she disappeared from my life until two years ago, when Spin told me he'd met a woman lawyer who was leading a demonstration against Gulf-Tex's drilling operations on Indian land in Oklahoma. When he described the woman as smart, beautiful, part-Indian, and a lawyer for the Cherokee Legal Defense Fund, I knew right away who it was.

I told him we'd been classmates in law school, but for some reason I didn't tell him we'd lived together for a year. Maybe it was because she'd dumped me, or maybe it was because I was still interested in her, I don't know. Guys tend to brag about former girlfriends, but only when they're conquests, and I definitely hadn't conquered Tacoma.

Because I knew her, Spin put me on the company's land rights negotiating team, and that put Tacoma and me back in touch. When the drilling rights confrontation ended he was so impressed with her negotiating skills he asked her to join the company and "change the world from the inside" for a while.

She played his offer smartly and accepted on condition he'd make a five-million-dollar gift to the Cherokee College Fund, which was raising money to build a new school on the Diwali Compound near Dallas, where her part-Cherokee grandmother lived.

When Spin promised he'd do it, Tacoma joined Gulf-Tex as one of its lawyers, and a year later became house counsel. Not long after that she became Spin's adviser on a wide range of problems, some of which, frankly, stepped on my turf.

As I mentioned, we have this competition with each other, which meant I was not only in love with a complex woman, but a rival. And if that weren't enough, there was another complication between us that was as big as a house. But there's no need to get into that right now.

Knowing I was still carrying a torch, Tacoma returned my interest with charm, innuendo, and whatever it took to keep the hook in my mouth. This year when I picked her up at her apartment to take her to the party, I gave her a silk scarf and she gave me a leatherbound volume of *The Sun Also Rises.* I had visions of returning to her apartment after the party for a drink, but by the time we reached the country club, I knew, once again, that it wouldn't happen.

Why a man tortures himself with an impossible love I don't know. None of the clichés—that he wants what he can't have, or that he loves a challenge—explain it. All I know is that we'd started something that was good but hadn't gone far enough.

Tacoma was still talking to Jenny and Joe Wright when Audrey caught my attention and gave me an unusually serious stare. "You have to get over her," she said.

"Longing is good for the soul," I said.

"It's not your soul I'm worried about, it's your hide."

She read my reaction: *What are you talking about?*

"I have something to tell you," she said, but just then the orchestra struck up a few chords to get everyone's attention. Audrey turned and looked at the band, then back at me. Instead of finishing her thought, she patted me on the arm and headed for the dais.

SPIN STEPPED UP TO THE MICROPHONE to speak. When Audrey got to the riser he helped her up, drew her close to his side, said something private to her—they both laughed—and, with one arm still around her waist, took the microphone. They looked incredibly good together.

"Ladies and gentlemen . . ." He was smiling handsomely. Everyone stopped talking and turned to the riser. It was the traditional highlight of the party, the moment when he announced holiday bonuses. "I want to welcome all of you to our annual Christmas shindig."

The men in the audience responded with hoots and "Let's hear it for Santa Claus!"

"This is a party," Spin said, "so let me give you your presents and get on with the celebration."

More applause and whistles.

The spotlights caught the diamond studs in his tuxedo, shooting sparkles across the room. He was enjoying his moment of patrimony, and why not? He was admired by people on five continents, but this was his family and he was their provider, a corporate knight who ran the castle and slayed the dragons. He knew everyone's name in the room, not because he was a great politician, which he was, but because he genuinely cared. I couldn't have been prouder that I was his exec.

"So here's the deal this year," he said. "In the next few days all of you will receive five hundred shares of the company's stock, and . . ." He waited for a response the way a comedian waits for a laugh, but there wasn't one. Only dead silence.

They weren't buying it.

A woman behind me wearing red bows on her shoulders whispered to her husband, too loudly, "There goes the trip to Cancún."

Spin said, "And before you start moaning about getting stock instead of cash, let me tell you why."

Anticipation clogged the air.

"Because of you folks," Spin continued, "we are on the eve of a revolution in the oil business. Opportunity is ours in a way we never thought possible. Because you've worked hard despite trims and closed rigs, we've been able to pour every penny of profit into research and development to make a miracle happen. And now we're almost there."

He stepped away from Audrey and strolled a few steps across the dais, taking the spotlight with him.

"What am I talking about?" he said. "All I can tell you is its code name: Black Eyes. When it finally goes public, we're going to see oil in places you never imagined possible, and when the technology pops, the company's stock is gonna pop with it. Friends, roughnecks, and countrymen, lend me your patience. What you're receiving tonight is better than cash—it's a piece of the future."

The applause started in the front row, then rippled back and increased as it went. He'd won them over. He beamed and waved, then stepped down from the riser, reached back for Audrey, gave her a lift down, and the two of them began working the room.

Spin stopped at the first couple he saw, grabbed the man by the arm, shook his hand, then, smiling confidently, walked from person to person kissing the wives and hugging the husbands. These were his people. Without him the company was nothing, but he made them feel they were more important than he was.

I saw Tacoma coming toward me—then, from the other direction, Spin coming at me with Audrey. Spin reached out to me with both hands and pulled me to him in a bear hug. "Joe said you want to see him tonight," he said, patting me on the back. Over his shoulder I saw Audrey shaking Tacoma's hand, both of them gorgeous and smiling.

I turned to Spin and said, "Yeah, I asked him to meet me at the lab."

"We got a problem?" he said.

"Nothing that can't be handled," I said. "Our 10-Q is coming due and we're running out of time, that's all." The 10-Q was a quarterly disclosure form the company had to file with the Securities and Exchange Commission.

"That sounds more like Tacoma's bailiwick than yours," he said. He was right, but I wanted to get a handle on the problem first.

We broke our embrace, then Spin turned, reached out, and gave a hug to Tacoma. "Merry Christmas," he said. Audrey pulled me into an embrace of her own.

I said, "What did you want to tell me?"

She said, "Just this: If you ever need me but think you shouldn't come to me, I want you to come anyway, understand?"

"Sure," I said. "What have you got in mind?"

"Nothing in particular," she said, making it clear she did but didn't want to say. She gave me a kiss on my cheek and pulled back with a smile. "Merry Christmas, Max."

MOST OF THE PARTYGOERS were still dancing when Spin and Audrey walked outside into the chill air and headed for their car. It was half past one, and the party would go on deep into the night. There was still a case of Jim Beam at the bar, but the boss and his wife would see no more of it tonight. At least, not at the party.

Puck Tarver, Spin's bodyguard and driver, stood beside a gleaming black Cadillac Deville waiting for Spin and Audrey to arrive. After the tragedy on Wild Stallion sixteen years before—it was known around the company simply as "the accident"—Puck's collapse on the crane's controls had turned him into an untouchable, even though it wasn't his fault. It turned out that while visiting his father the night before, he'd borrowed his pill case of Excedrin without realizing it contained tiny nitroglycerin tablets meant to combat his dad's angina. When Puck popped the three Excedrins in the crane cab the next day, a nitro tablet not much bigger than a pencil point had apparently stuck to one of them and he'd chewed it up. The instant it touched the underside of his tongue, it lowered his blood pressure so far and fast he passed out. Taking pity on him, Spin said he shouldn't be financially ruined as well as publicly disgraced, and because Spin needed a driver and bodyguard, Puck got the job. It had worked out fine for both of them. Puck's gratitude was matched by his loyalty.

I, on the other hand, got blamed for nothing that day, although I felt responsible for everything. I always wondered if people saw through me.

Other CEOs who'd come to this special Gulf-Tex party

were climbing into their GMC Suburban "limos," but not Spin. His fellow moguls considered his Cadillac Deville a down-home touch of reverse snobbery, but Spin couldn't have cared less. He thought Suburbans were a cliché, and besides, he'd grown up poor and was proud of it. Once, during a TV interview, he said his view of money was the same as Jerry Garcia's of the Grateful Dead: "The only difference between having money and not having money is when you find a closed-up pistachio, instead of cracking it between your teeth, you throw it away." As a rich populist, Spin knew how to live high *and* low—from patent leather to dirty boots—and the guys in the company loved it. Of course, I knew him well enough to know he was proud of being poor only as long as he was rich. Real poverty scared the shit out of him.

He slid into the car after Audrey and sat on the edge of her dress by accident.

"Sorry," he said.

She didn't say anything.

"Tired?" he said.

"A little."

The tires crunched on the white gravel as Puck circled the tree-lined driveway toward an iron gate.

"Nice party," he said.

"My favorite night of the year," she said.

Puck drove through the gate onto a suburban street and sped toward their ranch an hour away.

"How do you think the gift of stock went over?" Spin said.

"The wives would have been furious with you if they weren't so in love with you," she said. "But they'll get over it."

"Loving me or being furious?"

"Both."

"I know they want cash," he said, "but it's all up to Black Eyes now."

"You've bet the ranch on one horse, you know."

"I don't think so. I spent the day with Joe testing the new software and it looks like he's got the answer."

"What was the problem?"

"AVO something-or-other."

"Has he field-tested it yet?"

"Tomorrow."

"So you aren't sure he's got it yet."

"There's no reason to think it won't work on the platform the way it does in the lab." He took her hand and brought it to his lips. Closing her eyes, she rested her head on his shoulder and touched his hair.

He smiled at her and said, "You looked beautiful tonight."

"I should have worn my red Valentino." Not opening her eyes.

"I should have given you a diamond to go with it."

AT THE TURN DOWN THE LONG driveway to the house, Audrey saw a fence glowing white in the moonlight and remembered their first time together. She and Spin had slipped out of her parents' house at two in the morning, taken a pair of horses out of the barn, and ridden into the pines to find a place to make love. She hoped she'd never forget that night. She was sentimental and possessive, and some of the things she loved to possess most were the special moments that had marked their twenty-five years together.

They pulled around the driveway and came up to the front entrance. Puck stopped and got out and walked around to Audrey's door, but she locked it and rolled down the window. "Go get Lightning, would you, Puck?" she said. Lightning was Spin's yellow Labrador, a dog who loved Spin the way Lassie loved Timmy. Puck went to the house to get him. Spin looked slightly confused. Audrey stared at him.

"Don't get out, Spin," she said. "Your suitcase is in the trunk. If I forgot something, you can buy it."

"What's going on?" he said.

She pulled a piece of paper out of her purse and handed it to him. "Read it later," she said. "I'm not in the mood to talk about it tonight."

"What is it?"

"I could have forgiven a roll in the hay if that's all it had been, but this woman is taking your time, energy, and heart."

"Aud—"

"It's taking away too much, Spin—how you look at me,

what you say to me." She thought about that a moment. "Worse, what you no longer say."

She unlocked the door and got out. Puck was coming down the steps with an unattached leash in his hand and Lightning galloping out in front. Audrey stooped and gave the dog a head rub, took a kiss from him, said "Good boy," then ushered him into the backseat of the car with Spin. To Puck she said, "You can take Mr. Patterson to his next stop now."

"Yes, ma'am."

"And where would that be?" Spin said after her.

Walking up the steps with her back still to the car, she said, "Just drop the reins on the pony, Spin. I'm sure it knows its way to the barn by now."

TACOMA REED'S WHITE SHEATH was hanging on the closet door like a piece of museum art. Max had dropped her off around midnight, and although she should have been tired, she couldn't sleep. Lying in bed in an oversized cotton T-shirt, she was reading a draft of the company's 10-Q and watching an Audrey Hepburn film. Every now and then, when Hepburn looked particularly gorgeous, Tacoma's eyes drifted back to the dress. One moment she couldn't believe what she'd paid for it, the next she couldn't believe it was hers.

She reached into a bowl of popcorn and turned the page on the form, thinking less about the company's cash flow than about another Christmas week she'd be spending alone.

Since going to work for Gulf-Tex, she was making good money for the first time in her life. She hadn't been poor working for the Legal Defense Fund, but neither had she been able to buy a Narciso Rodriguez or a Badgley Mishka without going hungry for a month. Sometimes she felt guilty about it, but she was trying to get over that. She'd never felt the need to choose between abject poverty and wretched excess; if you could do well as well as do good, why not? Besides, last year she'd donated as much money to the Legal Defense Fund as she'd been paid by it during the previous two.

She'd lived in a studio apartment the first couple of years she was in Houston, then bought a two-bedroom condo penthouse overlooking the city. The furnishings were simple: white walls, blond wood, overstuffed chairs, and a mix of modern expressionist paintings and Native American art. She had a gorgeous Cherokee blanket, a shallow basket, a pair of beaded baby moccasins, and three rugs that had belonged to her grandmother. The bright colors in the Indian art brought the space to life and the earth tones soothed and connected her to the land she considered her spiritual home.

Thinking she heard the front door close quietly, she turned down the volume on the TV. Only one person had a key to the apartment. Could that be him? Tonight?

She jumped out of bed and walked into the hallway just as he was closing the apartment door behind him. He was still in his tux and bow tie, and next to him was . . . Lightning? Sitting on the floor was a suitcase and a duffel bag.

Uh-oh.

"I could use a drink," Spin said.

Barefoot, she padded through the darkened living room to a cabinet tucked into a corner, saying, "What a surprise." Lightning looked at Spin, got a nod, and followed her. After pouring two fingers of Maker's Mark into a heavy crystal glass, she carried it into the bedroom, where Spin was already stripping and tossing his clothes onto a chaise. The shower was running. Lightning came into the room and lay next to the lounge and rested his chin on the floor. Spin took a swallow of whiskey and headed for the shower.

She turned off the television set, gathered up the legal papers she'd been reading, and pulled off her T-shirt, trailing her black hair through the neck hole. She went to her walk-in closet and put on a silk, spaghetti-strap nightgown.

He came out of the bathroom with his hair wet and a towel around his waist. After another sip of whiskey, he sat on the bed and reached out and pulled her to him. Her skin pebbled under the soft touch of his fingers.

"What happened?" she said.

Slipping the straps over her shoulders, he kissed her gently and pushed the gown lower, exposing the sensitive skin above her breasts. Then he pointed at his tux jacket on the chaise.

She rolled off the bed and found the piece of paper Audrey had given him when she when she'd got out of the car. It was a copy of an e-mail he'd sent Audrey earlier that day, but instead of beginning "Dear Audrey," it began "Dear Tacoma."

She climbed back on the bed and read it. *I can't wait to see you at the party tonight. I want you to know how much I appreciate what you've meant to me this year—the great work you've done, and the great person you are to me and everyone else in the company. I love you, Spin. P.S. Don't wear any underwear tonight, not even a thong.*

In a lapse of attention as old as betrayal itself, he'd sent his wife a message intended for his lover.

"Oh, no," Tacoma said.

He said nothing.

She said, "You shouldn't have sent it."

"No shit."

"I mean you didn't *need* to."

"I wanted you to know how I felt."

She reached out and touched his cheek tenderly. "I already knew how you felt. What you really wanted to tell me was not to wear any underwear."

He didn't argue.

She said, "And I already knew that too."

IT WAS MIDNIGHT WHEN I got to the lab, and Joe, his wife, Jenny, and his brainy assistant, Angela Song, were already there. The room was dimly lit by a hologram—a three-dimensional block of light the size and shape of a refrigerator—that was hovering in the air like Obi-Wan Kenobi in *Star Wars*. Jenny had lived with Black Eyes for years but had never seen it in operation, so Joe was showing her how it worked. Still in their party clothes, they looked out of place in the lab, but Angela looked as if she lived here, which, for the most part, she did. She'd been invited to the company party, of course, but, knowing Black Eyes would be tested in two days, she'd decided to work instead. If she had a personal life, none of us was aware of it.

The hologram floating in the air was a picture of the deep earth that had been obtained by a sonar "camera"—a kind of underground radar—then downloaded into three powerful Beowulf computers, manipulated by a sophisticated software program into a picture, and converted by lasers into a three-dimensional light form the human eye could see. There were waves of color in the block—grays, browns, and occasional spots of yellow—showing different parts of the earth's substrata. It was as if Joe and Angela had taken a huge apple corer, stuck it thousands of feet into the ground, lifted it out, and dangled it in front of us on an invisible string.

This was the end product of Black Eyes.

Sitting at the keyboard with a joystick, Angela killed the hologram and turned up the lights. Joe handed me a Dr Pepper and said he needed to take a few notes while he had them in mind.

The cool, quiet laboratory we were sitting in had been built inside an old Gulf-Tex warehouse that had once stored company rigs and equipment, but now was the birthplace of this great new device. In the middle of the room was a U-shaped console surrounding the laser pads—one on the ground, one ten feet high—that sandwiched the six-foot-high hologram between them. The only sound was the soft whir of computer fans cooling the computer's chips and circuits.

Although I wasn't an engineer, I'd worked with Black Eyes long enough to understand its basic technology. Holograms themselves were not new; they were used by businesses, universities, and magicians like David Copperfield to present images as diverse as classical paintings, financial pie charts, and disappearing elephants. The trick wasn't creating an image; it was gathering and interpreting the deep-earth data that formed it.

Joe went to a white board and turned to Jenny, a marker in hand.

"There are various ways you can see beneath the earth, honey," he said. "Used to be that the best way was to drill a hole and pull out a sample. Only problem is, it costs millions of dollars to drill twenty thousand feet down, so you'd better be pulling up more than sand and rock."

He took the cap off the marker.

"Once you have a hole in the ground you can see a few hundred yards around it with a nuclear resonance machine, but that still doesn't get you very far."

"What about those machines people use to find coins and metal in the ground?" Jenny said.

"Magnetometers? They can see through earth about six feet."

He drew a line across the white board, then beneath it another line running parallel to it. "This line"—the top one—"represents the sea's surface. This one"—the parallel line below—"is the seabed five thousand feet below. Here"—he made squiggles beneath the seabed—"is the deep earth we want to see. The best way to explore it is with sonar—sound waves, pings, vibrations, and acoustical signals."

He drew a torpedo-shaped device on the seabed.

"We run small, self-propelled submarines along the bottom of the sea that send sound waves into the earth and bounce them back as echoes, or what are called reflections. Receivers record them, and depending on their size, amplitude, and frequency, we can tell a lot about the substances they touched. Rock, sand, shale, water, oil, gas, empty space—all of them have their own acoustic signatures. The torpedo receives the echoes, sends them to a boat or buoy on the surface, and it transmits them to us at Wild Stallion."

He drew a representation of the platform in the sea.

"We gather up the data, feed it into these computers, and based on what the signatures show, make a three-dimensional underground map."

"Seismology?" she said.

"That's right. Oil companies use it every day. So do earthquake watchers."

"So what's different about Black Eyes?" she said.

"Black Eyes takes sound waves far deeper than any other technology."

"How much deeper?"

"That's classified." He smiled and said, "But not from you, honey. Right now, you can hire a sonar company to map an underground area about ten to fifteen thousand feet deep." He drew lines below the seabed to indicate the depth. "Black Eyes can go fifty thousand." He drew lines three times deeper.

"What's that do for you?" his wife said.

"It allows us to locate vast new fields of hydrocarbons—oil and gas—all over the world. Sources of oil so deep nobody knows they're there."

"So what's the problem?"

"You want to tell her, Max?"

I got off the counter and went to the white board. "At conventional depths there isn't a problem, but at unconventional depths—watch."

Angela dimmed the lights and worked the controls on the panel. A moment later, gray and white light began fizzing in the air again like aspirin dropped into water, except the particles were coming together instead of separating. A moment later a hologram shimmered between the two black pads and began to turn color.

"What are we looking at, Angela?" I said.

"A slice of Exxon's Valhalla field," she said.

"OK," I said. "Black Eyes can look beneath the ground in real time, but it can also take what it finds and store it in the computer for later analysis. Large parts of the Gulf have been surveyed acoustically and the data placed on hard drives. That's what we're looking at now, not a live picture. Out on the platform, we'll scan the substrata live and interpret it as we see it."

I picked up a laser pointer.

"This gray area," I said, "is shale. This brown area is sand."

Angela moved the hologram southward through the earth—or, more precisely, through the data forming a deep-earth picture that had been collected by Black Eyes and stored in the computer. Speckles of yellow began to mix with the brown, gray, and beige.

"What's that?" Jenny asked.

"Yellow signifies gas," I said. "It's lighter than water and oil, so if you're looking for oil, you'd probably want to look beneath it. Right, Joe?"

"So far, so good," he said.

Angela dropped the monolith deeper into the earth. Speckles of yellow began to come together and turn orange.

"This orange area is denser gas mixed with oil sand," I said. "Keep going."

She dropped the glass elevator another two thousand feet down. Green blotches appeared like measles, then a rash.

"Traces of oil," I said of the green. "We love the color green, don't we? Now watch."

Angela took the hologram another thousand feet down. The hologram turned orange-green in large hunks, then showed waves of bright green. Then it turned all green.

We were in the middle of an oil field.

"If you look at the coordinates"—the numbers were on the edges of the hologram and changed as fast as Angela moved it—"they tell you that this is the Valhalla field Exxon is producing now."

"Does Exxon know you've got a picture of their oil?" Jenny asked.

"Oh, sure, they've hired us to help them produce the field more efficiently."

"I still don't see the problem," she said.

"Take us a little deeper," I said to Angela.

She dropped another four hundred feet. Now the green began to be mixed with blue.

"What's blue mean?" Jenny said.

"Water," Joe said. "To most people it's the stuff of life, but to an oil company it's the stuff of bankruptcy."

Angela brought the hologram upward into the green oil reservoir, hit some keys on the control board, and turned the entire field from green to . . . blue.

"Oil and water have similar densities and attributes," I said. "At shallow depths, Black Eyes can distinguish one from the other well, just like most seismographs, but at super-depths it can't."

"Why's that?"

I handed the laser pointer to Joe.

"We're not sure," he said. "If the water's been saturated with gas, it can show up as an oil field, and conversely, certain oil fields will show up incorrectly as water. The problem goes both ways."

"Is it a hardware or software problem?" Jenny said.

"I think it's hardware," he said. "If we had more powerful and precise sonar, I think we'd get better data."

"That's his opinion," Angela said. "I think the answer is in the algorithms we're using to tell us what we're looking at."

"And there's your horse race," I said.

Joe lowered his laser pointer and sat on the console. "We've split the lab into two groups: an Alpha team, which I head, and a Beta team Angela heads."

"I expect to beat him," Angela said.

"I hope you do," Joe said.

Jenny could see why we were so obsessed with this thing. It was like being on an enormous treasure hunt. Once it worked at unexplored depths, it would be stunning.

"How close are you to solving the problem?" she asked.

Joe held his thumb and forefinger a quarter inch apart. "Based on what we're seeing now, one blip and we'll have it. But it's a crucial blip. You can't drill fifty thousand feet without being sure you know what you're going to hit."

"How long will it take to fix it, honey?"

He shrugged. "Could be a day, could be a week. Or longer."

"It's gonna happen on our next field test," Angela said.

"We're taking the prototype back out to Wild Stallion," I said.

"When?" Jenny asked.

"Day after tomorrow," Joe said. "Soon as Spin gets back from Washington."

"Wish I could go out there with you," she said.

Joe loved that. At last his wife saw firsthand why he was working so hard and why he was so passionate about it. Once Black Eyes worked, Gulf-Tex would license it to every exploration company and government in the world, and all of us would be smack-dab in the middle of a revolution.

I looked at my watch and said, "I only need a minute, Joe."

"I'll walk you to the gate," he said.

I said good-night to Jenny and Angela, and Joe and I left the room. Walking down a corridor, I said, "I just want to be sure everything's on track for the day after tomorrow. Anything you need? Any problems?"

"We're good to go," he said.

"So is Spin," I said. "His speech to the UN Development Fund is in two weeks."

"What's he going to say if it doesn't work?"

"Nothing. We'll have to cancel. You can imagine how he feels about that."

"Actually," he said, "there's something I want to tell you confidentially, OK?"

"Of course."

"It's one of those things you don't see coming until it's too late." He stopped and spoke in the semilit hallway. "Jenny asked why we were looking at Exxon's oil field as a test instead of our own. Good question. I've stopped surveying our own reserves."

"Why?"

"Because Black Eyes was giving us an accurate picture of them."

"Accurate or inaccurate?"

"Accurate."

"Why's that matter? Uh-oh."

"Got the picture?"

Yes, I assumed I did. He was saying he'd discovered that the company's proved reserves were smaller than we thought. "How bad is it?"

"They're less than half of what we thought they are, give or take."

Shit. Estimating reserves was a subjective exercise based on the oil you could find, market price, lifting costs, and other factors. But still, this was a gross shortfall.

"Listen," Joe said, "everybody knows an oil company's proved reserves are inflated. This isn't so bad, is it?"

"Any time you restate reserves, it hurts the company's stock," I said. "A sixty percent write-down is big."

We moved on and reached the door.

Joe said, "If we hadn't used Black Eyes on our own fields, we wouldn't know this. Does that help us out of a jam?"

"It doesn't matter *how* we found out, just that we found out. Does Spin know about this?"

"I'm telling you first."

I stepped into a light drizzle and turned back to say good-night. Joe was a good man—honest, smart, and hardworking—an engineer who wanted to invent things, not somebody who wanted to get mired in the complications of law, finance, and regulatory problems. If Black Eyes worked in the deep earth—not just as a good seismology machine that could see what we already had—it would solve the reserve problem by dwarfing its importance. And if it didn't work? That I'd get to discuss with our house counsel, Tacoma Reed.

"What should I do?" he said.

"Make Black Eyes work."

TACOMA WATCHED SPIN GET off the bed, pull on a robe, and walk into the living room. Lightning raised his head and watched the bedroom door until Spin returned with a vodka for her and another bourbon for himself. He lifted his clothes off the chaise, dropped them on the floor on the other side of Lightning, and sat facing her on the bed.

"What do we do next?" she said.

He took a drink. "I'm sure she has a divorce lawyer lined up," he said. He reached down and found Lightning's chin.

Tacoma didn't want to complicate Spin's life, but she was tired of being the "other woman" and couldn't help feeling better now that the secret was out. Guilt about their affair had plagued her from the first day they'd flirted with each other, but, as she often reminded herself with a touch of self-loathing, not enough to stop her. She did her best not to think about it. In time, she'd learned to be as successful at denial as she needed to be.

She loved him for many reasons, not just one. He was powerful, wealthy, and dynamic, of course, all qualities any woman would find hard to resist. But even more important were the qualities that lay beneath the glitz. He cared about doing something worthwhile with his life, not just accumulating money. He loved his employees, his children, Max, and his family. He worked hard and played hard without embracing the superficial trappings of the rich. Most of all, he loved her and showed it with affection and generosity.

What she loved most about him, though, was that he respected her opinion on everything that mattered, whether it was personal or professional. He treated her as his partner, not a trophy—a rare quality in a wealthy man.

And then there was the spice of their relationship: the physical touching, the inventive sex, and the perverse allure of his being unavailable because he was married. She knew that this attraction was deeply shallow and might one day come back to bite her, but until that happened, it was an aphrodisiac she allowed to work on her.

The only thing that troubled her was the unknown. When you were in an affair, there was always this gauzy romantic filter between you and reality that meant you didn't know each other the way you would if you lived together. They had not been tested by a crisis or the mundane day-to-day life of a couple. True character, she knew, emerged only in those situations.

For a year Spin had said he wanted to leave Audrey, but he also had a public life that would have been damaged by an ugly divorce triggered by a juicy affair. Look at the executives who were poster boys for corporate morality and public rectitude: One minute they were media heroes, the next they were "outed" as adulterers with lavish perks and ridiculous privileges. He didn't want to be in the pantheon of corporate hypocrites. Not if he could help it.

There were other complications as well. His control of the company was woven into Audrey's life and her position as a major shareholder. They had children he loved and didn't want to hurt. Tacoma knew that at some level he still cared for Audrey—not with the passion he'd once had, but with respect and fondness for what they'd formerly shared. It was important to Spin not to denigrate it, and Tacoma understood that.

She also knew that Audrey took no prisoners, and if she ever found out about her husband's affair, she'd come down on him like a ton of drilling mud. Tacoma dealt with it by ignoring the consequences and trusting that everything would somehow turn out right. Spin had never let her down in the past, and there was no reason to believe he would now. She had no desire to make bitchy demands that could blow up his corporate position, his reputation, or his future political life, not to mention his fortune. And he appreciated her for it.

Now that the moment of truth had finally arrived, her new lightness of being was freighted with worries. Secret affairs usually ended badly when they were exposed, which meant their relationship would soon be tested.

"Let's make a list," she said, playing the lawyer. She rolled across the bed and found a pad and pencil on the nightstand, rolled back, and lay on her stomach. "Number one: On a scale of one to ten, how rough is Audrey gonna be?"

"She'll try to tear me limb from limb."

"Mm." She doodled and put a question mark next to that one. "How about your kids?"

"They'll be hurt."

"Even if you tell them the truth?"

"You mean that I traded in their mother for a younger woman?"

"Is that what you think you've done?"

He reached down for Lightning's ear. "I'm talking about what people will think, not how I really feel about you."

"You aren't usually bothered about what people think."

"These are my kids." He took a drink and laid his head back on the chaise and looked at the ceiling. "Audrey didn't deserve to find out this way. I feel like a shit."

"About you and me?"

"No, about me and her. We've been a pair for twenty-five years, and any way you cut it, I betrayed her." He lifted his head and faced her. "I shouldn't be talking about this. You'll think I don't love you, or I'm blaming you or I still love Audrey or something."

She got off the bed and sat on the chaise next to him. "If you didn't feel bad about her, I'd think something was wrong with you." She laid her hand on his.

He reached out and straightened the shoulder strap on her gown.

"What else are you worried about?" she asked.

"The girls," he said. He'd tried not to be a workaholic dad

who spent too much money and too little time on his kids, but by the time they'd hit their teens, the pattern was set. In the last few years, since they'd gone off to college, he'd made a valiant effort to reconnect with them.

"Just when we were getting close again, I'm doing this to them."

Tacoma felt like a home wrecker. "Maybe they'll understand better than you think."

He reached out to her. "Regardless, this is my fault, not yours."

"Come on," she said, "I'm in the middle of this, too."

He held her hand, trying to be supportive.

"How are you going to feel being the target of gossip?" he said.

She wanted to say she didn't care how the world judged her, but she did. On the other hand, it was too late to do anything about it. "Don't worry about me," she said. "If this means we're finally going public, I say, great."

He pulled her into his arms and said, "I'm crazy about you, you know that?"

She pulled back and looked at him. Despite the mess that lay ahead, she felt the excitement of an adventure. "This isn't going to be as bad as you think, Spin."

He said, "Everything can be handled if the money can."

She didn't know what he was worth, but she thought it was more than enough to handle Audrey's demands. "Is that going to be hard? She's already a wealthy woman."

"It's not about her wanting to pad her bank account, it's about my humiliation and ruin."

Tacoma was playing a game she didn't fully understand. "Relax. She can't have it."

"Don't be so sure."

He reached out for his tumbler and took a large swallow of whiskey. Setting the glass on his chest, he said, "My accountant puts my net worth at a billion dollars, Tee. Most of it's in company stock, a little in cash, and the rest in the house and the ranch. Believe me, she's going to go for it all."

"How much can she get?"

"Texas is a community property state, which means she could get *half*."

"That's not so bad, is it?"

He looked like he'd just been shot. "You want me to give her *half a billion dollars*?" His jaw muscles rippled.

It was the first time money had come up between them. The size of his fortune—its importance and dominance—made her feel like David facing Goliath.

She reached out and smoothed down his hair with her long fingers, then stood up, raised him off the chaise by his hand, and led him to the bed. His new, official freedom was giving her an unexpected sensual rush.

She pushed him onto the bed, pulled down his robe, drew her nightgown over her head, and shook out her black hair. She began kissing him on his neck, mouth, and chest, taking her time, massaging his shoulders, then kissing him more. Her fingers drifted down his sides, lightly raking his skin. When he was ready, she straddled him, leaned forward, and began her oval movement.

"Let go, baby," she said. "Everything's gonna be fine."

"Do you know what the press is going to do with this?"

"The press loves you."

"They'll trash me."

"You're overreacting."

"They'll dig up everything they can find on me."

"What's to dig up?"

"Everybody has something."

She kept up the same slow pace. After a while, she said, "Like what?"

"That feels good . . ."

After some more time had passed, she said, "What are you worried about?"

"You know . . . when two people have been married as long as we have, they know things about each other . . . oh, man . . . things that should stay private." He closed his eyes and escaped into another world.

She continued massaging him with the center of her body. "It's not important," she said.

"Everybody hates gossip," he mumbled, "until they hear it, then they love it . . . take power from it . . . and before you know it . . . God, you know what to do, baby . . . before you know it, it's like a weapon in your enemy's hands . . . the board members you've got boxed in start getting pushy . . . the guy you cut a deal with wants a better deal . . . that's it, do it just like that . . . the governor takes an extra day . . . to return your calls."

She turned off the bedside light and went to work. Before long she had to draw back to exhale and shiver. A minute later, so did he. She thought her timing and control were excellent. If only she could do that with everything in life.

She lay next to him and placed her palm on his damp chest. When they'd both cooled off, she pulled a cover onto them and rested her forehead against his ear. Sex didn't put her to sleep, it energized her. When he laid his hand on hers, she decided he was awake enough to talk.

"What's the one thing you wouldn't want anyone to know?" she said.

After a long silence, he said, "It happened too long ago to matter."

"Tell me."

He turned on his side with his back to her, saying nothing. She touched his shoulder. He turned onto his back again, awake and restless. Darkness invited disclosure.

"I was just a kid."

HE LAY THERE WITH ONE EYE closed and traced the lines of a shadow on the ceiling. "My father left Corpus Christi the day I was born, and my mother did what she had to do to keep our noses above water. Everybody loved her because she helped the poor even though she was dirt-poor herself."

He adjusted his pillow.

"After years of scrimping and saving, we managed to get a mortgage on a small house on Sanchez Street in the barrio. It was the biggest day of my life—I finally had a room of my own. I hung out with the guys on the block, learned Spanish, and made money selling whatever I could get my hands on, including a few things that fell off the back of a truck. My favorite way of making cash was selling *pescador* on the beach."

"What's that?"

"Fish grilled on a stick. I had this dog that all the beach girls fell in love with, so we were a perfect team: He got their attention, I sold them the fish. He knew exactly what we were doing and did it like a pro. God, I loved that dog."

"What was his name?"

"Lightning. Same as my boy here." He took a minute to remember him. "He was a Lab, too. I found him in a thunderstorm."

He turned onto his side.

"My mother worried about my street life and made me go to church every Sunday. She was a dreamer, a religious hippie who thought God's love was all anyone needed. Naïve as hell, but the only person in my life who mattered. When I was thirteen, I decided it was time to become the man of the house, so I took my first legitimate job."

"What'd you do?"

"I was a cotton-candy spinner at the county fair. Twenty bucks a day plus a nickel for every order I took. I sold more than all the other spinners combined." That was how he got his nickname. He remembered those days for a moment. "One night my mother came home and told me the preacher needed heart surgery and she'd put a second mortgage on the house to help pay for it. I couldn't believe it. I asked her how she expected to pay off the first mortgage, never mind a second, and all she said was 'God will provide.'

"I stormed out of the house furious as hell. I hated her, but of course I loved her, too. She was the anchor in my life and the only person whose love and approval I craved. But just when I thought I could handle the house thing, she really did it to me."

"What'd she do?"

"Gave away Lightning."

"Why?"

"We were moving into a rooming house that didn't allow pets."

Tacoma touched him. "You must have been crushed."

"Actually, when I think about it, I still am," he said. "A few nights later I hitched a ride in a pickup truck and headed out to a ranch where I was going to pick cotton the next morning. On the way, we came across a Cadillac that had run off the road and hit a telephone pole a few minutes before."

He reached for a glass by the bed and took a drink.

He could still see it as if it were yesterday.

Bobby pulled the pickup off the side of the road and stopped a good twenty yards away. There was smoke and steam pouring out from under the hood and the smell of burned rubber rolling in through the windows. The driver must have fallen asleep, or maybe he was drunk. The car door was closed and there was no sign of life inside.

Thirteen-year-old Spin had got out and started for the Cadillac when the ranch hand yelled at him.

"Hold up there, boy," he said. "If that thang got a busted gas line, it's gonna blow." He squinted at the car, dropped his cigarette, drove it into the dirt with his boot, and opened the door to the truck. "You wait here, I'll go fer help." He got in, turned the pickup around, and stuck his head out the window as he shifted into first gear. "Stay away from that thang, you hear me, boy?" The pickup's tires spewed dust and headed toward a gas station about five miles back.

As soon as the taillights disappeared, Spin walked up to the car and touched the door to see if it was hot. It wasn't, even though smoke was still pouring out from under the hood. He cupped his hands at his eyes and looked through the window. The driver—a man—was slumped forward, unmoving.

He pulled the door open. The driver was pinned against the steering wheel, his eyes closed, blood dripping from his mouth. Spin smelled liquor mingled with hot steel and rubber. He thought the man was dead until a red bubble billowed out of his nose. If the guy had any chance of surviving, Spin had to get him out.

He reached in and took his arm and tried to pull him away, but he was pressed too hard against the steering column. Spin kicked the door open and reached in again, this time grabbing the man by his lapels. That's when he felt something hard inside his coat.

It was a wallet.

He pulled it out and found it bulging with hundred-dollar bills. The mere sight of them made his mouth go dry. He took them out and fanned them like playing cards. He'd never seen so much money in all his life. Who was this guy? A gambler? A banker? A thief? Whoever he was, his luck had finally run out.

And Spin's had finally turned up.

He stuffed the money into his pocket and placed the empty wallet back in the driver's pocket, then stepped back from the car. He was about to try to pull him out again when it occurred to him that if he saved the man's life, he'd accuse Spin of stealing his money.

Spin sat on the ground thinking about what to do when the fire glowed orange under the car's hood. He had only a few seconds to pull the man free.

He stood up, stepped back, and watched as the car went up in flames.

"Were you hurt?" Tacoma said.

"Was *I* hurt?" he said. He looked at her with amazement.

"What's so odd about that?" she said.

"You're the first person who's ever asked." He sat up. "No, I wasn't hurt, but the man in the car didn't survive."

She reached out and rubbed the back of his hand.

"Instead of picking cotton, I went home and counted the money and hid it. It was three thousand and fifteen dollars. I needed five thousand to pay off the mortgage. The next day I went to a racetrack where I used to spend Saturdays hustling drinks and cigars for tips." He stopped to recall it. "I loved that place. All those rich guys in their fancy suits, their good-looking women and shiny cars and big laughs. I wanted to be one of them so much I couldn't stop looking at them."

"You certainly got that wish," she said.

"I wasn't old enough to place a bet, so I got one of the vendors to do it for me."

"What'd you bet on?"

"I put the three grand on a horse named Gusher who was going off at four-to-one. Not the favorite, but I liked his name, the track was dry, and the sheet said he liked hard turf. I went to the rail with my ticket in hand and watched." He stared her in the eye.

"What happened?"

"He came in second."

Her mouth fell. "What did you do?"

"I waited for the crowd to settle down and went to the cashier's window and collected six and a half thousand dollars." He pulled her face close to his. "I bet on him to place, not win." And kissed her.

"Then what?"

"I took the money home. My mom was waiting when I got there."

"Where have you been?" his mother asked.

"Out," Spin said.

"Your supper's on the table," she said, pulling on a sweater. "I'd reheat it but I'm late for church."

"Mom?"

"What, dear?"

"We don't have to move."

"Not for a while, no, it will take the bank several weeks to—"

"We don't ever have to move."

He took an enormous wad of bills out of his pocket and held them out for her to see. She looked at them with disbelief, then looked at him, then looked back at the money. She put her hands out slowly, as if it might not be real, and he placed the greenbacks in them.

"Six thousand dollars," he said.

"Oh, my goodness," she said softly. Tears welled in her eyes and she opened her arms and pulled him to her and rocked him back and forth, kissing the top of his head.

"Some's for the preacher," hc said, putting his arms around her.

He held her tight, too. He could have held her forever.

"Bless you," his mother said. "Bless you, bless you, bless you. And thank you, Lord, thank you."

After giving him another squeeze, she opened the door to leave, then came back and gave him another hug and kiss. Shaking her head in amazement, she backed toward the door again, staring in adoration, wiping the tears from her eyes.

Spin stood on a cloud of love. Being kissed by her was so rare it was amazing, being hugged and praised even more so. Making her cry with happiness? A first. He listened over and over to the love he heard in her voice.

After she'd gone, he was hungry so he put on a clean pair of jeans and headed out to find his pals and buy them steamed baby goat on fresh tortillas with hot sauce and cold beer. He put on his best pair of sneakers, too, although he didn't have to. His feet hardly touched the ground.

Spin lay on the bed with his ankles crossed and his hand on Tacoma's back. Her head was on his chest.

"When she hugged and kissed me, I'd never felt anything like it," he said, playing with her hair. "For the first time in my life I felt powerful, and, I don't know . . . *loved.* I mean, I knew my mother loved me, but I never felt it before. I knew then and there that money was the key to everything."

Tacoma said, "Your mother didn't ask where you got it?"

"She didn't have to. She knew it came from God."

He kissed Tacoma on the back of her neck and got up off the bed.

"Did you ever find out who the man in the Cadillac was?" she said.

"He was a preacher from Monroe, Louisiana."

"One preacher dies so another could get his heart fixed?"

Spin put out his hands in a robe-covered shrug. "Two hearts got fixed that night."

"Do you believe you were right?" Tacoma said.

"That my heart got fixed?"

"That you can steal for a good cause."

"Up to a point, everyone believes that," Spin said.

"Not me."

He laughed. "Come here, Mother Teresa."

She came to him and he held her close. "Ask Cornelius Vanderbilt and the Rockefellers and all the other robber barons if it pays to steal. Ask the fine upstanding citizens who build statues and name foundations and universities after colossal thieves. Ask politicians and popes."

"I'll call them first thing in the morning."

He smiled. "If they were honest, they'd tell you everybody who makes a fortune does something they don't want people to know about. And you know why?"

"Because they're ashamed?"

"No, no, no. Because they don't want to get caught."

IT WAS TWO IN THE MORNING but they were too wired to sleep. Both of them were wearing robes, and Tacoma was making scrambled eggs while Spin sat at the kitchen table. Lightning sat at the door to the kitchen waiting to see what landed in his bowl.

"Money," Spin said, "isn't about six-thousand-dollar shower curtains and gold-plated toilet bowls. The assholes who do that sort of thing make the rich look so obnoxious you don't want to admit you're one of them."

"You want cheese or onions?" she said.

"Cheese." He got up and opened the refrigerator door and found a jar of salsa. It wasn't ideal huevos rancheros, but at this hour it would do. "Money's about freedom and security. And if it's big enough, the power to do something good in the world."

Spin had many expensive things—a huge house, a car and driver, a private plane, a chef, good food and great wine, to name a few. But he drew lines at things that struck him as juvenile and excessive: art he didn't really appreciate, a yacht he seldom used, a birthday party with toga-clad girls and ice sculptures of boys peeing vodka. He didn't mind that his wealth was known to the world—that was part of his persona—but conspicuous consumption turned him off. He tried to keep his wealth tasteful and, when it came to details, private.

She took the pan off the burner while the eggs were still wet and Spin took over. He scooped off a portion for Lightning and let it cool, then laid in the cheese and a dollop of salsa. He turned the eggs easily, once.

His pals who accused him of cultivating a phony regular-guy image missed the point. He drove a '57 Chevy from the ranch into town and wore jeans with torn knee-holes and a pair of scruffy loafers, but it wasn't for effect, he really *liked* being down and dirty. The trick was doing it on your own terms, when and where you liked, not because you had to.

Using a spatula, he placed a helping of eggs on two corn tortillas and placed some plain eggs in Lightning's bowl. After pouring orange juice for himself and Tacoma he joined her at the table.

"Here's to a great new year," Tacoma said, raising her glass.

"Here's to," he said.

The older he got, the less his money was about champagne wishes and caviar dreams and the more about the story of the burning Cadillac. Making money was how he kept score. It was the sign of success that had transformed him from a street urchin into the hero-prince his mother loved. Without money—big money—he'd always see himself as the runt in the barrio: invisible, unwanted, rubbish. So money wasn't just a means to an end, in many ways it *was* the end: the bottom line of his identity, the true measure of his worth. He didn't go around admitting it because he knew it shouldn't be this way, but he knew it was true and he didn't deny it, least of all to himself.

He couldn't live without big money and he couldn't live without being loved and respected by the woman in his life who mattered most. As a child that had been his mother, then it was Audrey and his daughters, and now it was Tacoma. She was the "testimonial woman" whose love and adoration healed his narcissistic wound and held the key to his self-esteem.

She took another bite and said, "If everything goes bad, you can always be a short-order cook."

His smile covered the spiritual shiver the image gave him.

She said, "You don't need money to be loved, Spin. I'll love you whether you're rich or poor."

"Another tortilla?" he said.

"No thanks."

He got up and put a couple of tortillas on the griddle and stood watching them turn brown. Love him whether he was rich or poor? His mother used to say the same thing, but it wasn't true. *Everyone* said that, even the songs that claimed the best things in life were free, but he knew better.

When they'd finished eating, he cleared the table—a habit from childhood—while Tacoma returned to the bedroom. After making sure Lightning had water in his bowl, he turned off the kitchen lights, walked to the duffel bag he'd left in the hallway, lifted out a package, and brought it in. Laying it on the bed, he said, "Merry Christmas."

"What is this?" she said.

"Open it up and see."

She lifted a long, beautifully wrapped package, thinking, what has he done? With her brow furrowed, she tore the wrapping off, saw what it was, and nearly stopped breathing.

It was a clear Lucite box holding a beautiful, long Indian pipe. Its bowl was made of catlinite, a soft, reddish stone that had been polished and hand-carved, and it had a long ash stem with file brandings on the side. She opened the top of the box and carefully lifted it out. Hanging from the bowl were strands of coral and turquoise beads, a silver peace medal, and an eagle feather. Closer to the mouthpiece, on the stem, was a fox-fur wrap for the smoker's hand. A museum-quality piece, it must have cost a half million dollars.

"My God," she said quietly.

Spin said, "It's the pipe smoked in 1836 by Governor Sam Houston and a Cherokee chief named Colonel Bowles to commemorate their agreement that the Cherokees would never be driven out of Texas. Naturally, Houston's successor kicked them out, but that's another story. Do you like it?"

"It's stunning." She admired the stars embedded in the catlinite. Putting it to her mouth, she mimicked smoking it, then offered it to Spin, who did the same. They promised each other they'd always keep the peace between them and live by the treaties they reached as a pair.

It was easy to say when you were clueless about what was going to happen next.

After placing it back in the display box and setting it on the bedside table, she brought her mouth to his and kissed him. He turned her over and made love to her on the chaise. After lying there awhile, listening to music and feeling warm, Spin started to get up, but she held him back.

"Not so fast," she said, turning him over. "There's another pipe I want to smoke."

I MET TACOMA AT THE DOOR to her office at 8:00 A.M. and told her about the reserves problem. By nine sharp she'd convened a meeting of seven people—her private "wise men's council"—to discuss what to do.

She came into the conference room wearing a chocolate-brown suit, librarian's glasses, and an air of self-confidence, reminding me yet again that whether it was business or personal, she had this enormous presence that commanded people's attention and respect. She sat at the head of the table, turned off her cell phone, and went to work.

"According to information from the lab," she said, "the proved reserves we've reported to shareholders, the SEC, the New York Stock Exchange, and our analysts may not be as big as we say they are."

Sitting at the table in addition to Tacoma was Richard Linzer, a securities lawyer in my old law firm; Joe Wright, who could tell us what he and his team had discovered about the company's reserves; Julie Branch, a geologist on his team who'd taken the actual readings; Champ Carter, the chief financial officer, who knew what the company had stated as its reserves in the past; and John Fineman, the chief operating officer, who was fierce, smart, and loyal; and me.

"Joe, tell us what you've got," Tacoma said.

Joe explained that in the course of trying to get Black Eyes to give him reliable sonar readings at extreme depths, he had scanned the company's reserves and discovered they contained less than half of what the company thought. When he realized he was getting a pattern of shortfalls, he stopped and reported his findings to me.

Tacoma said, "I want to get a handle on this immediately and make recommendations to Spin. How big a problem do we have here, guys? What, if anything, do we have to disclose, and when do we have to disclose it?"

Champ Carter said, "If Black Eyes isn't perfected yet, why do we have to disclose anything?"

Joe Wright said, "At the relatively shallow levels where our reserves are located, Black Eyes is the best data gatherer out there."

John Fineman said, "That doesn't cut it for me. Disclosing something iffy could depress the stock price below levels justified by what we really know, and that would be a hell of a disservice to the shareholders. Maybe the reserves are lower than we think, maybe they're not. We don't know for sure."

"If we have to disclose," Tacoma said, "how much time do we have?"

Richard Linzer, our outside counsel, said, "We've got four weeks till our next 10-Q is due. But depending on where we come out, we've got the street and the exchange to consider, too."

"What do you think, Max?" she said.

I said, "Even if the securities law doesn't require disclosure, we don't want to forget the *Wall Street Journal*. Stories like this have a way of leaking, and when they do, they're bigger than they would have been if we'd put them out ourselves."

Tacoma queried everyone, listened to their answers, and defined what she wanted next. She asked for a geological report from the engineers, a market impact prediction from the CFO, a legal opinion from outside counsel, and recommendations from everyone. She wanted everything we discussed held tight until Spin reached a decision as CEO, and she reminded us that if a director on the audit committee got wind of this, he or she would automatically require disclosure regardless of the law, wisdom, or damage to the stock price. No one in the room was to sell any shares they owned until further notice.

After that, she started moving systematically through her checklist, starting with a detailed discussion of case law, SEC regulations, and Sarbanes-Oxley, legislation that deals with disclosure obligations.

I had to get to the airport, so I got up to leave. Tacoma motioned for me to come over to her and said, "Tell Spin the nature of the problem, but don't give him a tilt on the answer yet, OK? Tell him I'll have a report and recommendations tomorrow."

I nodded and left the room, thinking, she's good. On all levels.

SPIN WAS ON THE PHONE IN the backseat of his Cadillac Deville. Puck was at the wheel, moving along a back road on his way to the private air terminal at Hobby International. When they got there, Spin's jet would be warmed up and waiting.

On the other end of the line was his wife.

"Tell me what you want to settle this, Audrey," he said.

"I'm entitled to half of everything you've got," she said. "In fact, if you figure in the stock I brought to the marriage, I'm entitled to more than half."

"Get real," Spin said. "Your stock was worth crap and you know it. I'm the one who made it into something."

"That's debatable."

"You can't question the record."

"And you can't question my contribution to your success."

He covered the phone and talked to Puck: "Get on the phone and make sure Max is at the plane. I want to be off the ground in ten minutes." To Audrey: "I need a number."

"If you agree right now, three hundred million," she said. "If not, the number goes up every day."

"Even as punishment this is ridiculous."

"I'm looking at my watch," she said. "Another minute gone by, another ten thousand you owe me."

"Would it help if I apologized?" he said.

"God, no, I'd faint."

"I didn't want this to happen."

"Come on, Spin, you always get what you want. You broke

the faith between us, you betrayed me, humiliated me, and hurt me. So guess what? I'm pissed."

"I would be, too, but I wouldn't try to ruin you."

"How long has this been going on? You and Tacoma?"

"Audrey, listen—"

"We're wasting time. Another minute, another ten thousand."

Angry silence. "OK, I'll see you in court."

She laughed. "You and I both know you aren't going to court."

"Why not? I've got nothing to be ashamed of."

"Oh, please," she said. "We've been married too long for you to say something that stupid. The tabloids will make an issue out of the way you brush your teeth."

"I'll ask for a sealed record and a gag order," he said.

"Think you'll get one?"

"Why not?"

"Fine, then you'd better get a plumber, too," she said. "Stuff this juicy has a way of leaking."

"Are you blackmailing me now, Aud?"

"I'm giving you a chance to pay me what I'm entitled to or kiss my gorgeous ass."

He didn't respond.

"You do remember my gorgeous ass, don't you, sweetie? The one you poked every night while you were banging Tacoma's in the afternoons? I'm sure you've told her all about our bedtime stories, but in case she's forgotten, I can always give her a front-row seat at the trial."

"Don't be a son of a bitch, Audrey."

"And don't you start calling me names. You'll lose that fight, too."

"I'm at the airport, I gotta go."

"Ticktock, ticktock. Three hundred million and counting."

She hung up without saying good-bye.

THE PLANE BROKE THROUGH the clouds and lowered a wing to make a slow-turning descent toward Reagan National Airport. Looking out the window, I saw a white carpet of snow, a toy-sized Capitol, and a lit-up Christmas tree on the White House lawn.

After we landed, Spin and I took a waiting car to the White House, cleared security at the northwest gate, and walked up the driveway to the front door. It was like entering a founding father's cozy house. The Marine Orchestra was playing Christmas carols and the halls were decked with holly, poinsettias, and tasteful ornaments.

There were introductions to congressmen and senators who championed the environment; the head of the Wildlife Association and the Sierra Club; movie stars like Tom Hanks and Bruce Willis; handshakes, cups of eggnog; and soon we were in the midst of the ceremony that had brought us here. Spin and three other honorees were being presented with the Preserve America Presidential Award for protecting America's cultural and natural heritage. In Spin's case, safeguarding Native American burial grounds on Gulf-Tex drill sites had done the trick. That and a few well-placed political connections. Men in his circle basically gave awards to each other.

I wondered why Tacoma wasn't with him. It was her confrontation with Gulf-Tex that had led to the company's new land preservation policy. If Audrey had come along, I would have understood why Tacoma wasn't there, but Audrey hadn't.

After the ceremony, we walked to the Blue Room for a reception. The first person to shake Spin's hand was the president, who grabbed the arm of a passing senator so the three of them could chat.

"He's onto something that could change everything," the president said of Spin. He shook my hand before being led away to continue working the room.

"What are you up to?" the senator asked.

Spin said, "We think we've got a new way to find oil."

"That won't get you elected to office, that will get you crowned. Where's Audrey?"

"Year-end obligations."

"I expected her to be here measuring the room for curtains."

They both laughed.

"The two of you make a hell of a team," the senator said.

"I'll tell her you said so."

"I'm serious. With her at your side you could go all the way."

"I've never even run for dogcatcher," Spin said.

"Politics is about exposure, money, and charisma, not experience," the senator said. "Ask Governor Schwarzenegger. If you come to Washington too soon, you get bored, lose focus, start messing around with the girls, wreck your marriage, and the first thing you know you're some burned-out hack."

Spin smiled, patted the senator on the arm, and moved away gracefully, saying hello to more well-wishers. He looked as if he belonged in the White House. I could tell by the way people talked to him that they thought so, too. Oil was big and dangerous, and so was the Oval Office. Oilmen had to know when and how to gamble big, and so did a president.

After he'd worked the room, we slipped away, found our car, and returned to the airport. The airplane door was pulled shut as the engines whined; a few minutes later we were on our way back to Houston. When we reached cruising altitude, the company's flight attendant came into the cabin offering drinks and canapés.

Although I'd come along to watch Spin get his award, I also had to work, so I opened my briefcase. Spin had his necktie down, his head back, and his eyes closed, looking more tired than I'd ever seen him.

"Want to work?" I asked. "I've got the Kerr-McGee papers."

"Are you happy with the numbers?" he said, not moving.

"I am, and so's the controller."

"Then go for it."

When documents required in-house counsel to sign off, I sent them to Tacoma with a note that Spin had approved and she reviewed them and passed them back to him with her signature and comments. He trusted her signature recommendations implicitly, as he did mine, and rarely second-guessed or reviewed them.

"Gotta give you a heads-up on something, Spin," I said. "In the course of using our oil fields as a Black Eyes testing ground, Joe inadvertently discovered that our reserves aren't what we think they are."

"Fabulous. How bad is it?"

"Don't know. But Tacoma's on top of it."

The telephone chirped. He picked it up and put it on the speakerphone. "Hello?"

"It's me," Audrey said. "Three hundred fifty million and we're done with this."

I started to get out of my seat to give him privacy, but he waved me down.

"I'll give you two-fifty."

"Not a chance," she said. "It gives no value to the stock I brought to the marriage."

"You know how I feel about that. Why don't we submit the valuation question to binding arbitration?"

"I'm listening."

"The arbitrator decides what the stock's worth and the records are permanently sealed. No court proceedings, no appeals, no press conferences, leaks, or gossip about anything having to do with us or the marriage. When the arbitrator finally rules, we both accept the number he comes up with and it's over. We announce to the world we've split with smiles and kisses."

"You must have White House fever," she said.

"What's your answer?"

There was a long pause. "I'll do it on condition you post a bond for the whole amount if I win."

"A bond for five hundred million *dollars*?" he said.

"Plus interest. I don't want to win the arbitration and find out the well's run dry."

"Good God, Audrey, I'd have to lose an entire billion before you didn't get paid."

"The way you chase ass, you could do that in a month."

Spin's fingers were clenched in a fist. "OK, if I post the bond, do we have a deal?"

She thought it over. "Yes—as long as the numbers are based on your net worth today, not your net worth at the time the arbitrator rules."

I saw his eyes flash. He made a quick assessment of what she'd just said and liked it. If Black Eyes worked and drove his stock up, the increase in value could pay the whole amount she was asking for and leave Spin's fortune untouched. Only if Black Eyes fizzled and the stock tanked would he be hurt by agreeing to a big settlement based on his current net worth. I knew what he was going to do before he did. He was a gambler, and gamblers are optimists. He expected Black Eyes to work.

"All right," he said, "I'll have my lawyer call your lawyer."

"Spin?"

"What?"

"We were a hell of a pair, kiddo. Family, friends, money, adventure—we knew how to do things nobody else could do."

"That's true, Aud."

"So tell me: Is she worth it?"

Spin didn't answer.

"I'll answer for you," she said. "She's not." She hung up.

We'd hit a pocket of air and the plane lurched. My coffee cup went sliding and I reached out and grabbed it just in time. He pushed the button for the flight attendant and she arrived with a tumbler of Wild Turkey. He took it and ignored a plate of hors d'oeuvres.

"You use private e-mail?" he said to me.

"Sure."

"Then let me give you a small piece of advice: Always check the address line before you hit the Send button."

"IT'S BEEN COMING A LONG time," Spin said.

"I'm sorry to hear it," I said.

He had no idea how sorry I was. Now that he was getting divorced, Tacoma would be headed for a new chapter in her life and it wasn't going to be with me. I've known about Spin and Tacoma's affair ever since I came barging into Spin's office a year ago and caught them disengaging from a tight-as-ticks embrace. They were embarrassed and showed it. I was crushed but didn't show it. I knew right away that I needed to drop my lust for her, but knowing and doing were two different things.

Oh, yeah: Their affair is the problem I mentioned earlier that's as big as a house.

There's probably never a good time for a married man to reveal an affair, but Spin *really* didn't want Audrey to find out right now. He wanted to demonstrate Black Eyes to the world first and milk its pure-gold publicity without muddying the water with an ugly domestic brawl. That was the other reason for his agreeing to a potentially huge settlement with Audrey. By valuing the stock with a private arbitrator instead of in court, he hoped to keep a War of the Roses hidden from view.

What a shame it had to happen. His Law of Unintended Consequences—that unforeseen events occur amid even the most carefully laid plans—had finally come home to roost.

"Is there anything that would save the marriage?" I said.

"Leaving Tacoma, maybe," he said, "but I can't do that."

Of course you can't.

He picked up his glass and held it the way I imagined him holding her arm, touching her the way I had once touched her myself, caressing her the way I'd caressed her. The sweat on the glass wasn't condensation, it was the perspiration she and I used to create in that sacred place between her breasts. When he drew the tumbler up to his lips, I swallowed dry spit. I loved everything about Spin except his love for Tacoma, and for that—but only that—I hated him big-time.

"If you don't mind my asking," I said, "what happened to you and Audrey? You seemed like the perfect pair."

"We were," he said. "She's smart, loyal, and presentable everywhere from the White House to 7-Eleven."

"Did the romance burn out?" *Or is the sex with Tacoma just too good to pass up?*

"Tacoma appeals to my better angels," he said. "She believes in me and makes me think I can do something important in the world besides make money. She makes me want to live up to her expectations."

How disappointing. My hero sounded like just another rich guy who wanted a beautiful woman to feed his ego. I wouldn't have minded so much, I suppose, if he hadn't chosen the wrong one.

"You're giving up a lot, Spin."

"It's worth it as long as Audrey doesn't bankrupt me." He looked at me. "You trying to talk me out of this?"

Hell yes! "Just playing devil's advocate," I said, but he'd seen through me. I could feel my cheeks blushing. What an idiot. Lancelot loved Guinevere, but at least he had the sense to shut up about it in the presence of King Arthur. Spin had no idea I'd ever been involved with Tacoma, much less that I still wanted to be.

Well, maybe he suspected something. He wasn't blind.

He downed the last swallow of liquid amber and said, "You and Tacoma—how come the two of you never hooked up?"

Yep. "You know how it is," I said, straining for plausibility. "First year of law school you're just trying to survive."

He looked at me as I talked. "You know something, Max? For all the skills you have, lying isn't one of them."

Nope.

"She and I were roommates our first year," I said, "but it didn't last."

"Why not?"

"She's always had an eye for the older, more sophisticated guys," I said with a small smile. But that wasn't the real answer and he knew it.

The real answer was the Macy's escalator accident that happened a couple of months before the end of the first year of law school. I froze in the face of danger that day, and you can't do that with the woman you love. It brought back every rotten feeling of inadequacy I'd had since I'd blown it that day at Wild Stallion and put my father's life at risk. She'd done her best to talk me out of my self-hatred, but I couldn't do it. So we split.

"I should have said something to you about Tacoma and me before now, Spin, but the time never seemed right, and after a while it felt too late to bring up, if you know what I mean."

"I do," he said.

"I also thought it was up to her to tell you, not me."

"You're right about that."

Great, now *she's* busted.

"It doesn't matter," he said with a smile. "I just didn't want something unstated to come between us."

Too late for that, Spin. We're both in love with the same woman, even if I don't stand a chance.

Besides, it *did* matter to him, I could tell by the way he turned away and pretended to read a magazine. He didn't like having his trusted VP for Special Projects keep him in the dark about something important, and he didn't like wondering why neither Tacoma nor I had told him about our history. He had the upper hand with her in every way imaginable, and she'd done nothing to make him doubt she was his, but his controlling personality had been put on guard and it would stay on guard from this point forward.

Jealousy is not only despicable, but embarrassing. He didn't like the green-eyed monster grinning at him and he liked it even less that I could see it.

"We'll be landing in Houston in ten minutes, Mr. Patterson," the stewardess said softly, interrupting the silence we'd lapsed into. "Is there anything else you need?"

He shook his head, picked up the magazine, and continued to pretend he was reading.

I picked up a document and did the same.

THE DINING-ROOM TABLE IN Tacoma's living room was carefully set with red accents and sprigs of holly. White candles burned in clear-glass candleholders casting a pleasant glow on the linen napkins and shiny silverware. Sitting nearby was a serving plate of poached salmon with tomato rosettes and blini dressed with red caviar.

Champagne glasses sparkled in the soft light, and a bottle of Cristal cooled in an ice bucket. This was the first Christmas they'd spend together, the first time Spin hadn't sent two dozen red roses with an apology for being absent.

They were decorating a small tree that stood on a table in the living room, or at least she was. Spin's voice boomed out of the second room she'd turned into a study as he talked to a famous divorce lawyer named Bob Cohen. For the last hour he'd been on the phone scheming, planning, and working out an approach to the arbitrator who'd decide what Spin owed Audrey for her stock. This wasn't how Tacoma had imagined spending their first holiday together.

She heard him hang up, hard. When he walked into the living room, he looked steamed.

"Are you hungry?" she asked, holding an ornament. Audrey was putting him through the wringer and he was showing it. Tacoma had never seen him as distracted as he'd been in the last few days.

"Not yet. I need another drink."

"Champagne?"

"Bourbon."

He'd already had one, but she didn't want to argue. Support was the name of the game, even if some people called it enabling.

"She can't humiliate you if you don't let her," she said, handing him a tumbler of mahogany liquid.

He groaned.

"Hey, I'm just trying to help," she said.

"Then you have to understand the rules of the game. If she gets half my money, she wins. Period."

Tacoma walked to Spin's chair and sat on the armrest. "She's not going to bankrupt you, darling," she said, massaging his shoulder. "You have to get that out of your mind. You're being haunted by ghosts of childhood poverty."

"Right now I'm being haunted by the hit I'm gonna take if we have to restate our proved reserves," he said. "You know, I had an idea about how we could delay announcing—"

"Come on, honey, don't," she said, touching his lips. "I may be sleeping with the boss, but business is business, especially when we're talking about the SEC."

"Sure it is," he said. "Trust me, the tape recorder is off."

He took a drink, looked at his watch, and stood up. "I have to go to the office."

"Now?" She looked at the table and candles. "Dinner's ready, and I want to give you my Christmas gift."

He walked to a chair to pick up his jacket. "Bob Cohen needs a file. We're going into arbitration right away. I'll be back as soon as I can."

She flapped her arms at her side in exasperation and accidentally smashed the ornament she was holding against the table. "Dammit!" A streak of red appeared on her palm.

"What'd you do?" he said, walking over to her.

"Just go!"

"Let me see—"

"It's nothing! Go get your divorce file!"

He took her hand, pulled a handkerchief from his pocket, and laid it on the cut. After walking her to the bathroom, he put her palm under a stream of warm water, patted it dry, and opened the medicine cabinet to find a bandage. She sat on the toilet lid holding a dry washcloth on her hand.

After he'd dressed the wound, she left the bathroom and walked into the study. He caught up with her at her desk.

"Come here," he said, pulling her into his arms.

She resisted. "Your file—"

"To hell with my file."

He lifted her up and laid her on the desk, knocking a clock, papers, and a lamp onto the floor. The bulb flashed and burned out, leaving moonlight streaming through the window, making her skin radiant with a blue-white glow. He kissed her wildly and began unbuttoning her blouse, pulling at it, letting it drop to the floor, then went to work on her bra. She didn't help. He didn't want her to.

Her breasts were exposed, her nipples dark and hard. She raised them to him as if she feared he might forget to caress them, but the air was cool and his hands were warm, and when he touched her, she exhaled with a whisper.

He unbuckled his belt; she took over until his pants were on the floor alongside his shirt and shoes. She liked it that their prelude to sex wasn't zipless. It prolonged the agony and made them both crave each other more.

His right hand cradled her neck. Her hand reached down and found what it wanted. His other hand slid beneath her buttocks and lifted. The nails on her other hand dug into his back. He entered her slowly, then went for depth.

Startled, she moaned, then trapped him with her legs. They moved in a heated rhythm they'd practiced many times but never understood.

He stopped. "Max told me the two of you had a thing."

She blinked at the ceiling to get her bearings. "What?"

"When you were in law school." Both of them holding still.

"That was . . . ten . . . years ago," she said.

"Why didn't you tell me?" Pinning her hands above her head.

"Because it has nothing to do with you and me. We all work together and I didn't want the tension . . ."

"I hear you, but I still don't get it."

She looked into his eyes. "You know—" She started to

argue then suddenly changed course. "Sorry, baby. I should have told you."

He started moving again. "How important was it?"

"We were law students. Everything was secondary . . . uhn . . . to getting through the first year."

"Why'd the two of you come apart?" Moving faster. An exorcist with a divining rod driving the devil out of her body.

"It just fizzled . . . the way things do," she said, feeling each stroke. "Mm. Mm. Mm."

"Tell me."

"Only thing I'm gonna tell you is . . . you're jealous."

"You're right . . . and you're gonna pay for it."

"Oh, really? Imagine my horror. Mm. Mm."

"You make me . . . crazy," he said, breathing hard.

"I like making you . . . crazy."

"What do you want?"

"You."

"How?" he said.

"This . . . way."

They moved against each other rhythmically and relentlessly, searching for the point of no return.

"I don't want to be . . . just another guy . . . in a long line of guys."

She pressed her calves against his back to draw him in deeper even though he was already there. "You're . . . mm, mm, too much . . . you're the only man in my life . . . in my imagination . . ."

She opened her mouth and pulled his to hers before he could respond. After that, they made love in the moonlight the way lovers do when love is threatened and jealousy looms large and nothing can satisfy a man's fragile, needy soul except the consuming lust of two lions in the wild.

WE HAD THE HOLY GRAIL OF the oil industry in our hands and were about to see if it worked. Everybody moved quicker and spoke quieter now. Black Eyes was like a ghost waiting to be set free. Its presence and promise were everywhere.

I could have come out to Wild Stallion on Spin's helicopter, but I left early and took the service boat instead. I wanted some distance from Spin, and besides, I loved getting out of the office and standing on deck in the sun. In my head I was a lawyer/vice president, but in my heart I was still a roughneck wannabe.

Bluebeard had nothing on the men who drilled offshore. Oilmen used lasers and computers instead of cannons and sabers, but they were still pirates in search of buried treasure. The only difference was the booty was black instead of gold.

I was feeling the intoxication of the hunt when Wild Stallion loomed on the horizon. The minute I saw it, I thought of Dad and how he would have loved the high-stakes game we were playing. He would have put everything on the line for it; in a way, he already had. I'm not a superstitious guy, but I felt he was out there with us and that what we were doing was partly for him.

After boarding the dock in a calm sea, I took the lift to the main deck where Spin, a group of roughnecks, a company geologist, and the members of Joe Wright's A team and Angela Song's B team were preparing to go to work. I entered the doghouse, closed the door, and let my eyes adjust to the lack of light. Angela was working the control panel and Joe was sitting next to her. "We've got good signals from the transmitters," he said, and the room grew quiet. The sonar signals on the small underwater torpedoes reached across the seabed a radius of twenty miles and pierced the earth as deep as ten. Oil within that range would appear in the hologram. If the system worked.

We were going to test Black Eyes in real time today, not collect and download the data for later analysis in the lab. The sonar torpedoes were prowling the Gulf floor and sending back digital images of what their "pings" saw beneath the seabed. A moment later, a hologram fizzed up and hovered in the air, revealing what the sonar was picking up live as it swept the earth's bowels.

"At this depth, we're seeing the substrata reliably, but this isn't where the big boys hunt," Joe said. "Take her down, Angela."

Angela worked the controls and lowered the earth-piercing sonar to a depth of ten thousand feet. The coordinates on the edges of the hologram changed as the computer dug deeper with its sonic echoes.

"What we're going to do," Joe said, "is show you BP's Thunder Horse field, which is here," pointing to a chart. "It's twenty thousand feet deep. We know what it looks like because BP logged it from the drill and gave us a composite picture."

British Petroleum, he explained, had found a reservoir at five thousand feet, continued drilling and testing it, and eventually hit "pay" on a vertical slope that went at least twenty thousand feet down. It was a rare find and rarer still to have a field that deep that was charted. "We're going to ping it and see if Black Eyes gives us a picture that matches what we know is there."

"If Black Eyes works at twenty thousand feet," Angela said, "it should work at fifty. The issue isn't range, it's analysis."

"So we hope," Joe said.

She maneuvered the computer's coordinates to the Thunder Horse region, and soon we were seeing the gold speckles of gas-saturated brine, then gas sand, then the rich, green spots of oil sand.

"We're at seventeen thousand feet," Angela said.

"While you're working the live feed, show us what BP already knows is down there."

Angela worked her mouse on a large monitor showing her control options. A moment later, the hologram changed color and structure in a blink.

"This is what it actually looks like down there," she said. "It's what is known as the BP Delta crib." The hologram was called a crib because when it was empty, it resembled a corn crib made of chicken wire. She hit more options and the hologram returned to the live picture Black Eyes was projecting to us—the so-called Live Echo crib. Now it was a matter of matching up the two cribs and seeing if Black Eyes gave us a picture of what was already proven to be there.

She maneuvered the system into the coordinates of the BP Delta. No one spoke; everyone was riveted to the rectangular crystal ball. Spin's expression was unexpressive, Joe's cool, Angela's nervous.

"We're at depth," Angela said. "Should be on the coordinates."

"Switch to Black Eyes and see if the location is right," Joe said.

Angela selected some options and made the switch. All at once, the Black Eyes Live Echo hologram resembled the BP Delta hologram, except that it wasn't in color yet, only monochromatic grays, whites, and blacks.

"We're at ground zero," Angela said.

"All right," Joe said, "let's see what we've got."

Angela worked the keyboard and mouse to choose her options. Frame Highlight: click. Capture Streaming Reflections: click. Color Code: click. The Black Eyes hologram began turning color, the monotones giving way to yellows, tans, and oranges.

The large field of oil sand turned green.

"Looks good so far," Spin said quietly.

"Switch back to BP Delta," Joe said.

The hologram showed the oil field as it had been surveyed by BP again. It, too, was green.

"Switch back to Live Echo."

The hologram showed the field Black Eyes was sending us live.

The two looked virtually identical in shape, content, and, most importantly, the color green, the color of oil.

"My God," Spin said, "I think you've done it."

There was a noticeable relaxation of tension. People who'd been as immobile as statues finally moved.

Joe said, "Move east a hundred feet. Do it live."

Angela worked the joystick and moved the hologram.

The colors shifted as the sonar probe moved. The green depicting oil sand shimmered and broke up like a TV program in a thunderstorm. Everyone took another breath and held on. The only sound was the squawking of seagulls outside the door.

The color green appeared, but it was laced with streaks of blue.

"Reload," Joe said.

Angela hit the option.

The green broke up again, then returned. This time, it was mixed with even more blue.

"Reload," Joe said again.

No one spoke. All eyes were on the patient on the operating table.

Angela reloaded and clicked Perform Analysis and Color Code.

This time, the reservoir known to hold oil turned entirely blue.

Not green for oil, blue for water.

Shit.

"What is it?" Spin said.

"Not sure yet," Joe said. But actually he was, or at least he was sure of the only thing that mattered: the problem of accurate analysis and presentation hadn't been fixed.

Joe and Angela worked the options systematically and calmly, but the results were the same each time: Black Eyes could see deeper than any commercial sonar system in existence, but at depths that mattered—twenty thousand feet and below—it still couldn't reliably and consistently distinguish oil from water.

We had the grail, but it wasn't holy. Not yet.

SPIN STOOD TALL IN HIS COWBOY boots and buttoned his Armani jacket.

"Listen up, everybody," he said. "This is a disappointment, but it's not a setback. We're still on the verge of making this thing work." He looked around the room and captured every pair of eyes there. "How many times did the Wright brothers get stuck in the mud before they flew? How many rockets blew up on the launchpad before they reached the moon? We're closer to a dramatic breakthrough now than we were yesterday, and yesterday we were so close we could smell it. So don't get discouraged—all that can do is hurt us. Believe me, we're going to find the answer."

Faces brightened.

Spin said, "I want everyone to go home and come back after the holidays ready to start fresh. Joe?"

"Sounds good to me," he said. "And Spin's right. You can't have this many pieces of the puzzle and not find the one that's missing." A couple of his technicians nodded. "When we come back, Team A will pick up at the lab where we left off, and Team B will work out here on the platform with Angela."

Everyone moved around and started packing up various odds and ends. Spin took Joe and me aside.

"You need to take a break, too, Joe," he said.

"I thought I'd take off tomorrow."

"That's not enough," Spin said. "I don't want to see you in the lab till after New Year's."

My cell phone rang. I checked the message window but didn't recognize the caller's number.

"Hello?" I said, stepping outside the doghouse.

"Max? Bob Cohen here." It was Spin's divorce lawyer. Spin had asked him to review the documents he was going to submit to the arbitrator and tell him what kind of case he had. "I was trying to reach Spin at the office and Charlene said he was with you."

"He's here but he's in the middle of something right now. Is there anything I can do?"

"We've looked at everything in the file, and we're all in agreement that the arbitrator is going to rule for Audrey."

I was afraid of that. "Any wiggle room?"

"Not really. I'll be glad to go into the reasons if Spin wants, but I know he's waiting for a bottom line, and I wanted to give it to him."

My phone beeped with another incoming call.

"Thanks, Bob, I'll relay the message."

I took the next call.

"Hello?"

"Max, it's Charlene." Spin's private secretary. "Bob Cohen is trying to reach him—"

"I just talked to him."

"OK. Did Tacoma reach you?"

"No, what's she want?"

"She's on her way over to Linzer's office and asked me to give you a message ASAP." Uh-oh, Linzer must have given her an opinion on the reserves disclosure issue. "She said . . . have to . . ." The line broke up.

"Say again, Charlene, I couldn't hear you." The chopper engine was whining.

". . . has to disclose! G-Tex has to disclose!"

She repeated it enough times to make the bad news clear.

I hung up and looked out at the sun bouncing off the royal blue water. Black Eyes' failure was like invisible rain on the horizon. The divorce lawyer's news was like an invisible squall on its way, and now the disclosure requirement was a coming storm.

There were times when I wanted to see Spin blown off course with Tacoma, but never did I want to see him sunk. After all, I was on the same ship with him.

"IF I LOSE THE ARBITRATION, how much time do I have before I have to pay Audrey off?"

"Thirty days," I said.

Spin and I were in his helicopter on the way back to Houston. He sat doodling on a pad as I broke the news about Bob Cohen's opinion.

"There's more," I said. "Richard Linzer says the company has to restate the value of our reserves."

"When?"

"End of the quarter."

He doodled more.

"You got any more good news?"

"No mas."

He finished writing and turned the page. "So let me see if I've got the picture. My stock's lost fifteen percent of its value in the last ninety days, it's going to drop another fifty to seventy percent on news that we don't have the reserves we thought we had, and I'm looking down the barrel of a gun at a half-billion-dollar bullet from Audrey."

"I'd say that just about sums it up."

"You have a nice day, too."

He kept turning his pen in a circle with his fingers and thumb, staring at it, thinking, expressionless, a gambler with all his chips on the line. I'd seen him in this position before. He was trying to figure out how to fill an inside straight and steal the pot.

I wanted to know what he had in mind. After a long silence, he picked up the telephone and dialed a number.

"Joe? Spin here. Instead of taking the day off tomorrow, let's take the plane to New Mexico and climb Darth Vader's Tower."

I couldn't hear what Joe was saying, but he must have been considering it. The two of them had rock climbed together for years and swore that nothing cleared the mind like an eight-plus vertical climb with no prepositioned bolts, small finger crevices, and a partner you could trust.

I had my own slippery slope to climb now. I had to pitch in and help Tacoma find a way to restate the company's reserves with the least amount of damage to the company and Spin's holdings. Most people think oil companies are always rich and that oilmen know how to manipulate the market to keep them that way, but that wasn't the way it worked. Oil stocks in general were down—they'd been falling the last two quarters—and Gulf-Tex's was sliding ahead of the pack. For every point the stock fell, Spin suffered an equal decline in his Gulf-Tex-loaded portfolio. Climbing a rock wall was an easy concept for an oilman.

Spin hung up and settled back in his chair, then lifted his glass and downed its contents. "Whatever else you may be in life, Max, don't be a goat. Anything is better than that, even a lamb chop on somebody's plate." He looked over at me with something on his mind. "Are you ready?"

"Sure am," I said. When he didn't say more, I said, "For what?"

"You're about to take a big step into the future. Stay awake."

SPIN'S CADILLAC DEVILLE PULLED up in front of the office, but he sat in the rear seat not moving. Puck's eyes caught him in the rearview mirror. "Everything OK, boss?" he said.

Spin didn't reply. He hated his vulnerability and hated what he was contemplating, but now that he'd lost Audrey, Tacoma was more important to him than ever, and the thought of losing her was impossible to imagine. When Audrey was in the dark about his affair, he and Tacoma had been free and easygoing, but now that everything rode on her, his expectations were different.

He hadn't seen this latest wrinkle with Max coming.

He decided not to do it and opened the door, but as he started to get out, the gnawing feeling hit his gut again. He closed the door and sat back in his seat.

"I'm taking the jet to New Mexico tomorrow," he said to Puck. "While I'm gone, I want you to do me a favor."

"Whatever you say."

"I want you to keep an eye on Tacoma."

"You want me to drive her somewhere?"

"No, I want you to keep an eye on her. You know what I mean? Without her knowing." He felt his face flush at the sound of his words.

"No problem, boss," Puck said.

Spin liked Puck's tone of voice: It was flat, businesslike, and nonjudgmental; he knew what to do. Spin opened the door and got out.

Puck said, "Anybody in particular I'm looking out for?"

Spin put his hand on the door to close it, then leaned in

and said, "Tell Wally"—his second bodyguard and pilot—"I want to lift off before six A.M."

"Will do," Puck said.

"And in answer to your question, yeah. Max."

He closed the door before he had to suffer any more of the embarrassment of his personal insecurity and Puck's deep understanding of it.

THE SUN WAS HIGH AND BLINDING, but Joe and Spin didn't notice. They were focused on a more basic problem: how to keep from falling a thousand feet to the desert floor.

Both men clung to the north face of the sheer rock with resin on their fingers and rubber climbing boots on ledges only an inch deep. There was a forty-foot rope between them. On this particular leg of the climb, or "pitch," Spin went first while Joe "belayed" him, or anchored him to his own harness and a steel ring in the rock. Fighting the weight of their own bodies, they cursed the birds that glided past them cackling with laughter. Even more, they cursed the occasional cold gusts of wind that stiffened their fingers.

But mostly they tried to control themselves—their muscles, coordination, agility, and fear. Not that you could climb without fear. Without it you not only endangered yourself but felt no sense of elation. Still, at the moment, "victory of the spirit" was the last thing on their minds. Balancing on their fingertips and toes was the only thing that mattered.

Spin had chosen climbing as a sport because it was a parallel universe to his own. He liked conquering the anxiety of falling off a rock so he could climb the mountains in his business and social worlds. He'd always possessed the nerve to avoid disgrace and failure in life, but conquering the fear of losing his entire fortune—of being poor and powerless—was out of the question. He had a better chance of flying like one of those birds.

More to the point, he had a better chance of getting Joe to do what Spin needed him to do to save the company and Spin.

They'd been climbing for two hours and weren't far from Never-Say-Die Plateau, a small ledge where they could rest, have a bite of lunch, and take on the last, toughest part of the route—the "crux"—before topping out and rappelling back to the desert floor.

Spin knew Joe hadn't climbed since his baby was born. It scared Jenny too much, so he'd given it up. But he missed it, and when Spin had suggested the climb, Jenny had told him to go for it.

Spin had other things on his mind besides climbing. He could have talked to Joe on the telephone or in the office, but out here you could speak in more than nine-second sound bites and do it with some long-range perspective. There was nothing like climbing, sailing, or crossing a desert on bikes to get perspective. Most people thought these were the self-indulgent games executives played, but for men like Spin, they were pathways to solutions, not detours. Both men wanted this climb.

So far there hadn't been any false steps. Their handholds had been good, and after more climbing they reached the plateau. With his climbing harness anchored to the cliff, Spin sat on the ledge, drew a Nalgene bottle from his small pack, spilled some water over his head, squirted some on his face, and drank a long, slow draft. Sitting nearby, slung to the same anchor, Joe unscrewed the cap on his bottle and took six swallows.

The sky was clear and the land spread out before them for miles. Clouds dotted the wild blue yonder, and hawks rode air currents like kites, holding still in midair until they swooped down to check out the two-legged aliens who'd confused themselves with a winged species.

"I needed this," Joe said, taking in the vastness of it all.

"Me, too," Spin said. "Makes you understand what really matters, doesn't it?" He went silent against the majesty of it all. "Look at that."

A hawk glided in circles, coming closer. Both men sat still, their eyes glued to the bird. It came close enough to reveal its eyes, then rose imperiously and soared away.

"It's a good thing we love the land the way we do," Spin said. "I'm proud of what the company's done to protect it."

"We'd better protect it," Joe said, "the way things are going at the lab, we may be farming it."

"There are worse fates," Spin said, "but I don't know what they are. I wouldn't survive a day as a farmer. I chopped enough cotton as a kid to know I could never work a single acre, much less forty." He retreated from the ledge and stooped next to his backpack to pull out a penknife, a hunk of cheese, and a baggie with some bread and sausage.

"What are we going to do if Black Eyes doesn't work?" Joe said.

"It's not an option," Spin said.

Joe opened his backpack. "We're so close. Six, nine months and we'll have it."

Spin cut off a hunk of sausage and handed it to him. "Unfortunately, we haven't got that much time."

"Why not?" Joe said.

"We're out of cash."

Joe put the piece of sausage in his mouth and chewed. "With your connections, surely you can raise more."

"Not if I'm not around to try."

Joe didn't understand.

Spin said, "I may end up owing Audrey over five hundred million dollars in a divorce settlement. If that happens, I'll be busted."

"Jesus, Spin, I had no idea."

"People assume the rich are rich forever, but it ain't so."

"What are you going to do?"

"That's what I want to talk to you about."

SPIN HANDED A HUNK OF FRENCH bread to Joe. "They say you should never put the cart before the horse, but sometimes you have no choice, know what I mean?" Spin said.

He tore off a hunk of bread in his mouth.

"Take our situation," he said. "You need time to make Black Eyes work and the company needs the cash to fund your lab. The only way we're going to do that is to show the world that Black Eyes is for real."

"I thought that's what we were doing."

"I don't mean in six months," Spin said. He cut off a piece of cheese and put it in his mouth and stared at Joe. "I mean now."

Joe turned away, put his plastic canteen of water to his mouth, drained most of it, and screwed on the dangling cap. "How do we do that?"

"We reveal Black Eyes to the world next week, exactly the way we've been planning to. We invite everyone to see it in action and give them a demonstration so stunning it sends the company's stock through the roof. We raise enough cash to buy you time to finish your work, keep the company running, get the takeover vultures off our back, and let me pay off Audrey."

Joe rolled a grape in his fingers. "After we announce it, what next?"

"You make it work."

"And if I can't?"

"There is no can't."

Joe put the grape in his mouth and chewed it. He spit out two seeds. "One question."

"Fire."

"Have you lost your mind?"

"I've never seen things more clearly."

"It's fraud!"

"It's nothing more than putting the cart before the horse."

"If it doesn't work, it's ten years in jail!"

"Only if someone gets hurt," Spin said, "and we're not going to let that happen."

"We don't have to hurt anybody, we just have to get caught!"

"We won't."

"Why not?"

"The odds are against it."

"You kidding me?" Joe said. "Cover-ups are like sitting ducks!"

"Actually, it's just the opposite," Spin said. "For every cover-up a reporter finds, a hundred more work. We just don't know about them because, by definition, they can't be seen."

"This is crazy, Spin." Spin didn't answer. "Even if I wanted to go along, I don't know how long it will take to get it to work."

"Doesn't matter. Once we announce it, you can have as long as you need." Spin held out a piece of cheese. Joe took it and Spin pushed a piece of sausage into his own mouth. "No need for me to make a point of it, Joe, but when it comes to cover-ups, you and I are already batting a thousand."

"Don't be an asshole, Spin."

"Just citing precedent."

"Not to split hairs," Joe said, "but *we* didn't do the last cover-up."

"In my book, if someone doesn't blow the whistle when they see a foul, they're on my team."

"Not in mine."

"Then what are you?"

Joe pulled off a piece of bread and rolled it into a ball. "I'm a whistle-blower who didn't have the balls to blow it."

"Christ, Joe, don't be so hard on yourself. You did what was right at the time and you know it."

Two hawks glided fifteen feet above their heads, checking them out. Joe threw the piece of bread into the air, but they let it fall.

"All right," Spin said, "I don't blame you for balking. Frankly, I don't like it either, but hear me out." He went back to his backpack and pulled out a small plastic bottle of Cytomax. "Black Eyes is no longer our company's biggest asset, it's our *only* asset. Our reserves are less than half what we thought and we've mortgaged the company to the hilt. If we don't leverage Black Eyes now, we're going down the tubes, Joe. Everyone in the company will be out of work, and it won't result in a few rusty barbecue grills, it'll mean long-term unemployment in a shrinking job market."

Joe drank another swig of water.

"We've got hundreds of employees depending on this company to feed them. People with mortgages and car payments and tuition bills who've put their lives on the line for us."

"You can stop with the violins," Joe said.

"I love these people," Spin said.

"So do I, but not enough to go to prison for them."

"I would," Spin said. "In a heartbeat."

Joe moaned. "Come on, Spin, you're not going to shame me into this."

"If I could pull it off alone, I would, but I can't."

"I can't show the world Black Eyes works when it doesn't! Who do you think I am? Houdini?"

Spin placed the leftover cheese back in a bag and sealed it. "You don't have to be Houdini to pull this off. Listen to how it works."

"WHEN I WAS IN MY TWENTIES," Spin said, "I was a sonar officer on a navy submarine." He started unscrewing the plastic top on the Cytomax. "It was a Wolf Class nuclear sub that stayed submerged for three months at a time and went to depths that are still classified. My job was to map underwater valleys in the deepest part of the Gulf of Mexico where we could hide our missile subs in case there was a nuclear war.

"One day, my deep sonar gave me a picture I recognized as an oil field. I told the exec about it, but he said forget it, our orders were to chart the seabed, not look for dead dinosaurs. I tried to convince him that a big oil find was as important to the national defense as a map, but he told me to go back to my station and shut up."

Spin took a swig.

"I plotted the reservoir in my field manual anyway. Not that I needed to—I can give you the coordinates from memory."

"Where is it?" Joe said.

"In a place called Damnation Alley."

Joe looked surprised "That's in Mexican waters, isn't it?"

"It is, which is another reason nobody's ever drilled for it. So here's the deal. After I announce we've got Black Eyes working, we demonstrate it in Mexican waters where everybody knows we have no prior knowledge of a reservoir."

"How do you get permission to do that?"

"Mexico wants American companies to drill in joint ventures with PEMEX. We steer Black Eyes into Damnation Alley searching for oil. You program Black Eyes to give us a hologram showing an oil field at the coordinates I remember. Black Eyes finds it and that's it."

"Finds it or appears to find it?"

"If you've fixed the problem by the time we do the demonstration, Black Eyes will actually find it, and if you haven't, it will *appear* to find it. Either way, since we know the field is there, we'll hit 'pay.'"

"What's that get us?"

"Everything! Showing the world how Black Eyes works will get us millions in deposits, and when we actually hit the reservoir, the whole world will be clamoring to license Black Eyes. Wall Street will throw money at us and, with our political contacts, so will everybody else. All we need is one success and we've got it made."

Spin got to his knees and leaned forward.

"We avoid bankruptcy and everyone in the company gets rich. Five years from now, Gulf-Tex will be bigger than Exxon and Shell put together."

"And if the oil field isn't there?"

"It's there."

"Humor me. What if it isn't?"

"You want me to state the obvious?"

"Yes."

"We're burned. Nothing left but ashes."

"That's attractive."

"If we don't try, we're definitely ashes."

"But we'd still have our self-respect."

"Self-respect doesn't pay the bills, Joe. Sure, it's a gamble, but we both love this company too much not to try it."

"But not the money," Joe said.

"Not what money?"

"It's not the divorce settlement that's driving you, it's your love of the company and Harry Homeowner's mortgage."

"Don't be a cynic, Joe. The only people who think money's evil are people who don't have any. The company's well-being is my life. If it survives, so do we, and vice versa."

Joe tossed another wadded ball of bread into the air. The hawks ignored it.

Spin said, "If we pull this off, you'll be so rich the only thought you'll have about money is how to spend it."

"Jenny and I have enough," Joe said.

"You never have enough. What about your dream house? Vacations anytime you want them, anywhere in the world? The best educations your kids can have?"

"I've got my 401(k)."

"Not if the company's stock is worthless, you don't."

Joe didn't answer.

"Look, we've got one of the great inventions of the twenty-first century in our hands—and we're gonna lose it because we won't buy a lousy six months to make it work? Now, *that* would *truly* be criminal."

Joe sat quietly.

Spin got to his feet and circled him like a hawk. "We're not Enron shitting in its own hat, Joe. We're not the idiots who ruined WorldCom, and we're not looting the company or cooking the books."

"No, we're just cooking up an oil field."

"But we're not! We're doing what Black Eyes is going to do when it works anyway! We're just accelerating the clock by a hundred and eighty days! Maybe less!"

"You keep saying that as if you know I can solve the problem."

"Because I know you can! And so do you! You know the system inside out! It's your baby!"

Spin saw a look on Joe's face he'd seen before. He was thinking algorithms and impedance and the logic of a system that should have worked long ago. He was thinking he was only an inch away.

"Let me ask you something," Spin said. "Could you preprogram Black Eyes to show us a reservoir without Angela knowing about it?"

"I suppose so. We've split the lab into two groups."

"And no one on your team would need to know, either?"

"No one but me. But I've still got a problem with this."

Spin saw the wheels turning and went quiet. His sense of how to exploit a man's weaknesses—when to nudge, badger, and bulldoze, when to soothe, stroke, or let him alone—was superb.

The monkeys in Joe's head were battling for his soul: *It's wrong—do it anyway—you'll get caught—you'll get away with it.* Some people called it corruption of the soul. Spin called it human nature.

"We're all sinners," he said softly. "Why not turn that lemon into lemonade by sinning for something good? A cause, a better life, a better world?" He waited. "Your family's welfare?"

After a minute, Joe took a third ball of dough in his fingers.

"How much would I get?" he said.

"Ten million down," Spin said. "All cash." Joe said nothing.

The hook was in Joe's mouth; all Spin had to do was set it. "Plus another ten million in stock at today's price. If we make Black Eyes work, who knows what it'll be worth three years from now? Twenty million? A hundred million? Two hundred? You'll be rich beyond your dreams."

Joe threw the wad of dough into the air with a sidearm toss. This time a hawk picked it off before it reached its zenith.

Spin said nothing. He didn't need to. He'd just witnessed a universal truth that applied to every living organism on earth, even the hawks who flew on the edge of heaven: Give them enough bread and they're yours.

All he had to do now was seal it. Before the day was over, he'd find a way. He had no choice.

MY OFFICE WAS DOWN THE hall from Tacoma's, but we talked on the phone as often as we did in person.

"Hey, you," she said.

"I sent down some papers for Spin's signature yesterday," I said.

"I already took care of them," she said.

"You alone?"

"Yes."

"I wanted to give you a heads-up on a conversation I had with Spin. About us. You and me."

"He already told me."

"I tried to sidestep it, but he looked me in the eye and called me on it."

"You've never had a good poker face," she said. "But you shouldn't have sidestepped it anyway."

"Did it complicate your life?"

"No, he's fine, no big deal," she said.

She made it sound like it didn't matter. I didn't like that either.

"I think you made a mistake, you know," I said.

"With what?"

"Walking out on us in law school."

She took a moment. "I didn't walk out, I was pushed, and why are you telling me this now?"

Because I still love you. "Take it as a Hallmark card and forget it."

"I'm flattered, Max, really I am, but I don't want to complicate things between us. We have too much work we have to do together."

"That reminds me," I said, "when I was on the phone with Dick Linzer this morning, he asked for an explanation of the addendum to Joe's lab report, so I put one together and e-mailed it to him. Copy to you, of course."

After a pregnant pause, she said, "You did that without checking in with me first?"

"I thought it would be one less headache for you."

"Excuse me, Max, but that 'headache' is my job!" She was pissed. "Are we in a turf battle here?"

"No, no, I was just trying to give you a hand and lighten the load."

"Thanks, white boy, but next time, just butt out, will you? You're Spin's executive vice president and dog robber, not mine."

She hung up.

I hung up, too, then leaned back in my chair and threw a pencil at the ceiling. I keep doing the same thing over and over—I keep trying to show her that I'm effective—that I'm not frozen at the controls—that I can push the right buttons, hit the right switches, and pull the right levers—that I can keep that payload from hitting my brother and stop that escalator from nearly breaking Tacoma's neck. I wear this super-can-do effectiveness like a badge, but it's really a mask, and even though I know it, I can't seem to take it off.

The escalator incident at Macy's was Wild Stallion all over again.

A couple of months before we split, we were in Macy's department store riding up an old escalator with wooden slats on the steps when a long silk scarf she was wearing caught in the moving handrail. She'd tied the scarf in a fashion knot at her neck, and we couldn't get it loose as we continued moving toward the top. I pushed past people and ran down the steps to the base, opened the control panel, and hit a red button and stopped it just as her scarf rounded the handrail curve at the top and pulled her head down to the floor.

Seeing what had happened, an assistant manager ran over and tried to loosen the knot, but it was pulled too tight. She was starting to turn blue from strangulation.

"Back it up!" the manager yelled down at me.

I looked at the controls and saw a toggle switch with arrows pointing in two directions, one for reverse and one for forward, but I wasn't sure which did which. "Back it up!" he kept yelling. "She can't breathe—back it up!" If I hit the switch the right way it would release her—but if I did it wrong, it would break her neck.

I froze.

Again.

A security guard ran up to the panel, hit the toggle switch, and backed the escalator down, releasing the scarf. It took an oxygen mask and an X-ray of her neck to make sure she was OK.

She was, but we weren't. When I told her I'd frozen, she understood—she'd known about my dyslexia and how it had made me push the crane controls the wrong way and drop the Caterpillar engine onto the deck. That scar she could cope with, but not the sense of impotence it renewed in me after the Macy's incident. Feeling inadequate and guilty all over again, I pulled away from her. She stayed loyal and hung in for the rest of the semester, but as I said before, it didn't work out. She left to spend the summer in Washington, D.C., met the professor, and never came back.

Until Spin brought her back into my life.

I tilted my chair forward and picked up the pencil from my desk. What was the point? She and Spin were inevitable. I could run the company single-handedly and it wouldn't impress her, change her mind, or change anyone else's opinion of me, either. *You can't run the tape backwards, Max. You can't even reverse an escalator. Stop trying.*

I put the pencil in a tray and went back to work.

"LET'S CLIMB," SPIN SAID.

He and Joe picked up their packs, slipped them onto their backs, and scanned the ledge for anything they might have left behind. Seeing nothing, they sorted out their gear—the bolts, hangers, carabiners, and steel devices they'd drive into the face of the wall so they had something to hang on to. When they were done, Joe handed Spin the climbing rope, and Spin put it through the belay device on his harness. When the line was secure, he let Joe know by saying, "I'm on belay."

Joe looked up the vertical wall, shifted his backpack, then checked one more time to make sure his climbing harness was tight and the figure-eight knot on his rope was finished with a fisherman's knot. Everything looked ready, so he slipped his fingers into a crack, put his foot on a small ledge, and said, "I'm climbing, Spin."

Spin played out the rope through his belay device and watched Joe move slowly up the cliff. When Joe was in shape he could climb degrees of difficulty in the elevens, but when he wasn't, he should have limited himself to fives. The pitch he was climbing now was an eight-plus and the hardest part of the entire route. He was in over his head, but like a lot of guys who come off the couch to climb, he thought he could handle it.

Spin thought so, too.

Joe trended off to the left side looking for places to pound his steel gear into rock. Drifting farther to the left, he finally stalled. The rock had become utterly featureless—no place to put fingers or toes, no cracks for gear. He was also somewhat overextended now, which meant he'd climbed farther than he should have, but there was nothing he could do about that.

"Watch out for me, Spin!" he yelled, and Spin tightened the rope that ran from himself to Joe through a carabiner twenty feet up.

Joe's hand groped the smooth surface in search of something that would let him defy gravity: a quarter-inch ledge for his toes; a tiny, vertical side-pull for his fingers; a crack, an irregular surface—anything to keep him levitated. All he found was sheer rock washed smooth by centuries of ocean, wind, and rain.

He felt the wall for a tiny crack that would take a steel camming device. Before he found it, his right foot slipped; then his left hand; then his entire body started to slide off the rock. His inner ear measured his physical existence in a matrix of weightlessness, air pressure, adrenaline, and fear.

He slid a few feet down the wall—hung on his fingernails—and heard Spin yell out his name. It didn't matter; Newton's laws took over.

His feet noticed the next step he took, then the rest of his body felt it, too: the soft, enormous, cosmic openness of space.

Standing on the ledge, Spin watched Joe fall past him headfirst—his rope had gotten between his legs and flipped him over—and bounce off the side of the cliff.

Spin's anchors—a bolted hanger, an equalizer, and a Spectra cord—held fast under the load, but now he had a partner hanging upside down a thousand feet above the ground.

Spin responded as if he were under attack: no thought, all reflex and adrenaline-fed reaction.

He steadied himself and waited for his partner to stop spinning. The line was taut, the anchors still holding.

"Joe?" he yelled.

No answer.

"Joe!"

He must have knocked himself out.

"Joe—can you hear me?"

Waiting for a reply.

From a distance: "I . . . hear you!"

"How bad is it?"

"Can't tell."

"Check it out."

Don't die on me now, Joe. I've got your life in my hands and you've got mine in yours.

"Nothing broken I can find," Joe yelled.

"You know what to do, right?"

Two hits on the line said yes.

They communicated by tugs, grunts, and words, but mostly by parallel thinking. They were two men with one mind speaking the unspoken language of trust and single purpose. One miscalculation and they'd both die.

"OK, swing forward," Spin said.

Joe didn't move.

Spin spoke telepathically, *I've got you, Joe! Trust the rope! Swing out!*

Joe leaned forward as far as he could, righted himself, and stretched out his hands in search of a fingerhold. Spin had fallen once himself and knew what was going through Joe's head: *Disregard the heart in the mouth, be practical, stay focused.*

Spin grabbed the safety line, fed it through two biners, and began working Joe upward a few inches at a time with the careful work of two spiders spinning a web.

THIRTY MINUTES LATER THEY sat on the ledge bathed in sweat. The summit was still forty feet above them, but they'd decided they'd had enough for the day. Only a hawk would sit atop Mount Olympus on this trip, and one did, looking down at them with its black, unblinking eyes.

Joe took a drink of water and put his head back. The sun lit his face like a Titian painting. "You saved my life today, Spin."

Spin took out a Nalgene bottle of water and handed it to him. "No more than you're gonna save mine," he said.

He had him.

SIX OF US WERE FLOWN OUT to Wild Stallion on a company helicopter and told we'd be briefed when we landed. I'd never seen an executive meeting held on a drilling platform before and hadn't been informed why, which was unusual. Whatever was going on, it must have been important. The air was electric with anticipation. Not even the occasional flashback to the fire sixteen years ago put a dent in it.

We landed on the helipad and walked down the steps to the doghouse on the main deck. Spin, Joe Wright, Angela Song, and Tacoma were already in the corporate offices on the subdeck where the living quarters and foul-weather safe rooms were located. The six of us who'd come out on this particular shuttle entered the doghouse, and a few minutes later the other four joined us. Spin took off his hard hat, unbuttoned his coat, and sat on the edge of the control console.

"All of you know we've been working on the Black Eyes project for several years, and you know how close we came in our last field test to making it work. Well," he said, opening a can of Pepsi, "that day has finally come."

There was silence in the room. Even the seagulls stopped squawking.

"Joe has just made a major breakthrough that's going to turn Black Eyes into the most revolutionary technology since the invention of the drill bit. The world's known reserves are declining and nobody seems to care. Black Eyes is going to give us another century of energy, and if we have any common sense, we'll use that time to find alternative sources of energy before the wells run dry. He'll give you an overview of how he made it work in a minute, but first, I want to set our agenda."

He took a drink of soda.

"A few days from now, I'm going to announce Black Eyes to the public and invite people from around the world to see it in action. Our plan is to scan an area of the Gulf where there's been no prior exploration and see if Black Eyes can find an oil field at depths never encountered by a seismograph. If it happens, we'll be selling licenses to Black Eyes like lottery tickets."

He turned to a chart on the wall behind the console and took out a red laser pointer. "We'll be exploring here in an area known as Damnation Alley. As you can see, it's in some of the deepest water in the Gulf. It also happens to be in Mexican waters, but that's good because it's virgin territory. PEMEX has agreed to let us explore as long as we give Mexico ninety percent of the product."

He turned back to the group.

"And if you think that's a bad deal, think again. Once we prove the technology works, we can find oil anywhere in the world."

He got off the console. "Max, I'm putting you in charge of thc announcement." His cell phone rang; he checked the incoming number and signaled me with his finger to take over the meeting.

"Janine," I said to the head of corporate public relations, "we'll need an oil-patch reporter with impeccable credentials to cover the field test."

"I know the guy," Janine said, "but he won't pull any punches."

"That's OK, credibility is the name of the game. Jimmy, I'm sure Spin's going to ask you to put together the best bunch of roughnecks you can find."

"I'll start with our own guys and go from there."

"Dave," I said, "you need to line up the best drill ship you can find on short notice."

"I think Asherman's got one available," Dave said.

"If they foot the bill, we'll split our ten percent with them. Assuming Spin agrees."

Tacoma said, "When you talk to them, make sure they understand there can't be any leaks or trading in Gulf-Tex stock. This is inside information."

"Got it."

"Same for everyone in this room," she said. "Nobody buys a share of Gulf-Tex stock from this moment until the public announcement. And no leaks!"

Spin got off his cell phone, finished outlining the plan, and said, "Any questions?" There weren't any. "All I can say is this is the most exciting moment in the company's history." He turned the meeting over to Joe and motioned to Tacoma and me to join him at the door. Outside, we headed for the helipad.

Walking alongside him, I said, "Do you really think you can tell this many people about Black Eyes and not have it leak?"

"Here's how it works," he said. "If you tell something to one person, you *might* keep it a secret; if you tell two, there's an eighty percent chance you won't, and if you tell three or more, you haven't got a prayer."

"You just told a whole roomful."

His answer was a devil's smile.

"You *want* it to leak?" I said.

"Got to prime the pump," he said. "We want investors to be eager."

"Who's gonna leak it?" I said.

"Deliberately, nobody. One of the guys will tell his wife why he's working late, she'll complain about it to her hairdresser, the woman sitting next to her will tell her husband, he'll tell a golf buddy in the locker room, and by tomorrow morning a Wall Street arb will be instructing his trader on the floor to buy. Leaks are like ice melting on glass, Max: They're invisible, untraceable, and impossible to stop."

We boarded the helicopter, which was already warmed up, and lifted off for the twenty-minute trip back to the office. Tacoma was already in the front seat working, her Prada backpack—her version of a purse, briefcase, and shoulder bag in one—at her feet. I felt a distinct coolness from her that made me think she was disciplining me for my gaffe with Dick Linzer. For Spin's sake, she was also making herself as pure as Caesar's wife.

"Where are we with the divorce?" Spin asked.

"The arbitrator has the papers," I said.

"Has Bob Cohen argued the case yet?"

"He has."

"What's he think?"

"Could go either way."

"That means it's bad news," Spin said. He turned to Tacoma. "What's happening with the stock?"

"Down two points since the opening bell," she said. "But so's the whole energy market."

"We leading the decline or following?"

"Leading," she said.

The company stock wasn't in a free fall yet, but it was going down.

"Black Eyes can't happen too fast," Spin said to himself.

As far as I was concerned, the whole situation was perfectly suited to what I did best: The company was in heavy seas, the captain was at the helm with steely eyes and the heart of a lion, I was his first mate, and we had to weather the storm or sink. This was why I was in the oil business. This was why it was so good. This was why, if you loved tension and adventure, you couldn't do better. Damn the torpedoes, full speed ahead.

THE NEXT MORNING WAS A different matter. My phone rang.

"Hello?"

"Max? Bob Cohen here."

"What's up?"

"The arbitrator ruled."

"And?"

"We lost."

Nuts.

"What's the price tag?"

"Spin owes Audrey half a billion dollars plus fifty million in interest, costs, and miscellaneous reimbursements."

"Have you told him yet?"

"I'm telling you first."

Right, here's the bad news, go tell the boss, and kiss your ass goodbye. "Between the two of us, Bob," I said, "what's Spin worth after paying this off?"

I heard the clacking of keys on a computer keyboard. "Can't speak to his real estate holdings, but his stock is worth four hundred and ninety million."

"Jesus," I said. "He's underwater."

"By about sixty million," Bob said. "Of course, the stock could go up."

"Or how about this, Bob: It could go down." I swiveled to see my computer screen. "It's down three since the opening bell." It was hard to imagine Spin being insolvent, bankrupt, and stone-cold broke. "You're the lawyer on this, Bob, you should tell him."

"I would but I'm late for a meeting."

"How long will it last?"

"About a week."

He hung up before I could say the "bull" in "bullshit."

I snapped my phone closed, called Spin, and gave him the news.

He was in classic form. He said it came as no surprise, not to worry, he had thirty days to pay her off and by then we'd be in clover.

The guy had balls the size of cantaloupes. I wished I were going to New York to see him in action.

AS IT TURNED OUT, I DIDN'T HAVE to go to New York to see him speak; Tacoma had arranged a live feed from the UN media center. She was already in his office when I got there.

"Hey, you," she said.

"Hi."

"Pull up a chair, he's about to go on," she said.

On the wall of Spin's office was a large monitor and a multimedia delivery system with cable TV, satellite feeds, closed-circuit broadcasts, DVD, VCR, and other forms of visual and audio internal corporate communications. By hitting the right buttons, he could communicate with supervisors at the warehouse, the laboratory, building security downstairs, and the company's offices on Wild Stallion. The cameras on the drilling platform sent their pictures to a digital videotape that recorded and held them for forty-eight hours, then cleared them for the next feed. Tacoma was recording Spin's closed-circuit speech, which we were seeing live.

I tried one of the remote controls and got a CNN news anchor talking about a rumor that Gulf-Tex Oil was about to announce a new technology in the oil exploration business. In anticipation of the announcement, the anchor said, the company's stock had spiked shortly before trading closed the day before.

"You want some of my sandwich?" Tacoma asked, pushing the plate toward me.

"What is it?"

"Tomatoes, lettuce, eggplant, and roasted peppers."

"No thanks," I said.

She laughed, and her eyes triggered the feeling I'd had the first time I'd seen them. It was an indelible feeling, like the first time you rode a roller coaster. Her lemony perfume and white blouse still occupied most of the space in my head. I suppose it always would. Even though she was out of reach—or maybe *because* she was out of reach—she was still the prize. I could be three feet or three miles away and still feel her magnetic field.

By the time I realized I was staring at her—I was remembering her hailing a cab on a hot summer day—it was too late, she'd already noticed. I wanted to walk over and tilt her head back . . . make her drop her sandwich and reach up for me . . . feel her full lips against mine, hear her whisper things in the language only the two of us understood—

"Max?"

"Uh-huh?"

"Can you figure this out?" She was in front of the bank of controls. She hit a button and the closed-circuit transmission came on the screen. "Never mind, I think I got it," she said, and backed up to the coffee table, pushed her sandwich aside, and took a drink of iced tea.

On-screen, a distinguished official with gray hair and a slight Southern accent was introducing our boss. There was polite applause as Spin walked to the podium. When it ended, he smiled at the camera.

"Ladies and gentlemen," he said, "thank you for welcoming me . . ."

". . . to the United Nations Development Fund Annual Meeting."

A second camera swept a large meeting room where people were having lunch and others sat on a dais. The audience included key staff of the UN Secretariat, a dozen ambassadors of oil-exporting countries, twice that number of people from oil-importing countries, consular staff, industry representatives, the press, and everybody who mattered.

Spin took off his reading glasses, stood straight, and spoke to the audience without notes.

"Oil is the largest prize on the planet, which makes it the world's greatest source of conflict. A handful of nations that control most of the earth's fossil fuels will continue to exert wildly disproportionate influence over the rest of the world, both industrialized and emerging."

He was commanding and at ease. The camera liked him.

"Ladies and gentlemen, imagine a world where the mystery of what lies beneath the earth no longer decides people's fate, where the hands of the map drawers no longer cause wars, hate, and terror. I ask you to imagine such a world, but you won't have to imagine it for long. A technological breakthrough rivaling Fulton's steam engine, Nobel's dynamite, and Einstein's fission will soon put that world within reach. Its technical name is Four-Dimensional Deep Earth Sonar, but its better name is the one given to it by the men and women who invented it: Black Eyes."

He stopped speaking, the lights dimmed, and a screen behind him filled with the Black Eyes prototype. And then it cut to Wild Stallion and a demonstration of how Black Eyes worked.

As Tacoma and I watched, she said, "You know what? He really is going to win a Nobel Prize."

I couldn't be sure of that, but I knew I was proud to work for him and help make Black Eyes a reality. It was central to everything that mattered now: the company's success, Spin's reputation, our employees' well-being, my future. My future not just with Gulf-Tex, but, I suspected, with Tacoma, too. If I had one.

THE NEXT THREE DAYS WERE a form of controlled pandemonium. Spin stayed in New York to be interviewed by national television, radio, and the pencil press, then meet with Goldman Sachs, Prudential, and half a dozen other investment bankers. Tacoma flew to New York to join him while I stayed in Houston to work on the licensing agreements Gulf-Tex would be using to sell the technology.

For the next week, there were as many interviews with Spin as there were with political figures and celebrities. Rumors started that once Black Eyes found oil, Spin Patterson would run for the Senate, look toward the White House, and eventually be canonized.

By the time Spin and Tacoma returned to Houston, the news was full of even more Gulf-Tex stories. Photo ops of Spin and Black Eyes were all over the place, and so were simulated pictures of the device, including a fancy clip of a hologram showing a hunk of the earth floating in the air with large areas of green, orange, and yellow in it.

Press calls came from all over the world, but more important were the inquiries from prospective buyers: oil companies, exploration companies, government agencies, universities, nongovernmental agencies, entrepreneurs, and wildcatters. Until something like this happens, you forget that everyone needs energy and that, sooner or later, it brings them to petroleum ore and gas.

If the news was big, the stock movement was bigger. In a matter of three days the company's shares went from five to eleven, a huge increase. Seeing the stock move that far that fast made everyone in the investment world a little crazy. Some people sold off their holdings under the assumption that the price had become too speculative, but it didn't put a serious crimp in the upward curve. It zigged and zagged, but at the end of each day it was still climbing.

The minute Spin got back to Houston he started organizing a field test of Black Eyes for prospective buyers. So many potential licensees wanted to see it in operation we had to limit organizations to two representatives each.

If the field test worked, we'd have more customers than we'd know what to do with. As it was, deposits from would-be buyers were already pouring in. Even if they were conditional on satisfactory proof that Black Eyes worked, cash was cash, and it was flowing. The result gave Gulf-Tex immediate revenues, made Wall Street happy, and created projections that drove the stock through the rafters. Everyone, it turned out, was against buying blue sky until you showed them a patch of it for themselves. Then they wanted it like oxygen.

It was a classic Spin Patterson game of nerve: hang the technology out for everyone to see, give them as much due diligence as they wanted, be transparent about the pluses and minuses of the system, and make it work. It was the kind of strategy he was known for. All or nothing, boom or bust.

There must have been some doubters someplace in the industry, but if there were, they weren't inside the halls of Gulf-Tex. Around the office there was a sense of excitement verging on hysteria as we watched the stock continue to soar. Bank accounts were emptied as people bought into Spin's vision of the future. The five hundred shares worth $10,000 he'd given everyone at Christmas were now worth $50,000 and climbing. Everyone was buying stock as fast as they could—draining their pension plans, mortgaging their homes, borrowing from friends and relatives, emptying their kids' piggy banks—doing whatever it took to grab on to the tail of a shooting star.

Every day for the next forty-five days the stock went up and we got richer and richer, at least on paper. And who was to say stock wasn't money? Unless you held it in your 401(k), all you had to do was call your broker, sell, and just like that your bank account got fatter. The color green was running through the veins of everyone in the company.

Hearing that the employees were on a buying rampage, Spin called a "town hall" meeting inside the company to talk some sense into them. The minute he walked into the auditorium, the place erupted with applause, whistles, and victory signs. He took the stage and told everyone the same thing they'd seen on the news about Black Eyes, then ended by advising them not to bet the ranch on a technology that showed great promise but wasn't proven yet.

Everyone listened, applauded politely, then went out and bought more stock. Most of the men in the company had wives who worried about overextending themselves, but their husbands either didn't listen or bribed them with flowers, dishwashers, or plane tickets to Italy. One guy wheeled a new refrigerator up to the kitchen door before telling his wife he'd mortgaged the house to buy more shares.

Not to worry. When you're watching a stock grow to the sky, it doesn't occur to you that it might stop one day. This was everyone's moment to win the lottery, hit the jackpot, and get in on the American Dream. Every capitalist cliché you've ever heard kicked in and pushed the people of Gulf-Tex to go as far as they could go. *I can't miss. Slam dunk. I'm rich.*

How did I know this was everyone's mind-set? First, because everyone in the company talked about it; second, because when we filed our 10-Q and wrote down the company's oil and gas reserves by 58 percent, it hardly put a dent in the stock price; and third, this morning I bought five hundred shares, sold them at noon, and used the profits to buy two hundred more. What more proof did I need?

Carpe diem.

IT WAS THE FIFTEENTH DAY of the month—the ides of March to be exact—two months after the Black Eyes announcement, and for Spin it couldn't have been a more important day. He was thirty days overdue paying Audrey, who'd given him twenty-four more hours to make good on her judgment or she'd foreclose on his half-billion-dollar bond. Having strung her out as long as he could, he was on a conference call with his stock portfolio manager at Salomon Smith Barney and his personal banker, Borden B. Bishop III, discussing the Gulf-Tex stock price and whether it had peaked.

"The curve is flattening," his broker said. "Until you find oil with this new invention, a lot of the play is going out of the stock."

His banker said, "Are you still getting deposits from prospective licensees?"

"Yeah," Spin said, "but they're slowing. I think next quarter's revenues are already reflected in the stock price."

"I agree," the broker said. "You could get another upward spike when you do this field test you're gonna do, but until then I don't see anything happening that's going to give the stock a boost. When you doing that test?"

"Mid-May," Spin said.

"I'd take some profits now, buy back in before the test, and ride it up on some more good news later, assuming you have some."

"If I sell now," Spin said, "what's my after-tax net?"

"On how much of your stock?"

"All of it."

His broker took a second to calculate the figure on his computer.

"Eight hundred fifty million dollars and change," he said.

"Sell it," Spin said.

"How much?"

"Everything."

That quieted the conversation.

The broker said, "We'll have to do this on a controlled program or you'll depress the price. And you'll have to file."

"Do what you have to do," Spin said, "but sell."

His banker said, "Spin, I think you want to hold back a little so you can remain a shareholder in the company."

"Of course, keep a few hundred shares in my account. And Borden?"

"Yes?"

"When the money hits my account, give me a call. I'm a month overdue writing a sizable check."

"Will do. And congratulations, Spin. You're a very rich man."

AUDREY'S CHAUFFEUR, JACKSON, brought a package into the kitchen that had just been delivered by messenger and set it on the counter. "It says open at once, Mrs. Patterson," he said, and left.

Audrey's cocker spaniel, Mobil, sat down, licked his chops, and cocked his head to the side, waiting for something to happen. She pulled a kitchen knife from a drawer and sliced open the wrapping. Inside was a bottle of Cristal and a white envelope, and inside that was a card and a cashier's check.

The check was for $550 million. The card read simply, *Aud: I believe this settles all accounts in full. Spin.*

She laid the check on the countertop and opened the bottle of champagne without chilling it. When the cork popped, she poured it into the dog's water bowl and invited him over.

"What do you think, Mobil?" she said, holding his head close to hers and rubbing his ears. "Does this settle all accounts in full?"

He pulled away and shook his head no the way dogs do when their ears have been rubbed too long.

"Exactly," she said.

He barked once and went for the champagne.

THE BABY NEEDED TO BE FED and Christopher needed to be held. Both were crying at the same time, which was rare; usually one waited for the other to stop before starting.

Jenny was glad Joe was home.

She opened her nursing bra and fed her baby girl. Joe picked up Christopher, who had a stomachache, and rocked him gently. Ordinarily he sang to the kids, but not tonight. He was preoccupied with problems at the lab and showing the strain, but cradling Christopher helped ease the boy's pain and Joe's, too.

"You alright, honey?" Jenny said.

"Of course," Joe said. "Why wouldn't I be?"

"I don't know, you seem a little tense."

He didn't reply.

She said, "Maybe it's because it's your birthday. I hope you're not feeling old. You're not, you know."

"I'm feeling old, but not because it's my birthday."

Jenny rocked in a chair and held her baby close. "I thought we should take a look at an SUV this weekend. What do you think?"

"What's wrong with the station wagon?" he said. "OK, Christopher, you're gonna be fine, listen to Daddy."

"It's a broken-down piece of junk," she said.

"I don't want a new car."

"What's the point of having all this money if we don't buy a few things now and then?" she said.

"I don't like it!" Joe roared.

Christopher started crying.

"For God's sake, Joe," Jenny said in a low, determined voice, "what's gotten into you?"

Joe sat rocking Christopher again, shushing him and finger-combing his fine, blond hair.

"I'm working too hard," he said.

"Way too hard," Jenny said. "When's it going to end?"

"Tomorrow," he said. "Definitely tomorrow."

They sat there quietly, tending their kids. After a while Sarah was finished and Christopher was finally asleep. They carried them into their rooms and closed the door.

Jenny said, "I left a grocery bag in the car. Would you mind bringing it in?"

Saying nothing, Joe walked out the door and headed for the garage.

Joe paused on the stone path to smell the May blossoms on the vines by the door. The moon was half-full and the spring air was sweet, reminding him of evenings when he was a kid and new flowers told him summer was on the way. It felt as if those days were hidden behind a sheet of bulletproof glass now, as if everything meaningful and good had become hostage to a fraudulent fortune. Staring at the moon, he made up his mind once again: Tomorrow it would end. Tomorrow for sure. He was pulling out, regardless of the consequences.

He opened the door to the garage, reached inside, and flicked on the light.

"SURPRISE!!!"

He jumped back from a roomful of people who were laughing and clapping and blowing birthday kazoos. Music on his workshop stereo started up.

"We got ya!" one of the roughnecks said.

Angela Song came up and gave him a hug.

Jenny appeared at the door, smiling. Joe turned to her, cocked his head, and said, "You dirty rat," and the two of them embraced.

Others came up to him to congratulate him and pat him on

the back: his staff members and their spouses, Angela's team, Max, their roughneck friends—Musselman, Eddy J, Harley, and Dutch.

The music stopped and there was a recorded trumpet entrance. Everyone parted, and there in front of him was a shiny new Ford SUV. The crowd said, "Oouuuuu."

Joe turned to Jenny, who was dangling the keys in her hand. He took them and went to the cab and opened the door. Taped to the steering wheel was a manila envelope with a red ribbon on it.

He peeled it off and looked at Jenny again.

"Go ahead," she said, "open it."

He tore off the flap, reached inside, and pulled out a stock certificate of five hundred shares of Gulf-Tex common. When the crowd saw it, they began applauding.

Dutch walked up to him, took the certificate, and held it high, a beer in hand. "Here's to the man who turned this paper into gold!"

Everyone cheered and lifted their glasses.

Joe smiled and closed the door to the SUV, then found Jenny and pulled her into a long embrace. At the end of it, whispering in her ear, he said, "I'll be right back."

"Where you going?" she asked.

"Get me a beer, would you?" he said, backing toward the door. He smiled grandly, waved, and said, "Got to see a man about a horse!"

Joe hadn't taken ten steps before he found himself leaning against the kids' swing set, crying. All these people so happy and grateful for wealth that was built on a lie. And he created it. After a moment, he dried his face in the crook of his elbow, then sat on the swing seat and listened to the sounds of the friends who'd come to honor him and laugh and play music in his workshop. His tears splattered on the dirt where the kids' feet had worn away the grass. If he were slipping down the face of the Darth Vader's Tower right now, he would simply have let go.

"What is it, honey?"

He felt Jenny's hand on his shoulder. Turning, he pulled her to him and buried his face in her midriff. "There are going to be some rough days ahead," he said. "I just want you to know I love you more than ever."

Rubbing the back of his neck, she said, "What rough days?"

He didn't answer.

She said, "You really are working too hard, sweetheart," and kissed the top of his head. "Spin couldn't be here, but he said to tell you your birthday present is a week's vacation in Cozumel. For two—I almost forgot to add that." She stooped in front of him and smoothed back his hair. "I've never been more proud of you, Joe."

He reached out and touched her face. She kissed the palm of his hand and turned back to him with a big smile. "Have you ever been to Mexico?"

Staring at her, he saw innocence in her face he'd never noticed before. It was amazing what a little extra money could do to make people's lives lighter and better. "I've been to Mexico, but not Cozumel," he said, and gave her a smile. "Who knows? Maybe we'll like it so much we'll never come back."

"If that's what you want, that's fine with me."

He stood up and kissed her and held her tight. "That's all I need to know."

She pulled back so she could see his face in the light of the workshop. After drying the wetness around his eyes, she said, "We better get back inside, don't you think?"

The two of them walked arm in arm back to the garage.

MY BROTHER WILL AND I WERE in my BMW Z4 with the top down and the wind whipping around our faces heading for O'Reilly's for a beer and a sandwich.

"Everybody with two dollars is betting on Gulf-Tex," I said.

"You included?" he said.

"Me included."

"Be careful, Max."

"About what?"

I drove past an exit sign.

"Hey, you missed the exit," Will said. "You having trouble reading again?"

"No, it's not my dyslexia," I said, grinning. "I need your help with something."

I pulled off the highway and took the exit ramp faster than I should have, but the car held the road and I was feeling good. Up ahead was a strip mall with an electronics store that sold computers and cameras. I pulled into a parking space, cut the engine, and reached into the backseat for my little digital camera.

"It's broken," I said. "I'm gonna leave it here to be fixed."

We got out and entered the store. Will can't get within a hundred yards of a camera shop without being drawn into it like a boy in a hobby shop.

"What can I do for you gents today?" a salesman said.

I handed him my camera and said it was broken. He toyed with it a second and handed it back. "There's only one remedy," he said.

"What's that?"

"A new camera."

We laughed.

He turned and lifted a box off the counter behind him. Inside was a new Sony videocam with everything on it. Will picked it up and turned it in his hands as the salesman told him it did everything but take out the garbage. After fiddling with it a minute, he set it down and looked at his watch.

"We gotta get to O'Reilly's," he said.

The salesman put the camera back in the box and slid it across the counter. "Why'n't you take it for a spin?"

Will raised his eyebrows. "You're lending me a new Sony?"

"Nope," the salesman said. "I'm giving it to you."

"What's going on?" Will said, looking at me.

I gave him a big grin. "Go ahead, it's yours."

"The hell it is."

He was getting the picture.

"How about that," I said, picking up my little camera, "it works after all." I gave him a hug and he slapped me on the back.

"You're crazy," he said. "Rich and crazy."

Gulf-Tex stock pumped us all full of helium and made us feel a little bigger than before. Money was fun. Money was freedom. Handled with the right attitude, money was simply the best.

And, handled wrongly, the worst.

JOE WAS STILL WORKING AT eight thirty that night but he wasn't any further along than he'd been that morning, or the morning before. Sometimes the deep sonar transmitted an accurate picture of the physiology of the earth, and sometimes it didn't. He still thought the problem was in the transmission, not the computer program that interpreted it, but he was beginning to wonder if Angela might have been right after all. Maybe it was a software problem.

It had been four months since Spin had announced Black Eyes, and the more Joe worked on the problem, the more a solution eluded him. And now time had finally run out. In less than forty-eight hours, it wouldn't be his boss and coconspirator who was looking over his shoulder, it would be the world.

The phone rang but he ignored it. When it continued, he checked the caller ID and saw that it was Jenny.

"Hi," he said.

"How are you, honey?" she said.

"Still here."

"Come on home, we miss you."

"I've got to get this thing ready for tomorrow." He and Spin were going to do a dry run the next day and get it ready for the big event the day after that.

"How's it going?"

It doesn't work! I'll have to fake it! "OK," he said.

"You'll be fine. You always are."

Everyone believed in the magic of the machine except the guy who'd invented it. "I'll be there in an hour," he said.

He hung up, finished typing in the new set of instructions he'd been working on, and waited.

Once again, they failed.

"Damn it!" he hissed, and threw the pages of notes into the air. He stared at the mess, then gave in and rubbed his eyes under his glasses. He was going home. He got up and put on his jacket.

When he reached the door, he stopped. Someone had pinned an article from *Oil Industry News* on the back of it with a headline that read THE PROMISE OF BLACK EYES and a subhead that read, *Joe Wright Named Industry Engineer of the Year.*

He tore it down, crumpled it up, and threw it across the room, missing the wastebasket. Staring at the computer's red and green lights, he put his hand on the light switch, then pulled away. His shoulders slumped and he returned to his desk, where he picked his notes off the floor and went back to work. He had one other idea he hadn't tried. If it didn't work, there was only one thing he could do.

And it was ugly.

WHEN THE HELICOPTER TOUCHED down on Wild Stallion's helipad, the pilot told Spin he was getting reports of a weather system forming in the Gulf to the southeast. It was a little early for a hurricane—the season usually started at the end of May—but they had to keep their eyes open.

Spin told the pilot to hustle back to the warehouse, pick up Angela Song and the rest of the crew, and return. He wanted to meet with Joe first, then bring in everyone else who'd have a role to play the next day. He and Joe had to make sure the fake program was loaded into the computer and operating flawlessly, and that Joe was comfortable at the controls.

The pilot powered up the rotor blades, lifted off the platform, and headed back to Houston before Joe and Spin had climbed down to the main deck. The sky was calm but filled with a gray thickness that blocked out the sun. Spin didn't want to dawdle, so they headed straight for the doghouse. When he slipped the key into the lock, Joe put his hand on the door and held it closed.

"I can't do this," he said.

Spin straightened up. "Can't do what?"

"Fake the test."

"You have to," Spin said. "The whole world's gonna be here tomorrow."

"I can't."

Spin touched Joe's arm to comfort him. "Listen, Joe, I know how you feel, you're under terrific pressure and so am I, but we've got to keep our nerve and stick with the program."

"I'll never find the solution," Joe said. "I've been at it for months. It's not there."

"You'll find it," Spin said.

"But we're telling the world we already have it! If anybody finds out—"

"Nobody's gonna find out!"

"Don't be so sure. Angela's starting to ask questions. I can't keep her out of my black box forever."

"All we need is one more day."

"All these people and engineers coming out here—they're gonna be on to us!"

"Take a deep breath."

"I can't sleep, I can't face Jenny, I can't even talk to my team."

"You're just jittery. Get us through tomorrow's dog and pony show, take that vacation with Jenny, and you'll come back a new man."

"A vacation won't do it, Spin. I need to put an end to this."

"You think backing out now will *end* it? It'll just be the beginning! The dice have been rolled, Joe! We've passed Go! We back out now, we're talking scandal on a scale you wouldn't believe! Think of your family!"

"I am! Other families, too! We've got everybody in the company mortgaging their houses to buy stock! My own wife gave me five hundred shares of Gulf-Tex for my birthday! Can you believe it? Five hundred shares of worthless shit tied up with a little red ribbon, and I'm the one who created it!"

"You're a rich man, Joe, and if you keep your nerve, you'll be richer still."

"You aren't listening, Spin! I *can't* get it to work!"

"Yes, you can! And if you can't, Angela can!"

A gust of wind kicked up a piece of paper and sent it across their feet.

"I've made an appointment to see a lawyer," Joe said.

"What kind of lawyer?"

"A white-collar guy to help get me out of this mess."

Spin walked in a small circle and came back. "Now listen to me, Joe. Talking to a criminal lawyer would be the biggest mistake of your life."

"That's not how I see it," he said. "What I see is you running the stock through the roof and selling off your holdings. Probably more than you needed to pay off Audrey. Did you?"

"Did I what?"

"Sell more than you needed to pay her off?"

"I sell according to what my brokers think makes sense."

"That's what I thought," Joe said. "You sold big."

"Stick to the issue, Joe. If we take Black Eyes out to Damnation Alley and prove we can hit it big, we'll have enough revenues to justify the stock price at twice its current level. We're talking about finding an elephant field! Ten percent of it will give us enough cash to carry the company another year or more, which is plenty of time for you to get Black Eyes working!"

"Come on, Spin, there's no oil field out there and you know it. You never saw it on that submarine, and you never plotted the coordinates of it. If you had, you and PEMEX would have figured out how to drill it by now. You gave me a cock-and-bull story just to get me to rig Black Eyes, and like an idiot I went for it."

"You're wrong, Joe. Completely wrong."

The wind was picking up fast. They put on their hard hats and tightened the chin straps.

"What you did took balls," Joe said, "I have to give you that. You bet everything you owned that I'd find the answer, and if I had, you would have pulled off one of the greatest shell games in history. But I haven't got the answer, and nobody's sorrier about it than I am."

The wind fluttered the flaps on their jumpsuits. Spin paced again, rubbing his neck beneath his chin.

Joe said, "My career's ruined, Spin, but it's not too late to keep other people from going down the tubes. God help me when Jenny finds out."

"Listen to me, Joe, the only way this gets out of hand is if you—"

They heard the sound of the steel derrick groaning in the wind above their heads.

"We better get inside," Spin said. He opened the door to the doghouse and they entered. A gust of wind shook the building. Spin pulled his cell phone from his pocket and dialed. "This storm is coming faster than I thought."

His secretary, Charlene, answered. He told her to call the chopper and have it come back right away. "Let's load the program, Joe. We've got to be ready tomorrow."

Lightning lit up the room.

"Can't do it, Spin."

"Come on, Joe—"

"I can't!"

"You have to!" Smacking the console with the flat of his hand.

Joe stared at him impassively.

Spin grabbed his friend's jumpsuit below the neck. "Think, Joe, think! We're on the tiger's back! We get off now, we're lunch!"

A bolt of lightning hit so close by they could smell the burned ozone after the crack, but neither man moved. Spin's cell phone rang. He ignored it as long as he could, waiting for Joe's answer, then opened the flip and put it to his ear. "What is it?"

Charlene said, "The pilot says you and Joe should get on the helipad immediately. He's got a small window but it won't last long."

"Got it." Spin hung up and turned to Joe, but instead of getting him out of there, he said, "We've got enough time to get this done."

Spin went to the window. The sky was black and the wind was blowing debris across the deck. A loose rope was beating the top of the doghouse. They heard the sound of the chopper engine approaching.

Spin said, "I'll tie him down."

He exited the doghouse, leaned into the wind, and made

his way toward the steps up to the helipad. When he got to the base, he saw the chopper bobbing on a sea of turbulent air, the pilot working hard to set it down. If he made it, they'd have to board immediately and leave.

Spin waved his arms in an X motion, got the pilot's attention, and shook his head no. He pointed both hands away from the deck, telling him to depart. The pilot pointed downward—asking if he should come in—but Spin shook his head and pointed away again.

The pilot gave him an OK sign and pulled back on the yoke. The helicopter lifted, tilted toward Houston, caught the enormous tailwind, and disappeared.

Spin grabbed his hard hat and struggled back to the doghouse.

SPIN OPENED THE DOOR AND slipped inside. The howl of the wind was rising.

"He couldn't get down," he yelled. "We gotta get below!"

Waves slammed against the semisubmersible's pylons, shaking the platform with earthquakelike tremors.

Spin tossed Joe a yellow slicker and pulled one on himself. They tightened the chin straps on their helmets and Joe pulled on his gloves. "Where are your gloves?" he yelled at Spin.

Spin shook his head, he didn't know. "Let's go!"

They opened the door and bent down and took baby steps toward the stairwell that led to the offices and safety quarters below. Pieces of debris were now flying missiles in the rising, hurricane-force wind.

A piece of torn tarpaulin hit Spin below the knees, knocking his feet from under him. He landed on his butt and skidded in the wind across the slippery surface toward the edge of the platform. Rolling onto his stomach, he flattened himself on the deck a few feet from the edge and lay still. Joe got on his hands and knees and crawled to him.

"You OK?" he yelled.

"Yeah, let's go!" Spin said.

They crawled to the safety cable ringing the platform, grabbed it, stood up, and began working their way hand over hand toward the stairwell. Lightning flickered on their all-weather gear and the steel cable. Another fifty feet and they'd be there.

A burst of blue ripped through the air above their heads—so

close the lightning and thunderclap were simultaneous—then they heard the *zizz* sound of burning steel. They looked up and saw a crane arm dangling from the derrick. The wind twisted it and broke it loose, slammed it onto the deck between the two men, slashed through the safety cable, and slid into the void. Dancing on one foot, Joe grabbed the restraining cable, but with a break in the middle it wasn't taut.

Holding on to the end of it, he went over the side.

"JOE!" SPIN YELLED, REACHING for the cable. It played out over the edge and snapped tight against the end that was still screwed into a turnbuckle on a stanchion.

Spin dropped to his stomach, wrapped one arm around the stanchion, and looked down over the edge of the platform. Joe was dangling two stories below, high above a snarling sea, the cable wrapped around his gloved hands, the loose end whipping in the wind.

Spin used his leg to anchor himself to the post, then grabbed on to the cable with his bare hands and pulled. It was no use: There was too much weight and the cable was too wet and slippery.

He looked over the edge again, his hands trembling and bleeding.

Joe was still holding on with one hand and using the other to gather in the loose cable and coil it around his thigh—once, twice, three times—making a jerry-rigged climber's seat to take the weight off his hands.

"You're secure at this end!" Spin yelled.

Joe nodded. The platform was groaning as if the world were trying to pull it from its moorings. After resting a moment, Joe pulled himself up, suspended himself with one hand again, and tightened the cable around his thigh, raising himself upward a few inches at a time. It was smart, but Spin couldn't tell how long he could keep it up.

Don't die on me now, Joe. You're all I got.

He recalled seeing tools on the truck next to the doghouse.

"I'm going for a winch!" he yelled.

Spin swiveled on his stomach toward the doghouse, let go of the stanchion, and crawled toward the truck. When he reached it, he grabbed the tailgate handle and pulled himself into a standing position. The vehicle was rocking in the wind.

He loosened the tie-down line on the tarp. The wind got under it and ripped it away like a handkerchief. In front of him was machinery but no winch. He saw a toolbox—reached for it—pulled open the top—and spilled the contents across the bed. Pushing through the tools frantically, all he saw was a wrench. He grabbed it, thinking he could wrap the cable on it and pull Joe up, then he dropped onto his stomach and crawled back to the post.

WHEN HE REACHED THE EDGE of the platform, he looked down and saw Joe dangling ten feet away, the cable coiled four times around both thighs.

"No winch!" Spin yelled.

Joe lifted himself another six inches and tightened the coil. His breathing was hard, his face strained and bulging.

More lightning and cracks of thunder.

Spin lay on his belly and looked down at the man he'd worked with, laughed with, and climbed with for twenty years, dangling above a bottomless black hole. "Two more pulls and I can reach you!" he yelled.

Spin wound the wrench into the cable like a stick into a kite string and turned it, shortening the cable and helping Joe up. The rain and wind were getting worse.

After another upward hoist, Joe's hands were nearly within reach. Spin anchored his legs around the cable stanchion, leaned over the edge of the platform, and extended his hand.

Joe hoisted himself one more time, muscles spent, his movement as slow as cold honey, wrapping the cable around his thigh to keep himself from slipping down. He looked up at Spin, then slowly extended his hand. Spin reached for him the way he had at Darth Vader's Tower—quickly and instinctively, one climber to another—and grabbed his wrist.

I've got him in my hands!

He pulled until Joe's free hand reached the platform and pawed the wet, slippery surface, searching for an edge to grip.

Spin held tight. *Everything is in my hands!* He mustered

his strength and pulled, fighting gravity and weather and the lubrication of blood and rain on his palms. Joe's eyes were close enough now to show his fear.

Then something strange happened: Spin saw the preacher in the Cadillac. Suddenly, everything went into reverse: his plan for Black Eyes, his hopes, his dreams, the moral assumptions that made him a civilized man. *But you can trust him—he kept his mouth shut once before—why shouldn't he do it again?*

His brain shrieked back at him, *It's not about staying silent this time—he's not going to fake Black Eyes to begin with! He'd rather face his wife and prison before that! You know it's true! You know it!*

Spin had half a second to make a decision.

"Joe!" Spin yelled. "I'm sorry!"

Joe's eyes showed confusion—*Sorry?*—then turned bright with understanding.

Spin waited as long as he could—every instinct he had told him to hang on to Joe's hand—and then let go.

Joe's other hand swiped wildly at the platform, found nothing to grip, and fell away.

SPIN LOOKED OVER THE EDGE and saw his friend jolt to a stop ten feet below and swing in the violent wind, his body held in place by the cable wrapped around his thigh and tangled around his waist and chest. He wasn't moving and his head was tilted down as if he'd passed out.

Spin rolled onto his back and tried to gather his thoughts. Was he dead? He looked down again and saw no sign of life. Maybe his neck had snapped when he reached the end of the cable. Maybe he'd died of exhaustion. Maybe he'd died of a broken heart.

Spin's own heart was pounding wildly.

He turned onto his back again, lifted the wrench in his bleeding hands, and slowly placed the mouth of the wrench on the shank nut that screwed the cable into the turnbuckle. Turning it to the right would keep it from coming loose, turning it left would disconnect it.

He turned it to the left.

After several more half-turns, he could feel the cable shank coming loose and wiggling under the weight of Joe's body. One more turn and it would come free.

He made the turn.

The cable pulled out of the turnbuckle and disappeared over the side like a tape measure being zipped into its case.

Spin leaned out and watched Joe drop away. Blown outward by the hurricane, he missed the safety net three stories below, hit the net's frame, windmilled, and continued falling toward the sea.

A small voice in Spin instantly cried, *Bring him back!* but another—bigger and stronger—shouted, *You did what you had to do!*

He rolled onto his back and stared into a closed-up sky. A phrase kept coming to mind—*cold-blooded killer*—but he told himself it didn't apply to him, he was a decent man, a good man, a CEO responsible for the survival of his employees, a respected leader who'd helped thousands of people all over the world, a man who was honored and adored, a man people expected to be president someday, a candidate for a Nobel Prize. Once he got Black Eyes working, there'd be millions of lives he'd save and make better.

He closed his eyes and prayed for understanding.

What had happened was awful but it wasn't of his own making. It was a hurricane, a natural disaster, an accident, like a burning Cadillac by the side of the road. It was an . . . *opportunity*. His mother's voice said it again: *God will provide.*

He opened his eyes and saw a flash of lightning appear in the clouds like a cosmic wink.

God knew. God understood.

My God—what have I done?

HE TURNED ONTO HIS STOMACH, teeth chattering, and crawled back to the doghouse. He had to get a grip on himself and do what he had to do.

First, get rid of the evidence.

A hundred-forty-mile-an-hour wind was rocking the trailer back and forth on its dolly like a dragster waiting for a green light. He crawled to the chocks holding the wheels in place and pulled them out. Small pieces of debris lashed his forehead and face, but he paid no attention. Squinting, he found the door handle on the truck, pulled himself into a standing position, and slid into the driver's seat.

He reached for the ignition—his shaking hands jangled the keys—started the engine, and put it into reverse. The truck felt ready to take off and fly, but he wasn't afraid. He'd just killed a man. The idea of death—even his own—seemed strangely acceptable.

He turned and looked out the back window, then ran the rear bumper of the truck up against the trailer. With the wind helping, the two vehicles moved back toward the edge of the platform. *Not too fast or you'll go over the side.*

He heard the screeching of steel as the trailer skidded against girders and equipment. He pushed the accelerator down and continued driving the trailer toward the stanchion that had held the safety cable. If he survived, he had to make sure no evidence was left on deck except the remains of a hurricane.

The truck and trailer were moving faster toward the edge.

He saw the wrench he'd used sitting on the passenger seat, grabbed it, and jammed it against the accelerator. The engine redlined and the truck picked up speed. He was in a moving coffin.

He pushed the door open frantically, fought the wind that tried to hold it closed, and finally flung himself out. The stream of air sent him cartwheeling past the trailer toward the platform's edge. He spread his arms in search of something to grab and felt his body slam into a huge diesel engine.

He lay against it watching the truck continue to push the trailer toward the void. The wind deafened him as the trailer tore through the stanchion and the restraining cable and toppled over the side, followed by the truck.

He hadn't just swapped Joe's life for his own, he'd swapped something just as dear to his heart: Black Eyes. It was gone.

The wind's ferocity was increasing. He had to get off the platform or he'd be pummeled by debris or swept into the sea.

He dropped to the deck and tried to press himself flat against the surface. His head bounced up and down in the wind but he felt no pain. Every nerve in his body was focused on reaching the stairwell and the safety quarters below. He began crawling toward the door an inch at a time, trying to stay below nature's radar. *You got me this far, God, bring me the rest of the way.*

That's when he saw a tiny red light blinking through the driving rain. Instantly, he knew it was a security camera. He lifted his head to see it better.

That was a mistake.

The wind hooked under his chin and lifted it, then got under his neck, chest, and stomach and blew him into a standing-upright position, stretching his arms out to the side like a scarecrow's. His lips, cheeks, and slicker rippled as the wind-tunnel air lifted him onto his toes and danced him across the platform like a puppet on a string.

He flailed.

His hands found a rope, tried to grab it, and missed.

His body continued sliding.

He felt himself moving helplessly toward the edge of the platform.

He went over the side.

MY PHONE RANG AT 7:00 A.M. Tacoma was the last person I expected to be calling at this hour and, even less, crying.

"What is it?" I said.

"There was an accident on Wild Stallion." She paused to get control of her voice. "Spin was swept over the side. The Coast Guard found him an hour ago in the platform safety net."

"Is he alive?"

"Barely. They're bringing him to the hospital now." Her voice cracked again. "Joe's missing."

My God. "Does Jenny know?"

"I don't know. You better call her."

"I'll meet you at the hospital."

"There's something else, Max. Black Eyes was blown off the platform, too."

"It's *gone*?"

"Not a trace."

We hung up and I dialed Jenny.

TACOMA WAS WAITING AT THE emergency entrance to the hospital when the ambulance pulled up. The doors opened, the EMTs jumped out, and a second later, there he was, strapped to a gurney.

Having spent time in the great outdoors, Tacoma had seen her share of raw anatomy—animals being eaten, skulls drying in the sun—but the flayed skin of Spin's hands, face, and neck and the blue-white bone poking out of his arm made her stomach churn.

She took a breath, wiped her mouth, and walked to his gurney.

The painkillers were kicking in now, distorting his perception and driving him toward disconnection. Still, he was conscious enough to see her shiny hair and black eyes rolling toward him as if out of a dream. *Tacoma.*

His dilemma came into focus with her face. She was the only person he trusted to see what the platform cameras had captured, and yet . . . if they'd captured him unscrewing the cable, he couldn't imagine letting her see it. He couldn't stand the thought of her shock and condemnation . . . her opinion of him meant everything to him . . . but he needed someone to look at the tape . . . destroy it if necessary . . . if he didn't, he could go to prison . . . who else could he trust . . .

A rock . . . a hard place . . . He needed to stay awake.

Tacoma followed him on the gurney into the receiving room. The moment it stopped, she leaned down to him to speak in a whisper. "Didn't your mother teach you to come in out of the rain?"

He nodded and tried to smile, but the skin on his face was too swollen and bruised to flex. He wanted to ask her how badly he was hurt, but that could wait, the other thing couldn't. The drugs were rapidly pushing him toward premature sleep.

"Come . . . here," he said, his voice raspy and unrecognizable.

She leaned down and touched him, helping him stay conscious. An orderly started pushing the gurney again. Moving down a hallway, he sensed she was falling behind and heard someone tell her to wait in the lounge. *No! Stay with me!*

"Ta . . . coma," he groaned.

The gurney reached a double door and was parked next to a wall. She caught up with it.

"What is it?" she said softly.

"My . . . office."

The seductive pull of the painkillers was winning.

"What about your office?"

"Video . . . tape," he said.

She looked perplexed.

"Cameras," he said.

He felt warm velvet spreading through his body. He needed to make her understand . . . before his eyes closed.

He felt movement again—the gurney was starting up, or maybe it was the medicine, he couldn't tell. A tinny voice in his head told him it was only a matter of seconds before his consciousness burned out. Tacoma's voice already had. As if drifting down a long hallway, he heard her last words:

"What about them?"

What about what?

He no longer knew what she was talking about.

He no longer cared.

BY THE TIME I GOT TO HER HOUSE, relatives and neighbors were already there and friends from the office were still arriving. Jenny sat at the kitchen table staring at a blue-and-white baby rattle. Not crying or speaking, just staring.

One of the neighbors said, "He's a great swimmer, Jen."

Another said, "The Coast Guard's got every boat they own out there."

"All the oil service boats are out there, too," someone added.

She toyed with the rattle.

The phone rang. Angela Song picked it up and talked in a low voice. Hanging up, she said, "The Coast Guard's still looking." Her eye caught mine and she shook her head.

I set a glass of water on the table next to Jenny, squeezed her hand, then left the room to make some calls and see what I could find out about the search and Spin's condition. I called Audrey, but Jackson said she was out. I told him what had happened and asked him to let her know as soon as possible. As for Joe, the situation hadn't changed: People were still looking for him, but nothing had been recovered except wreckage blown off the platform.

Hope for his survival was going flatline.

I walked into the living room and found Jenny sitting on the sofa with two-and-a-half-year-old Christopher hanging on her knee, frightened by the presence of so many somber people and an impending sense of doom. She rocked the baby gently in her lap. I stooped in front of her.

"What can I get you?" I asked.

She shook her head.

I stared at her a moment to be sure, then touched her arm to go.

"Spin," she said. "You can get me Spin."

I sat on the sofa and asked her what she meant, but she didn't answer. I realized it wasn't something specific, it was undirected anger at the man she suspected was responsible for her husband's death. As a lawyer I'd seen it before: Even if the cause of death was a natural disaster, relatives wanted to find someone to blame, someone real who could be tried and convicted. Nobody had ever punished God for anything.

I stuck around for a while, feeling useless. When it was clear there was nothing I could do, I headed to the hospital to see Spin.

TACOMA ENTERED SPIN'S OUTER office, which was in turmoil. News of the disaster had reached every floor and employee at Gulf-Tex, but nowhere was the activity and panic greater than in Spin's executive suite. His assistant, Charlene, red-eyed and solemn, fielded phone calls and tried to keep reporters, friends, and the curious at bay. Spin was in critical condition in the middle of surgery.

There was no news about Joe.

Tacoma stopped to talk to Charlene. They hugged each other and commiserated.

After entering Spin's office, Tacoma sat at his desk, put her head down on the mahogany surface, and felt the tears start to well again. Then she reminded herself that Spin was counting on her and straightened up. The large-screen monitor on the wall was dark. She turned it on and saw the main menu appear. Carrying the remote, she walked over to it.

She hit a button that brought the building entrance onscreen—someone was talking to the security guard at the desk—then a live picture of the warehouse—it was quiet—then Joe's laboratory—it was filled with people milling around looking stunned and confused.

She brought up Wild Stallion. The first three cameras, evidently disabled by the storm, showed black-and-white snow, but the fourth camera was still working. Gulf-Tex roughnecks and Coast Guard officers were meandering on deck, looking for evidence of what had happened. Scattered debris showed the storm's aftermath, but nothing that helped find Joe.

Standing at the monitor, she heard the quiet spinning of the digital videotape recording what the cameras had transmitted during the storm. She brought up the menu, placed her cursor on the Replay icon, and hit Select. The monitor blinked and divided into four screens that showed what the four platform cameras had captured.

Using Fast Forward, she stopped-and-started her way through the recording: Spin and Joe coming aboard, the two of them disappearing into the doghouse to work. Fast Forward. Clouds rolling in, the sky darkening. Fast Forward. Everything in rapid motion, Mother Nature on amphetamines.

She hit Play and saw events at normal speed.

Rain. Spotlights illuminating the deck.

She hit Fast Forward again, and Play.

More rain. Canvas tarps and debris being swept across the deck and blown out to sea. Despite the wind, the bolted-down camera remained impervious to the storm.

What's Spin so concerned about?

She waited and watched.

Spin moving into range, Joe next to him. The two of them talking, gesturing normally, holding on to their hard hats as the wind picked up.

Snow on-screen, the transmission momentarily broken.

A gust of wind blowing a loose board past them like a missile, the two of them ducking. Disappearing from view. Now coming back, crawling to the safety cable, grabbing on, pulling themselves to their feet, ten yards apart, trudging toward the stairs that led to the safety room below.

A huge piece of metal structure—a boom or piece of a crane—falling across the deck.

She hit Stop, Rewind, and Play, this time zooming out for a wider angle.

She saw the hunk of metal hit the cable, sever it, and bounce off the platform. Joe dancing on one foot, trying to get his balance, the broken cable in his hand.

Joe blown overboard.

She saw Spin staggering into view toward Joe, dropping to his stomach, crawling to the edge. Grabbing the stanchion that held the other end of the cable. Putting his head over the edge, looking down.

Her heart was beating as if she were watching it all in real time.

The screen turned to snow—broken transmission—then the picture returned.

Spin pulling on the cable. Impossible to lift. Joe apparently on the other end. Spin yelling down at him.

Snow breaking up the screen, then a picture.

It was eerie seeing it without sound.

More snow. Broken transmission. Blips and occasional glimpses of the platform and Spin. Now a picture again.

Spin crawling to the truck behind the doghouse, out of the camera's range.

She tried the other cameras, but they were out of commission. She returned to the wide angle on camera four and saw Spin crawling back to the stanchion, a wrench in hand. Trying to wrap the cable around it to pull Joe up.

Snow.

More snow. The picture gone.

She chose camera three.

Nothing but snow.

Back to camera four.

Snow.

Snow.

Now picture: Joe's hand in Spin's. Spin trying to hold on.

Snow.

Spin alone, Joe not in the picture. My God—he's gone—Joe is gone. Spin crawling under the turnbuckle that held the cable—the cable must have been holding Joe—Spin moving the wrench back and forth on the shank to keep it tight so Joe didn't fall.

She hit Rewind, Play, and Zoom In.

It was hard to see. Sometimes it looked as if he was turning the shank to the left, sometimes to the right, but of course he wasn't turning it to the left because that would have loosened it.

She hit Rewind, Play, Slow Motion, and Zoom In, but still

couldn't see what was happening. Why did she need to? She didn't. She hit Stop, took a drink of water from a plastic bottle, and hit Play. Zoom Out.

Snow.

She stopped the playback, took a head-clearing breath, then got up to leave. Spin was in surgery and needed her. She had to get back to the hospital.

SPIN WAS IN THE SURGERY for three hours. When they wheeled him back to his room, Tacoma was there waiting. An oxygen tube was in his nose and IV needles punctured his veins. Bandages covered the cuts on his hands, neck, and face, and his left arm was in a cast. Waiting for him to wake up, all she could do was dip a small sponge into a bowl of ice water and wet his lips. The doctor said he'd been lucky, his tendons would heal and so would the cuts. As long as there was no infection, the prognosis was good.

"He has a strong heart," the doctor said.

She nodded and smiled wanly.

The doctor said, "And from what I hear about him, a good one, too."

She nodded again.

It was ten o'clock that night when he finally opened his eyes. His daughters had waited in the lounge during surgery and stayed at his side in his room until the nurse said visiting hours were over and they had to leave. When Tacoma saw them walk through the reception room, she slipped into Spin's room.

"Hey, you," he heard her whisper.

"Hey," he said.

"How do you feel?"

"Can't tell." His voice sounded like a metal rasp on plywood. "Am I in one piece?"

"Thanks to some stitches."

His eyes faded. "Hope you like scars."

She smiled and said, "Scars are sexy," but he knew she was trying to be brave. She'd only seen him tall, powerful, and decisive, never frail, drugged, and helpless. It must have come as a shock.

The nurse entered and said it was time for Tacoma to go. She stood and gathered up her bag and jacket.

"Where are you going?" he asked groggily. He winced with pain and toyed with the morphine button but didn't press it. There was something he had to deal with before she left. "Did you get it?"

She pulled a black cassette from her open bag and held it up for him to see.

"What was on it?" he said.

She took a small paper cup and poured herself some water. After drinking it, she said, "The transmission was pretty broken up." Her slender fingers fiddled with the smooth plastic covering.

"How broken up?"

"Lots of static."

"So . . . what did you see?"

"I saw you risk your life to save Joe, and I saw you pull on the cable so hard your hands were a bloody mess. I saw you get thrown by the wind against a huge engine and disappear over the side of the platform."

He closed his eyes and waited for the next shoe to drop. "Nothing else?"

"Like what?"

"I don't know, it's all a blur. I remember having trouble . . . tightening the turnbuckle on the cable . . ."

"I saw that," she said.

"You did?"

"With a wrench."

"He was still holding on to the cable. . . . I screwed the nut on tight, but it didn't hold. The storm ripped it out of the turnbuckle." He felt her lay her hand on his. "I couldn't save him," he said.

"You did your best," she said.

"It wasn't enough." He closed his eyes and lay still. "How much of a beating am I gonna take on the videotape, babe?"

"Why would you take any at all?"

"If it gets out and it's blurry, the TV gossip channels will turn it into a mystery like Diana's death."

"No way, darling. It's clear you did all you could. You'll come out smelling like a rose."

"Ever smell a rose after it's been dragged through the mud?"

She looked at him a moment, then picked up a pair of surgical scissors lying on the bedside table and put the tip of them into a small space on the cassette. There was a loud crack as she pried off the lid.

"It's not going to happen," she said.

Her fingers worked into the box and she pulled out the silvery tape. She slipped it between the scissors' blades and sliced it in two, then cut it into small pieces. After dropping them into a trash bag, she leaned forward and gave him a kiss on his forehead. "See you tomorrow," she said.

"Baby?" he said. "I love you."

"I love you, too."

As she was leaving, he performed a medical miracle on himself.

He started breathing again.

"SELL!" THE INVESTMENT FUND manager said. "Every last share." He didn't look up from the sandwich he was eating or the report he was reading.

"You sure?" the young analyst said. He stood in front of the manager on the forty-fourth floor of a Wall Street hedge fund. "Just because the prototype went into the drink doesn't mean they can't build a new one."

The manager looked up. "Black Eyes is finished. The inventor is dead, Patterson is a wreck, the company's licensing agreements will go into default, and their revenue stream is going to dry up." He pushed his horn-rimmed glasses up the bridge of his nose and turned to a different report on his desk. "We swung for the fences and struck out."

"But it worked before—"

The manager ripped off his glasses. "Number one, we don't know if it worked, and number two, even if it did, by the time the company rebuilds it—if they can—Exxon, Shell, and Kerr-McGee will be ripping off Gulf-Tex's patents and inventing a better mousetrap."

The analyst who'd recommended Gulf-Tex's stock stood like a chastised schoolboy. "I think the stock's coming back. You watch."

"Steak dinner on me if it does," the fund manager said, shoving his glasses back on and turning a page. "Now, sell it and move on."

That conversation, or one like it, was taking place wherever Gulf-Tex stock was owned.

I GOT THE CALL TWO WEEKS after the storm. They'd found Joe's body. Some of his clothes were intact, his gloves were on, and the restraining cable was still wrapped around his legs, but he'd been pretty badly chewed up by sharks and the current. Even though they knew who it was, the majesty of the law required someone to identify him. Spin was still recovering, so to keep Jenny out of it, I volunteered. As her friend and the godfather of little Christopher, it was the least I could do.

Naturally, Jenny insisted on going with me anyway. She wanted to see him one more time so she'd have "closure." I went with her to the morgue, put my arm around her shoulder, and held her hand as they drew back the sheet. I expected her to cut off my circulation, but instead her hand went limp and cold. She cried. It was bad. Closure? When you see your husband ravaged, what you got were nightmares, bitterness, and sorrow, not closure.

Driving her home, I found her silence painful. She'd not only lost the man she loved, she'd lost a husband, provider, and the father of her kids. With no job or income and a pension plan that was close to worthless, maybe bitterness wasn't in the cards after all. She had no time for it.

I'd never thought of Jenny as particularly angry or obsessed, but in the last two weeks she'd decided Spin was the "bad guy" more each day. Sometimes it was based on what she knew, sometimes on what she imagined. Joe had worked so hard he'd become moody and cryptic; he'd started smoking and drank too much—things he'd never done before—and he couldn't sleep. Spin's manic drive to make Black Eyes work had cost her husband his peace of mind and caused him to take risks he shouldn't have taken. Those were the simple facts she chose to interpret against Spin, but she suspected something even darker.

Spin had survived and Joe hadn't. It didn't take much to turn that into something ugly. The softness I'd always seen in her eyes was no longer there.

When I dropped her at her door, she invited me in, but I knew she was just being polite so I took a rain check. It was a hot day for the first of June. I pictured her awake all night with open-eyed dreams, and I pictured Joe's broken body on the slab. After lingering a moment, I gave her a hug and left thinking there was unfinished business here, something good had to come out of this somehow, but I didn't have a clue what it was.

FOUR MONTHS LATER

OCTOBER FIRST

IT WAS AMAZING TO SEE THE devastation that could happen to a company in four months.

I temporarily returned to my old law firm to help them liquidate the company. After that, I wasn't sure where I'd go or what I'd do. At the moment, my work consisted mainly of carrying boxes of Gulf-Tex documents to the bankruptcy lawyers and watching them cut the company into little pieces. As a lawyer, I'd seen this happen before, but seeing it happen to my own company was like watching my own autopsy.

Shortly after the hurricane, the stock went from sixty-seven dollars to six dollars, then almost stopped trading. By mid-July, Gulf-Tex's licensing agreements with oil companies and countries around the world had all gone into default. The company owed cash deposits it no longer had, and the projected profits that had driven up the company's stock now looked like an upside-down hockey stick. A bankruptcy trustee was appointed, everyone was laid off, and the company closed its doors.

The company's assets—the Galveston warehouse, Wild Stallion, two rusting platforms that had already been abandoned, and a pile of drilling equipment—were sold off for peanuts to an oil-patch scavenger called Shotgun Salvage, Inc. I wanted Spin to buy the only asset that really mattered—the software, books, drawings, and proprietary rights to Black Eyes—but the bankruptcy trustee, citing conflict of interest, wouldn't allow it, and they, too, were sold to Shotgun at fire-sale prices. The prototype was still lying at the bottom of the Gulf, but, even if it could be found, it wouldn't have mattered.

With its chief designer dead, the market considered it worthless.

Shotgun Salvage apparently didn't understand that. Viewing the technology as still mythical, they hired Angela Song to string together some computers, call it a prototype, and, as they say so delicately on Wall Street, "put some lipstick on the pig" before putting it up for auction.

That was fine with her. It put her back to work in the same lab she and Joe had worked in for years. Like all the king's horses, she tried to put Humpty Dumpty back together again, and not just cosmetically. She was convinced she could do the real thing. She didn't know how Joe had made Black Eyes work in the spring, since he hadn't given her his lab notes or explained what he'd done, so she was left to her own devices. But she'd always believed her Beta team solution was better than his solution anyway, and she still did. It would be slow going because she had to work alone, without her team. Shotgun was paying for a tube of lipstick, not a fashion show.

No one took her optimism about Black Eyes seriously except Spin, Tacoma, and me. It may have been a long shot, but somewhere in the back of our minds we heard a voice—Joe's—saying, *It's gonna work.* Angela was smart, driven, and inventive, and nobody had shown more confidence in her abilities than her boss. She possessed a dogged, matter-of-fact way of solving problems the way inventors usually do. Lightbulbs, steam engines, nuclear fission: She was a member of the club.

And then there was Spin. He was still living in Houston, but he was no longer a major player. He didn't even have a "shop" to go to during the day; the corporate offices were up for lease. He and Tacoma took a trip to Mexico, and when he got back, he busied himself with Sierra Club problems and some informal lobbying with the state legislature on behalf of environmental bills. All good stuff he could throw his body and soul into, but not his heart. That was still with Black Eyes, and he made no pretense about it.

He didn't see much of his beloved employees anymore. In the first place, they were busy digging out from unpaid bills, looking for work, and dealing with the bankruptcy fallout that had affected them personally. Bless the IRS. Turns out that stock losses suffered in your 401(k) can't be used to offset personal income, assuming you had any.

That aside, the guys who six months earlier had been stomping their boots for Spin Patterson no longer had the same warm and fuzzy feeling for him, and who could blame them? He'd sold out at the top while everybody else's stock was locked into their 401(k)'s, forcing them to ride their savings and retirement plans into the toilet. It may have been legal for him to get out while they couldn't, but that wasn't the point. It felt like shades of Enron and other corporate rip-offs.

Even though he'd done nothing illegal, Spin's press notices put him in the slush pile of infamous executive pirates. Spin Patterson—protector of the environment, political do-gooder, Houston social maven, visionary risk-taker, Johnny Appleseed of fossil fuel energy, Nobel Prize shoe-in, next governor of the state of Texas, and potential president of the United States—was now little more than a cardboard figure who dined at a country club on the hundreds of millions of dollars he'd bilked from his poor, downtrodden former employees. When asked about their plight, according to the political cartoons, his answer was to let them eat cake.

And then there was the flip side of that stereotype. Former employees—disheartened, financially drained, their pension plans ravaged—were portrayed as innocent salt-of-the-earth victims of yet another greedy CEO. Never mind that they'd taken a great ride *partly* of their own accord, and never mind that they'd disregarded Spin's warnings not to overinvest. Never mind that they'd scratched the greedy little tickles in their own bellies with new toys, cars, boats, trips, and overspending that now seemed preposterous. Never mind that they'd been as human as Spin. They were forgivable and he wasn't.

For the most part, that double standard made sense: If you're paid to be Big Daddy, you have to act like Bid Daddy. But knowing him to be the good man he was—complicated and flawed, but with a caring, generous heart—I thought calling him names was simpleminded and excessive.

Spin was probably right to keep his head down for a while, even though that included with me. I called and tried to see him several times, but he always had an excuse, so I stopped. Even though he was busy with some legislative projects, I assumed he was still recovering from his injuries, Joe's death, and the trauma of losing Black Eyes.

Besides, he wasn't exactly an object of great financial pity. He still had three hundred to four hundred million dollars, a beautiful apartment—he purchased Tacoma's penthouse and gave her a joint tenancy in it—a car and driver, an exec-jet lease, time to travel, a sailboat in Cancún when he wanted it, and, best of all, the woman he loved.

With the company gone, I thought Tacoma would be out of my life completely, but to my surprise I was wrong. We didn't see each other much, but we talked every week about Gulf-Tex cleanup matters, or conspired with each other to get Spin back into the game. She was the one who told me he was working on environmental bills and reading up on Cherokee history, both of which were fine, but that was like a diesel engine pulling a little red wagon.

I thought his interest in the Cherokee nation meant he'd finally make the gift to the college fund he'd promised Tacoma, but she said no, not yet. I thought that was a shame, but she didn't seem daunted by it. She still assumed he'd do it.

It was good staying in touch with her by phone, although I missed seeing her in person. Bankruptcy or no bankruptcy—apocalypse or no apocalypse—that never seemed to change.

Every week Wall Street heard rumors that other companies were pursuing deep-sonar 4-D technology. That really lit a fire under me, even though, for some reason, it didn't ignite Spin. Unless Angela could make her solution to the Black Eyes problem work soon, what remained of the technology would be overtaken by events and fresh innovation and it wouldn't bring enough money at auction to pay the lab's electric bill.

I called Tacoma. We agreed we couldn't let that happen, we needed to shake Spin out of his lethargy. I spent a week putting together a strategic plan for the resurrection of Black Eyes, and Tacoma arranged a dinner for the three of us. We were determined to start over. Like old times.

IT WAS THE FIRST TIME I'D SEEN Spin since he'd left the hospital. He looked good, even though you could tell he was still on the mend. He was a bit underweight, his left arm was slightly atrophied, and the grip in his hand was weak, but the scars on his face were mostly gone and his smile was back. Generally speaking, you wouldn't have known by looking at him that he'd taken a near-death beating from a hurricane.

We sat in his and Tacoma's living room drinking red wine and catching up. If Spin was still a little off his game, Tacoma never looked better. The Mexican sun had given her skin a fabulous copper glow, and her hair and eyes were bright. She was glad to see me and made no bones about it. As usual, I had trouble trying to keep my feelings for her under control.

It was annoying as hell being in their apartment and seeing the intimacy of their lair: the newspaper they'd been reading, the coffeemaker they shared, the comfort of Lightning wandering around the room with ease. He sat next to my chair with his head back, enjoying the scratching strokes of my fingers. At one point I found myself petting him and looking at Tacoma at the same time, hoping she saw a connection. If she did, she didn't acknowledge it, and a good thing she didn't. It was a harmless flirtation on my part, but inappropriate.

Besides, it wasn't why I was there.

"You ready to get back in the game?" I said to Spin.

"I'm busy," he said. "I'm headed to San Francisco tomorrow to meet with the Wildlife Association on a new initiative to—"

"I'm talking about Black Eyes," I said.

He squeezed a tennis ball in his left hand, strengthening the tendons in his arm. "What's going on?"

"Angela's working on finding a solution until it goes on the auction block. I made a lawyer's call to see if Shotgun would sell it outright, but they have no idea what it's worth, so they're committed to an auction."

"Unless she finds a solution, it's worthless," he said.

"I think we should get ready in case she does." I pulled a one-page memo out of my jacket and gave him and Tacoma a copy. "It's a simple start-up plan," I said. "One, we incorporate so we've got a vehicle to work with. I suggest BEP, Inc."

"What's it stand for?"

"Black Eyes Phoenix. You know, we're bringing it out of the ashes."

She didn't roll her eyes. Good sign.

"Two," I said, "you contact your key shareholders and tell them you're back in the game and want to line up some money."

"No one will put money into this without a technical breakthrough," he said.

"If they were willing to put millions into it before it was field-tested, why not invest enough to make a comeback?"

"Because that's logical, and logic doesn't drive investment decisions. Dreams do, and this one died when it went to the bottom of the sea."

"Not in my book," I said.

He squeezed the tennis ball and read my three-point agenda. "What else?"

"Three, we monitor what Exxon and the other labs are doing, as best we can, and try to stay ahead of them."

"How far along are they?"

"Angela says a couple of them are putting serious money into 4-D Deep Earth Sonar, but she doesn't think any of them are nearly as advanced as she is."

He finished reading the memo and looked up at Tacoma, who was still reading. "What do you think, baby?"

"It costs virtually nothing and it positions you to bid on Black Eyes if it looks like something good is going to happen."

More squeezing of the ball, more thinking. He was like a heavyweight champion who'd lost his title and wanted to get back in the ring. He just couldn't take the first step.

"Alexander Graham Bell," I said, "filed his drawings of the first telephone at the U.S. Patent Office, and two hours later another inventor came in and filed virtually the same plans."

"Two hours?"

"True story. You know who that other inventor was?"

"No idea."

"Exactly, nobody does. He disappeared from the history books without a trace." I took a drink of wine. "The breakthrough's gonna happen, Spin, the only question is, are you gonna be Alexander Graham Bell or some guy who disappears into the mist?"

Setting my glass down, I spilled some wine on a stack of magazines on the coffee table. "Sorry," I said, and lifted the top magazine to wipe it off. Tacoma handed me a napkin and said not to worry.

Beneath the lifted magazine was a stack of notebooks with the Gulf-Tex logo on the cover. I recognized them instantly as Joe Wright's lab notes. Obviously, Spin had been reading them.

I grabbed one and held it up. "And you want me to think you're not interested," I said. Black Eyes was still his obsession, his contribution to humankind, his beautiful balloon that would take him above the world.

I knew we had him.

We raised our glasses, then got down to the earnest business of what to do next. We were starting over, just the three of us—no Gulf-Tex, no platforms, no employees, no Wall Street investors—nothing but Spin's original vision, his personal seed money, and our shared conviction that what had brought us to the brink of success before could bring us there again.

I would have toasted the moment with a "Carpe diem," but the last time I'd tried that it didn't turn out so well.

THREE MONTHS LATER

CHRISTMAS EVE

IT WAS CHRISTMAS EVE AND I was back at the Oak Creek Country Club exactly twelve months after the most upbeat party in the company's history. Passing by the ballroom, I could still imagine everyone dancing and drinking and whooping it up the way they did the year before when they were high on Jim Beam, good jobs, good times, and a miracle maker called Black Eyes. Gulf-Tex, as it turned out, was a lot like life: If you wanted to make God laugh, tell him your plans.

The decorations in the members' dining room were the usual candy canes, Christmas trees, hot pepper lights, and poinsettias. Dinner with Spin's girls wasn't exactly an occasion to look forward to, but he and I were working together again, and I was still part of the family, and the dinner was a tradition, so there I was. It wouldn't be the same without Audrey, though. I missed her. She'd invited me to a separate dinner with her girls the next day, but I'd have to skip it for a family affair of my own.

Entering the dining room, I saw Spin and maneuvered through the tables of millionaires to join him. Sitting next to him was the other half of my heart, Tacoma, looking great, as usual, although even before we spoke I felt an unexpected estrangement from her. After the apartment meeting in October that had reignited Spin, she and I hadn't spoken much or seen each other.

Spin rose and gave me a hug and kiss on the cheek, which I returned. His scars were virtually gone now, and the grip in his left hand was strong. He wore his signature

Armani suit and a Christmas tie, and his physique was back to normal.

After saying hello to the girls, I leaned down and kissed Tacoma hello and smelled a hint of the spicy perfume that fit her perfectly.

"Hey, you," she said.

I sat down and she handed me a napkin, and that's when I noticed the diamond engagement ring on her left hand. Oh, wow. I suppose it shouldn't have been a punch in the stomach, but it was.

After spreading the napkin on my lap, I drank some wine, smiled a lot, and we all made nice in a slightly formal, stilted way. The more Tacoma and I talked, the more I thought she had changed. Something in her was missing: her ambition. Her edge. Her independence. Even the touch of mystery she usually had. Overdressed and sitting in this fancy room full of rich people, she resembled something I never expected to see her as: a trophy. You could say it was sour grapes, and no doubt some of it was, but it was more than that.

The upshot for me was a touch of unexpected liberation. Seeing her there as someone's prize, and feeling my respect for her diminish, I felt the ghosts of Wild Stallion and Macy's—the ghosts that had made me feel inadequate and unworthy of her—diminish, too. *Stop beating up on yourself, Max. She's no longer the person you loved. You've got nothing left to prove.* But if there was liberation in the moment, there was also sadness.

I had a piece of business to announce before dinner turned completely social: The International Petroleum Association was having its annual convention in Tampico, Mexico, this year and had invited Spin to come down and talk about the state of deep-earth sonar. Shotgun Salvage's auction of Black Eyes was scheduled to take place just before the convention. With a little luck, Spin might have more to offer the convention than war stories and a weather report. Announcing the return of Black Eyes would be spectacular.

Spin really lit up and said the invitation was the best Christmas present I could have given him. Whether it was going to happen or not, the date gave us a target to shoot for to make Black Eyes work. He was more energized than I'd seen him since the hurricane. We drank to our progress and discussed other subjects.

I turned to Trish and Barbara, who at twenty-two and twenty-four resembled each other more than Audrey or Spin. Blonde, lean, and well-groomed, they led privileged lives and made no apologies for it. I'd always thought they had none of Audrey's wit or Spin's brains, just their money. Ostriches had sand to bury their heads in, the Patterson girls had Neiman Marcus. But since the accident they'd paid more attention to Spin, and he'd done the same with them. It was as if the three of them were trying to break through the insulation that had been built up between them over the years by too much money and a spoiled life.

Spin understood their soft upbringing and refused to give up on them. Since the hurricane he'd spent time with them one-on-one and worked hard to engage them in something more meaningful than shopping. In effect, he'd rediscovered them and, having done so, realized that he loved them more than he knew. I'd never seen him pay attention to them like this. It was nice to see.

A waiter appeared at the table.

"Can I get you a drink, sir?" he asked.

I turned and tried not to show my surprise when I realized it was Jim Francesca, one of the guys who'd laid pipe for Gulf-Tex for years. His formality with me—and my being at Spin's table—embarrassed me. Spin showed no sign that he even recognized him, which only made it worse.

"A Scotch for me, thanks, Jim," I said, saying his name conspicuously.

"Mr. Patterson?" Jim said.

"I'll have another, thanks," Spin said. When he left, Spin said, "Do you know him?"

"Yeah, and so do you. He's Jim Francesca, one of your roughnecks. I went to high school with him."

Spin looked confused, then chagrined. "I should have remembered."

Barbara scoffed and said, "Did you see his shoes? Dad, you should complain about that to the maître d.'

Spin let it pass.

Trish said, "I don't care who he worked for, he shouldn't dress like that in the club. What do you think, Randy?"

Randy—Trish's boyfriend—shrugged.

Tacoma's eyes caught mine and said she wanted to throttle Trish as much as I did.

Spin said, "Don't sound like a brat, Trish. You're a better person than that."

Trish stood up theatrically and walked away.

"Here we go," Spin said. "No question who she takes after."

"You don't have to insult Mom," Barbara said.

Spin drank some of his whiskey. He held his liquor well, but I'd never seen him drink this much. Being worth a few hundred million while his bankrupt employees were serving him caviar on toast points evidently didn't make him happy. He wasn't guilty about being wealthy—he never had been—but neither was he indifferent to the people who'd worked for him and had once worshipped the oily water he walked on.

He took a drink again and said to Barbara, "If your mother had been reasonable with a settlement, none of this would have happened." The "none of this" wasn't defined, but you got the idea.

Barbara's face reddened. "Would you go find Trish?" she said to Randy. The boy shrugged and got up.

Sensing a brewing storm, Tacoma wanted to get away from the table. "She may be in the ladies' room," she said. "I'll go check." She stood up and followed Randy out of sight, leaving Spin, Barbara, and me behind. I said, "I'll go with them," but Spin asked me to stay.

Barbara instantly turned on her father. "How dare you say if there was a different settlement none of this would have happened! There never would have been a divorce if you'd kept your hands off Pocahontas!" Before he could react, she said, "And if Pocahontas had kept her hands off your fucking totem pole, *none* of this would have happened!"

Spin turned bright red. Ordinarily he would have blown

his top, but instead he said, “You don’t know anything about Tacoma, and you don’t know anything about your mother and me, and even if you did, you can’t talk to me that way!”

Barbara stared at him until tears filled her eyes, then she looked away shaking her head in lip-curled disgust.

To my surprise, Spin got up, sat next to her, and put his arm around her shoulder. “Come on,” he said, rocking her gently. “We don’t need to fight. You and Trish are the most important people in my life.” A few people at nearby tables gawked, but Spin didn’t care. Making up with his daughter was all that mattered.

I admired what he did, although I still felt bad for everyone involved. Barbara’s comments about Tacoma were unfair, Tacoma wasn’t there to defend herself, and Audrey was taking a beating without knowing it. “I’ll find out what’s taking Trish so long,” I said, and got up.

Spin nodded good-bye, then kissed Barbara’s hairline and continued hugging her. I said good-bye and left before Tacoma and the others came back.

What a difference a year makes.

I WAS BEHIND THE WHEEL of my Z4 making my way to Jenny's Christmas party, watching the cultural landscape of Houston morph from country club champagne to backyard beer and kids' swing sets. The deeper I got into my old neighborhood, the more obvious the contrast was. I never used to notice it—or if I did, I guess I didn't care—but now that Gulf-Tex had disappeared, and with it a hunk of my life, my old roots mattered. Funny how that works, isn't it?

I was arriving later than I'd told Jenny I would. I had gifts for her two kids, one of whom, Christopher, was my godson, and hoped they were still awake. With a party going full blast, I assumed they would be.

I turned the last corner, slowed, and pulled into Jenny's driveway, which was full of pickups and motorcycles, all in need of a wash. I could see the lights on the Christmas tree twinkling inside the house. Maybe the holiday spirit I'd missed at the country club was here.

After getting out of the car, I threw my suit jacket and tie in the backseat, pulled on an old windbreaker, and headed for the porch. The yard had been all but abandoned since May: The grass was scruffy, leaves lay in the weeds, and the jungle gym was rusting. I picked up a swing seat that was broken on one side, looked for the S-hook that should have held it, couldn't find it, and lowered it gently back to the ground.

Entering the living room, I said hello to pals on the fly and made my way to the kitchen for a beer. On my way in, I saw Jenny through the dining-room arch trying to round up three-year-old Christopher, who was running around on a sugar-cookie high.

Jenny looked beautiful. The only difference between now and a year ago was that now she was a widow with two kids. Small stuff like that.

"Did you bring Santa Claus?" Christopher said as he ran over to me and gave my knees a hug.

"Hello, big boy," I said, and picked him up and held him in one arm. Jenny gave me a kiss on the cheek and said, "I'm really glad you're here."

Behind her the TV was playing *It's a Wonderful Life.* In the corner, the Christmas tree stood tall, its lights blinking red, green, and white. Beneath it was a stash of presents for the kids.

"Mommy won't let me open a present," Christopher complained.

"She's right, you have to wait for Santa," I said.

There were bottles of beer in ice-filled tubs, one of which was leaking on the kitchen floor, and crushed cookies and red and green sprinkles were crumbled into the rug. Christopher wiggled out of my arms and toddled over to the tree. Jenny took her eyes off him and looked at me curiously. I gave her a perplexed look back—what? She started to tell me when we both saw Christopher getting ready to eat a glass candy cane he'd taken off the tree.

We both jumped at him at the same time, our hands colliding. I picked him up while Jenny took the ornament and put it back on a branch, then we pointed out the things on the tree that were not for eating. Her hand was on his back and so was mine, touching lightly.

Someone interrupted with a question about food. Jenny said, "Excuse me a minute, would you?"

"Go ahead, I'll watch him," I said.

She gave me a glance and walked toward the kitchen. A female voice yelled, "Would somebody turn down the music or turn off the damn TV set? I can't take both at once!" A few minutes later Jenny returned and took Christopher out of my arms.

I wandered off toward the kitchen where Musselman, one of the roughnecks, had taken the cowling off the stove and laid it on the floor.

"Ned," his wife was asking, "why have you got that thingamajig on the floor in the middle of a party?"

"I'm trying to fix it."

She looked at me and said, "Just like he fixed the exhaust pipe on the dryer."

He patted her on the ass and said, "I've got your exhaust pipe right here, honey."

She messed up his hair and walked away.

I was watching them without realizing Jenny was watching, too, this time with her baby girl in her arms. She looked at me and said, "I see some friends of yours coming through the door."

It was my brother, Will, and Dutch. They found their way to the kitchen where Dutch shook hands and checked me out.

"Suit pants? Where you been, boy?"

It was an accusation, not a question.

"Hey, don't pick on my little brother," Will said. "That's my job."

I said, "Ha, ha," and took a swig of beer. They were right: Jenny's party was the opposite of the one I'd left at the country club. The number of waiters was considerably smaller—like zero—and the drink of the evening was beer instead of Maker's Mark. The only similarity was a certain amount of stress in the air, which, like the stress at Spin's table, ultimately came from Gulf-Tex.

As Will, Dutch, and I talked, my attention drifted to a small group of guys huddled by a bay window. The way they were talking looked far too serious for a Christmas party.

Something was going on.

"YOU WANT TO SEE SOMETHING cool?" Dutch said to me. Christopher was in my arms again, chewing on a rocking-horse cookie.

"I'll watch him, Max," Jenny's sister-in-law said.

"Grab a beer," Dutch said.

I grabbed one and followed him out the door, unbuttoning my cuffs and rolling up my sleeves as I went. We walked across the yard toward Joe's workshop adjoining the garage, and when we got there, Dutch opened the door and ushered me inside.

I don't know what I expected, but this wasn't it. Five guys stood in front of a workbench leaning against it with their arms folded and ankles crossed. After Dutch closed the door, the only sound in the room was the hum of fluorescent lights. It reminded me of the time a bunch of us got together to raid old man Stoner's peach orchard. The atmosphere was thick and dark with plotting.

First there was Harley, who was smacking a piece of pipe lightly in his hand. A primo motorcycle junkie, he was a big guy with a red beard who dished out more than he took, and he could take a lot.

Next to him was Lucas, a quiet man in his late fifties who had four kids, two in college, and a sick wife in a nursing home. Of the group, I guessed nobody had been hurt by the stock crash more than he had.

Dutch's being here kind of surprised me. A family man with three kids, he'd once worked in my law firm as a paralegal before admitting that all he'd ever really wanted to do was work on an offshore rig. We'd gotten it arranged.

Musselman was a hardworking man with a live-in girlfriend. Tough but a straight arrow, he had a good sense of humor until it ran out. At the moment, he was fresh out.

Eddy J I didn't know well enough to peg, except he was married with a family. Something told me I'd know him better before this get-together was over.

And then there was my brother, Will.

"What's up, guys?" I asked.

"Not my 401(k)," Musselman answered.

I grabbed a chair Jenny was evidently stripping the paint off in her spare time, turned it around, straddled the seat, and folded my arms on the back. This was their party, not mine, but I had a pretty good idea why I'd been invited.

"WE'RE HURTING, MAX," DUTCH said. "We haven't worked for months, our savings are shot, and nobody's hiring. We got mortgages, car payments, and grocery bills to pay. Most of us got wives and kids. The bankruptcy killed our health care, and COBRA isn't covering us anymore. I don't expect a Purple Heart for putting my butt on the line for G-Tex, but I didn't expect to take a joint of drill pipe up the ass, either."

The other guys were dead still. Six bulls, and me the matador.

Harley said, "Everyone who worked for the company's being treated like a piece of shit. Tell him what you did this morning, Lucas."

The older man said nothing until silence compelled an answer. "I put Dot in a new nursing home."

" 'New'?" Dutch said.

A twitch started up under Lucas's eye.

Harley turned to me and said, "Golden Rose Nursing Home? I wouldn't put my dog up there."

"How about you, Eddy J?" I said. "What's on your mind?"

"Nothing except I don't know how to live without money."

"Musselman?"

"I'm not a lawyer, but I didn't think we lived in a country where one guy puts eight hundred and fifty million bucks in his pocket and everyone who made him rich gets Ozzie's dog biscuits."

"What does he eat, Max?" Harley said. "Champagne and caviar?"

"I'm not his chef," I said.

"Oh, that's right, you're just his VP for special projects."

I could feel my white shirt and suit pants blinking in neon. I got off the chair and paced around the half-lit space at the end of the room. Jenny had accumulated things from the laboratory—Joe's desk items, boxes of books, photographs of him with Angela and his team. Off to the side in a jumbled coil was a long piece of cable with a tag tied to it from the Houston Police Department. It must have been the restraining cable Joe had clung to during the hurricane. Why it was here I didn't know, but seeing it was a little eerie.

I turned back to the guys, found an S-hook on a work counter, dropped it into my pocket, and circled back to the chair.

"What about you, Will?" I said to my brother. "What are you doing here?"

"Same thing everybody else is. Something stinks when families have to wrap up last year's Christmas presents to give their kids."

Harley said, "Guys who were working rigs for G-Tex are sitting around union halls like a bunch of beaners from Reynosa. The fuck's that all about?"

"We bought the company's stock in our 401(k)'s," Eddy J said, "and couldn't sell it for a year? And while we're trapped like rats, the CEO runs the price of the stock through the roof, sells it for a gadzillion bucks, and hammers us with personal bankruptcies?"

Harley said, "Why wasn't his stock locked up like ours? How's he get to skim the cream while we're stuck in a mud pit?"

Eddy J said, "And don't tell me about the fine print. We already read that."

I walked to the end of the room again and saw Joe's stuff.

"Anybody got anything else to say?" I asked.

No one spoke.

"OK, what's the point?" I said.

"You're our quarterback," Dutch said. "Call the play."

"We don't want anything more'n what's ours," Eddy J said.

Harley said, "Personally, I don't want that, I just want him dead."

These were the guys I'd gone to school with, drunk beer with, gone to weddings, christenings, and more than one funeral with. They were the salt of the earth, but somehow they'd all gone bonkers. Joe's stuff—the safety cable and the photographs—made his presence tangible. I walked back to the chair.

"If you guys had a stack of poker chips and a couple of cigars in here," I said, "you'd be the law school definition of a backroom conspiracy."

Dutch stepped forward. "I don't think you—"

"Shut up, Dutch. Joe's dead, and we're standing in his workroom bitching about our 401(k)'s? The guy who tried to save Joe—a guy who put bread on our table the last sixteen years—isn't here to defend himself, and we're talking about him like he's a thief? A few months ago you were whooping it up for Spin like a bunch of teenage girls at a rock concert. What's changed?"

I didn't give them a chance to answer.

"I'll tell you what's changed," I said. "Your bank accounts."

They didn't try to answer.

"This is a guy who's done good things for us since the day I lost my dad." I looked at Will. "Is this how you feel about Spin now, Will? You want to screw the guy who pulled you out of a mud pit?"

He didn't answer.

"There isn't one of you who wasn't as happy as a pig in shit when the stock was up, but now that it's gone south, you're a bunch of crybabies."

"He wiped us out," Harley said quietly.

"Only because you got greedy." I turned to Dutch. "Everybody in this room bought too much stock, including me. Why take it out on Spin? He told us not to do it, for Chrissake."

They were going broke and I was giving them a speech

instead of moral support, but I was pissed and they were on the verge of doing something stupid. I needed to nip it in the bud right now.

"You think he deliberately put Gulf-Tex into bankruptcy?" I said. "You think he's no better than the CEOs who are doing hard time in Leavenworth?"

I walked up to Harley and stood nose to nose. "Guess what. I worked with Spin every day and I know him better than anybody in this room. I know what happened to the company, too. We didn't go down because he cheated, we went down because he gambled. He had the guts to put everything on the line and invent something that would have saved the company and made us all rich."

I stepped away from Harley and found another target.

"So Black Eyes didn't survive a hurricane, what does? He cut his hands to ribbons trying to save his best friend."

"No way," Eddy J said. "Spin bet the ranch on Black Eyes and the minute it came time to prove it, the prototype got conveniently dropped to the bottom of the sea."

"Gosh, Eddy J, thanks for that insight, I never looked at it that way." I turned to the others. "If Spin was powerful enough to make a hurricane, surely he was powerful enough to make Black Eyes work."

Dutch said, "That hurricane was the biggest piece of luck he had since he married the boss's daughter."

I looked at my watch. "You guys want me to do you a favor, fine, I'll do you one: I'll pretend this meeting never took place." I pushed away from the counter. "I'm going back into the house and finish my beer and wish the widow of a great friend merry Christmas."

"You don't have to go to the house to do that," Jenny's voice said. She stepped into the room from the shadows by the door.

"What are you doing here?" I said.

"It's my house, Max. But you're right, I think it's time for everybody to get back to the party."

There was a lot of slow movement as the guys shuffled around and headed out the door. Jenny stood and let them file out first. Her eyes were dark and her lips pale. I couldn't tell how long she'd been standing in the room. We heard Harley's motorcycle start up and the gears click into place. I put my hand on the small of her back and guided her out of the room. Two more car doors slammed and the cars left.

We stepped outside into the cool air and stood still listening to the party drift across the lawn from her living room.

I said, "I'll grab my jacket and go."

Back at the house I went to the bedroom where the coats were piled on the bed. Jenny went to the baby's room and picked her up—she was hungry—and brought her into the bedroom where I was pulling on my windbreaker. She closed the door, lifted her sweater, and put her baby to her breast.

I glanced at her a moment and she looked back, natural and unself-conscious.

"I better go," I said.

"I'll walk you out to the car."

WALKING ACROSS THE YARD, I stopped at the jungle gym and asked her to wait a second. After pulling the S-hook from my pocket, I picked up the dangling swing seat, coupled it to the chain, and gave it a push. It squeaked as it swung back and forth. "Needs a drop of oil," I said.

She looked wistful. "I've forgotten what it's like to have a man around the house."

When we reached my car, I dug into my pocket for the keys.

"You OK?" I asked.

"It's my first Christmas without him," she said. "Once I get through a whole year, I'll be fine."

The ambient light masked our faces, making conversation easy. She rubbed her fingers sensually along the sleek silver fender of my Z4.

I reached out and took her hand. Finding the right words wasn't easy; I wanted to be supportive but respectful, personal but appropriate. "Is there anything I can do to help?" I said.

"A while ago I thought so, but when I heard you talking to the guys in the room, I changed my mind."

"About what?"

She hesitated. "I don't think this is a good idea, Max."

"Why not? We're not doing anything wrong," I said.

"But you know me, I tend to say what's on my mind."

"Go ahead, tend away."

She took a moment. "Listening to you tonight, I thought, this is the real Max I'm hearing now, not the golden boy the guys looked up to in high school. This is the grown-up Max, my husband's friend and the godfather of my son, someone who I might have fallen for under different circumstances. Then I thought, you know what, Jen? You'd rather live in a poorhouse for widows and orphans the rest of your life than spend a single day with this guy."

My hand froze. She pulled hers away kindly.

"You used to be on our side, Max. Now you play for the enemy."

I cleared my throat.

She touched the car again, this time as if it were a reptile. "How much does he pay you?" she said.

That pissed me off. "Not as much as he paid Joe."

She wheeled around and slapped my face. "Don't you ever talk about Joe like that!"

It felt like the slap I'd taken from Dad when I'd tried to stop him from cutting off Will's foot. Once again I felt my cheeks burn, and once again I was only making matters worse by being there.

I reached for the door of my car. "Not every tragedy is the result of foul play," I said.

"That's your opinion."

"What's yours?"

"That you're naïve."

"About what?"

"Spin."

I opened the door a couple of inches. "For some reason I can't seem to shake this annoying habit I have of refusing to label people murderers based on barroom gossip."

"I see," she said, "you want hard evidence." She put her hand on the door to keep me from opening it. "When they found Joe's body, his legs were still wrapped in the safety cable. Doesn't that seem a little strange?"

"In a class four hurricane?" I said. "Not really."

She looked at me as if she were searching for someone she couldn't find. I got in the car, plugged in my key, and rolled down the window.

"Thanks for the cookies," I said, and started the engine.

She bent down close to the window. "If you want the truth about Spin, talk to your brother."

I gunned the engine. "About what?"

She started to back away, but I reached out the window and grabbed her wrist. Even if she was the mother of my godson, I'd had enough of her cryptic bullshit.

"Ask him about *what*?" I said.

She looked straight through me. "The accident."

"What accident?"

"The one that killed your dad. Joe said it wasn't what it appeared to be."

That came out of nowhere. "What is that supposed to mean?" I said, but she didn't answer. "And how would Joe know?"

She looked at me coldly, trying to decide whether to trust me or not. "He said he knew what happened out there that day but he didn't have the nerve to tell anyone. I believed him, because sometimes it ate him alive."

"*What* did?" I said.

"Max—I don't know. He wouldn't tell me."

I hated circles inside mazes.

"What am I supposed to do with this information?" I said.

"I told you, ask Will," she said. "Joe said he knows."

I let go of her arm. There were no friendly good-byes on either side. She turned back toward the house and I dropped the car into gear and left.

IT WAS LATE CHRISTMAS NIGHT, which meant the State Highway Patrol was on the lookout for speeding drunks. I qualified on only one of those counts: I was driving like a maniac toward Will's house ten miles away, thinking about what Jenny'd said to me. What Will does know about Wild Stallion? What did Joe mean?

I took a corner at eighty-five. A rich man's car has its advantages. The cable I'd seen in Joe's workroom was bothering me. *"You want evidence? The cable was wrapped around Joe's body."* I took the next corner on all four wheels. Mostly.

I tried to put Jenny's anger into perspective. When it came to her and the guys, everyone who was still close to Spin was guilty by association these days. My temporary job with the old law firm was more than the guys had. I wore a suit and tie and I didn't have a haunted look in my eye. I had an apartment and a BMW Z4. I could probably feel guilty enough about my good fortune to give it all to the Salvation Army, but when it came to joining a conspiracy against Spin, forget it.

I'm still the quarterback, guys. Get used to it.

I took the next corner like the last. I knew the road; I'd driven it since I was sixteen, got my license practicing on it two weeks before Dad died. I tried to clear my head but Jenny's female instinct was still under my skin.

I came up on the fork between Route 80 and Perdido Road, the turnoff to Mom and Dad's house, which was now Will's. I put on the turn signal and moved into the right lane, but instead of turning I pulled onto the shoulder and stopped.

What did Joe have in mind? What was Jenny talking about? If I couldn't forget it, how could I pursue it?

I could do what she suggested and call Will, but if he knew something big about Wild Stallion and hadn't told me all these years, why would he tell me now? I needed information first. The number one rule of a trial lawyer is never ask a hostile witness a question unless you know the answer.

There was one place where the facts about that ugly day could be found.

Remember the investigation that followed the fire? Remember your testimony about what you saw happen that day? Remember the investigator's questions? Start there.

I turned off my direction blinker—I'd hit the wrong one anyway—then peeled back onto the gravel road. Not toward Will's house, but in the opposite direction. The direction I wanted to go in.

My dyslexia didn't always win out.

CDS OF CHRISTMAS CAROLS sung by Bing Crosby and Etta James, an empty bottle of Dom Pérignon on the glass-top coffee table, a melting bucket of ice, a plate of untouched chocolate truffles and strawberries. The floor was strewn with boxes, wrapping paper, and ribbons—a cashmere sweater, a silk tie, tissue paper littering the sofa.

Tacoma had made the apartment beautiful for Christmas with sparkling lights and a large pine tree decorated with shiny ornaments. It was the first time she'd made a big deal out of Christmas, but it was the holiday Spin loved most, and, as he'd pointed out, it was nice to celebrate it without lies, secrecy, and an early departure for home.

Inside the marble bathroom, white candles lined the bathtub, scenting the room lightly. Music wafted out of hidden speakers, and damp towels lay on the floor. Another fell from Tacoma's body before she wrapped herself in a robe that had been one of Spin's presents.

He came up behind her and put his arms around her, slipping his hands under the soft fabric. He kissed the nape of her neck and ran his hands up and down her body, finally bringing them to rest on her breasts, cupping them and lightly caressing her nipples. She closed her eyes and let her head fall back onto his shoulder. The robe was half off now, slipping down.

"It's a great present," she said.

"And your humidor was inspired," he said, and kissed her neck. He moved his right hand down the outside of the robe and stopped. "What's this?"

"What's what?"

"This—in the pocket."

She came out of her reverie. "I don't know—what is it?"

He reached in and pulled out a rust-colored suede pouch. "I have no idea."

"Spin—what are you up to?"

She took the pouch, untied the silk string, and dropped the contents into the palm of her hand. The dimmed globe lights around the mirror hit the necklace and sent sparks of light flying onto the bathroom walls. Tacoma's mouth opened in astonishment as she held up a delicate platinum chain of pure white diamonds, each a half carat.

"Oh, my God," she whispered.

"Put it on," he said.

She draped it around her neck, bent her head forward, and lifted her hair so he could close the clasp. When he had, he kissed the spot where the necklace lay flat on her skin.

Her robe fell to the floor. Standing naked in front of the mirror, she looked back at him and touched the extravagant gift at her neck. The stones were on fire.

"It's beautiful," she said.

"Not half as beautiful as you are."

She turned and put her arms around his neck. He led her toward the bedroom door. She pulled back and stopped. "I'll be there in a minute," she said, giving his hand a squeeze.

He walked into a passageway to the bedroom and shut the door.

Tacoma closed the bathroom door and turned back to the mirror. Her body was lovely—the soft light shadowed the muscles in her belly—but she was focused on the diamonds ringing her neck. She touched one of them and pressed it into her skin until she could feel the pain.

Why'd she do that? Why the negative feeling? What was wrong with her?

She straightened the necklace and watched the diamonds glint. It had been months since she'd done any serious work in her professional life. OK, so she'd been on a long holiday, was that a crime? It had been months since she talked to the

Cherokee College Fund chairman about Spin's promised gift, but these things took time. Even if it never happened, she'd given it her best shot. Why cut herself up about it?

She touched the stones one at a time.

Did she feel . . . guilty?

Or did she feel . . . hollow?

She let go of the diamonds and stared into her own eyes. Despite herself, tears began to flow. *Something's wrong. Stop kidding yourself.*

This wasn't the moment to think it through. Sensing too much time had passed, she ran cold water on a washcloth and pressed it against her eyes, then lifted her robe from the floor and put it on.

What was the point of doing that?

She let it fall back to the floor and walked into the bedroom tall and regal, wearing nothing but a beautiful necklace that sparkled like Cleopatra's eyes but still made her feel like Mark Antony's slave.

A slave? Before the night was over, that would be the least of it.

THE FIRE ON WILD STALLION was once again front and center in my life. Over the years, various things had taken me back to it in a flash: a photograph of Dad on the rig, watching Will put on his prosthesis, the smell of burned metal from a shorted-out lamp cord. But this wasn't nostalgia, this was a search for something new.

I showed my pass to the night guard on the main floor of the office building. He'd seen me pull all-nighters before, but never on Christmas Eve. You're right, I said, it's ridiculous, but if you guys have to work tonight, why shouldn't I? He gave me a symbolic high five and I walked to the elevator.

I got off at my floor, used my electronic card to enter, and walked to my temporary office. After turning on the lights, I opened a file folder on my desk—I wanted a pretext for being there if security came sniffing around—then headed out the door to the file room where I sat at the filing system computer, took it out of sleep mode, and clicked on the alphanumeric search function.

I typed in the name of the insurance company that had covered Gulf-Tex's losses from the Wild Stallion accident seventeen years before. I'd never looked at the file because I'd had no reason to. I'd been in the crane's catbird seat and seen everything that had happened that day—I didn't need to be reminded by someone else's eyewitness account. The file was in a locked steel cabinet that only partners had access to. I went into my wallet for my partner's security card.

As the computer started listing files, I felt the ugliness of the fire wash over me once again. I swiped my security card through the magnetic field and, using the computer's search function, found the location of the files I wanted in Drawer 16. I got up and went for it. The card opened the electronic lock on the drawer and I pulled it open.

My fingers moved through the file tabs, found the file I wanted, and pulled out a brown manila accordion envelope. Sitting at a nearby reading table, I pulled loose the rose-colored strings that tied the envelope flap and looked inside.

A file folder was marked "Witness Depositions." I opened it and breathed in the smell of musty transcripts of interviews conducted by an insurance company investigator. Thumbing through the pages, I found the service boat captain's description of the fueling operation, and the drill manager's explanation of how the Caterpillar engine hit the fuel line and cut it in two. It felt strange seeing the most crippling events of my life reduced to these dry, verbal accounts.

I found my own deposition next, opened it, and began to read. The investigator's questions, and my answers, outlined the accident with a vividness I'd blurred over the years.

My own testimony described the Caterpillar engine moving toward the mud pit, Puck Tarver collapsing on the console, my momentarily trying to revive him, and my taking over the controls—or trying. Reading about them, I felt the pit of my stomach aching all over again: the dead intercom, the frustration of not knowing what to do, of not being able to hear anyone tell me, the near panic of having a runaway train in my hands and not being able to stop it.

I described the cargo knocking Bud Hightower into the sea and come swinging back. I described putting my hand on the lever—not sure which way to push or pull it—not sure what it would do—unable to figure out the arrows—and dropping the payload onto the deck. I described seeing it roll into a roughneck and knock him into the mud pit, then climbing down the crane ladder and running over and realizing I'd knocked my own brother into it.

Strike that—I hadn't knocked him in, the payload had.

Sure it had.

Reading the account, I felt the frustration, fear, and failure of that day come over me in a fresh wave of impotence. Trying to avoid it, I looked up from the deposition and stared at the filing cabinets across the room, but all I saw was Will in the mud pit . . . the fuel hose spewing diesel fuel onto the deck . . . the liquid rolling into the pit. Once again I heard that word that still jolts me whenever I hear it yelled: *"Fire!"*

I closed the deposition and wiped the sweat off my forehead with my handkerchief. The heat must have been turned up; the room was stifling hot.

After getting up and walking around the room a moment, I came back to sit at the desk and found Spin's deposition.

SPIN'S RECOLLECTION SEEMED matter-of-fact.

Q: Where were you standing when the fuel hose was severed?
A: About twenty yards away from Mr. Hightower.
Q: What were you doing?
A: Walking toward the other side of the platform, as I recall.

Not quite. I remembered seeing him stop and look up at Puck and me in the crane operator's cab. Our headsets weren't receiving transmission, but Puck's mike was still working. When Puck asked Spin if he could hear Puck talking, Spin gave us a yes salute. I read on:

Q: So you didn't see the crane operator slump forward on the controls?
A: No.
Q: And you weren't in communication with him at the time?
A: No. I could hear him, but he couldn't hear me.
Q: Did he say you should give him a signal if he could hear you?
A: Yes. And I did.
Q: Shortly after that, did he ask you another question?
A: What kind of a question?
Q: Did he say, "If it's still a go, give me a signal," or words to that effect?

A: If what was a go?
Q: Please just answer the question.
A: I don't recall anything like that.
Q: Were you in charge of dropping the Caterpillar engine at the mud pit?
A: No, no, that would have been the deck supervisor.
Q: So, if the crane operator said to you, "If it's still a go, give me a signal," he wouldn't have been referring to his delivering the payload to the pit.
A: No, but as I said, I don't recall his asking me that question.
Q: And if someone in the vicinity who was wearing a headset claimed to overhear the crane operator ask you that question—"Signal if it's still a go," or words to that effect—that claim would be incorrect?
A: It would be incorrect. I suggest you ask Max McLennon about that. He was sitting right next to Puck the whole time.
Q: This deposition is about what you know, Mr. Patterson. I take it your testimony is that you have no knowledge that such a statement was made by Puck Tarver?
A: It makes no sense.
Q: Does that mean you have no knowledge?
A: That's right, I have no knowledge. But I wasn't in the cab. You really should ask Max about this.

I turned back to my own deposition and paged to something I'd read.

Q: Now, Max—excuse me, may I call you Max?
A: Sure.
Q: Now, Max, you said your headset wasn't working and neither was Puck Tarver's. How do you know his headset wasn't working?
A: I heard him yell into his mike and say something like "My headset's not receiving, I can't hear you, Spin. If you can hear me, give me a signal."
Q: Did Spin give him a signal?

A: Yeah, he waved at us.
Q: What happened after that?
A: Nothing. Puck talked to him some more, took some aspirin for a headache, then worked the controls to bring in the payload. Then he collapsed.
Q: You said he talked to Spin some more after getting the hand signal. What did he say?
A: I couldn't hear.
Q: Why not?
A: He cupped his hand around the mike so Spin could hear him better. The noise in the cab was pretty loud.
Q: But hadn't he just talked to Spin without cupping his hand around the mike?
A: Yeah, but he had to yell when he did, and that makes it hard for the listener to understand.
Q: So you didn't hear what Puck said to him when his hand was cupped around the mike?
A: No, it was too noisy.
Q: So if someone else in the vicinity were to claim they overheard Puck say, "Give me a signal if it's still a go," or words to that effect, you didn't hear that?
A: No, sir.
Q: If Puck had said those words, would you have any idea what he might have been referring to?
Counsel: Objection.
Q: You can still answer, Max, this is a deposition, not a trial.
A: No, sir, I wouldn't know. Spin wasn't standing at the mud pit, so I don't get why Puck would say something like that.

I closed my deposition and found my brother Will's. After the usual questions and answers, they got into the same subject matter.

Q: Where were you when the diesel engine started moving across the deck?
A: Standing near a mud pit.

Q: Doing what?
A: Waiting for the crane operator to lower it.
Q: Were you wearing an intercom headset?
A: Yes.
Q: Were you in communication with the crane operator?
A: Yes.
Q: What happened next?
A: As I was waiting, the diesel engine swung past the drop point and knocked Mr. Hightower off the platform.
Q: Did you see it hit him?
A: Yes.
Q: Did you talk to the crane operator?
A: I tried, but there was no response.
Q: Did you look up at the cab?
A: Yes.
Q: What did you see?
A: Puck was collapsed against the front window of the cab and my brother, Max, was standing next to him waving at us and pointing at him.
Q: Did you talk to him over the intercom?
A: Like I said, I tried, but he was on the same channel as Puck and couldn't hear me.
Q: OK. Now, shortly before Puck collapsed, did you overhear him talking to someone on his intercom?
A: No.
Q: You didn't overhear the crane operator trying to communicate with Mr. Patterson?
A: I wouldn't have heard that, they would have been on a different frequency.
Q: The question isn't whether you *would* have heard that, Mr. McLennon, the question is whether you did hear that.
A: No, I didn't hear that.
Q: So if someone overhead Puck say to Mr. Patterson, "Give me a signal if it's a go," or words to that effect, you have no knowledge of such a statement having been made?

Counsel for the Witness: Objection.

Q: Let me rephrase that. If such a statement had been made, Mr. McLennon, it is your testimony that you didn't hear it?

A: Never heard it.

Q: And you have no knowledge of it?

A: That's right.

Q: Thank you.

I CLOSED THE TRANSCIPT AND opened a deposition of someone named Dougie Bender, the twelve-year-old son of the service boat captain who was delivering the diesel engine to the platform the day of the accident. According to the transcript, Dougie was learning how to be a ham radio operator, liked to ride on his father's boat when he could, and listened to radio traffic between the ships and rigs.

After the accident, Dougie Bender said he'd overheard conversations between Spin Patterson, Puck Tarver, and Will McLennon, the roughneck in charge of bringing down the Caterpillar engine. According to Dougie, the crane operator and the roughneck were talking down the payload when suddenly the crane operator, Puck Tarver, switched communications channels, stopped talking to Will McLennon, and started talking to Spin Patterson.

For some reason, Puck was having trouble hearing Mr. Patterson, and when he tried to fix the problem, he cut off his reception from everyone. Apparently not realizing what he'd done, he kept asking Spin Patterson for "a signal if it was a go," but he couldn't hear Mr. Patterson's answer. But Dougie Bender could. And so could Will McLennon—Dougie knew this was so because he heard Will saying to the crane operator, "You're on my frequency, Puck, not Spin's. Can you hear me? You're on my frequency." But the crane operator couldn't hear anyone even though they could hear him.

As for what "signal" the crane operator was looking for from Spin Patterson, the boy had no idea. He was in a service boat a hundred feet below the platform.

Dougie may not have known what the signal meant, but the investigator thought Will McLennon did.

And now, so did I.

I put away the transcripts and began searching other files. The insurance investigator evidently thought there was something fishy about the accident, but in the end he couldn't prove it. The next file I read showed a hefty insurance payment settling all claims.

After that I came to a file that made no sense at all. In addition to the insurance payment, a confidential trust had been set up for my brother, Will—a large trust created by a company I'd never heard of, but one that had all the earmarks of a "shell" designed to protect the identity of whoever had set it up. What was that all about?

The file held an accounting of payments the trust had made to Will over the years, and an accounting of what he'd spent the money on: our family, the mortgage, ordinary bills, my sister's wedding. Then another surprise: It included my college and law school tuition.

My *tuition*? I knew Will wrote the checks for it, but I thought the money came from the insurance settlement for Dad's death, not a secret trust. That had never been in the picture.

I opened more files.

The next one that caught my eye was a toxicology report on Puck Tarver following his collapse. It stated what I already knew: that he'd accidentally chewed up one of his father's nitroglycerin pills, which lowered his blood pressure and caused him to pass out.

But next to the report was something else: a copy of an internal memorandum written by Puck's lawyer, a woman in a Houston law firm. Marked "Confidential—Attorney-Client Privilege—Work Product Privilege"—the lawyer stated that she'd interviewed Puck's mother and discovered that his father did, indeed, own a vial of nitroglycerin pills, but hadn't opened it since returning home from a heart bypass operation two years earlier. The vial had been sitting unused on a shelf beneath the sink, sealed tight. If some of its nitro tablets had been mixed into her husband's box of Excedrin tablets, it hadn't been mixed in by him or her.

That left only one person who did the mixing: Puck.

I read the report twice. The first time, I asked a question: *Puck Tarver took a nitro tablet on purpose?* The second time, I answered it: *I thought it was an accident—I testified it was an accident—but he took it on purpose! He passed out on purpose—or maybe even faked it!*

I pictured him setting the course of the payload and falling over against the cab window as it headed for Bud Hightower.

With my blood pressure rising, I searched for files on Bud Hightower. After a few minutes, I found one and started reading. It was the partnership agreement between Spin Patterson and Bud Hightower that defined their working relationship in Gulf-Tex and their respective ownership of the company's stock. I searched the terms and conditions for something I wanted to know: If one of the partners died, what happened to the partnership's assets? The answer was simple: The surviving partner inherited everything.

I felt myself moving into darkness like a bat moving into a cave. Now I knew what Joe Wright wouldn't talk about, not even to his wife. Now I knew what the insurance investigator was trying to prove but couldn't because he didn't have all the files, only witness testimony. But I had all the files, and I didn't need to prove a thing. I just wanted the facts.

I felt my scalp itch. The pieces of the puzzle were coming together like chunks of a hologram. Forget more coffee to stay awake, I'd never sleep again.

THEY SAY THAT IN EVERY MAN'S life, a time comes when the son becomes the father and the father becomes the son. For me and Spin, it happened around 7:00 A.M. on Christmas Day.

I was in my office watching the sun come up, thinking about the files I'd read all night, my head buzzing from lack of sleep and my chest aching from a case of heartburn. Not the kind you get from too much pastrami, the kind you get from too much truth.

I looked at my watch. It was time to get moving.

Before Mom went into the hospital, she, Will, and I used to visit Dad's grave every Christmas Day—his favorite holiday—where we told stories, laughed, and ate some holiday cookies. After Mom died, Will and I continued the tradition, more at my insistence than his. We'd been a close family, and I thought the ritual would help keep us that way. It was the only time of the year I could look at Will without feeling guilty about his lost foot.

I locked up my office door, left the building, and headed out to St. Mary's Cemetery. It took me an extra twenty minutes to get there because I missed the turnoff. Not because of my directional dyslexia, but because I had other things on my mind.

Pulling into the parking lot, I watched the cold, gray drizzle streak my windshield. My back was aching from sitting in a chair all night, I was unshaven, and my Christmas mood was anything but merry.

I took a spruce wreath off the top of my Z4, tried to wipe the sap off the canvas, and carried it up the soaked path toward our parents' graves. My suit was rumpled from wearing it all night, and the light rain wasn't smoothing it out. I was late. When I came over the gentle rise, Will was standing near the ground-level plaques that marked the graves, the canvas bag of our family ornaments beside him.

"Where have you been?" he asked without a hello. He'd never been happy visiting Dad's grave. Now, for the first time, I knew why.

"I had to pick up the wreath," I said.

"Like you didn't know that when you set your alarm clock?"

"Merry Christmas to you, too."

He looked at the wreath. "Put it down and let's get out of here before the rain gets worse."

I laid the wreath between the two grave markers, but before I could straighten it he stuck out his foot to adjust it.

I hit his foot out of the way with my fist.

"What is *wrong* with you?" he said.

"Keep your shoes off it or you'll be wearing two plastic feet instead of one," I said. I had a chip on my shoulder I wanted knocked off so badly I was pushing it off myself.

He opened the canvas bag that held the ornaments we had as kids. Every year we put one or two on their graves. "You look like you spent the night in a bar," he said, pulling out a blue-and-gold one.

"I spent it at the office," I said.

"What'd you do, take a wrong turn again?"

"I went in to read some files." It was starting to drizzle harder. I reached in and pulled out a shiny red ornament with my mother's name written on it in silver paint.

"Did you bring the Christmas photograph?" Will asked.

"Forgot."

"Naturally. You've only had three hundred and sixty-four days to remember."

I looked him in the eye and realized that even though I'd known him all my life, I didn't know who he was. The ornament in my hand was the one Dad had given Mom on their first Christmas together, his sentimental favorite.

Seeing it, Will softened and said, "Remember when we almost broke that thing? The tree started to fall and we jumped up to catch it and Mom stepped on my foot and pulled off my prosthesis and no one knew whether to laugh or cry? And then you"—he gave me an accusatory look—"picked it up and threw it to me like a football?"

He laughed.

I wanted to laugh, too, but I couldn't. I put the ornament back in the bag and pulled out one with red and green stripes.

"You know what your problem is?" he said. "Too much education and not enough humor."

"Speaking of education," I said, "how much of my college tuition was paid for by Spin?"

His silence revealed a raw nerve.

"None," he said. "I paid it out of the settlement."

"I know the checks were drawn on your account, but where'd the money come from?"

"The insurance company. What's on your mind?"

That's all it took. The chip got knocked onto the ground.

"WILD STALLION," I SAID.

Will laid the ornament on the head of Mom's marker and stood back to take a look. "That meet with your approval?" he said.

"Why'd you perjure yourself, Will?"

He kept staring at the ornament without answering. "I think it's better over here," he said, moving it.

"Why'd you say you didn't hear Puck Tarver talking to Spin from the crane cab?"

"I don't know what you're talking about."

"I'm talking about your deposition taken by the insurance investigator," I said. "The twelve-year-old boy who overheard Puck asking Spin if it was still a 'go.' The hand signal he asked for if it was still a 'go.' "

"If *what* was a go?"

"You tell me."

"I think you had too much to drink last night."

I stepped closer to him. "Puck didn't pass out on the controls of the crane by accident that day, he deliberately aimed the diesel engine for old man Hightower and then passed out."

Will looked more serious than I'd seen him in a long time.

I said, "He and Spin had it prearranged that he'd whack Bud Hightower if Spin gave the final go-ahead. But Puck's headphone went out, so he asked Spin for a hand signal to confirm it."

"What signal?"

"This one." I raised my hand to my forehead in a salute, as

if I were shielding my eyes from the sun. "Remember seeing him do that?"

"You kidding me? That was seventeen years ago."

"I do."

Silence.

"What's your point?"

"I think the little boy overheard Puck ask Spin for a signal to whack Hightower, and I think you overheard it, too. The only reason the boy's testimony didn't stick is because there was no one to back him up except you, and you refused. You understand what I'm saying? You overheard Puck asking Spin to confirm the move, and you saw Spin give a salute that meant yes, but you lied and said you didn't. The question is, why?"

His face reddened. "You accusing me of being part of a hit on Bud Hightower?"

"You tell me."

"Fuck you."

"Problem was," I said, "the hit didn't go down the way it was supposed to. After old man Hightower got knocked overboard, the payload swung back on deck, cut the fuel hose, and knocked you into the well."

He began trembling. "Bud Hightower didn't die because of some bullshit effort to kill him!" he said. "He died because *you* didn't have the guts to stop the payload from knocking him off the platform! You had the controls in your hands and froze, little man! You lost your nerve and copped out! And now you want to blame it on a crane operator who was out cold when it happened!"

I felt my eyelid twitching and my tongue go dry. "Puck faked his collapse," I said.

"Bullshit. You want to see a fake collapse? Look at your fuckin' dyslexia. You been using that as an excuse to wuss out for years!"

"Shut up!"

He put his nose in my face. "You want to see what you got for wussing out that day, Max?"

He pointed down at his missing foot. "You took away my foot, but that's not all you got."

This time he pointed at Dad's grave.

I slugged him in the chest to push him away. Instead of falling, he brought his fist around and laid it on my nose.

There was a flash behind my eyes, blurred vision, and the ground rushing up to my face. I lay there a moment, then rolled onto my back and tried to clear my head.

What I saw was a double image of Will coming at me. He jumped on top of me and straddled me, his right fist drawn back for another punch.

"If I thought Spin killed old man Hightower," he said, "why in God's name would I protect him? It would mean he killed Dad and cost me my foot!"

"Only one reason I know," I said, and rubbed my fingers together in the universal sign of money.

He brought his fist down again. I deflected the punch this time—grabbed his arm—pulled him over—and we rolled onto Dad's brass grave marker. But Will ended up on top of me again.

"I saw the trust agreement!" I yelled up at him. "He's been paying you all these years!"

"Bullshit!"

"You lied to the investigator! You said you didn't hear Spin and Puck talking about making it a go!"

Will's breath was steaming, his nostrils flaring.

"You fucking Judas!" I said.

He swung and hit me on my jaw.

"What else did you do for Spin?" I said.

This time he swung at me so hard he lost his balance. I arched my back, pushed him off, and grabbed him as the two of us rolled over grunting and struggling for position.

We heard a crunching sound, stopped, and I backed away on my knees. Strewn all over the ground were the remains of the family ornaments. Will stopped, picked up a broken rocking horse, and sat on his butt looking at it.

After a minute, his face turned long and sad. After a longer wait, he finally had something to say.

"You're right about the money," he said, "but you're wrong about Bud Hightower. Spin wasn't trying to kill him, he was trying to deep-six the diesel engine. Bud Hightower just happened to get in the way."

"Why was Spin trying to lose the engine?"

He picked up another piece of the broken ornament. "He said the company had to take delivery on a Caterpillar diesel engine it couldn't use, so the idea was to swing it out over the platform, drop it into the sea like it was an accident, and file an insurance claim. Problem was, it didn't quite work out that way. Puck accidentally took one of his father's nitro pills and fainted, and instead of dropping into the water, it swung back onto the deck."

He tried to fit the pieces of the broken horse together.

"When the insurance investigator asked me to back up what the kid overheard Puck say to Spin—the give-me-a-signal-if-it's-a-go thing—Spin told me the insurance company was trying to get out of paying the claim by saying he and Puck had deliberately killed Bud Hightower."

"Go on."

"Spin said if I backed up the kid, it would cost him a fortune to defend himself and the false charges would ruin him. He said he'd eventually win the case because, if he had to, he'd admit the insurance scam, but he said if he had to pay a fortune in legal fees to defend himself and have his reputation ruined, he'd rather pay me. Us. The family."

He wiped his eyes with the back of his hand and fiddled with the pieces of the glass ornament.

"I told him I wanted to know what really happened that day," he said. "I said I wouldn't lie for him unless he told me, so he did."

He put down the broken ornament.

"And you believed him?" I said.

"Of course I did. He was admitting insurance fraud, for God's sake!"

"What about Bud Hightower?"

"I'm telling you, his death was an *accident*! For cryin' out loud, Max, why would Spin want to kill his own father-in-law?"

"Because, asshole, he found out that Bud Hightower was

secretly negotiating to sell Gulf-Tex to the Japanese, who were going to sell off the reserves and liquidate the company. If Hightower lived, Spin's career was over. If Hightower died, Spin inherited the whole company. Puck Tarver didn't take a nitro pill by mistake. He took one after killing Bud Hightower so he had an excuse."

A stun gun couldn't have done it better. "I don't believe that," Will said. "You have no proof."

"Yes, I do, and when we get back I'll show it to you." I stood up to go. Will sat there looking at the grass, still not buying it. "Even if you thought it was just an insurance scam," I said, "why'd you go along with it?"

It took him a while to speak. "When Dad died, I became the man of the house with no way to make a living," he said. "We had the insurance money, but it wasn't enough to handle Mom's hospital bills and take care of you and Uncle Tad. I wanted to put you through school, pay off the mortgage, and help everybody the way Dad would have." His face was tight. "Even though it was an accident, Spin felt responsible for Dad's death and my foot and wanted to make things right."

"So you decided to lie for him."

"Why not? You think I was gonna let some jerk-off assistant DA crucify Spin with a big lie about Bud Hightower's death? What for? So he could put Spin's head on his wall and run for state senator or something? The insurance investigator's lie was a hell of a lot bigger than the one Spin asked me to tell. If I'd told the truth, what was that gonna do for me and my family?"

I picked up the pieces of an ornament, put them into the bag, and got to my feet.

Will said, "Spin loved us and said he'd take care of us, and he's been true to his word. The trust he set up kept Mom out of a snake pit nursing home and put food on the table! And it paid your tuition!"

"You gullible son-of-a-bitch." I started to walk away.

He got to his feet and followed me. "You can be holier-than-thou all you want, but you've made more out of this scam than any of us!"

That was like a noose thrown around my neck. He was right. All these years I thought Dad had died to save my brother after I'd knocked him into the mud pit, but the truth was that Dad's death—one way or another—had benefited us all.

I turned away toward my car. All these years I'd thought Spin's generosity had been out of love and affection, but it was just hush money to my brother. Worse, it had worked. He owned him and me the way he owned everyone else in my family. The way he owned everyone he knew.

I hated him for killing Bud Hightower. I hated him for killing Dad. I hated him for making me think it was my fault. I hated him for using my testimony about Puck to help make his cover-up work.

I hated him for taking Will's foot and corrupting his honesty. I hated him for buying me off with tuition money and gifts I didn't have the common sense to question. But I also hated myself. Will was right: I was looking at a mirror for the first time since the accident, and I detested what I saw.

I got in my car and ripped out of the parking area. After running an orangish red light and nearly getting wiped out by a truck, I slowed down and headed home at a reasonable pace.

I like *doing* things more than *thinking* about things, but doing things without thinking first was going to make the Wild Stallion fire into a bigger disaster than it already was. I needed to figure it out. When I did, I'd know what to do.

FOR THE NEXT FEW DAYS I questioned everything I knew about the accident. Why hadn't I seen what was happening? What else was I missing?

Those favorite photographs of mine on the wall—Spin wasn't smiling at me out of friendship, he was gloating because he knew I was an idiot. My car—I hadn't earned it, it was paid for with Dad's blood. My job with the law firm—Spin hadn't introduced me to the hiring partner, he'd bought my way in. You name it, I rewrote it.

All the time that was going on, the anger rumbling inside me was getting louder. I wanted to call the DA and unload on Spin, but all I had to offer was a theory and a handful of attorney-client-privileged files the DA couldn't use, none of which, taken separately or together, was enough to indict a high-profile, wealthy, powerful, heroic citizen of the Lone Star State. Even if I managed to convince an ambitious assistant DA to open a case, Spin would have answers, explanations, and alibis. By the time he and his lawyer got done with me, I'd be kicked out of the firm, sued for slander, and given a chance to practice bankruptcy law on my own behalf.

I needed more ammunition and a better aim before I made a move on Spin. After all, he'd taught me the first thing to think about in a situation like this.

If you're going to shoot the boss, don't miss.

IT WAS AFTER MIDNIGHT BY the time I got there. The alley door to the garage was unlocked; I entered quietly, turned on my key-chain flashlight, and made my way through the door to Joe's workshop. When I got inside, I went straight for the cable. Something about it had bothered Jenny, and now it was bothering me.

I found it balled up with two manila tags tied to it. Written on one were the words *HPD—J. Wright Exhibit 12,* from the Houston Police Department, and on the other, *Evidence Locker Release—Return to Owner.* There must have been fifty feet of it, maybe more. Jenny's question—*If it was wrapped that tight around him, why didn't Spin pull him up?*—was the wrong one. Spin's hands were bloody testimony to his inability to do that. The question was, how did it come loose from the platform? Precisely because he *had* tried to pull him up, everyone assumed it came loose from the force of the hurricane or a piece of flying steel.

Maybe everyone had assumed wrong.

I fished my way through the tangled mess until I found the end that had been severed. It was frayed into a wild spray of tiny wires like a used Brillo pad. The impact of whatever had hit it must have been incredible.

I let go of it and continued following the cable toward the end Spin said had been yanked out of the turnbuckle. When I got there, instead of finding it frayed, it was still neatly housed in a steel jacket.

I looked at it carefully. Its threads were like new.

I touched them with my fingertip, not sure what to make

of them. The metal was pristine, not ripped out by the wind or a piece of falling steel. It looked like it had been unscrewed.

Unscrewed?

I tried to picture it. It took a while before it kicked in. Only one person could have unscrewed it. Sweet Jesus, had he done it again? First Bud Hightower, and now Joe?

I looked at the shank and listened to my gut. Yeah, he could have, and, yeah, he did. I heard myself whisper a short message to him: "Gotcha."

Turning to the bench, I found a wire cutter, returned to the cable, and snipped off the shank about six inches below the threads. I was putting it in my pocket when the overhead lights flashed on.

I wheeled around and saw Jenny standing at the door with a baseball bat in her hands.

"Max? What are you doing here?"

"I wanted to take another look at the cable."

She walked over to me. "At this hour?"

I pulled the cable shank out of my pocket and showed it to her. She asked me what it meant, but instead of telling her I let her connect the dots herself.

First, she cried.

Then she was furious.

WE WERE IN JENNY'S SUV IN the drive-through lane at an all-night McDonald's waiting to pick up hamburgers and Cokes. By the time we reached the window, I'd told her most of what I knew, suspected, or guessed about what Spin had done to Bud Hightower, my dad, Will, and Joe. Even though none of it surprised her, it was sobering and incredibly sad. Worse, it confirmed what she already believed about Spin.

We picked up the bag of food and drove out the exit.

"The problem is," I said, "knowing something is one thing and proving it is another." I opened the bag and gave her a double cheeseburger and Coke. "I want to nail him, but even if we put him in jail, it won't do much for the guys who lost their savings and their jobs." I ate a french fry.

"I can go through the notes Joe had in his computer," she said. "Maybe there's something in there that'll help."

We ate and drove back to her house in silence. She pulled into the driveway, turned off the engine, and we sat listening to the sound of her plastic straw sucking air out of the bottom of a plastic cup.

I said, "About what I said the other night—"

"Don't apologize. I shouldn't have slapped you."

"You made a good point."

She reached over and touched my cheek.

"Other one," I said.

She smiled and dropped her hand and the car went silent.

"What are we going to do?" she said.

We sat listening to crickets. "I want to put him away," I said.

"How?"

"Not sure."

"Isn't the cable enough?"

"No, he'll say he was trying to keep the cable tight in a hundred-mile-an-hour wind, he was lying upside down and confused about which way to turn the wrench. Something like that."

"Too bad the cameras were knocked out," she said.

"Yeah," I said. "Wait a minute—how do we know that?"

"I don't know—wouldn't we have heard something by now?"

I made a note to myself to talk to security.

Drumming our fingers.

"Prosecuting him isn't enough," I said. "He'd either be acquitted or cop a plea and end up as the rich and famous man everyone adores while everybody he screwed gets nothing."

Watching the rain start to splatter on the windshield.

"I want to hit him where he lives," I said.

"Where's that?"

"His pocketbook."

Thinking about that.

"How do you rob somebody like Spin?" she said.

"Don't know."

Turning on the engine.

"We have to sell him something," I said.

"Florida swampland?"

"He's too smart for that."

"What else is there? He's got everything he wants."

"I know." Then: "No, he doesn't. He still wants a Nobel Prize."

"How do we sell him that?"

"You know anybody in Norway?"

"Some guy who cans sardines," she said, turning on the AC.

"Wait a minute." I looked at her. "There's a way to sell him a Nobel Prize."

"There is?"

"A Nobel Prize and a whole lot more," I said.

"How?"

"You know."

"I do?"

"Better than anyone on the planet."

The sound of the AC fan.

She said, *"Black Eyes?"*

I stared at her.

"But it's at the bottom of the sea," she said.

"The original is. What about the new and improved version?"

"Where do we get that?"

"We build it."

"Without Joe? Not a chance."

"We don't need to build one that works, we need to build one that Spin *thinks* works. He's doing everything he can to make that happen already."

She turned on the windshield wipers. Thump, thump, thump.

"Spin knows more about what works and doesn't work with Black Eyes than we do," she said.

"But not more than Angela."

Watching the rain fall.

"You think she'd help us?" Jenny said.

"Don't know."

Thump, thump.

"Only one way to find out," she said.

"Not yet," I said.

"Why not?"

"If we're going to sell Spin some blue sky, I have to figure out how we won't get caught."

Thinking about it.

She said, "If we get enough on Spin to show he killed Joe, would the DA prosecute us for stinging Spin? We'd be doing it for the shareholders, not ourselves."

"I don't know what the DA would do."

She stared through the windshield. "You know what? That's enough reassurance for me. Let's do it."

The next question hadn't occurred to her yet: "What's *it*?"

After a while, I said, "I once saw this cartoon of two prisoners chained to a dungeon wall, one half-dead, the other squinting up at a small shaft of light coming through a grating high above his head. And the guy who's squinting turns to his half-dead pal with a confident look in his eye and says, 'Here's my plan.' "

"Yeah?"

"That's us, Jenny. Here's my plan."

ANGELA SONG WAS FIRST. Without her, we had nothing.

I drove to the warehouse to see her. It was seven in the morning, still dark, but she usually started work early and I wanted to catch her alone.

I pulled into a parking slot and got out. As a lawyer for the company, I'd been there many times and the guards knew me, so I headed in. The building, once a hub of activity, was now a graveyard for tons of old drilling equipment that would soon be auctioned off at humiliatingly low prices.

Walking down an unlit hallway, I saw the morning light coming through the high ceiling windows, casting an eerie gray pall on the remains of a once-proud company. There were drill shanks and rusty motors, piles of damaged pipe, a beat-up diesel generator, the guts of electrical panels and wiring. All kinds of things—wires, hoses, pumps—were gathered as the flotsam and jetsam of a modern corporate disaster.

At Angela's door I knocked. "Come in," she yelled. I found her glued to a monitor, her hand on a control-board joystick. "Have a seat," she said without looking up.

I sat next to her and watched her work. Hovering over the black pad in front of the console was a five-foot-high, 4-D hologram representing a piece of earth somewhere deep below the crust. There were gently rising and falling streaks of color indicating sand and shale. She was moving the hologram slowly through seismographic data that had been downloaded onto the computer.

"See this?" she said, pointing. "It's part of Deep Field 2303 drilled two years ago by Exxon, which means what you're looking at is water, not oil. When I use the first program, it comes up blue, as it should, but when I use the second, it comes up green."

"So why not stick with the first?"

"Because I get the reverse effect at other depths." She continued navigating. "One of these algorithms could solve the problem, or maybe a combination of them will do it. Or maybe none." She put the cube into pause mode, freezing it in midair, and turned to greet me. "So what are you doing here so early?"

"This," I said. I pulled the cable shank from my pocket and held it up. "It's the cable that held Joe before he died."

She reached out and took it.

I said, "It wasn't yanked out of the turnbuckle, it was unscrewed."

She kept examining it. "What do you mean?"

"I mean Spin said it was torn off the stanchion by the falling derrick, but it wasn't. It was unscrewed."

She let the thought develop. "While Joe was hanging on to it?"

I stared at her.

"My God." She looked at the cable again. "There has to be an explanation."

"There is," I said, "and it's not nice."

She dropped her hand into her lap and stared into space for a long time. "This is unthinkable."

She raised the shank and stared at it again. When the truth finally kicked in, tears began welling in her eyes. "Joe was such a good man," she said. "But so is Spin." She wiped her tears away with a tissue.

"Let's take a walk," I said.

ANGELA AND I STROLLED BESIDE her two greyhounds, Jiminy and Cricket, toward a field about a half mile from her apartment. They were a pair of graceful, retired racers she'd rescued from the pound, and they loved her for it as much as you'd expect.

On the way, I told her I wanted to get the goods on Spin and take his money with a sting, but I couldn't do either without her.

"Here we are," she said, entering a wide-open grassy area. She reached forward and released the dogs from their leads. They took off like four-legged birds, flying over the ground. I loved seeing them run.

"What makes you think you can separate Spin from his money?" she said. "He's a sophisticated man."

"He's also ambitious, and Black Eyes is his ticket to greater wealth and immortality."

She pulled two tennis balls out of her bag and handed me one, then took the ball from Jiminy's mouth and threw it into the field. The dog was running before the ball left her fingers.

"I'd have to put together a new prototype," she said, "do a bench test, and write up fake notes showing how it works." She took the ball from Cricket and handed it to me.

I threw it hard. "You'd also have to take it out to sea and demonstrate it."

"That's a problem," she said. "It'll be a perfectly good seismology machine at normal depths, but it won't be the deep-earth detector that makes Black Eyes special. Spin's no fool, Max. He knows a lot about the technical side of Black

Eyes, and I can't take a prototype out to sea without the company knowing about it." She stooped down and rubbed Jiminy's ears. His tongue was out and he was panting.

"If I can solve those problems, are you on board?" I said.

She sat on the ground and let her dog lick her chin while she tussled him behind the ears.

"I don't know, Max. I'm an engineer, not a con artist." She continued hugging her dog.

"If the sting works," I said, "you'll be bankrupting Joe's killer and helping put him in jail."

"And if it doesn't?"

"You'll be ruined and could do time yourself."

Her dog turned his head up and licked her face.

"I keep thinking of Joe," she said.

"So do I. And my dad."

"What about your dad?" she said. I had let it slip out. She put her hand under my chin and turned my face to hers. "Look me in the eye. What about your dad?"

I didn't want to talk about what Spin had done to my father, brother, and me. It felt private, like a disgrace. But I needed her help, so I told her about Bud Hightower's death, the fire at Wild Stallion, and Will's foot. The whole thing.

"I'm stunned," she said.

"Spin's good side and dark side live in close harmony."

She stood up, put the leads on the dogs, and stuck out her hand to say good-bye.

"If they give me a laboratory," she said, "I suppose I could get some work done."

"If who gives you a lab?"

"The state Department of Corrections," she said. "Count me in."

I SAW HER BENTLEY PARKED in front of the garage. Jackson was polishing it in his famous red suspenders, his white shirtsleeves rolled up. I waved hello and he waved back.

I went to the front door, rang the bell, and was greeted by Phillip, the butler, who showed me into the foyer and disappeared. I smelled the fresh-cut roses and was preparing my pitch when I heard footsteps on the shiny marble floor.

"Hello, Max."

It was a Saturday afternoon, but Audrey was as elegant as usual in tan boots, faded jeans, a denim shirt, and a pair of many-carat diamond earrings. "To what do I owe the visit?"

"Hello, Audrey," I said, shaking hands. "It's been too long, I know."

"Hasn't it." She ushered me into a large, comfortable living room and asked Phillip to bring us fresh ginger tea. I sat on the sofa and she settled into an overstuffed chair. "Tell me why you're here," she said. "I know you too well to buy the let's-get-reacquainted routine."

"You once said if I ever needed you but thought I shouldn't come to you, I should come anyway," I said.

"I remember."

"That's why I'm here."

"What do you need?"

"I want to pull a sting on Spin."

She wasn't expecting that. She stared at me for a moment "You know something? You've got the balls of my prize bull coming in here asking me to join into some conspiracy against my former husband and the father of my children." She picked up the phone and dialed a number. I pictured the DA and that dungeon I'd described to Jenny.

"Phillip," she said into the phone, "we need that tea."

AUDREY HUNG UP AND STARED through me. "What, may I ask, has caused this sea change in your affection toward my ex-husband?"

I pictured my dad and Will. "It's personal."

"That's what I thought," she said. "One way or another, Tacoma's always in the middle of it." Phillip brought the tea, set it on a table between us, and left. She poured us both a cup. "Whatever it is, you've come to the wrong place, Max. The divorce is over, the girls are finally OK with it, and I'm moving on. Sugar?"

I nodded and she dropped in a couple of brown lumps. I hated to take the next step, but I took it anyway.

"There's more," I said.

"I thought so."

I picked up a spoon. "You and I have a bond I didn't know about until recently."

"What's that?"

"Wild Stallion."

She took a sip of tea. I settled into the cushions. "We both lost our fathers that day," I said, "but not the way we thought."

I told her about the Caterpillar engine, the intercom conversation between Spin and Puck, his fake collapse. I told her how I'd inadvertently helped cover it up with my testimony about the genuineness of Puck's collapse and how I didn't hear him ask Spin if the hit on Bud Hightower was still a "go." I told her about Will and the trust set up to pay him off. I told her that her father was secretly planning to sell Gulf-Tex to the Japanese, and that the prospect of losing the company had driven Spin nuts. She didn't say a word, but before I was done her eyes filled with tears. It was the first time I'd ever seen her cry.

When I'd finished, she sat quietly a few moments, then got up and walked toward the hallway leading to her bedroom. At the doorjamb she stopped and said, "Wait here," then disappeared.

IT WAS THIRTY MINUTES BEFORE she returned, but when she did, she was composed again. She sat down and looked at me with a sad fire in her eyes.

"What do you want?" she said.

I decided to focus on the sting, not a potential prosecution of Spin. Despite what Spin had done to her father, I wasn't sure she'd help put him in jail even if she could. If that day ever came, I saw no reason to involve her or her children.

"I need you to buy the rights to Black Eyes from Shotgun Salvage—secretly—and then turn around and have Shotgun sell them for you at auction. The amount you get for them as an undisclosed seller could range anywhere from nothing to millions."

She lifted the teapot and poured herself another tea. "So you intend to convince Spin to buy Black Eyes at auction for a big number and give him the mother of all headaches when he finds out it's junk?"

"Exactly."

"How much of the auction price do you want?"

"Enough to make the roughnecks whole."

"Appealing to my sense of fair play will get you nowhere," she said. She stood up and walked to the living room double doors and closed them, then returned to the chair.

A sip of tea. "Tell me what you have in mind."

I explained the plan: Angela pretends she's found a solution to the Black Eyes problem, we "test" it and make it look like it works, we leak the news to Spin, and he buys Black Eyes from Shotgun at auction. But unless Audrey bought the rights to Black Eyes first, Shotgun would reap the auction money, not us.

She showed no reaction. "First, you'll never sell anything to Spin based on a laboratory test. Somehow you'll have to fake the results in the field."

I nodded.

"Second," she said, "he'll hold on to his money until the very last second, which means you'll have to stay patient and not show your hand." She set down her teacup. "I'm not sure you can do that, Max. You're a bit transparent."

"My poker face is improving. Who will he use as his banker?"

"Borden B. Bishop III at First Texas."

"I know him."

"Then you know he'll guard Spin's money with his life. He'll want to have all the relevant documents in his hand before he lets Spin bid a penny of his money on anything. Third, if Spin suspects I'm the real owner of Black Eyes and I'm trying to get him to buy it, you're finished."

"How will he know?" I asked

"If I buy Black Eyes from Shotgun, I'll have to file a public notice with the Patent Office that I'm the new owner. That'll tip him off."

Hm. That was a problem. "There's only one solution," I said.

"What's that?"

"Instead of buying Black Eyes, you'll have to buy the whole company."

That made her blink. "Buy Shotgun?"

"It's the only way to keep the patent ownership unchanged and mask what you're after. You can buy Shotgun though a shell company without revealing you own it."

"What assets does it have?"

"Oil-patch junk."

She looked at me over her teacup.

"If the sting works," I said, "you'll make a fortune."

"And if it doesn't?"

"You can sell Shotgun for what it's worth and come out even."

"Even?"

"Close."

She smiled. "You certainly are sure of yourself."

"I've never been more unsure of myself in my life."

I lifted my cup.

She kept me waiting a moment, then lifted hers.

She was on board.

THE MOONLIGHT STREAMED down on the white aluminum siding as I took the key out of the mailbox, slipped it into the lock, and opened the door. The house was dark, no sign of life. Even the crickets had stopped chirping.

I walked to the small lamp next to my brother's living-room reading chair and turned it on. Laid out before me was the landscape of his life: newspapers, a biography of Stonewall Jackson, the smell of tobacco, a ticking clock, the time, ten after twelve. Much had happened to Will in this small sanctuary since the accident, but I'd never really noticed before. A war of attrition had been fought in choked-down silence, invisible transfusions of support had been made to everyone around him, day in and day out, never recognized or appreciated by any of us, least of all by me. It was too late to wake him, so I decided to stretch out on the sofa and talk to him in the morning.

I sat on the couch and was pulling off my shoes when I saw Will's slipper by the ottoman. Not two slippers, one. The sight of it stopped me cold. Morning wasn't soon enough. I got up and went to his bedroom door and rapped gently.

"Will?" I whispered. "You awake?"

No sound.

I opened the door. There was no rustle from the wrought-iron bed, only a sonorous snore.

Standing by the bed I looked down at the man who'd prostituted himself to help his family. He was still sleeping, unaware that I was there. I tried to imagine the pain and honor of loving a family the way he'd loved us. He'd done his duty beyond the expected, but all I'd seen at the cemetery was his corruption, not his sacrifice.

I reached out and laid my hand on his shoulder. "Will—wake up—it's me, Max." I squatted next to the bed and balanced myself on the balls of my feet.

He stopped snoring and turned toward me onto his side, opened his eyes, and stared at me, sleepy but partially awake. His right hand rose from under the sheet, pushed it out of the way, and dropped onto my arm. Then he closed his eyes and started going back to sleep.

"What do you want?" he groaned.

"I need to borrow your camcorder," I said.

" 'S'in the closet," he said, pulling his hand under the pillow and burrowing his head in. He didn't want to hear me yak about how I understood what he'd done for us over the years.

I pulled the sheet up a few inches onto his shoulder and left. After getting the camera out of the closet, I returned to my car. I'd have to extend an olive branch to him another time, when his loyalty to Spin was no longer unshakable. In the meantime, I had work to do.

IT WAS SUNDAY AFTERNOON, which meant she'd be at the Boys and Girls Club in southwest Houston teaching tennis to disadvantaged kids, some of them Indian. I drove up to the courts, got out of my car, and watched through the chain-link fence as she showed a little girl how to do a backswing. Watching her was worth the trip. She was wearing a white tennis dress with a short skirt and below-the-ankle socks that accentuated the length of her legs. Her skin was tan and smooth, her piled-up hair a little loose, as if it were about to fall apart. I thought I'd gotten her out of my bloodstream at Christmas, but according to the temperature of my bloodstream, I was wrong.

I wasn't all that astonished.

When the lessons ended, Tacoma told the kids to pick up the tennis balls and came off the court. She was surprised to see me.

"I didn't know you played tennis," she said, closing the gate.

"I don't," I said, "but that doesn't mean I don't need a lesson."

"You need a lesson, all right, but not in tennis." She toweled off her long neck. "What brings you out here on a Sunday afternoon?"

"Can we find a place to talk?"

She nodded toward a picnic table across the way. After picking up her soft-leather backpack, she walked backward, yelling, "Make sure they're all in the basket, Billy," then turned and continued toward the table. When we got there, she took out a plastic bottle of water from the backpack and sat. "What's on your mind?"

"Joe Wright. I talked to the former head of security at Gulf-Tex, who said there was nothing on the videotape from Wild Stallion the day of the hurricane."

"And?"

"I talked to Charlene, who said you spent some time in Spin's office the morning after the storm."

She unscrewed the cap on her water. "What are you implying?"

"Nothing, just wondering if you had any idea what happened to the videotape."

She took a drink. "What makes you think the cameras even worked that day?"

In court, an answer like that is evidence of nothing, but in life it's a full confession. "Three of them didn't, but one did."

"I don't think I like the tone of this," she said.

"The hurricane wasn't the only thing that killed Joe," I said.

She set down her bottle and didn't take her eyes off me.

I said, "Spin didn't do all he could to save him."

She frowned.

"He unscrewed the cable from the stanchion."

She didn't respond.

"While it was holding Joe."

"Bullshit."

"I know you don't want to hear this—"

"Bullshit!"

"But I can prove it."

She sat toying with the plastic cap. "You know Max, this is about as low as you can go. I know you want me to leave Spin, and I know you still have this ridiculous need to prove yourself to me in some way, but calling him a killer is outrageous."

"This isn't about you and me, this is about him and the evidence."

"What evidence?"

"This." I pulled out the cable shank from my coat pocket and laid it on the table. After looking at it a moment, she picked it up. "Notice that it wasn't yanked out of the turnbuckle," I said, "it was unscrewed."

She toyed with the safety nut a moment, turning it on the perfectly formed threads, then laid it down.

"You don't know what you're talking about," she said.

"You're in denial."

"I know what happened."

"You mean you know what Spin *told* you happened."

"I mean I saw it with my own eyes." She let that sink in a moment. "You're right, one of the cameras caught it on tape."

Your honor, the prosecution requests a five-minute break.

She picked up the shank. "I saw Spin use a wrench on this thing, but he wasn't unscrewing it, he was trying to tighten it so it wouldn't come loose in the storm. Which, of course, is completely consistent with the shredded hands he got trying to *save* Joe, not kill him."

"Where's the video?"

"I destroyed it."

"You *what*?"

"I didn't want it to end up in the hands of the *National Enquirer*," she said, "or people like you."

"It's evidence and you're a lawyer, Tacoma. Do you know what you've done?"

"Yes, and if I had to do it again, I would." She stood up and got ready to leave. "You're disgusting, Max. Spin has been like a father to you. Why you'd want to smear him like this is beyond me." She walked away, saying, "Absolutely beyond me."

I unscrewed the cap on my water and took a drink. I wasn't going to get her to leave Spin, and I wasn't going to get her to come over to my side. I wasn't going to put my hands on the videotape, and I wasn't going to enlist her as a witness to what she saw. I wasn't even going to walk her to the car.

If I wanted a lesson, clearly I'd have to find another instructor.

"HI, HONEY, I'M HOME." TACOMA entered the apartment with warm feelings and a bag of groceries. She was going to fix Spin's favorite dinner: a succulent roast chicken with sautéed spinach, silky mashed potatoes with roasted garlic, and a bottle of Young's Sirah.

She set the groceries on the kitchen island and found a Milk-Bone biscuit for Lightning, who followed her in and sat down to join her in conversation. "What did you guys do today?" she asked him. He answered with a cocked head.

Spin came in wearing jeans, loafers, and a sweater and put his arm around her waist.

"Hey, you," she said. She gave him a kiss and handed him the bottle of wine. "How was your morning?"

"Fine, how was yours?"

"Good. The kids are getting the hang of it. One of them is a regular little Venus Williams."

"I want to bring Trish and Barbara out to see them next Sunday," he said of his daughters. "They love tennis and they're good at it. Maybe they'll get interested in helping out."

His cell phone rang and he answered. "Hello, Puck, what's up?"

There was a long silence as he listened. Slowly, he drifted away from the kitchen into the living room, out of earshot. When he returned, he picked up the wine bottle but didn't say anything.

"You seem a little preoccupied," she said, reaching for a saucepan.

"I'm having a problem with Max," he said.

"What kind of problem? Would you hand me a stick of butter?"

He handed her the butter and cut the tinfoil top off the bottle of wine. "He's not returning my calls. When we get to the petroleum convention in Tampico, I'll need a speech." He had worked hard trying to round up money and support from friends and investors in case Angela made Black Eyes work and he reacquired it.

"Maybe he's busy with other clients." She turned on the oven.

"I'm paying him to work for me." He pulled a corkscrew out of a drawer.

"Smell this," she said, holding a bunch of rosemary beneath his nose.

He put the corkscrew into the cork. "Have you seen him lately?"

Was he psychic or was he spying on her? "As a matter of fact, he dropped by the tennis clinic this afternoon."

"Nice," he said. "He won't return my calls but he follows you around like a horny puppy dog." He pulled the cork out of the bottle with a pop.

She turned away from the oven. "What's the matter, Spin?"

"Why's something the matter?"

"I know you."

Holding the cork, he began unscrewing the corkscrew with half-turns. "He only works on Black Eyes as long as he thinks it will get you into bed, that's what."

Ah, the green-eyed monster was rearing its snarling head. If Angela didn't get Black Eyes to work and he didn't buy it, he was going to drive her crazy.

"I can't read his mind," she said, "and I have no . . . interest . . . in trying." Her eyes had become fixed on the corkscrew. He was turning it to the left, and it was about to . . . come out of the cork.

"OK, I admit it," he said. "I'm jealous."

"You have no reason to be." She couldn't take her eyes off his hands.

He caught her staring. "What?"

"Nothing."

He pulled the corkscrew out, sniffed the cork, and laid it on the counter. "We'll talk about Max later."

"There's nothing to talk about," she said. "Nothing at all."

TWO DAYS AFTER I SAW AUDREY, she called. "Watch how you address me in the future, young man," she said. "You are now speaking to the proud owner of Shotgun Salvage Company, Inc., of Houston, Texas."

"How'd you do that?"

"My lawyers formed a shell company, made an offer to Shotgun's seventy-two-year-old owner, and gave him twenty-four hours to take it or leave it. He took it."

"Congratulations, you're also the proud owner of a glorified junkyard."

"I'm keeping the employees in place so there's no rocking the boat. Pretty exciting, huh?"

"Live it up. The thrill you're feeling may be the only thing you get out of this."

TACOMA SAT ALONE AT THE desk in the study of her apartment, her telephone in hand.

"Bob Bryson," a voice answered.

"Hello, Mr. Bryson, my name is Tacoma Reed and I'm a lawyer here in town who's researching an industrial-safety issue for a client. I found your ad in the *Oil and Gas Journal* and wondered if I could ask you a question?"

"Fire away."

"It's about temporary safety cables on drilling platforms. I've got a client who's concerned that a cable he's installed while they're rebuilding the perimeter might come loose, and I'm wondering if that could happen?"

"Well, there are all kinds of safety restraints on platform perimeters—railings, nets—"

"This is a temporary cable held by turnbuckles."

"—but I was about to say, I've never seen any of them come loose by themselves."

"How about from vibration?"

"What kind of vibration?"

"Machinery, diesel engines, drill heads. A storm, perhaps."

"No, they're made to withstand those things. The shanks have a safety nut with a reverse thread on them, so if there's vibration or wear, the nut tightens on the shank instead of backing away."

"I see."

"Once they're installed and inspected, the only way you're going to get them loose is with a wrench."

A long pause. "Thank you, you've been a big help."

"Not at all."

She laid the receiver in its cradle so softly she couldn't hear it touch. Soon the room began to jiggle and jump through her tears.

Sensing something was wrong, Lightning came over to her and gave her a sympathetic nudge. She reached out and rubbed his ears, then got up, crossed the room, and dropped into a leather club chair. Lightning followed and laid his chin in her lap. She wiped her eyes and blew her nose and sent painful sighs toward the ceiling.

In a near whisper, folding her handkerchief, she said, "Houston, we've got a problem."

"I DON'T KNOW WHAT TO DO."

Tacoma sat on the other side of my desk looking shaken and confused. The door to the office was closed and my calls were being held. She'd called early that morning and asked to see me as soon as possible. Of course I agreed.

We sat in the privacy of my office with coffee cups in hand. She said she'd had no doubts about Spin's innocence and integrity after seeing the video of the hurricane and talking to him at the hospital.

"Then I saw the corkscrew," she said.

"Corkscrew?"

She told me that when she saw Spin unscrewing a corkscrew from a cork, it had brought the videotape back to mind and she'd called an engineer.

"When I heard what he had to say, I felt betrayed on so many levels I can't tell you," she said. "Spin's been such a huge person in my life."

"So have you in his," I said. "Nobody's approval means more to him than yours."

She took a drink of coffee.

"Did he really do it, Max?"

" 'Fraid so."

"Why?"

"Money. He's convinced that without it, he's nothing."

"But that's so wrong!"

"You and I may know that, but he doesn't."

"He cares about so much! The company, the environment, oil, energy, Trish and Barbara! And me!" She sank into her chair. "What happened to me? How'd I misjudge him so badly?"

"That's easy. You fell in love."

"I came to Gulf-Tex thinking I could do good and live well at the same time, and wow. I let it all slip away." She ran her hand through her long, black hair. "You know what I've done to get the five million he promised the college?"

"What?"

"Nothing."

Her forehead was furrowed.

"Don't be so hard on yourself," I said.

"When I think of all the people in the company losing their jobs . . ." She set her coffee cup on the table and stood up. "Thanks for listening to me, Max."

"Where are you going?"

"Home. The police. My grandmother. I don't know, I'm confused. What he did was horrible, but I can't imagine turning him in."

"Wouldn't matter if you did," I said, getting out of my chair. "The cable's not enough to convict him. He can explain it away."

"I could testify to what I saw on the videotape."

"You didn't see anything definitive. And where's his motive? He cut his hands to ribbons trying to save Joe, and everyone knows he loved him and needed him to make Black Eyes work."

She sat back down.

"Besides," I said, "the people he screwed in the company don't care about seeing him do time as much as they care about getting their money back."

"There's no way to get their money back. That toothpaste is out of the tube."

"Maybe." I sat on the edge of my desk and told myself that beneath the silk and diamonds was a heart that was true, that her disappointment with Spin was real, that it was the reason she was here. I told myself we still had this connection, this potential, and I could trust her. So, I did. "Then again, maybe not."

"Come on, where are they going to get that kind of money?"

"How about from the guy who ripped them off?"

"Spin? He'd sooner die than lose his fortune."

"What if he doesn't know he's lost it?"

She sat there trying to compute the idea. "A *robbery*?"

Careful how much you give up, Max. She's still his girlfriend. "I'm working that out."

Her eyes flashed and she sat forward in her chair. "I don't know what you have in mind, but whatever it is, I want to help."

"Hang on—"

"Whatever you have in mind, sooner or later you're going to need somebody on the inside to make it work."

"If he found out—"

"I can handle him."

"I'm not so sure about that." She seemed to like the idea awfully fast. "Why are you so quick to get involved? The way I see it, you have a pretty good life with him as things are."

"Everybody thinks I'm a gold digger, but I'm not," she said.

"People will always talk—"

"It doesn't matter. The point is, I want to do what's right."

"What's that mean?"

"I want to help the people who lost their savings, and I want to get my hands on the money he promised the college." She came over to me and stood too close for comfort. "If I help you, will you help me?" As I looked at her, she reached out and touched my cheek. "Thanks, Max."

"Hang on," I said, "I haven't decided anything yet."

"You decided the minute you told me."

True, I wanted her on my side. True, I wanted her in my bed. True, I wanted *her*—period.

She said, "Don't worry about me staying with Spin, I'll be fine." Then she smiled at me and said something I wished she hadn't. "Trust me."

WE SAT IN A BOOTH AT A DINER near the warehouse.

"What's the setup?" I asked.

Angela said, "I've taken the data from British Petroleum's discovery of the Zapata oil fields and programmed it into the computer. Our Shotgun team will put Black Eyes to work out on Wild Stallion, record the trial on videotape, and when the right time comes, I'll pull up the Zapata profile and make it look like we've found a new oil field fifty thousand feet down. Nobody's ever looked that deep."

"You sure Spin won't recognize the field as Zapata?"

"It's possible," she said, "but I doubt it."

No sense debating it, it was a chance we'd have to take. "Good luck," I said.

"Same to you." She looked scared. "We're going to need it, aren't we?"

"Not really," I said confidently, giving her a reassuring smile.

Tons is what I thought.

HONESTY, SINCERITY, AND THE TRUTH. As they say in the theater, once you know how to fake those things, you've got it made.

It was Tuesday morning and we were headed out to Wild Stallion to pull off the biggest fraud since Enron, except this time it was the good guys who were stealing the loot instead of the crooks. In the supply boat with me were Angela and Jenny. The sun was shifting upward, leaving light blue traces in its wake. You couldn't have picked a better day—or one more different from the day the storm had hit the platform.

Audrey had put one of her lawyers in charge of Shotgun and kept her identity as the new owner a secret. Not even Angela knew. If Spin smelled a rat—especially one wearing his former wife's perfume—the sting would be over in a flash. She had become our biggest ally, giving us everything we needed to pull off the fake test: a service boat, a working generator, and enough equipment and money to make Black Eyes function. Or, rather, *appear* to function. I had Will's video camera ready to record Black Eyes' grand "discovery" of a deep oil field.

Honesty, sincerity, and truth. Fake those things and you've got it made.

We reached the platform around noon, climbed up to the main deck, and went to work. Angela took her place at the control desk in the doghouse while I set up the camera at the end of the console. When Angela said she was ready to go, we dimmed the lights and got started. The video camera was on, recording everything.

She made contact with the seismology transmitters stationed on the seabed floor—the eyes of Black Eyes—and received a good signal. After checking her inputs, she was ready to scan. She was going to pretend to look for oil deposits fifty-five thousand feet deep, or ten miles down. That capability was the supposed genius of Black Eyes.

All eyes turned to the black pad on the floor in front of the console. A few moments later, blinks and blots danced in the air above it as a hologram took shape.

Working the controls, Angela coaxed the image from an empty crib into a three-dimensional block of earth hovering a foot off the ground. Inside the frame was a live, real-time picture of what Black Eyes was sonically "seeing." At the moment it was only what any good seismograph would see, but when it came time to "see deep," Angela would make a seamless transition from active sonar to canned data and give us what appeared to be a live picture of the deep earth. At least, that was the plan.

At the top of the hologram was a gray mass shot through with lines indicating cracks in the substrata. You could see different textures of the earth—shale, sand, and granite—as the sonar moved through it.

As Black Eyes descended, the colors of the substrata began changing from gray to browns and tans, the warm tones we were looking for. I continued to videotape the hologram and everything we said and saw.

Angela placed a laser pointer in the middle of the elongated cube. "Here's the five-thousand-foot mark. We're at the top of the Perdition fault."

The eyes of the machine moved deeper.

Jenny said, "What's that?"

"A field we played out twelve years ago. We're going deeper."

Angela worked the joystick and drove the sound waves far into the earth. The hologram's edges were beginning to fade with each foot it dropped. Images of subterranean mud, shale, and stone continued passing through the transparent cube as if it were a glass elevator dropping down into the earth. I left the camera running on the console and stepped over to Angela's chair at the control panel.

"We're into territory never seen before," she said. She continued working the controls like a pilot flying a space shuttle. I couldn't see anything except gray and brown masses riddled with striations.

Then it happened. A lit-up Christmas tree couldn't have looked better. Rising slowly into the monolith were green dots on gray, like a block of sand with frog-green measles, and dots of orange and red indicating the presence of gas. We were into the western edge of the Perdition oil field. You could see huge quantities of sand with oil strung through it like veins in a chunk of marble.

"Look at that," Angela said softly.

Jenny said, "It's working."

It looked so real, for a moment I thought it was. I hadn't even noticed the moment when Angela had converted the hologram from live images to her preprogrammed data. She knew how to take it from reality to illusion and back again without a hiccup.

I glanced over at the camera at the end of the console. The red lights on the camera indicated that everything was being captured on tape.

"Now," Angela said, "I'm going to take us east to a known water deposit and see what kind of reading we get. If it's blue, it's working."

"And if it's green?" Jenny said.

"Then it's lying."

She worked the controls, and even though I knew what was about to happen—it would be blue because she'd programmed it to be blue—there was something exhilarating about it. I understood why this thing had possessed Spin's soul. If it ever worked the way it was supposed to, it would change the world the way he'd dreamed it would.

Mesmerized, I watched as the invisible elevator moved laterally away from the orange and yellow gas back into the gray shale and dull earth. It moved fast until it began to pick up streaks of white—areas not captured by the sonar—and then streaks of light blue.

"We're coming up on the water reservoir," she said. "The last time Joe and I looked at this, the whole thing was green even though it's water. That really crushed us."

"I remember that," Jenny said.

I watched as the hologram came closer to Perdition. Angela read off the coordinates and I checked them on the chart. The light blue area began turning darker until it was a rich, royal blue. Then, without warning, Black Eyes moved into the center of the water reservoir.

The hologram began shimmering with what appeared to be an underground sea. Angela let go of the joystick and Black Eyes stopped moving.

"Oh my God," she said. "Look at that."

"It's blue!" I said.

She turned to me and Jenny. "It works," Angela said. "Black Eyes works!"

Will's camera was recording the whole act.

"FEAST YOUR EYES," I SAID. "You're seeing the equivalent of the oil industry's first landing on the moon." I put my hand under Angela's arm and lifted her out of the control seat. "Congratulations," I said, and gave her a hug. The three of us hooted and exchanged high fives. The camera continued to roll, recording the act that would eventually be played for Spin's eyes.

Jenny went to sit at the controls and put her hand on the joystick, turning it, pushing it forward, rotating the hologram in the air, onto its side, then upright again.

Angela saw her and returned to the console. "Here, let me show you how." But Jenny was already dropping Black Eyes deep into the earth.

It showed gray and black and more of the worthless cheese that lay below the Perdition field. I looked at the depth chart on the side of the screen and saw that it had descended to fifty-four thousand feet before Angela reached the console.

"Hold on there, cowgirl," she said, "you're going to outdistance your telemetry."

Jenny pointed at the hologram. "What's that?"

Little specks of blue and green in a long stream were hovering in front of our eyes. Angela stood looking at it, puzzled. Jenny got out of the controller's chair and Angela sat down. The quieter Angela became, the more Jenny and I closed in.

"I don't know," she said softly.

Once again, our eyes focused on the hologram. We were

at sixty thousand feet beneath the surface and still receiving a good signal. Something strange and unexpected was happening.

Angela worked the keyboard and the joystick with her right hand, and for a moment the hologram turned fuzzy. Then it disappeared, leaving nothing but the hologram's frame looking like a box kite without its paper panels. I thought we'd seen an illusion, but then the hologram vibrated back to life and hovered in front of us.

Jenny started to say something but Angela cut her off. The room went quiet except for the whir of the Beowulf computers. Black Eyes descended along the lines of the blue and green speckles.

"I think we're in a deep fault," Angela said.

"Which one?" I asked.

"Can't tell, we're beyond anything that's been charted."

She zoomed out from the large-scale picture so we could see it at a distance. Slowly, what lay beneath the fault began to emerge like a confetti structure suspended in midair, with specks of yellow gas mixed with blue water. Then a mass began to emerge in the shape of a megaphone. Black Eyes blinked off again, turned fuzzy, then started coming in.

"We're getting a picture," Angela said.

She tried to move the hologram downward, lost reception, and moved back to the bottom of the cone and held still. She clicked different options on the menu on the right of a screen. Aspect ratio. Resolution. Reimaging. Her hand returned to the joystick and once again she tried to drop Black Eyes into the deeper region beneath the cone.

This time it worked.

Emerging in front of us was a clear picture of the earth's deep substrata.

"We've got a real-time picture from a depth we've never seen before," Angela said. "The thing is still working at more than sixty thousand feet." She looked up at me. "I mean, it's *really working*!"

"SHUT OFF THE CAMERA!" I yelled at Jenny, who was standing closest to it.

She reached out and touched the power switch, laid her gloves over the top of the camera, and joined us at the console.

Up to now we'd been playing for an audience of one—Spin—but no longer.

Jenny turned to Angela and said, "You didn't tell us about this part of the sting. What's going on?"

Angela was still staring at the hologram as if she were drunk. "This isn't part of the sting. This is for real."

"What are you talking about?" Jenny said.

"My algorithm solution is working," Angela said in a whisper. "I was right and Joe was wrong. Black Eyes is *really working*!"

I looked at the hologram, but it looked like any other. "You sure?" I said.

"Let's check. Give me the coordinates of a huge water field," she said.

I opened the log of ExxonMobil's Hoover wells in the Alaminos Canyon and read off the coordinates of a reservoir. They'd logged it as water, not because they could see that deep with their seismograph, but because water had gushed up through their drill pipe. No one had ever seen seismic reflections at the depth of their find.

Angela moved the cube into the coordinates I'd given her. The gray striations of rock and brown sand became speckled with blue, then the whole hologram turned blue.

Black Eyes saw the water reservoir.

"Look at that," Jenny said.

Angela didn't talk. She worked the joystick and turned the hologram on its side, upside down, twirling it slowly in the air, looking at it from every angle. "It's not an illusion," she said. "Black Eyes is transmitting it live."

"You sure this isn't a quirk?" I said.

"I don't think so," she said. "But let's find out."

I grabbed a chart off the shelf, unfolded it on the counter, and turned a spotlight on it. It was a chart of the area below Alaminos Canyon in Mexican waters.

"We've got uncharted territory right here," I said.

Angela inserted the coordinates into the computer and worked the joystick. The hologram moved through time and space—if you could call thick earth "space"—like a hand passing through air. A few minutes later, we saw the ends of the drill pipes BP had sunk into what appeared to be an underground river of oil. She paused to show us. Some of their pipe was in a mainstream of hydrocarbons, some in tributaries, some in gray dry holes.

"Let's drop below their field and see what's beneath it," she said.

The hologram began moving deeper into the earth. Forty thousand feet—forty-five—fifty. We were into uncharted territory again. "It's beyond the range of any seismograph," Angela said.

"Go to the west," I said. "BP has always suspected a huge petroleum field in one of those underground mountains, but they've never been able to look that deep." I read off the coordinates I wanted her to check out.

The hologram moved thousands of feet below the end of BP's production pipe. We were now fifty thousand feet below the Gulf of Mexico seabed.

"Nothing there," I said.

Angela said, "Don't speak so soon."

A few small specks mingled in with the gray and tan.

The specks were green, the color of oil.

The room went quiet.

Angela moved the hologram laterally where the specks seemed to be more plentiful. We were like Hansel and Gretel following green bread crumbs into a forest.

She found more green spots. They led to still more.

All at once, the hologram turned completely green.

"What is *that*?" Jenny said.

"Hold on," Angela said.

She zoomed Black Eyes away to get a larger view.

The hologram stayed green.

She backed it away farther.

It stayed green except for a small portion of orange—a sign of gas—near the top.

She backed it away again until we were looking at five hundred cubic miles of oil beneath the Perdition field. If Black Eyes was right, we'd just hit on the most massive oil field I'd ever seen. Not millions of barrels. Billions.

"Look at that," I said. "It's the size of Lake Michigan."

"BP doesn't know it," Angela said, "but they're sitting on top of a Saudi-class reservoir."

I put my hand on her shoulder. She looked up.

"Good God, Angela," I said. "What have you done?"

THE DOGHOUSE DIDN'T ERUPT with hoots this time, it went silent. None of us could digest what was happening.

Jenny broke silence first. "We're rich," she said.

"What do you mean *we*?" Angela said. "We don't own Black Eyes, Shotgun does."

"But you've invented the solution," Jenny said. "Max is right, you're a genius. You have to get credit for it, don't you?"

"Hold on, guys," I said. "Who's got the rights to what isn't clear right now. Until we sort this out, we have to sit on this information like it's the gold in Fort Knox, OK? Not a word."

They both nodded.

"If this holds up," I said, "there's going to be plenty of money for everybody."

"What about the sting?" Angela said.

"Forget about it," I said. "We've got bigger fish to fry. Spin is a pauper compared to what Black Eyes is worth."

"Besides," Jenny said, "stealing his dream will crush him more than taking his money."

"You mean I'll finally be able to pay off my mortgage?" Angela said.

"You'll be able to pay off your mortgage and buy Spin's apartment for laughs," I said.

"This is gonna be an icicle through his heart," Jenny said.

It was starting to sink in. The room was filling up with awe, then excitement.

Jenny was out the door first, saying, "Hello, Spin? It's Jenny. I've got some great news you're absolutely gonna hate."

I CAME INTO WILL'S HOUSE carrying a canvas bag holding his video camera, a stack of about a dozen CDs showing the fake test of Black Eyes we'd recorded out at Wild Stallion, and a manila folder holding copies of certain files I'd taken from the office. He was sitting in his favorite chair watching a television show. When he turned and saw me come in, he clicked off the TV set and got up.

I set the canvas bag on the floor by his chair.

"Thanks for the camera," I said, reaching for it.

"Any problems?" he said.

"Nope, worked like a dream."

He took the camera and set it on the table next to his chair.

"What'd you need it for?" he said.

"I wanted to record a field trial of Angela's latest effort to make Black Eyes work."

"How'd it go?"

I shrugged. "She's still got a ways to go, but she's hanging in there."

"That girl never gives up," Will said. "You want a beer?"

"Nah, I gotta get back to the office. Maybe later."

He looked down into the canvas bag. "What else you got in here?"

"Copies of the field trial and some files I thought you might want to see."

"What kinda files?"

"The stuff we slugged it out over at the cemetery."

He looked sheepish. "That was like old times, wasn't it?"

"You're still the big brother I could never beat up," I said.

"And you're still my brainy kid brother I can't outsmart."

I reached down into the bag and pulled out the folder. "I wish to hell I didn't have to show you these."

He reached out and took the papers. "What're they gonna tell me?"

"They're gonna tell you that Puck Tarver faked his collapse, and they're gonna tell you why Spin killed Bud Hightower."

I saw his jaw muscles rippling. "Thanks, little brother, but I don't want to see this shit." He handed the files to me.

I didn't take them. "I know it's hard to swallow, but you gotta see what happened."

"No, thanks," he said, extending his hand.

"Listen to me, Will, he made assholes out of both of us!"

"I said, *no thanks*!"

"But—"

"I don't want to hear it!"

He threw the files across the room; the folder opened up and the pages spewed into the air and floated to the floor. Will's jaw was working hard now, his eyes were burning with hate and disbelief, and his face was red. I stared at him a moment, saying nothing, then walked to the side of the room, turned my back to him, and started gathering up the pages. When I was done, I stuffed the pages back inside the canvas bag, picked it up, and headed for the door. He didn't say anything as I went, and neither did I.

I knew we'd have another test of wills soon. And then I'd know what had really happened here in the living room.

WILL SAT ON A PLUSH SOFA IN front of a television set with a CD drive in it, a tumbler of whiskey in one hand, a remote control in the other.

"Watch this," he said to his host.

He turned up the volume. On-screen were the faces of the people who'd conducted the test of Black Eyes out at Wild Stallion the day before: Max McLennon, Angela Song, and Jenny Wright. A hologram hovered in the air like a mirage as Angela took Black Eyes through its paces. Reaching a depth no seismograph had seen before, it continued to go deeper.

Spin Patterson leaned forward on his living room ottoman and watched.

Tacoma Reed stood watching just as intently.

The three of them saw Angela find an underground pool of water to test Black Eyes for its reflection accuracy.

"Oh my God," Angela said on tape. "Look at that." Then Max said, "It's blue."

Will hit Pause.

Spin stared at the screen for a moment without commenting, then said, "Keep going."

Will touched the remote and ran the tape forward. When Angela got good deep reflections, Max said, "You're seeing the equivalent of the oil industry's first landing on the moon."

Will hit Pause and froze the picture.

Spin caught himself and turned. "What's going on?"

"What's it look like?" Will said.

"Don't play games with me, Will," Spin said. "Obviously,

it looks like Angela has made Black Eyes work—but I want to know what's *really* going on." Will lifted his empty glass and held it out to Tacoma, who took it and walked to the bar at the end of the living room.

Will enjoyed seeing Spin beg. "Watch," he said, and hit Play.

Will, Spin, and Tacoma watched Jenny sitting at the console, then Angela taking her place, then Angela puzzled to see Black Eyes transmitting pictures from depths never seen before.

Angela saying, "It's *really working*!"

Max immediately saying, "Shut off the camera!"

Will hit Pause again and the tape froze.

"You want to know what's really going on?" he said to Spin. "Everything you just saw was fake."

"Fake?"

"Fake. A show. Bullshit." He emptied his glass and set it down. Spin motioned to Tacoma to fill it up again. She brought the bottle to Will's glass and poured.

"What you just witnessed," Will said, "was a deliberate effort to make you think that Black Eyes works. It's an elaborate con game to get you to buy Black Eyes even though it's a worthless piece of junk."

Spin looked at him blankly. The blood was at his neck and rising. "Go on," he said.

"Go on with what?" Will said. "It's a sting! Max and Angela and Jenny are stinging you!" He took another drink.

"Why?" Spin said.

"Why?" Will rolled his eyes toward Tacoma, signaling to Spin that he didn't want to say it out loud when she was in the room. Then, hoping Spin would understand, he said, "Max brought me some files from the office. Depositions and transcripts from years ago." The silence that followed told Spin all he needed to know: *Max knows what you and Puck did to Bud Hightower! What caused the fire! He's pissed!*

Spin got it and rubbed the back of his neck. "He should have come to me first."

"He came to *me* first," Will said. "We duked it out Christmas Day at our parents' grave." He took another drink.

"What is *happening* to that boy?" Spin said, and got up and paced. "Does he really think he can get away with a *sting*?"

"He certainly does," Will said.

Spin looked at Tacoma and shook his head, then back at Will. "How'd you come by the video?"

"Max had a stack of them in my camera bag. It wasn't that hard."

"I appreciate this information, Will," Spin said.

Will said, "I thought you would," and kept staring.

Spin said, "Are you looking for . . . a more concrete expression of appreciation?"

"Actually, yes."

"How much?"

"A million dollars."

Spin looked stunned, then laughed. "Will! After all the cash I've given you over the years—you want a *million dollars* for something you owe me anyway?"

"I don't want it for the information I just gave you," Will said.

Spin looked confused.

"I want it for this."

WILL PICKED UP THE TV REMOTE control and hit Rewind, backing the disc up to the point where Max was saying, "Shut off the camera!"

"Now watch," Will said, and hit Play.

On-screen, you could see Jenny's hand reach for the on-off switch on top of the camera—hit it *twice* instead of once—first stopping the recording briefly, then turning it back on before she laid her gloves over the top of it and joined Angela and Max at the console.

"She thinks she's turned it off," Will said, "but she hasn't. Now watch what the camera picked up."

Angela could be seen staring at the hologram.

Jenny: "You didn't tell us about this part of the sting. What's going on?"

Angela: "This isn't part of the sting, this is for real. My algorithm solution is working. I was right and Joe was wrong. Black Eyes is *really working*!"

Spin, Will, and Tacoma watched the videotape as Angela maneuvered Black Eyes into the Exxon-Mobil Hoover wells and found a water reservoir, then watched as she took it into uncharted Mexican waters. She zoomed out to the big picture, but no matter how far she went, the hologram stayed green. They'd found an enormous oil field.

"Look at that," Max said. "It's the size of Lake Michigan."

Stunned silence.

Jenny: "We're rich."

Max: "We have to sit on this information like it's the gold in Fort Knox."

Angela: "What about the sting?"

Max: "Forget about it. We've got bigger fish to fry. Spin is a pauper compared to what Black Eyes is worth."

Jenny: "Stealing his dream will crush him more than taking his money. . . . Hello, Spin? It's Jenny. I've got some great news you're absolutely gonna hate."

Will hit the Pause button.

Spin blinked. He was no longer thinking about the sting, he was picturing the Saudi-class oil field fifty-five thousand feet beneath the Gulf. Untouched. Pristine. Waiting to be produced.

Tacoma broke the spell. "If Black Eyes really works," she said to Will, "why are you bringing it to us?"

"A bird in the hand," he said. "Max and Angela don't own Black Eyes, Shotgun Salvage does."

"Does Shotgun know it works?" she said.

"No," Will said, "but how long will that last? And even if Max screws them out of it, you need money to develop a thing like this. How's my thirty-three-year-old lawyer brother and his whiz-kid pal from MIT gonna do that?" He held Tacoma's eyes. "I want mine now."

Spin licked his lips. "I'll give you two hundred fifty thousand dollars for the disc, take it or leave it."

Will stood up. Spin couldn't tell if he'd offended him or sold him on the offer. Then Will put out his hand.

"Deal."

SITTING ON THE EDGE OF HIS living-room chair, Spin was more animated than he'd been for months. Across from him were three former shareholders in Gulf-Tex, and listening on the other end of the line on a speakerphone were two former investors who'd been the biggest supporters of Black Eyes. Tacoma sat on the sofa with a yellow legal pad on her lap and a pencil in her hand, taking notes.

"I can't go into the details yet," Spin said, "but I've got reason to believe that a new Black Eyes prototype has been built and that it works the way Joe said it would. If I manage to acquire the rights to it—and I think I know how to do that—I want to know who's in and who's out."

"How much you want?" a disembodied voice said through the telephone.

Spin said, "I'll put the first fifty million in as a loan and test the product. If it works, I'll convert the loan to equity and you guys can match my fifty with ten each. That's what we need to market this thing."

There was silence all around as each potential investor waited for another one to respond. Finally, one of the men in the room said, "If Black Eyes works as advertised, I'm on board. How about you, Fred?"

"I've always thought it was a winner—if it works. You demonstrate that, Spin, and I'm in."

The other three said the same.

"I don't want a penny from any of you yet," Spin said, "but if this goes the way I think it will, we're back in business, guys. I'll keep you posted."

SPIN AND I SAT IN A DUCK BLIND at six in the morning waiting for a covey of sleeping mallards to wake up and feed in a pond—or what Texans call a tank—a few feet away. Spin had called the night before and said he'd heard some news about Angela's research he wanted to discuss and he was going duck hunting in the morning. A car would pick me up at 4:00 A.M., good-bye.

I got my gear together, the car came, and I met Spin at the Gulf-Tex preserve where he'd created an environmental sanctuary and a place to hunt birds. Huge, pillbox-shaped oil storage tanks rose in the background as we entered the duck blind at the edge of a pond. We sat on stools, opened a thermos of coffee, and waited. Sensing that the adventure he was born for was afoot, Lightning waited, too, alert and ready.

"So when were you going to tell me about Angela's breakthrough?" Spin said, standing to stretch.

"Never," I answered. "How did you find out?"

He gave me his trademark smile. "Nothing about Black Eyes escapes my attention, surely you should know that by now." He rubbed Lightning's head and told him to be patient, they'd get there soon.

"Let's put our cards on the table, Max," he said. "I know about the new prototype, and I know about the successful test—assuming it was successful."

He broke the barrels on his Remington twelve-gauge over-under and loaded two shells of steel shot. Lead, a pollutant, was no longer legal in Texas, thanks in part to Spin's efforts.

"But a sting?" he said, shaking his head. "I'm disappointed in you, Max, I have to tell you."

I stood up and poked the barrel of my Winchester out the gun slit.

He said, "I could have you disbarred and prosecuted for conspiracy."

"Go for it," I said, aiming my weapon at an imaginary duck. "The minute you put me in a courtroom, I'll lower the boom on you."

"For what?"

"Joe." I looked at him. "You know the cable they found wrapped around his body? Turns out it wasn't ripped out of the stanchion, it was unscrewed."

A sly smile crossed his face. "First a sting, now blackmail? You certainly have become ambitious." He was trying to stare me down as if I were a kid, but I wouldn't let him. "What do you want, Max?"

"Until yesterday I would have said a piece of the millions you made at the expense of your shareholders and employees."

"And today?"

"Nothing. I've got what I want."

"You sound awfully sure of it," he said.

"Sure enough to know I don't need you."

The sound of a duck quacking. We looked out the slit and saw a bird drop gracefully and glide onto the water. Any second now, the covey would follow. We got our guns into position.

"Here they come," Spin whispered. Lightning's ears went up. More squawking, and there they were, wings backstroking the air as they touched down.

Spin fired the first shot; we fired the next ones simultaneously, and I fired the last. Spin's bird fell into the water while mine turned and fell into a stand of tall reeds. Lightning backed up to the door like a kid asking permission to go outside and play.

We left the blind and walked to the edge of the pond. Lightning had his eyes fixed on Spin's bird in the center of the tank. Spin barked, "Lightning!" and the Lab bounded forward, jumped into the freezing water, and swam straight for it. When he got there, he took it in his mouth and swam back. After coming out of the water, he walked proudly to Spin, who took the duck and dropped it into his game pouch and told Lightning he was a good dog. Lightning understood everything he said.

The dog shook off his coat, sat on his haunches, and looked up at Spin, then me, then back at Spin, saying, What about Max's bird? Spin pointed at the reeds where it had fallen. Lightning stood up and aimed his nose in the direction of Spin's hand.

"Lightning!" Spin yelled again, and off he went. When he'd swum halfway across the pond, he turned, looked back at Spin for more hand directions, saw him motion to the right, and swam toward the reeds. After getting there, he disappeared into the grass, emerged a few seconds later with the bird in his mouth, and swam back to us.

"Go to Max," Spin said, and Lightning brought the duck to me. I bagged it and stroked Lightning's head; he shook off the water again and stood panting, ready for more. But this tank was finished for the day. We grabbed our gear and tramped through the underbrush toward the next blind.

"How did it come to this, Max?" Spin said. "All these years we've been like father and son."

Father and son? At one time the thought was as natural as spring, but now it was profane. "Some things are too late for me to do anything about, Spin, but Black Eyes isn't one of them. It's mine now, it's that simple."

"You know me better than that, Max."

Yes, I did. I pictured Sun Tzu's *The Art of War* on his bookshelf. Business wasn't business with Spin, it was war. But I'd learned from him how to use battle tactics myself.

He said, "There's no reason to walk a horse when you can ride him, Max. Why don't we work this thing out together? You have the prototype and Angela's solution, I have the money and contacts to bring it to market. What I'm doing with Black Eyes Phoenix puts us in position to sell it worldwide. Part of it belongs to you."

Lightning stopped, sniffed the air for ducks, and continued on.

Spin said, "We can fight each other or we can cooperate and do something spectacular—light up whole continents, open hospitals, build schools, not to mention make ourselves rich beyond our wildest dreams."

"I didn't say I wanted to fight you," I pointed out. "I said I don't need you."

"You're a good lawyer, Max, but you're not an oilman."

"True, but you're not the only oilman in town," I said.

His eyebrows arched. "You telling me you've got someone else backing you?" He stopped walking and looked me in the eye. Then he smiled. "You never could bluff worth a damn, Max."

"This isn't poker." I turned and started to walk away.

"Don't turn your back on me!" he said, grabbing my arm.

I dropped my shotgun, turned, and charged him, hitting him chest high and knocking him to the ground. Before he knew it I was straddling him and pulling his field-jacket collar so tight across his neck he couldn't breathe.

"Before we go into the business of saving the world," I said, "I want some justice for my father!"

He tried to speak, but couldn't. His fingers clawed at his collar. When his lips started to go white, I eased up my grip.

"I never wanted to hurt your dad," he croaked. "I loved him."

"Loved him enough to kill him."

"You don't know what you're talking about—"

"Bullshit! I read the files! You took out Bud Hightower because he was going to sell the company, and Dad got caught in the cross fire."

More coughing. A long, penetrating stare at me.

"When you're trying to help people, sometimes an innocent victim gets hurt," he said.

I leaned down with my face close to his. "You're not a fucking general, and my dad wasn't in your fucking army. He was your friend! He trusted you and gave you everything he had!"

"That's my point. I wanted to save his job, too."

I wanted to smash his face. And I might have if Lightning hadn't cried and pushed his cold nose into my neck. I let go of Spin and got up.

"It was all an accident," he said. He lay still a moment, then sat up. "When it comes to your dad and your brother, I've tried to make up for what happened even though it was an accident."

"I don't want your blood money," I said.

"Come on, Max, you know about lawsuits and damages. Sometimes money is the only thing we have to work with."

"What about Bud Hightower?" I said. "His death wasn't some inadvertent piece of collateral damage."

"I'll never admit to killing him," he said, "even though the son of a bitch deserved what he got. I busted my ass to pull the company back from the brink, I gave people jobs, I made him and the shareholders rich, and he decided to throw it all away so he could line his own pockets. It was like he was destroying his own family!"

He stood up and brushed himself off. "You move pretty fast when you want to. I'll have to remember that." We picked up our guns and started walking. "When I was thirteen," he said, "I had to decide between saving myself or a guy in a burning Cadillac."

"I wonder how that turned out."

"When you make a choice like that, Max, you learn two things: First, you learn never do it again, and second, you learn how to do it again if you have to. I think about that night with regret, but if I have to—if it's me or the other guy—I'll do it again."

"Is that a threat?"

"Not at all," he said. "I don't need to threaten you because you have to work with me whether you like it or not."

"And why's that?"

"I own the patent to Black Eyes."

He rested his gun on his arm and stood looking at the horizon. For some reason, I hadn't thought about the patent.

"I didn't sell the patent to Gulf-Tex," he said, "I licensed it to the company with a reversion back to me in the event of the company's insolvency, bankruptcy, or sale. The bankruptcy trustee didn't sell the patent rights to Shotgun Salvage because he never had them to sell."

I thought I'd pinned him but he'd flipped me.

"We're in a Mexican standoff, Max. You've got Angela's new and improved Black Eyes, and I've got the patent to the system she's improved. One without the other is worthless, but together they're gold. If either of us is going to get a nickel out of this thing, we have to put what we've got into a partnership and own Black Eyes together. I'll send you an agreement soon as it's drawn up," he said. "Take time to read it if you want, but you'll have to sign it either way."

I turned and walked away, giving my back to his gun. Not smart, but the next best thing to giving him the finger. After a few steps I stopped and turned back.

"You're really good with those hand signals, Spin. Good enough to tell a crane operator to swing a Caterpillar engine into a man's back."

He didn't smile this time.

"Send me all the agreements you want," I said, turning to go. "I'll put the new prototype on the bottom of the sea before I do business with you. Happy duck soup."

"HE'S PLAYING HARD TO GET," Spin said.

He was standing in the bathroom talking to Tacoma while she sat on the edge of the tub sipping a glass of water. He took off his hat and threw it toward the hamper, missing. Tacoma sniffed the bird dung and loamy mud on his clothes, then picked up the hat and put it in the bin.

"Who the hell does he think he is?" Spin said. "I taught him everything he knows."

"Maybe that's why he's so good." She hadn't seen Spin this worked up for a long time.

"He said he's got all the money he needs to market Black Eyes." With a rip of two buttons, he took off his field jacket and threw it down on the floor. Tacoma let it sit there.

"Maybe he does."

"Come on, he's a kid."

"Do you know anyone who'd back him?" she said.

"With that kind of money? Nobody."

Is he really missing it? "How about someone who wants something more than money."

"Like what?"

"Like your humiliation and ruin."

Spin sat down on the closed toilet. "You talking about Audrey?"

"Why not?"

He tugged his right boot. It didn't budge, then it flew across the room and hit the glass shower stall. He unbuckled his belt and took off his camouflage pants. "Even if she's behind him," he said, stepping out of his underwear, "no way is she stealing my invention."

He stepped into the shower and closed the door. "I've got no sense of humor these days."

Tacoma walked into her closet, picked up a manila file folder with a legal pad inside, and returned to the bathroom. "I'll make some eggs," she said. It was eight in the morning.

"All we know at this point," he shouted over the running water, "is that Black Eyes appears to work and Max seems to want it. Both are good signs, but before I put a penny on the table, I need to know if it's for real."

"How are you going to do that?" She opened the file folder and doodled on the pad nervously, making five-pointed stars. *Is this the time to ask him point-blank if he let Joe fall? How do you ask anybody that, never mind the man you love? How does he answer other than no? How do you know if it's the truth?*

"I'm not. You are," Spin said.

"I'm what?"

"You're going to get close enough to him to find out what's going on." He turned off the water, stepped out of the stall, and grabbed a fluffy white towel.

"Why would he let me do that?" she said.

"Because he's in love with you." Drying his back.

"He's over that."

"Sure he is. Every time he lays eyes on you he's like a kid with a hundred-dollar bill." He dried off his legs quickly and wrapped his arms around her. "You're a woman of many talents, my dear—lawyer, negotiator, and world-class flirt."

"Flirt?"

He kissed her and whispered in her ear. "I need you to do this for me, baby. I need you to get the partnership papers drawn up and signed, and I need you to find out what's he's up to. As for how, you'll figure it out." He walked out of the bathroom.

"Spin, I need to talk to you about something."

He didn't answer.

"Spin?"

A few minutes later he came back carrying a piece of paper in his hand.

"Spin, can we talk a minute?"

"Sure, baby, what about?" He handed her a check and said, "If you help me get Black Eyes back, this is yours."

She looked at the payee line and saw that it was made out to the Cherokee College Fund. The amount: five million dollars. The date it could be cashed: the day after the Shotgun auction.

Her first thought was *How great.* Her second was that he'd promised to give it to her with no strings attached, and now she'd get it only if she helped deliver Black Eyes to him. *And to think they called Indians "Indian givers."*

She decided to dwell on her first thought. So did he, which was the bed.

"If you want me to get a partnership agreement drafted, we haven't got time to fool around," she said.

"We've always got time to fool around," he said through the door.

She stuck the check and legal pad into the manila file folder, wrote *Partnership Agreement* on the tab, closed it, and stared at herself in the mirror. There were no tears this time.

THE PHONE RANG AT NINE AS I was getting ready to leave and take my hunting clothes to the laundry.

"Hello?"

"Hey, you."

It was the voice I wished I heard across my pillow every morning.

"Spin told me about your conversation this morning," Tacoma said. "He wants me to draft a joint venture agreement today. I wondered if we could get together tonight so I can present it to you for your signature." Very stiff and formal, as if Spin were listening. Maybe he was.

"I think I can manage that. What've you got in mind?"

"Someplace where we can have some privacy," she said.

"How about my apartment?"

"That's a little too private. How about the Blue Room?"

"On La Cienta?" I'd heard about this place but never been there.

"That's the place. About eight?"

"See you there."

"Oh, and congratulations," she said. "You and Angela must be flying to the moon these days."

"Things look pretty good," I said.

"Pretty good? Finding a reserve the size of Lake Michigan?"

So Spin was sending Tacoma to do his dirty work for him. Did he have any idea whose side she was on? Did he even have a clue?

Never mind him. Did I?

I CAUGHT ANGELA OUTSIDE the lab carrying a cup of coffee as she headed toward her desk.

"How'd the hunt go?" she said.

I opened the door to the lab and ushered her inside where no one could hear us.

"What happened?" she said, coffee steaming.

I broke into a grin. "He bought it!"

Her eyes widened. "He *did*?"

"The whole thing!" I said. "I told him I didn't need him, I've got a financial angel backing me—and he bought it all!"

"Holy cow!" She put her coffee down.

"Angela, you were so good yesterday I actually thought you'd made Black Eyes work. 'My algorithm solution is working,' batting those big, black eyes. 'It's the real thing!' "

"Look who's talking!" she said. 'Shut off the camera,' you said. 'Sit on this like it's the gold in Fort Knox! Forget about the sting, we've got bigger fish to fry!' You win the Oscar, Max."

"If I get it for acting, you get it for best technical effects—you moved from real time to canned images so smoothly I couldn't tell when it happened—and I was looking for it!"

She set down her coffee mug and raised her hands in the air, praise the Lord.

" 'The sub-Perdition fields,' " I said, mimicking her from the day before. " 'We're sixty thousand feet down!' "

"Fifty-eight," she said, "but who's counting? Does Spin really think Black Eyes works?"

"Of course he does! If I didn't know better, I would, too!"

Stirring my coffee. "You don't know how good it feels to take him. Everybody says I'm a bad poker player, but I bluffed him out of his jock."

"How did you get the videotape to him without his suspecting it?"

That was a bluff I didn't like. "I used Will."

"Will?"

"I picked a fight with him at his house and turned my back on him to give him time to swipe a CD out of my bag. I didn't know if he'd do it or not. I guess part of me hoped he wouldn't—but he did."

"Oh, Max, that has to feel awful. I told you to let me give it to Spin."

"He would have suspected you more than Will," I said. "Besides, I needed to know where Will stands, and now I do."

"Why's he so loyal to Spin?"

I shrugged as if I didn't know, even though I did. "If somebody supported you and your family all your life, you'd have a hard time believing anything bad about them, too. Besides, what's he going to do if he turns on Spin? How's he going to face himself? How's he gonna make a living?"

I took a drink of coffee. I understood Will's vulnerability, but even so it hurt to know he was still a traitor.

I said, "Things are going to get tough now that Spin's bought into the sting."

"I can make preprogrammed holograms as long as I have some idea what part of the Gulf we're supposed to be scanning," she said, "but if we have to demonstrate how the system works without knowing in advance where we're scanning, we're dead."

"Deep-earth sonograms all look alike to me. How can anybody tell one place from the other?"

"Oh, they can, believe me. If you know oil-field profiles the way Spin does, it's like comparing the Rockies to the Grand Tetons."

I had to believe her. "Keep inventing as many different scenarios as you can and put them on the hard drive," I said. "It's all we can do."

Her eyes wandered off, then her face broke into a devil's grin. "You know something? It's kinda fun being a crook!"

"Yeah, well, don't go crazy," I said. "Remember Murphy's Law: If something can go wrong, it will."

I WAS PARKED IN FRONT OF the Blue Room waiting for Tacoma to arrive when I decided to call Jenny and get her analysis of my conversation with Spin on our hunting trip. I told her Tacoma was meeting me in a few minutes to try to get me to sign a partnership agreement, but I didn't tell her I'd recruited Tacoma to become our man in Havana. I wasn't sure she'd believe it. I wasn't sure I did.

"You gonna sign it?" Jenny said.

"I have to," I said. "He holds the patent to the device Angela improved. Unfortunately, we need each other."

She held the phone away from her mouth and called out to Christopher not to put a crayon in his mouth. "I think you made a mistake telling him you know he killed Joe."

"Why?"

"It makes you a threat, and we know what he does to threats."

I could hear her talking to Christopher again, then she came back on the line.

I said, "He won't mess with me as long as I have Black Eyes and he thinks it works."

A midnight blue Jag pulled in and parked two cars over from me.

She said, "Keep in mind that he doesn't have to hurt you himself. He can hire someone to do it for him."

Tacoma got out of her car and walked up to the door of the bar. "She's here, Jenny, I gotta run."

"I don't trust her, Max. She's Spin's girl. You just don't see it."

"I'll bear that in mind."

She tried to pack in all she could before I hung up. "Remember the Godfather's advice to his son: The one who comes to make the peace will be the one who will betray you."

"Later."

"And don't forget something else!" she said.

"Jenny—"

"You're a fool for love!"

I CAUGHT UP WITH TACOMA at the door and she was looking great, as usual. If she was wearing jewelry, I didn't notice. First I had to get past her eyes.

She said, "Hey, you," and we gave each other a perfunctory hug. I opened the door to a softly lit room of candles and amber-filled liquor bottles behind a bar. The fragrance in the air—that lounge-lizard mix of whiskey, smoke, and perfume—filled people's heads with romantic expectations and things dark and hot. Couples sat in booths with hands touching and eyes focused on each other.

The Blue Room was supposedly the place where the rich, married men of Houston brought their mistresses. According to the story, an oil baron's wife had shown up there in search of her husband one night only to discover she couldn't get in without an escort. Lacking one, she left, hired a gigolo, and returned every night until her husband showed up with his girlfriend, at which point she pulled out a pearl-handled pistol and shot him in the groin. If he'd died, which he didn't, they might have closed down the place, but the men who came here weren't about to let a stray bullet in a domestic dustup deprive them of their sanctified privileges. Texans to the last, they feared .38 caliber vasectomies less than monogamy.

Tacoma and I were shown to a table in a corner. We ordered drinks—her usual vodka martini, a beer for me—and had hardly spoken before she pulled a sheaf of papers out of her backpack. I took them and held a votive candle over the first page. The title read "BLACK EYES PHOENIX, LLP—A

Texas Partnership Between Maximilian 'Max' McLennon and John B. 'Spin' Patterson."

"Has Spin read it yet?" I asked. There were two copies.

"He's read it and he's ready to sign." Once again, considering our intimate conversation in my office, she seemed awfully formal.

I opened the first couple of pages, tried to read them, couldn't, and looked up. She was leaning back with her arm stretched across the top of the booth, her black hair framing her face, her skin the color and smoothness of caramel pudding, her eyes reflecting the candlelight. Ordinarily a conservative dresser, she surprised me with a display of cleavage.

When it came to the work at hand, she had my divided attention.

"Trust me, everything's there that's supposed to be," she said, handing me a pen.

"You sure?"

"I am," she said, looking me in the eye and speaking to me without words.

I closed the document. "Tell me three things you'd want me to know about this document if you were my lawyer."

Giving me her enigmatic smile, she took back the papers, put on her librarian's glasses—God, she looked good—and turned to page twenty-two.

"Everything's fifty-fifty—ownership, voting rights, governing authority, division of profits," she said.

"That's a prescription for disaster," I said. "What if we can't agree?"

"The only alternative is to give Spin fifty-one percent, so don't fight it." She pointed at a paragraph on page twenty-three. "He's going to capitalize the partnership with a fifty-million-dollar personal loan. Until it's paid back with interest, you won't see a dime. I assume you have no problem with that."

"Of course not," I said. It was a standard provision, but even more to the point, it was meaningless. Although he didn't know it, the partnership was a vehicle for stinging him, not going into business with him.

"I just want to be clear that none of his money is going

into the partnership as an investment," she said. "It's a loan, not equity. You won't get rich when he puts it into the Black Eyes Phoenix bank account."

"Understood," I said.

She looked at me for emphasis. "It's an important point."

"I *got* it," I said. Important, yes, complicated, no.

She turned the pages on the agreement. "When you have some light to read by," she said, "take a look at paragraph thirty-five A."

I picked up the candle, moved it as close to the page as I could, and read. The paragraph said that if either partner died before the partnership was concluded, the surviving partner inherited all the dead partner's rights, title, and interests in the joint venture.

"What made him put this into the agreement?" I asked. It gave me the creeps seeing the same provision he'd written into his partnership with Bud Hightower that allowed him to take over the company when Bud died.

She shrugged. "It's boilerplate."

It also happened to be Texas law in the absence of an agreement to the contrary, but I didn't like it. "I'd feel better if a dead partner's interest went to his estate."

"What can I tell you?" she said. "This is what he wants. Besides, if you ask me, it's to your benefit; he's older than you are, which means he's more likely to die first."

"Actuarially speaking," I said.

"You think one of you is going to kill the other?"

"Ask Joe Wright."

She gave me an intense, disapproving stare.

"Why are you being so formal?" I said.

She blushed slightly and shook her head, so I let it go.

"What about the patent rights?" I said. "They're the only reason I'm considering a joint venture in the first place."

"It's all here. Spin will contribute his patent rights in Black Eyes as long as you get Angela Song to contribute hers, including her new solution." Another sip of her drink. "Assuming it *is* a new solution."

"Would we be here if it weren't?"

"Just looking out for my boss's interests." She was playing her role awfully well. Assuming she was playing.

"I'll read this tonight and call if I have any questions," I said.

"If you don't like something, you'll have to take it up with Spin." She picked up her drink and doodled on a napkin before taking a sip.

"Are you sure there's nothing else in here I should know about?" I asked.

She looked me dead in the eye. "You won't have any trouble with it. And while I don't mean to push you, I have to ask you to sign it by tomorrow."

"I'll do my best," I said. "By the way, where's my copy?"

"Once you sign, I'll get Spin's signatures and send you a duplicate original."

She finished her drink and looked at her watch. With business over, I wanted to talk personally.

"Tacoma, I—"

She shook her head as if she knew what I was about to say and didn't want to hear it.

"What?" I said.

She turned the napkin around and showed it to me. She'd written the words PLAY IT STRAIGHT. "Unfortunately, I have to run," she said. She signaled a waiter and pulled out a wallet. "This is on me."

"On you or Spin? I'm not letting him buy me a drink."

She gave me a weary smile but didn't answer. As she gathered up the file, a piece of paper slipped out of the envelope onto the table. Picking it up to hand it to her, I saw what it was: a check made out to the Cherokee College Fund in the amount of five million dollars. The date on the check was a few days away.

"This yours?" I said.

She took it, unhappy that I'd seen it, and said, "Thank you." Then she departed.

I left a few seconds later wondering if *she'd* played it

straight, and, if so, where straight had ended and duplicity began. I'd told Angela my poker face was getting better, but that was only half the problem. The other half was *her* poker face and how well I played the game.

"DID HE SIGN?" SPIN SAID, HANDING her a cup of Sleepytime tea.

Tacoma raised her hand to say no thanks and walked into the kitchen. Spin followed.

"Well?" he said.

"For God's sake, Spin, we met in a bar. What do you think?"

"What'd he say?"

"He's going to read it and call me in the morning. Run a hot bath for me, would you?"

"Is that all?"

"What else were you expecting?"

"I wasn't expecting anything, I'm just asking if that's all."

"Let's see," she said, tapping her finger on her lips and rolling her eyes up. "I think he also said hello, I'll have a beer, and good-bye."

"OK, Tacoma."

She stared daggers at him, then let her backpack slide off her shoulder, grabbing the strap before it hit the floor. She reached in, pulled out a silvery object, and tossed it at him without warning. He spilled his tea catching it. She walked out of the room, saying, "Listen for yourself."

He held the tape recorder up and looked for the Play button.

"This compulsion you have for recording things is going to get you into trouble one of these days," she called back.

He turned on the tape recorder and listened to the whoosh of background noise in the Blue Room, picking up pieces of conversation between Tacoma and Max. He flicked it off and followed her into the walk-in closet where she was getting undressed.

She said, "That's the last time I'm taping," pulling off a boot. "It really sucks, and when you know you're being recorded, it throws off your conversation."

"I need that signature, baby," he said, sitting on the bed.

"Then let me get it for you." Off with the other boot.

"I need it tomorrow."

"I'm dancing as fast as I can." Taking off her shirt.

He followed her to the bathroom door and spoke through it. "I'm not gonna spend fifty dollars, much less fifty million, for something that doesn't work! After you get his signature, there's more you need to find out."

No answer.

He downed his tea in a rush.

"I don't like this any more than you do," he said. "And I sure don't trust him when it comes to you. I never have."

"How about me?" she said. "Do you trust me?"

"Of course. Any reason I shouldn't?"

"Still waiting on that bath, Spin."

WHEN I GOT TO AUDREY'S house, Jackson said she was in the barn with the horses. I went over there.

Calling it a barn was an insult to the Ritz. There were well-groomed indoor trees, beautiful brick floors, and waxed pine timber. Hanging over the inlaid brick walkway was a huge crystal chandelier that had once graced the ballroom of the Dallas Hilton. It was early afternoon, and she was there to groom her favorite horse for a show and groom me for the Shotgun auction.

"Did he propose an agreement?" she said, lifting a brush.

"Got it right here," I said.

"What's he want?"

"He wants us to put Black Eyes into a partnership so we can sell it as a package. I put in the technology, he puts in cash and the patent rights."

"Have you signed?"

"Not yet. I'm playing hard to get."

She brushed the horse's flanks and talked to it quietly.

"How much will he bid at auction?" I asked.

"How much do you want?"

"Every penny he's got, but I need at least seven million."

"*Seven* million? You have to think bigger than that, my dear," she said.

"Fine with me."

She put two bridle lines on the horse to hold him in place, then walked to a wooden bar at the side of the stalls and poured us both a fresh lemonade.

"Here's how the auction is going to work," she said. "Starting at one o'clock, buyers will bid every hour until four o'clock, at which point the highest bid wins."

"Who do you expect the players to be?"

"The usual. Shell, Exxon, BP, Halliburton, a few other biggies, and a handful of bottom-feeders. In order to place a bid, a company has to prove they've got money to back up their offer, which means the big guys will qualify easily while the small companies will have to get a bank to stand behind them with a letter of credit. Since your partnership will be a new kid on the block, Spin will have to put up cash as security before he can make a bid. That's the first step to get him to put his money at risk."

She took a drink.

"That should be easy," I said. "The money he puts into the partnership is a loan, not equity. If he doesn't make the winning bid, he can simply take back his money."

"Easy? Not for Spin. He won't even lend money to a company he controls unless he absolutely has to."

"Awfully anal," I said.

"Believe me, he's not going to transfer a penny out of his personal account until he's sure he wants to make a buy. He's like a lion; if he smells the least bit of trouble, he'll leave in a flash."

"So we have to get him to fund the partnership first, then we have to get him to bid on Black Eyes."

"That's right. Only if he makes the highest bid and purchases Angela's new machine and software will the money belong to Shotgun. But once that happens, there's no way he can get it back."

"He'll sue for it," I said.

"Let him," she said. "It's a blind sale."

Salvage companies often sold equipment with no representations or warranties about the quality of what they sold, and with no recourse back to the seller if the buyer didn't like it. Sales were strictly caveat emptor—what you bought was what you got. Besides, as long as I had that cable shank, suing Audrey or me wasn't going to happen because it would make trouble for him he wouldn't want. Even if the DA didn't indict on it, it would be a scandal that would ruin him and he knew it.

She pointed at a bucket and I lifted it to her.

"So," I said, "how do we get him to put up more than seven million dollars?"

"My Swiss company will drive up the price," she said. "It'll be the last bidder to compete with him, I'm sure."

"I won't be able to help you at that point," I said. "The partnership agreement gives him sole discretion to bid or not bid."

"Oh, you'll be able to help. When we get near the end of the auction, I want you to call me and describe his attitude and demeanor. I know him better than Eve knew Adam. What you have to tell me will give me more insight into his bidding strategy than you can imagine."

"He hasn't told me where he plans to do business," I said.

"Probably in his apartment." She walked over to the fence, picked up a chestnut-colored English saddle, and laid it on the horse. "No one knows I own Shotgun, right?"

"Nobody."

She tossed the cinch and grabbed it under the horse's belly. "If he so much as *dreams* I own it, the sting is over."

She finished buckling on the saddle, gave the horse a carrot, and walked me back to my car.

"I won't see you again before the auction," she said. She handed me a card with a telephone number written on it. "Don't use my regular number; if he's scanning the room, he'll recognize it."

"Scanning?"

"He loves to ID telephone numbers and tape-record conversations. It's his idea of cheap intelligence."

"It also happens to be illegal," I said.

She broke into a big laugh. "Like what we're doing *isn't*?"

Somehow, I kept forgetting that. When you think you're doing something right, you have a tendency to forget the law.

She put her hand on my cheek. "You're such an interesting combination of innocence and guile, Max. It's a wonderful quality—but stay on your toes. We've got a lot riding on this."

"Not a lot," I said, "everything." I opened the door to my car.

She kissed me good-bye and turned back to her house. "'It also happens to be illegal,'" she said, parroting what I'd said as she walked. I could hear her laughing all the way to the front door.

THIS TIME, I TOLD TACOMA to meet me at my apartment. I wanted privacy. We had things to discuss.

She arrived wearing a pale silk blouse, a black sweater over her shoulders, a brown suede skirt, and tight leather boots. After her usual "Hey, you" and a hug, we walked to the living room, where she sat on the sofa and asked for a cranberry and soda.

While I was pouring her drink, she opened a legal file folder and lifted out a finished partnership agreement, which she laid on the coffee table. I set her drink on a coaster and sat next to her. She handed me a pen before I'd even read the first page.

"Mind if I take a look at what I'm signing?" I said. "It's just one of those funny lawyer's habits I can't kick."

"It's the same agreement I gave you at the Blue Room."

Paging through it quickly, I said, "You having any second thoughts about this?"

"The agreement? No, why?"

"Just wondering." Turning the page. "How about the sting?"

"No, but I wish you'd tell me how you're doing it."

"You know the rule: You only know what you need to know."

"What is this, the French Resistance?" she said. "If anybody's going to slip up because he knows too much, it's you. Spin knows you inside out."

"Not as well as he knows you."

She didn't particularly like that.

She said, "You don't think I'd rat you out, do you?"

"If I did, we wouldn't be here. But when a person is sleeping with a person, a person tends to say things a person might not otherwise say, if you get my drift." I turned the page but my mind wasn't on the document. "You are still sleeping with him, aren't you?"

"You know the rule: You only know what you need to know."

"Very *good,*" I said, and turned the last page. I pushed aside the papers. "If this were a real deal, I wouldn't sign it."

"Why not?"

"I don't like the terms."

"You didn't even read them."

"If they're the same as they are in the draft, I did. They are the same, aren't they?"

"Of course. So you're saying you don't like having a partner put a fifty-million-dollar loan into a partnership you own half of?"

"Not this particular partner."

"Who else could you get to back you?"

"With Black Eyes working? Twenty people, easily."

"But it isn't working, is it?" she said.

"Of course it is," I said, mustering all the bluff I had.

She rolled her eyes. "You need to sign this if you want to get Spin into the auction." Lifting a pen again.

"He'll think something's wrong if I sign too fast."

"We haven't got time for this, Max."

"I'll give him the agreement, but not without a fight."

"A fight?"

I came closer to her.

"Yeah, you know, I won't sign . . . unless."

"Unless what?"

"You make me."

She gave me a Mona Lisa smile. "Like I'm going to tell him that."

"Shouldn't be a problem if you're not sleeping with him."

"I didn't say that."

"If you are, better tell me now." I pulled her to me and she didn't pull away. Just that much give on her part—her not pulling away—flipped a switch inside me. All these years I'd blamed myself for my dad's death—and all these years I'd compounded that by blaming myself for letting down Tacoma—but now that I knew Spin had set me up, the guilt and self-loathing were gone. And with it, some kind of barrier between me and Tacoma.

So I went for it.

I kissed her cautiously—waiting to see if the Big No came booming out of the sky. When it didn't, we both took the next step together. Then the next, and the next, until we were pawing each other, bumping noses, and kissing each other's mouth, cheeks, and neck so desperately we didn't feel much of it.

She couldn't be doing this just to get my signature. It wouldn't be this good.

"We shouldn't be doing this, Max."

"We're not doing anything. We're lawyers. This is all hypothetical."

"Oh, in that case . . ."

More kissing.

"You want that signature, right?" I said.

"Can't go home without it."

"Then I guess you'll have to do whatever it takes to get it."

"You wouldn't pressure me that way, would you?"

"No, of course not."

More kissing.

"You're behaving as if you are," she said.

More kissing, then she broke away.

"I'm not thinking clearly," she said.

"Relax, I'll think for you."

"Oh, my God."

She backed onto the sofa and I thought it was all over. "What's gotten into you?" she said.

"I don't know, exactly. For the first time I can remember, I feel worthy of being with you."

"I never thought you weren't."

"I know, but I did."

She sat looking at me with a combination of curiosity and desire. I sat looking back. God, was I hot. But I had no idea where her head was.

She said, "If we were really negotiating at arm's length here, what would happen next?"

"Next would be the top button."

She stared at mc. I stared back. Neither of us blinked.

She unbuttoned the top button on her blouse.

"Then what?" she said.

"Another one."

She undid the next.

"See how easy it is when it's not for real?" I said. "We lawyers love hypotheticals."

She unbuttoned the one below that.

I stood up, took her by the hand, and lifted her to her feet.

"Where are we going?" she said.

"No place."

"Max, we're not going to your bedroom."

"Only hypothetically."

She stopped. I kissed her. She whispered in my ear, "We've gone far enough, don't you think?"

"Not yet. But we won't go too far. Trust me."

I took her by the hand and pulled her gently. She looked at me a moment, then came with me. We entered the room and I stood next to the bed. Another deep kiss, another button undone.

"So you're not sleeping with him?" I said.

"Max. What do you think?"

"Doesn't matter what I think, it only matters what you're doing."

"Not if we're just pretending."

"God, I don't know what to think," I said.

"Why don't you just sign the agreement and let me go?"

"Good idea. In a few minutes."

More kissing.

I took off her blouse slowly, laid it on the bed, stood her in front of me, and sat on the edge of the bed. She put her hands on her hips and measured my mind for all it was worth, which wasn't much.

I sat there and watched.

"Do I get the signature yet?"

"Almost," I said.

She took a deep breath, then her hands disappeared behind her back and unhooked her bra. When it came loose, she cradled it against her breasts. "Now?"

"Let's imagine you took it off all the way," I said.

She lowered her arms slowly, revealing herself. Oh, my. I thought I hadn't forgotten, but I had. At this point I thought she knew I'd give her the signature anytime she wanted, that my holding out on her was a charade, an excuse, a grown-up version of playing doctor-and-nurse.

She dropped the bra and unbuckled the belt on her skirt, unzipped its side, let the silk lining slip over her hips, and dropped it to the floor. She was wearing a sheer white thong with embroidered lace on the triangle.

I took off my shirt.

She stepped out of her skirt and stood in her boots and bikini, then piled her hair on top of her head and looked at me. The insides of her thighs were curved like the neck of a swan.

"How far are we going with this?" she said.

"As far as it takes to get that signature."

She stared at me a moment, then said, "I can't believe I'm doing this."

"You're not. It's virtual."

She let her hair cascade over her shoulders like a slow-motion waterfall, then took a step toward me, put her hands on my chest, and pushed me onto the bed. Lifting one knee, then the other, she straddled me.

"Are you going to give it to me now?" she said.

"Oh, yes."

"I mean the signature."

"That, too."

She shifted her weight, undulating slightly, then reached out and put her finger in my mouth. "Remember our last night together?"

"Nuh-uh."

"Do I have to remind you?"

"Uh-huh."

She leaned down and kissed me and her hair enveloped our faces in a private curtain. The softness of her lips made me dizzy. My hands fell onto her back and stroked her from the nape of her neck to the base of her spine. The seam between her legs found the rise in my jeans and caressed it with small movements. My hands were all over her.

I heard a voice say, "I love you," and realized it wasn't hers, it was mine—it was coming out of my mouth as if I were possessed. Trying to minimize it, I said, "I think about you all the time." As if that would help.

She undulated against me silently, massaging the words out of my throat.

I said, "They say Indian braves used to cut the hearts out of their enemies and eat them while they were still beating—is that what you're doing to me now?"

"Which fantasy are we in—cowboys and Indians or oil deals?"

I reached down to unbutton my jeans. She stopped moving and brought her face down to mine. I put my hand on her back and we lay still, breathing but not moving.

"I want to," she said, "but I can't."

"Why not?"

"I'm still in his bed."

I considered all possible meanings of what she said: She was in his bed alone, she was in his bed asleep, she was in his bed yakking—everything but the obvious.

"I'm sorry, Max."

SHE STARTED TO GET UP.

"Relax," I said, putting my hand on her shoulder. "You're safe."

"I'm also half-naked."

"More than half." I reached down to the bottom of the bed and pulled the down comforter over her. "It's not as if this is the first time we've been in this position, you know."

She reached up and pulled my face into her neck. I felt her body relax. "That was a long time ago," she said.

I looked at the ceiling for answers. "What happened to us?"

"You blew it."

"*I* blew it? You're the one who bailed on me for the guy with the hot car."

"Only after you made it clear you didn't want me."

"I didn't not want you."

"You sure fooled me," she said.

I pulled a strand of her hair over my upper lip and smelled the fragrance of her shampoo. "Why are you still with Spin?"

"Until a few days ago I didn't know what he'd done. I couldn't believe it. Sometimes, I still can't."

"I know what you mean, I stayed blind a long time, too. But if you put the facts together the way you would in a brief, you'll see."

She looked pained, although whether she was convinced or not, I couldn't tell.

"I need your help, Tacoma."

She nodded slightly. "I know what I have to do."

Did she? And what was that?

I ran my foot up her leg. "You've still got your boots on."

"I know."

"If we'd kept going, were you going to take them off or leave them on?"

"I didn't get that far in my thinking," she said.

She put her hand on my face and we looked at each other with no screen between us for the first time since law school.

"Remember the dreams we had?" she said.

"Sure do. I was going to be a big-time lawyer with a family, you were going to save the Cherokee Nation from the ravages of heartless industrial America. Now look at us. I'm a con artist and you're a rich girl in two men's beds."

"That's not what's going on here," she said.

"Really? Tell me, what is?"

"We're both trying to do what's right."

"What's that mean?"

She didn't answer.

Loving her was one thing, trusting her was another. Her silence reminded me that I couldn't do the latter. Not yet.

"The check he gave you for five million," I said, "if you think he's going to make good on it, you're kidding yourself."

She closed her eyes and pulled the comforter up to her chin. I thought she was thinking about that when she opened her eyes and sat up fast. "What time is it?"

I checked my watch. "Five thirty."

"Oh, wow, I have to get moving."

She ripped off the comforter, wheeled her feet over the side of the bed, and stood up. I lay on my side with my head propped in my hand and watched her dress. She grabbed her bra, held it up and turned it around twice to find the front, put it on, and hooked the back. Her blouse went on fast—buttoned from the bottom up—then her skirt, belt, and backpack.

I got up, put on my shirt, tucked it into my jeans, and tried to smooth down my alfalfa-wild hair. She said forget it, it was hopeless, and besides, she liked it that way. That I had forgotten.

"Walk me to the door," she said. She went back and picked up a hairbrush and dropped it in her backpack. When we got to the entrance, she said, "OK, Max, it's time to sign the agreement, no foolin' around."

"I already did," I said, handing her the manila envelope.

"*Before* you put me through all that?"

"Before."

"You bastard!" she said. But she was smiling.

She turned to say good-bye.

"What the heck just happened here?" I said.

"What do you think?"

"I think I said, 'I love you,' and your answer was something like 'Pass the ketchup.' "

"But we were both just pretending." She turned to leave, then stopped. "I think what happened is that we learned to trust each other again."

What a concept. Wouldn't that be nice. "Where will Spin be bidding—at your apartment?"

"You don't know? We're going out to Wild Stallion."

Wild . . . *Huh?*

"He's instructed Borden Bishop"—his banker at First Texas—"to be ready to transfer fifty million dollars from his personal account into the partnership account, but he won't give the word until he's ready to bid, and he won't bid until he's sure Black Eyes works."

"How's he going to do that?"

"With a test," Tacoma said. "He hasn't told you?"

"No. What kind of a test?"

"He knows of an oil field that's never been charted. Something he found when he was in the navy looking for places to hide submarines. He's going to give you the coordinates and make Angela demonstrate that Black Eyes can find it."

"What oil field is he talking about?"

"I don't know. It's in an area called Damnation Alley, about two hundred miles south of Galveston."

I hoped Angela knew where it was.

"I need to know where it is."

"Why? If Black Eyes works, it'll find it, right?"

"It works, but I still need to know."

She looked troubled. "I'll see what I can do," she said, and started to leave.

"Wait a sec." I reached out. "I shouldn't have said that."

"That Black Eyes works?"

"That I love you."

She put her hand on my cheek. "Don't take it back, Max. It came from the heart, and who knows, maybe someday . . ." She held me with her eyes, then gave me an uninspired kiss and left.

The minute she was gone, I called Angela and told her we had a new problem, then I jumped in the car and headed for the lab, stopping at a 7-Eleven to buy some sandwiches and coffee.

Where was Tacoma's head? What was her game? Where was the oil field? What kind of a test did Spin have in mind? What were Angela and I *doing*?

I knew how to find the lab. Beyond that, I knew nothing.

TACOMA PULLED INTO THE GARAGE and sat in her car. After waiting a minute, she got out and headed for the elevator. Entering the apartment, she found Spin sitting in the living room in his robe doodling on a piece of paper with a black Sharpie, a Scotch near his hand, Lightning on the floor at his side. The dog looked up, but Spin didn't.

"How did it go?" he asked.

She walked past him without answering, went to the bar, and fixed herself a Campari and soda. Saying nothing, she pulled off her boots, took a sip, and walked to the window to check out the Houston skyline. He came over to her and touched her back with his fingers.

She flinched.

"What?" he said.

She took the envelope holding the contract, turned, and shoved it against his chest. He tried to stop it from falling to the floor, then bent down and picked it up. Placing it on the bar, he watched her roam around, unsettled and edgy.

She crossed the room and sat in the large leather chair, putting her feet up on the arm. After taking another sip of Campari, she said, "So, how far did you expect me to go to get him to sign?"

"What do you mean, how far?"

"You know—how *far*?"

He walked toward her. "What's going on?"

She got up and crossed the room again. He followed her, grabbed her arm, and spun her around. She pulled away and raised her hands to stop him from coming closer.

"I'm not playing games, Tacoma. Tell me what happened."

"This isn't a game. I want to know how much of me you were willing to sell out to get what you wanted."

He leaned against the door to the terrace and examined her face. She knew he could see the fatigue in hers and the anger around her mouth.

"I didn't think I'd have to sell out any of you," he said.

"Well, you did," she said with no inflection.

"What did you do?"

"What you wanted me to do. I got his signature."

She walked to the bar without glancing at him as she passed by. After grabbing the manila envelope, she pulled out the contracts and laid them on a writing desk. Picking up a pen, she held it out to him.

"He's not going to cooperate until he gets a duplicate original." She opened a second copy for him and turned it to the signature page.

He took the pen from her hand and tried to get past the impersonal face she was giving him. He sat down, looked at the signature page, then flipped back and saw Max's initials on the corners of the rest.

"Did you sleep with him?"

"I did my part, now you do yours."

"I'm asking you a question. Did you sleep with him?"

"Keep this up and I'm walking out of here."

"You did, didn't you?" The electricity in the air was doubling with each exchange.

She took the pen from his hand, pulled off the cap, and handed it back to him. "You'll get my answer when I get your signature."

"Now listen, baby—"

"Don't 'baby' me, just sign!"

She was in a cold fury and she could see that it confused him. He wasn't sure which of his personalities to use on her—the charmer, the psychiatrist, the boss, or the lover.

She stepped to the curtain and opened a window. A breeze blew in and lifted the papers off the desk; he slapped them down on the mahogany surface, then turned on the desk lamp and put on his reading glasses.

"What did he say about the profit split?"

She didn't answer.

"How about the survivor clause?"

Still no answer.

He looked up. "Stop acting like a girl and be my lawyer, would you?"

"He signed and initialed every page without alteration."

He turned a page. "No problem with my control of the auction?"

"I told you, he didn't make a change," she said, her voice cracking with emotion.

This time when he looked up, tears were coursing down her cheeks. "What the hell is going on?" he said.

She turned away and walked to the bathroom. It was risky, but she thought she knew him well enough to know what he'd do next.

He signed the agreements fast, tucked them into the envelope, turned off the light, and followed her to the closed door.

"Come on, Tacoma." She didn't answer. "You did great!" He tried the doorknob. "Come on, baby, let me in."

She still didn't answer. He waited. After knocking once more, he gave up. With her heart pounding, she waited for him to say one thing more.

"The agreement's on the desk," he said. "I'll be on the sofa in the study."

Thank God! She could breathe again.

"THROW A DART," I SAID.

Pinned to the wall behind our tables was a chart of the Gulf of Mexico north of the line of demarcation between U.S. and Mexican waters. Damnation Alley lay on both sides of the line. The entire area was about two hundred square miles. If Spin had found an oil field with the navy's powerful, deep sonar, most likely it was in uncharted Mexican waters. Every oil field had its particular seismographic footprint, and every one had its own geographic coordinates. Without knowing which field he had in mind, creating a program that could "prove" Black Eyes worked in it was like a magician "finding" an audience member's birthday. You had to know what it was in advance.

We'd been at it for three hours. Angela had pulled up all the seismographic profiles she could find of oil fields similar to ones in Damnation Alley, downloaded them into the computer, and tagged them for easy upload when the time came. Still, what Spin had in mind was impossible to figure out. If he knew the target oil field as well as Tacoma said he did, there was a good chance he'd know that what she pulled up was a fake.

We'd done all we could.

"Let's get some sleep," I said.

We heard the buzz of the fax machine in the next room. Who was sending us something at three thirty in the morning?

I went and watched the machine give birth to a piece of paper with black markings on it. When it was finished, I carried it into Angela's console. She swiveled from her computer and took off her glasses.

"What is it?" she said.

I laid it on the table beneath a hanging lamp. "You tell me."

There were three mounds drawn side by side with a horizontal line about a third of the way down from their tops. Angela stared at it and said, "It's a drawing of a substrata mountain range. The horizontal line is the ocean floor, and the mounds are mountains."

"There's *mountains* beneath the floor of the Gulf of Mexico?"

"The size of the Alps," she said. "When the Ice Age ended, water covered them up and filled in the valleys with silt that formed the seabed, but some mountaintops still poke up through the ocean floor."

On the side of the middle mountain, deep below the seabed, was an oval with an X in the middle of it.

"It's Spin's oil field," I said. "X marks the spot."

She looked up. "Where'd this come from?"

I looked at the fax number printed at the top. "Tacoma's apartment," I said. We looked at the drawing more carefully. The letters "DA"—for Damnation Alley—were in Spin's distinctive handwriting. "She must have gotten her hands on Spin's sketch and faxed it to us."

"Unless Spin's the one who faxed it," Angela said.

"She's trying to help us . . . unless she's trying to set us up." I thought about our afternoon at the apartment. *What happened here today? We learned to trust each other again.* "I think she's trying to help."

"You don't say that with a lot of conviction," she said.

"I'm giving it all I got."

Angela looked at the sketch. "These mountains could be anywhere." She went to the computer, pulled up some digital charts, and turned them so we could see them from the side like the drawing. I looked over her shoulder.

She said, "Here are three mountains in the Damnation Alley range that more or less resemble the drawing."

"They look like just like it—nice work!"

She shifted the program to a new area. "But here are three more."

Oh.

She did it again. "Here's another three." And again. "I could do this for quite a while."

For the next hour she found mountains in groups of three and printed them out while I pinned them on the wall. When we had eleven triplets, she said she'd found all she had in the region. We stared at them.

"So which one is it?" I said.

"Don't know," she said.

"Pick one," I said.

"Max, I've reduced the area to the best pictures I've got."

I said, "Look at the wall and tell me which one of those mountain ranges has Spin's oil in it."

She stared at the charts for about thirty seconds, then raised her finger and started to point—then stopped. "I don't know."

"Yes, you do! Point to it!"

"I don't know! I don't know!"

She turned toward me, angry that I was putting her through this superstitious charade. "I sympathize, Angela, but it's all we've got. I trust your intuition more than mine, but if you won't pick one, I will."

She stepped aside and raised her hand, be my guest.

I looked at the charts. Off to the left was a mountain range that looked to be the largest of the bunch. "I say it's this one," I said, jamming my finger onto the western slope of the center peak.

She stared at it, then her eyes wandered elsewhere. She stepped up next to me and raised her finger. "More likely it's this one," she said, pointing at a range nearby.

I looked it over. "Why?"

"It's three clean mountain slopes, and the center one is slightly larger, like the drawing. The peaks rising above the seabed are close together, which means they'd make a good place for a submarine to hide. And there's no indication in the charts of any drilling in the area. It's clean."

I compared it to the drawing. She had a point, but who knew whether the center mountain on the drawing was accidentally larger or not? I handed it back to her.

"This is the horse we ride," I said.

"I'll program it," Angela said. "Go get some sleep. I'll meet you at the boat."

I wished her good luck and said good-bye.

When I got to the door to the parking lot, I stopped to zip up my jacket and pull up my collar. There'd be no more communication with Angela, Audrey, or Tacoma until we got out to the platform, and then it would be awkward at best.

What was Tacoma doing?

Too late to ask. I felt as if I were standing at the door of an airplane, and that only when I jumped would I know whether Tacoma had packed my parachute bag with nylon or confetti.

Jenny said, *You're a fool for love.*

Tacoma said, *Trust me.*

Angela said, *She could be setting us up.*

I stepped out the door.

Geronimo.

"THIRTY MINUTES TO GO TILL the first bid," Tacoma said quietly.

We were in the doghouse on Wild Stallion, just the four of us—Spin and Tacoma, Angela and me. I'd wanted to bring some roughnecks as part of the package, but Spin wouldn't have it. He knew Angela could work the system herself, and that's what he wanted.

We were half an hour from placing our first bid, assuming Spin decided to place one. Angela had guided the sonar torpedoes into a two-hundred-square-mile region Spin had outlined on the charts, and was receiving good signals from the surface-buoy relay stations.

Spin heard Tacoma say "Thirty minutes to go" but didn't answer. He was focused on the hologram pad he hoped would come to life and hand him the keys to the kingdom. We were like wildcatters trying to capture lightning in an oil can.

Angela sat at the control panel in the doghouse working the joystick and the keyboard, hoping her digital hand was quicker than Spin's eye. The lights in the room had been dimmed the way they usually were when a hologram was running. She'd entered the coordinates of Spin's unnamed oil field and was driving her seismographic eyes thousands of feet into the ground.

Or so it appeared to the eye.

I assumed she'd already switched from the real-time sonar signals she was receiving live from the torpedoes to the preprogrammed data of a deep oil field she needed to pretend she was seeing live. If she had done that, any minute now she'd reveal what Black Eyes "saw"—or seemed to see—eight miles below the sea. Once Spin examined it, we'd know how good her fake move really was.

"Twenty-five minutes to go till first bid," Tacoma said.

She had a cell phone in each hand: a Verizon phone connected to the auctioneer in Plano, Texas, and an AT&T phone with an open line to Borden B. Bishop III at First Texas National Bank. Bishop always made sure that his best client was served with attention and precision, day or night, whether it was from Bishop's office or home. At the moment, he was ready to transfer money from Spin's personal account into the partnership account if Spin gave the go-ahead. Unless we got that far, we wouldn't be qualified to bid.

Angela worked the joystick on the computer and clicked on the options she needed. The lasers sent their invisible light to a center point and, after a few seconds, little white specks and sparkles danced in the air creating an elongated, three-dimensional hologram in the shape of a corn crib. There were no colors in it yet, only whites, blacks, and shades of gray. As far as the eye could tell, the image was coming from the sonar's live feed, not, as Angela and I knew, from a preprogrammed image.

As she worked the controls, suddenly the entire image turned into living color: the tan and brown striations of earth, the purples of rock, the mauves of clay, and small streaks of white where no image had been captured. She rotated the rectangle in midair, turning the eastern side toward us.

We saw speckles of yellow turning to streaks of orange, then the most incredible color of all: green for oil. She moved the rectangle farther east and the coordinates on the "zipper" beneath it changed as fast as the system prowled the earth's interior.

All at once we were looking at a slice of oil that had no apparent boundaries. Like the last time, it looked so real I almost believed it.

The room fell quiet.

"Fifteen minutes till bids are due," Tacoma said.

Still staring, Spin said, "If this is accurate, there's no limit to what Black Eyes can do."

"It's accurate," Angela lied.

"Move the image farther east," Spin said. "I want to see how much of the field we've picked up."

She worked the controls and moved the monolith east. An oil field that existed only in Angela's hard drive and Spin's memory continued to reveal itself.

"Thirteen minutes," Tacoma said.

I tried to catch her eye and give her some telepathic support, but she was too focused to pay attention.

"Pull back," Spin said. "I want to see the field as a whole."

If we pulled back too far, it would reveal a profile of the entire mountain Angela had preprogrammed into the computer. If it matched his memory, he'd think he was seeing it live as the real thing. If it was different from what he remembered, he'd know he was seeing a canned version and we'd be busted.

Angela zoomed out, shrinking the size of the field to smaller and smaller proportions. The coordinates on the zipper changed with each click of the mouse.

Tacoma spoke to the banker. "Sit tight, Borden," she said, then to Spin, "Eight minutes to go."

Spin looked at the oil field, chewing a dry lip.

"Hold it right there," he said to Angela. The hologram froze. Spin looked at it more closely, then picked up a laser pointer and shot a beam of red light into the picture. Moving it around, he circled the profile of three rising masses of gray above the green oil field. "These look like three mountains," he said.

He dropped the laser to the coordinates on the zipper.

"But these aren't the coordinates I remember," he said.

"They're the coordinates you gave me," Angela said.

"I know," Spin said, "but I didn't give you the coordinates I remember."

Silence choked the room.

"Four minutes to go," Tacoma said.

I synchronized her time with the clock on the wall. Tacoma's expression was flat and professional, not a trace of concern, just doing what the boss asked her to do. Either I was right and she was the best actress on the planet, or Jenny was right and she was Spin's double agent.

Angela said, "I can't speak about the region you have in mind, Spin, because I don't know where it is. But the coordinates you gave me show oil."

"I don't want to rush you, Spin," Tacoma said, "but we're almost out of time. What do you want to do?"

He looked at the hologram and refused to be pushed. "Tell Bishop to transfer ten million dollars into the partnership account and wait for further instructions."

Tacoma spoke to Borden Bishop crisply. A few seconds later, she told him to stand by and lowered the phone.

"The money's in the account and Bishop's confirmed it with the auctioneer," she said. "We're qualified to bid up to ten million."

Spin continued to examine the hologram. Did he smell a rat?

"We've got one minute to place a bid," Tacoma said.

After waiting for what felt like ten, Spin spoke to Tacoma without taking his eyes off the hologram.

"Bid five million," he said. "Let's see who else is playing."

Tacoma raised the Verizon phone to her ear and spoke to the auctioneer in a cool, direct voice. "This is Tacoma Reed of Black Eyes Phoenix Partnership, ID code 2-BE-242. The partnership bids five million dollars."

We waited to see if she'd made it under the wire.

She flipped the phone closed.

"The bid's accepted. We're in the game."

SPIN SAT IN A CHAIR AND TOOK a drink of water from a plastic bottle. Setting it on the console in front of him, he spoke to Angela, who sat on his left. "I want you to go to these coordinates." He gave them to her from memory. "They're within range of the torpedoes."

The hologram we'd been looking at froze, then dissolved. Angela programmed the new coordinates into the computer. I did my best to communicate with her by eyesight: *You're doing great, Angela. Just use another fake program and show him some fake oil.*

I could feel her answer: *How do we know what he's looking for?*

And my response: *We don't—keep going!*

She worked the controls calmly, and in about ten minutes a new hologram began to form. Beneath it, on the zipper, coordinates were approaching the ones he'd given her, even though we were still seeing a picture she'd downloaded last night. Once again it looked like it was being transmitted live.

Tacoma was on the phone, talking quietly.

Angela turned the hologram to color. Slowly, as it moved, green speckles appeared, then green streams, then whole segments of a green core. Once again, Black Eyes had found oil—or so it seemed.

Spin began examining it and giving Angela directions. She turned the hologram on its side, rotated it, and spun it in a slow-moving circle. Thirty minutes of this, and still Spin said nothing.

Tacoma was writing furiously on a pad. After a few minutes, she lowered her telephone. "I've got the results of the first bid," she said.

Everyone looked at her and waited.

"Thirty-two companies have bid over a million."

"Like who?" Spin said.

Tacoma began reading. "ExxonMobil, Royal Dutch Shell, Chevron, Getty, Texaco, Unocal, and Continental. Kuwait Oil, Saudi Arabian Oil, Japan Petroleum, Bahrain National Oil, Iranian Offshore Petroleum, Petro-Canada, PEMEX, Elf Aquitaine." She turned the page. "Shall I go on?"

"Who made the top bid?" Spin said.

"Syntech Exploration."

"Who's that?"

"No idea."

"What'd they offer?"

"Twelve million."

Spin looked back at the hologram. "Give me something more, Angela. Dazzle me. Make me a believer."

Tacoma said, "We need to formulate our next bid."

"In a few minutes," Spin said. "I'm not even sure we're going to bid."

He turned back to the hologram. Angela stretched her fingers. Tacoma picked up her phone. I took a drink of water. Syntech Exploration was Audrey, but I didn't have a clue so far.

SPIN WORKED ON THE HOLOGRAM for the next twenty minutes, asking Angela questions and examining the reflections he thought were real, not programmed into the computer. I took out my cell phone, found Audrey's private number, and hit Send. If she answered, I'd step outside and tell her what was happening, get her advice, give her some help, and keep us on track.

She didn't answer. I hung up.

After more analysis of the sonar, Tacoma joined us at the console.

"If we're in the game, we have to bid," she said.

Spin rubbed his forehead, told Angela to hold on, and swiveled to Tacoma.

"Any reason not to bid?" he asked.

"Not at my end. How about you?" Tacoma said.

He stared ahead, thinking, then turned to the hologram. "This range doesn't look like what I remember, but it's been twenty-five years. See this?" He used the pointer. "The center mountain is much flatter here than I thought, and the deposit is lower."

"What do you want to do?" she asked.

He waited again, then said, "Tell Bishop to put fifty million into the partnership account and bid the whole fifty."

Surprised at that, Tacoma started to ask him a question, but he raised his hand and cut her off. He'd decided to make a high, preemptive strike and drive everyone else out of the auction. She opened her cell phone and walked to the other side of the doghouse to talk to Bishop. I had no idea where her head was. With five minutes to go, she called in the huge bid.

Spin went to the door, said he wanted to stretch, and stepped outside. Through the window I saw him walk to the hatch-covered mousehole—the hole in the platform where the drill pipe went through—and touch a huge cast-iron lobster claw that lifted the sections of pipe into place so that other machinery could screw it into the ground.

Angela got out of her chair and stretched, too. After that, we waited for the results of the last bid.

THIS TIME, ALL EYES WERE ON Tacoma as she listened and scribbled the results. She hung up and read from her notes.

"Six companies placed a second bid in excess of twelve million," she said. "Everybody else is out."

"Where are we in the pack?" Spin said, hoping he'd blown everyone else away.

"We're thirty million ahead of everyone except one," Tacoma said.

"Who?"

"Syntech."

"What'd they bid?"

"One hundred million."

Spin slammed his palm onto the console. "I knew it! There's been a leak!" He turned to me. "Who else knows about Angela's solution?"

"No one," I said.

Nice work, Audrey—if only you could see him now.

"Bullshit!" he said. "Syntech isn't paying a hundred million for the *potential* of Black Eyes, they're paying for something that works!"

"I'm telling you, nobody knows!" Trying to keep my lying, deceiving poker face credible with the man who saw through it best.

He pointed at Tacoma. "Find out who Syntech is, fast!"

"I've already got Whitacre on it," she said.

Already? How well did she need to play her role? Lew Whitacre was a lawyer-investigator who specialized in due diligence for oil companies, known as the "Matt Drudge of the oil patch." If anyone could scoop up rumors, gossip, and facts on short notice, he could. Spin walked to the door, signaled Tacoma to join him, and the two of them left the doghouse together. I didn't like it.

Angela immediately leaped up to talk to me. I shook my head—don't talk—Spin might have a bug in the room—and she sat down. I sat opposite her in Spin's chair and leaned close so we could whisper.

"I don't know what he's looking for!" she said.

"Doesn't matter, he's still on board!"

"But if he asks to see another deep field, what am I going to do?"

"Show him one. You've got more in the can."

"I know, but I can't keep doing this without him smelling a rat."

"Just do it, we've got no choice," I said.

I heard the door open.

"Here he comes."

TACOMA HAD HER VERIZON PHONE at her ear and her AT&T phone at her side.

"Got it," she said into the phone, and hung up. Turning to Spin, she said, "Syntech's a new company. Whitacre's never heard of them and can't find anyone who has."

Spin said, "Sounds like a company put together to take advantage of inside information. Is Whitacre calling who I told him to call?"

"He is. He'll call me the minute he makes contact."

Spin looked at me. I stared back. *Who's Whitacre calling?*

Tacoma said, "At fifty million, there's nobody left to take on Syntech except you, Spin. What do you want to do?"

"I already told you," he said.

"You sure?"

"Do it."

She opened her Verizon phone and speed-dialed. "Borden? Tacoma here. Spin wants you to put an additional hundred million dollars into the partnership account. . . . That's right, a hundred more from his personal account for a total of one hundred fifty million. I'll wait."

She doodled on her pad. Spin continued staring at me, looking for a twitch, a blink, a drop of sweat, a break in the façade that would give us away, but at this point if anyone had reason to sweat it was him, not me. The money he was dumping into the partnership account was only a loan but, as Audrey had predicted, merely transferring it from his left pocket to his right was nerve-racking. Obviously, Black Eyes still beckoned. Spin's greed and ambition were keeping us in the game.

"OK, stand by," Tacoma said into the phone. She lowered it. "The partnership account is funded," she said. "How much do you want to bid?"

"The whole thing," he said. Just like that.

It took all I could muster not to blink.

Apparently it was hard for Tacoma, too. "Bishop told me to remind you that you're playing with half your net worth," she said.

What are you doing, Tacoma? Don't talk him out of it!

Spin said, "Tell Bishop if he thinks I need to be reminded of that, he's the one who needs a therapist, not me."

Tacoma called the auctioneer, gave him the partnership pass code, and placed the bid. She repeated each sentence the auctioneer spoke to her: Yes, a bid of $150 million; yes, I know our conversation is being recorded; yes, I'll confirm the bid again. Spin nodded OK and she repeated it before hanging up.

Spin turned back to Angela as calm as a cat. He took a piece of paper out of his pocket and handed it to her. "Show me what Black Eyes sees at these coordinates," he said.

"What is this?" she said.

"Don't worry. Just show me."

ANGELA WAS ABOUT TO PULL up another one of her fake programs when the call came in. Tacoma raised the phone to her ear and listened. The lovely burnished color of her face flushed. She hung up.

"Syntech didn't fold," she said.

"What'd they do?"

"Jumped your bid."

"By how much?"

"Twice."

Now Spin's face flushed. "They bid *three hundred million* dollars?"

"On the nose."

Spin got up and started pacing. "What in God's name are they doing?" Tapping the console. "What do they know that we don't?"

"Logic would say they know Black Eyes works," Tacoma said.

"Either that or . . . where's Whitacre?"

"I called him five minutes ago and he said—" Her Verizon phone rang and she looked at the number in her window. "That's him now." Answering. "What've you got, Whitacre?"

She took notes again, saying nothing until she hung up.

"Syntech is a Swiss company whose principal place of business is the address you guessed," she said.

Spin hit his hand on the desk. "I knew it! Syntech is Audrey!"

He turned to me. "What the hell's going on, Max?"

"What do you mean, what's—"

"Don't mess with me, boy! My ex-wife just bid three hundred million dollars for Black Eyes. What's she up to?"

"I have no idea."

"I told you don't fuck with me!" His finger was in my face, the muscles in his neck taut. "Either you've cut her in because you know Black Eyes works and this is your way of stealing it, or you and Audrey are setting me up for a fall. Which is it?"

"I'm not playing a game and I've got no deal with Audrey—I haven't seen her in months!" Shit. Why'd I say that?

"Tacoma," Spin said, "call Puck."

He glared at me while she made the call and handed him the phone. "He's on the line," she said.

He spoke to his driver. "Puck? Call Jackson and ask him if he's seen Max at Audrey's house in the last six months. Tell him an honest answer is worth ten thousand dollars. Call me right back."

I pictured Jackson, in his white shirt and red suspenders polishing her car and waving hello to me the day I saw her and we cut a deal.

Tacoma said, "We haven't got much time, Spin. Bidding closes out at four o'clock." She looked at the clock on the wall and synchronized her watch with it.

"Angela!" Spin said. "What have you got on those coordinates?"

"Bad reflections," she said. "But hang on, they're improving."

I could hear it in her voice: *This isn't going to work.*

Tacoma said. "We've got fifteen minutes, Spin." The phone rang. "Hello?" she said. "Oh, hello, Jackson, this is Tacoma Reed. Sure can, just a minute." She handed Spin the phone. "He heard from Puck but he wants to talk to you directly."

Here it comes. Spin held the phone at his ear. "Jackson? Spin!" He made nice, laughed about something casually, and spoke in a voice that was friendly and relaxed. The contrast between his easy presentation to Jackson and his true state of mind was startling. What an actor. No wonder he could sell palm trees to Tahitians.

"OK," he said, "great to talk to you, and just remember, anytime you want to work for me, one call and it's done." Another friendly laugh and he hung up.

I waited for the ax to fall. Angela and Tacoma watched. He glared at me and said, "He says he hasn't seen you. Either you're telling the truth or Audrey's got him to lie."

I owe you ten thousand dollars, Jackson.

"Twelve minutes, Spin," Tacoma said.

"Get Bishop on the line," he said.

She used the AT&T phone.

"Angela?" Spin said. "I want to see what you've got, and I want it now."

"It's almost here," she said.

Tacoma said, "Bishop's on the line."

"Ask him how much I'm good for if I hypothecate everything."

"Everything?"

"Tacoma, if you take time to repeat everything I say, we'll *definitely* miss the deadline."

She talked to Bishop. "How much is Spin worth if he puts up everything he's got?" She waited, then lowered the phone. "He says three hundred million."

"Tell him I need fifty million more," Spin said.

She told him and came back. "He can't do it."

"Give me the phone," he said, reaching.

She handed it to him.

"Borden? Spin here. Listen, I'd say this nicely if I had time, but I don't. I need a total of three fifty mil, and I know you've got the authority to give it to me."

He listened.

"I've been doing business with your bank for what, twenty years? Have I ever pushed you?"

He listened.

"Three forty," Spin said.

He listened.

"Three thirty."

He listened longer.

"Three twenty-five, and that's my last offer."

He laughed.

"OK, it's *your* last offer. Just give it to me and I'll make us both rich." He smiled. "You're a good man, Borden. Now listen. Get it ready to be transferred into the partnership account but don't make the transfer unless I tell you to, understand? Put your finger on the trigger but don't squeeze." He listened. "Exactly. I'll tell you whether to pull it or not in the next ten minutes. Even if I fund the partnership with the three twenty-five, I may not bid."

He handed the phone back to Tacoma and turned to Angela. "Show me what you've got."

She touched some controls and the hologram fizzed in the air and turned color. There was the usual underground mix of rock, sand, and shale spiked with dots of water.

"Go west," he said.

She moved the hologram through the earth—or rather, through a program she'd put onto the hard drive that made it look as if she were moving through the earth—and slowly the colors shifted to yellow and orange.

And then green.

There was a pool of oil in the middle of the hologram. Spin examined it for what felt like an eternity.

"Read off the coordinates," he said.

I read them from the zipper at the bottom. He read them back to me and checked them off one section at a time. When he was done, he looked up without any expression on his face. I didn't like it.

"Congratulations, Angela," he said, breaking into a smile. "You've done something few people will ever do. You've changed the world."

She'd done it? Good Lord, I felt like a kid at a surprise party.

Spin looked at me and extended his hand to shake mine—or so I thought. Instead, he was pointing it toward the door.

"Come with me," he said, and got up.

"Where are we going?"

He didn't answer.

I stood up and followed.

SPIN WALKED ACROSS THE platform to the mousehole and stood on the hatch that covered it. Above us was a derrick that held the drill pipe, and behind us, on a massive crane-arm, was the empty cast-iron lobster claw that was used to grab pipe when drilling was under way. A yellow remote control the size of a shoe box that worked the lobster claw lay on the deck near our feet. Spin picked it up.

"When I was a roughneck," he said, "we didn't have a machine like this, we had to set pipe by hand."

He looked up at the sky. Instinctively I turned to see what he was looking at. It gave him just enough time to work the controls on the remote.

Hearing the electric motor start up, I turned back and saw the jaws swooping toward me. I pushed forward into Spin to get away, but he pushed me back into the claw's grip.

The pincers closed around my chest before I knew it.

Spin eased the grip enough to let me breathe and put his face in mine.

"Angela failed the test," he said. "The coordinates I gave her are for an Exxon watering hole. It came up green for oil when it should have come up blue for water."

He tightened the claws.

"Did she do that on purpose to throw me off the auction? Or is Black Eyes a fraud?"

"Black Eyes . . . works," I said. Talking wasn't good for my health; I could expel air easier than I could draw it in. But at least the pain masked my bad poker face.

"Are you and Audrey swiping it from me," he said, "or are you trying to get me to buy a piece of junk?"

"Told you, I'm . . . not working for Audrey."

He reached into my pocket and pulled out my cell phone.

Oh, shit.

After pushing the List Calls button, he found the last one I'd called, hit Send, and waited. After a moment, his face turned red. He put the phone to my ear.

"Max?" a voice said. "Hello?"

It was Audrey.

Spin pushed the Off button.

"You're a liar," he said, "but the amazing thing is, I can't tell which lie you're telling me." He pushed the control button and closed the claw another inch. "But you can."

I saw Tacoma running toward us, slowing to a stop as she saw what was happening.

"Spin—what are you *doing*?" she said.

"How much time have we got?" he asked her.

"Three minutes! My God, Spin—you're hurting him!"

"He can stop it with a single word."

I saw Angela coming up behind Tacoma, her hand at her mouth.

"Which is it, Max?" Spin said.

"Audrey and I . . . are trying to steal it," I said.

He looked into my watering eyes. "So you *are* working with Audrey! What's your objective?"

"To get this claw . . . off me."

He still couldn't tell which story to believe. "Are you stealing Black Eyes, or are you trying to sting me?"

"Spin!" Tacoma said. "If she was trying to sting you, she wouldn't have bid three hundred million dollars!"

"Not necessarily. Call Whitacre," he said.

"We haven't got time!" she said. "If you're going to make your bid, you have to call the bank and fund the account!"

"Make the call! I need to know what's happening!"

Tacoma punched a speed-dial number into the AT&T phone, then punched another speed-dial into the Verizon phone and held them to her ears. She looked back at me with worry on her face until someone answered and she turned away to talk.

"If you think Black Eyes is crap," I said to Spin, "let Audrey . . . have it."

"Her bid is the only thing that makes me think it's *not* crap," he said. "Nothing would please her more than stealing my dream and laughing at me all the way to the bank."

"Then . . . bid . . . for it."

He came close to my ear. "As my mother used to say, why guess when you have to be right?"

HE CLOSED THE CLAWS ON ME another notch. I felt the cartilage in my chest stretch and pain shoot through my neck and left shoulder. I needed to breathe deeper but couldn't.

"Talk to me, Max," he said.

Angela screamed, "Stop it, Spin! Stop it!" Crying.

Tacoma said, "The auctioneer wants to know if we're in or out!"

Spin didn't answer, just stared at me. "Don't be stupid, Max. Give me the answer."

"I'm your partner . . . not . . . Audrey's."

"Is that true?"

"Yes, yes . . . true."

Tacoma said, "I've got Bishop on the line. Does he put the three hundred twenty-five million into the partnership account or not? We can't bid until he does."

"Not yet," Spin said. Then to me: "Say it again. Give it to me straight."

"Black Eyes . . . works."

"For God's sake, Spin you're killing him!" Tacoma said. She leaped toward him and tried to pull him back, but he pushed her away.

"I want the truth!" he yelled at me.

Tacoma dropped her forehead into her hand, then lifted the cell phone but didn't dial.

"I told you to help me!" Spin yelled at her. "Now do it!"

Don't do it, Tacoma—don't stop him—help him make the bid! Fast! Before the pain makes me cave!

Tacoma recovered, dialed a number, and raised the phone to her ear.

Black circles began to form at the outside of my vision.

"Give me an honest answer, Max," Spin said.

I tried to speak but nothing came out.

He picked up a leather glove and stuffed it into my right hand. "Hold on to it!" he said, closing my fingers around it. "If Black Eyes is for real, keep holding it! If it's a fake, drop it!"

I could feel my lungs collapsing against each other, feel the pain of stretched fiber shooting up into my arm and down my back. My left shoulder felt like it was separating, but somehow I managed not to let go of the glove. Small breaths kept me alive. If I passed out now, I'd suffocate. *Hold on—another minute and he'll place the bid and we'll take him for every penny he's got.*

Angela was crying.

Black circles closing in.

Don't drop it—don't drop it—don't drop it . . .

"Drop the glove if it's fake," Spin said.

Tacoma said, "We've only got two minutes to bid, and we still haven't transferred the money into the partnership account!"

"Come on, Max. Tell me the truth."

Tacoma yelled, "Spin, the auctioneer is hammering us—he's got Bishop on the line asking if we're in or out!"

"It's now or never," Spin said to me.

I mustered all the air I could. "If I drop it . . . it's only 'cause . . . I'm passing out."

The spirals had closed in completely. I could hear a voice from down a long hallway mixed with the sound of my heart pounding in my ears. I heard Tacoma say, "It's now or never, Spin!" Heard Spin's voice say, "Give me the phone." Heard him say, "Borden? Spin. Transfer the money into the partnership account and tell the auctioneer we're good for a bid if I decide to make it. . . . That's right, the whole three twenty-five. Then sit tight. We're making no bid until I say so."

Heard the phone snap shut.

We're almost there. Money's in the partnership account. I can hold on, Tacoma! Make him do it! Make him bid!

Spin's voice was more distant. "I'm ready to bid, Max—tell me if I should. I'm not gonna bid until you tell me—"

My eyes closed and I felt myself passing out. Dying? Yeah, I suppose I was, if getting no air in your lungs makes you die.

I heard Tacoma's voice saying, "Spin! Wait!"

"Wait?" I must have been hallucinating. She couldn't be saying, *"Wait!"*

"Don't bid!" she said. "It's a fake!"

I couldn't believe it. She didn't say that. The pain must have fried my brain.

"How do you know?" he said.

"Audrey owns Shotgun! Which means she already owns Black Eyes! She's got you in a bidding war for a piece of junk she *already owns*! She's not at risk! If she wins the bid, she's just paying herself!"

Oh, Tacoma. No, no, no.

The last breath of air I owned escaped my mouth. I was going down.

I felt the lobster claw release an inch and felt oxygen strike my lungs like air on a cold winter day. Air rushing in and out of my throat.

The black spirals blinding me slowly began to disappear. I saw Spin holding the AT&T telephone. "No bid," he said to the auctioneer. "Black Eyes Phoenix is making *no bid*." He waited a moment and said, "That's right, the partnership is out of the bidding permanently. That's ID code 2-BE-242."

He hung up and came face-to-face with me. The claw still had me pinned even though I could breathe. Angela ran up to me and tried to pry it away. Tacoma looked at me with sympathy, as if she'd done me a favor instead of driving a silver stake through my heart. *You didn't save me, Tacoma, you screwed me. Another thirty seconds and I would have had him.*

Agent, double agent, triple agent—it didn't matter. She'd finally shown her true colors.

Spin said, "Nice try, Max." He patted my cheek like a coach, then hit the button on the remote, releasing the air in the pistons with a *pooosh*. I staggered out of the claw, bent over, put my hands on my knees, and breathed like a sprinter at the tape. My left shoulder was so stretched out of place I couldn't raise my arm.

"Max?" Tacoma said. I didn't look up.

"Let's go," I heard Spin say to her.

Angela knelt in front of me and examined my bloodshot eyes.

I mustered the energy to straighten up to take one last look at Tacoma, but she was already gone. I felt two ribs, or something in there, pop back into place.

And that was it. It was over. The sting, Spin's defeat, Audrey's revenge, money for the guys and their families, the sweet taste of victory, whatever chance I had at getting the goods on Spin for the DA—it was all over. And so was Tacoma. I finally knew everything I needed to know about her.

We'd never had a chance. Not even from the start.

IT WAS THE KIND OF WAKE the Irish understood best: a drowning of the spirit with spirits. We were at O'Reilly's Bar and Grill, "we" being the roughnecks—Dutch, Musselman, Harley, Eddy J, and Lucas—along with Jenny, Angela, and me. Audrey said she'd join us later; at the moment, she and a close friend, Johnnie Walker Black, were in the midst of a two-person wake of their own.

I told the guys I'd made a mistake defending Spin in Jenny's garage, told them I'd wanted to make it up to them with a sting, and told them I'd failed. They were impressed with the effort and tried to cheer me up with the best clichés they could find. "You can't separate a rich man from his money," Harley said. Dutch gave me a well-meaning pat on the back that sent a shot of pain into my shoulder and a shot of whiskey down my throat.

Trying to make me feel better only made me feel worse. It was like losing a game with a fumble on the last play. All I could think of was how close we'd come. Despite that, I made a toast to Angela and Jenny for having the guts to try. Then I toasted them all for being my friends.

After that, I wanted out. It was only eleven o'clock, but the combination of booze and painkillers was starting to take its toll. My left arm was still semi-useless, which suited me fine because so was I.

The failed sting was one thing; Tacoma was another. I still had to deal with that on more levels than one. By trusting her I'd betrayed everyone—the guys and their families,

Jenny and Joe—I don't know, Abe Lincoln and the American flag if I thought about it long enough.

Eddy J said, "You think Spin's gonna try to prosecute you?"

"No, it'd open him up to problems of his own," I said. As long as I had that piece of cable, he'd have to explain it to the DA, and I knew he didn't want to do that.

As long as I have the cable.

I pictured it in my car's glove compartment. It was locked up, but I felt a nervous itch about it. Time to check it out.

"I gotta go, guys," I said, and pushed away from the table.

I WAS APPROACHING MY Z4 when I saw someone closing the passenger side door. Coming closer, I made out a figure I knew in my dreams: Tacoma. She was starting to walk away when she saw me coming.

She stopped and leaned back against the door with her arms folded, glaring at me as if I were the one who'd betrayed *her.*

"I'd appreciate your getting off my car," I said. "I just had it washed."

"You were an idiot not to drop the glove," she said. "You could have been killed."

"What are you doing here?"

"Putting something in your car."

She looked at her watch, then turned to leave. I grabbed her by the arm. "Wait a second."

I let go and opened the passenger door and saw a manila envelope on the passenger seat. I unlocked the glove compartment and pawed through its contents: a car manual, an insurance certificate, salt and pepper packets from McDonald's. And, to my surprise, the cable shank.

"You really should put that in a safe place," she said.

"Like your hands?"

"You know," she said with a look of disgust, "I came here because I wanted to tell you—"

"You screwed me!" I yelled. "I believed in you—I trusted you—I thought you were on my side, but you were his spy the whole time!"

"I didn't betray you—"

"Bullshit! All you had to do was wait one more minute and we would have had the money!"

"If I'd waited another minute, you would have been dead!" she yelled.

"That's ridiculous! I could have survived sixty seconds and you know it!"

"Like hell you could! Your face was turning blue, and you couldn't see me or hear me—"

"Just one lousy minute! That's all we needed!"

"I'm telling you, you were *going to die*—"

"Then you should have let me!"

That turned the air silent.

"I mean it. If you were on my side, you should have taken the chance and gone for it."

She closed her eyes a moment, then looked at me. "You don't understand, Max, you didn't *need* to die." She reached for the door to my car. "Let me show you something—"

I held up my hand and cut her off. "Piss off, Tacoma. I don't want to hear it."

She stared at me a moment, trying to decide what to do, then smiled wanly and walked away. For the first time I could remember, I was glad to see her go.

IT WAS ONE OF THE FEW TRAIN crossings left in south Texas, and I had to arrive at it just as a double-engine diesel was pulling an endless line of freight cars at a jogger's pace. I sat watching the red warning lights blink on and off, left and right, and counted cars. When I reached fifty, I picked up the manila envelope Tacoma had left on the seat next to me and counted boxcars by the sound of their wheels clacking on the rail joints.

Fifty-one, fifty-two . . .

I opened the envelope and pulled out a copy of the partnership agreement—not a copy, my duplicate original.

Fifty-seven, fifty-eight . . .

There was nothing else in the envelope. Putting the agreement back, I noticed a sticker with an arrow and the words "Sign Here" stuck midway through the document, not at the end of the document where it was supposed to be. Besides, I'd already signed it at the apartment, so what was the point of the arrow now?

Clickety-clack, sixty-one, sixty-two . . .

I punched on the dome light and opened the document to the sticker. The subheading read "Partnership Capitalization."

Sixty-seven, sixty-eight . . .

I read it quickly. It made no sense.

Seventy . . . something. I finally lost count.

I read the next paragraph, which was headed "Partnership Shares," not noticing that the railroad warning bell had stopped and the gate had gone up. A pickup truck behind me laid on the horn.

I sat still and read to the bottom and turned the page.

Pinned to the next page with a paper clip was the five-million-dollar check Spin had given Tacoma for the Cherokee College Fund. Across the front of it, defacing it, was a note written in Tacoma's hand.

You know the rule: You're only allowed to know what you need to know. I couldn't tell you about this because you're a bad liar and I was afraid you'd give it away.

The truck roared around me with its passenger giving me the finger. I sat still, reading the agreement I'd signed, and let the other cars go by. When they were all gone, I laid my head against the back of the leather bucket seat and stared at the empty road ahead. Letting it sink in.

Oh . . . my . . . God.

THE RENTED YACHT'S ENGINES rumbled as the crew went through its final survey: food and wine on board, check; caviar in the refrigerator, check, a case of champagne in the galley, check. As soon as Tacoma arrived, they'd be ready to go.

"Where the heck is she?" Spin muttered to himself.

He was sitting on a deck lounge, a telephone at his ear, talking to Borden B. Bishop III, who'd set down his telephone to retrieve a document. Spin drummed his fingers. Tacoma should have been here an hour ago; all she had to do was pick up her bag at the apartment. He'd told her to let Puck get it, but she'd insisted on some last-minute packing, and now it was nearly midnight.

Spin sat up slowly, his feet straddling the deck chair. "What do you mean, you can't transfer the money back to my account?" he said.

"I'm holding the partnership agreement in my hand, Spin," Bishop said. "Paragraph 16 (D) (2) states that the money you transferred into the company is equity, not debt. I can't transfer partnership equity to your personal account, it's not yours."

"What are you *talking* about?" Spin said. "Until the loan's repaid, I *am* the partnership!"

A riffling of pages. "Not according to Paragraph 25 (A) (5)," he said. "It says that as of noon today, Maximilian McLennon became the sole general partner."

Spin stood up, knocking his mai tai onto the deck. "What the hell are you reading?"

"I told you, it's the partnership agreement. Tacoma brought it to me the day after you signed it."

"There's no way it could say that, Tacoma drew it up herself . . . Good God." He went silent.

"Spin? Hello? You there?"

"Call you back."

He flipped down the cover on his cell phone and stood up, started for the stairs, stopped, picked up the intercom handset and told the captain to stay put until further notice.

He walked down the hallway like a bull seeing red, wheeled around a corner, and broke into a run to his cabin. Entering, he saw the manila file holding the Black Eyes Phoenix partnership agreement, grabbed it, and dumped its contents onto his California king-sized bed. Turning the pages furiously, he found the paragraph Bishop was talking about and read it aloud. ". . . contribution to the partnership for purposes of qualifying it to purchase assets at auction, and to make such a purchase, shall not be a loan to the company but a capital contribution for the account of the general partner, Maximilian McLennon . . ."

He riffled to the signature page. His name was in his own handwriting, in original blue ink. He'd signed it! Tacoma had drafted it and presented it to him for his signature in the middle of a fight over Max—when he thought she'd slept with him—when she'd cried, and instead of reading the agreement, he'd done what she'd asked him to do and signed it!

And now his entire fortune belonged to Max?

To *Max*?

Impossible!

He broke into a clammy sweat.

The sting wasn't to get him to buy Black Eyes, it was to get him to transfer his money into a partnership altered by Tacoma to make Max the predominant partner!

He threw the papers across the room and cussed in shouts, some in English, some Spanish, some in the incoherent language of a man who'd been cheated out of a fortune. With his chest still heaving, he called Puck.

"Meet me at the boat!" he said. "But first, go to the basement and grab the gardener's overalls and that rubber tube I exercise with in the gym. . . . Don't ask, I'll explain when you get here! Bring a knife, too, and some cash. I've got some other things I need you to pick up, too. . . . No, no, I'll tell you later." He started to hang up, then brought the phone back to his mouth. "And, Puck? Make sure your Glock is cleaned and loaded."

I WOUND OUT MY Z4 AND HEADED back to O'Reilly's Bar, my cell phone at my ear. I'd tried Musselman, then Eddy J, and finally reached Jenny.

"Keep everybody there!" I said.

"Max?"

"Don't let anyone leave the bar! I'll be there in fifteen minutes!"

"What's going on?"

"Can't tell you on the phone!"

I could hear her telling everyone to stick around till I got there, and Harley saying, "He's gotta give me a better reason than that, I gotta get home to feed my pig."

"Tell him we won!" I yelled, taking a corner with one hand on the wheel.

Jenny said, "You shouldn't be driving drunk, Max."

"I'm not drunk! We pulled off the sting!!"

Just before she hung up, I heard her say to the guys, "He's blasted."

TACOMA LOOKED AROUND HER apartment one last time to make sure she hadn't left anything behind. She'd taken the blanket off the wall and folded it; she'd opened the glass frame and removed the baby moccasins; and she'd opened the Lucite box, taken out the pipe, removed the stem from the catlinite bowl, wrapped both pieces in towels, and placed them in her backpack. The blanket was too large to take with her, so she slid it into the closet, hoping to retrieve it later when everything was . . . what? Calmed down? She couldn't imagine that day would ever come. Not with the fury Spin would be in once he found out what she'd done.

Seeing nothing more to do, she pulled on her backpack, picked up her suitcase, and headed for the door. She had no time to waste. It would be a four-hour drive to the only place she felt safe: her grandmother's house at the Diwali Compound in Van Zandt County near Dallas. She turned off the light switch and opened the door.

A hand grabbed her wrist and forced her back into the room.

The light came on.

Spin looked down at her suitcase, then touched her backpack with his other hand. "Hello, babycakes. Planning on taking a hike?"

THE LIGHT WAS REDDISH ORANGE as I went through it, accelerating. I came up behind a slow-moving pickup truck and roared around it. Ten minutes later, I pulled into the parking lot behind O'Reilly's and picked up my cell phone to try to call Tacoma one more time. So far, I'd gotten nothing but her voice mail. This time, she answered.

"Tacoma, it's me!" I said, getting out of my car.

"I was just dialing you," she said.

"I read the partnership agreement! How in God's name did you do it?!"

"Max—"

"Why didn't you tell me?" Locking my car.

"Max, listen—"

"You've got to come back to O'Reilly's! Everybody's here!"

"Sounds like fun." The voice that spoke those words wasn't Tacoma's, but Spin's.

I slowed my walk.

Spin said, "Instead of O'Reilly's, why don't you join me at my favorite watering hole? We'll do our business and you can be on your way."

"Business?"

"A simple transaction: my money for Tacoma."

I heard his voice in the background as if he was talking to someone else on a second cell phone. Whoever it was, Spin said, "Go for it, that's him, he's talking to me right now."

He came back on Tacoma's phone. "I'll see you shortly, Max."

"Where are you?"

"Wally will tell you."

Wally? His pilot and backup bodyguard?

I felt a hand on my arm before I saw him. Wally took the phone away from my ear and nodded toward his truck a few steps away. Its headlights were on and the engine was running. The rest of his invitation was no less subtle: He simply unbuttoned his jacket and showed me a gun in his shoulder holster.

"Where are we going?" I said.

"Shut up and get in."

SPIN'S FAVORITE MIDNIGHT watering hole turned out to be St. Mary's Cemetery. Wally pulled up next to Spin's black Cadillac Deville, which was parked off to the side of the circular road, and cut the engine.

"Get out," he said.

I searched for a weapon, an argument, whatever I could find.

Pointing, Wally said, "Follow the yellow brick road." He lit up a cigarette and leaned back against his truck with his ankles crossed like a casual sentry ready to stop anyone who might be coming up the road, unlikely, at this hour, as that might be.

I followed it up over a gentle rise and down past Joe's grave. Five minutes later, I saw the flicker of a flashlight in the distance, then two. No voices, no sound.

I picked up my pace, and a few yards later things began to emerge: a white tent—the kind that shelter the bereaved at a burial—a backhoe for digging graves—a Ford pickup truck off to the side.

Low voices. Two—both male. Hearing me coming, someone whipped around a flashlight and shined it in my eyes.

"Over here, Max," Spin said.

I made my way off the road toward the tent. In front of it were empty folding chairs and, in front of them, a black hole in the ground waiting for a casket. The yellow backhoe stood next to the pit with its claw resting at the edge. Next to it was a pile of fresh-smelling dirt.

Standing up against the machine was Tacoma.

I stepped up to her and rested my hand on the silver piston that drove the backhoe's digger arm and felt its warmth from recent use. She was wearing jeans, a sweater, and her backpack.

"You OK?" I asked.

"So far. What's he going to do?"

"I have no idea."

Spin came up behind me. "Sign this paper," he said, laying it on the backhoe.

"What is it?"

"A modification of the partnership agreement restoring it to the status quo ante. I want my money back."

"What happens then?"

"You can go your merry way." He slapped a pen on top of the paper. I didn't pick it up. His jaw muscles rippled. "If you don't sign, there's always another way,"

"You mean the Bud Hightower solution?" I said. "Kill a partner and take his share?" He didn't answer. I picked up the pen but didn't remove the cap.

I heard a noise behind me and turned to see Puck pushing a large box made of raw pine with the Gulf-Tex logo and the word "compressor" printed on the side. What I noticed most was its size, which was roughly the size of a big casket.

Jesus, he couldn't be serious, could he?

"Come on, Spin. This has gone far enough."

Instead of listening to me, he and Puck walked over to the aluminum lowering device that cranked a casket into a grave and shoved it into place over the hole. Puck wiped his brow with a handkerchief, then grabbed the webbed cradle hanging from a chain and slipped it under the wooden box.

I looked over and saw Tacoma's face filled with terror.

"What are you doing, Spin?" I said.

He didn't answer.

"Aren't people going to find it a little strange to see a box sitting in their daddy's grave?" I said

Puck's flashlight lit the hole and I looked down.

Holy cow, it must have been nine feet deep. Now I understood: They'd dug out the bottom with the backhoe and made it deep enough to put a large box into it, bury it, and raise the grave's dirt bottom to normal depth. Now I knew where Jimmy Hoffa was buried: beneath someone else's casket. It was the last place on earth anyone would look.

My running heart increased its pace.

"You've made your point," I said. "Let's talk."

Puck slipped the second cradle under the end of the box and the two of them dragged it closer to the edge of the hole. Spin took up the slack in the lowering chain with a crank.

My mind was going lickety-split.

When the box was ready, Spin stepped over to Tacoma at the backhoe. "Sorry, baby," he said, "but I'm afraid this is it."

"Spin, for God's sake—" she said.

"I don't want to do this," he said, "but what choice do I have? You tried to bankrupt me, and if you'd do that to me, you'd turn me in."

"I could have done that long ago but I didn't," she said.

"Only because you wanted my money first. Why'd you do it, baby? What'd I do to you to make you do that?"

Tears were running down her cheeks.

"Talk to me," he said softly.

"You cut Joe loose and let him fall," she said, "and if you could do that to him, you could do that to me."

"Never," he said. "I'd die first." Now his eyes were watery, too, and his face incredibly sad, as if *he* were the one about to be buried. "We could have had it all."

"And you could have been great," she said. "You still could. It's not too late."

He stared at her as if maybe she was right, then took her into his arms. "I love you, you know."

"Then let me go."

"I want to, but how can I? Tell me."

"I don't have to go to the police."

"But you would. I know you."

"Not if my life depended on it."

He seemed rattled. He touched her shoulder softly and shook his head to get her to stop crying, but she didn't. She looked at him again and begged him not to do this.

He looked away a moment and pinched the bridge of his nose between his fingers. "I can't think straight," he mumbled. Then he said, "Get in the box."

"Spin—"

He raised his gun suddenly and pointed it at her head. Beads of sweat glistened on his upper lip. "Get in!"

"Spin, please!"

"I'll come back for you after I get my money!"

"I won't live that long!" she said.

"I'll make sure you do, now get in!"

"Please don't do this, Spin! Please!"

His finger tightened on the trigger. Seeing that, she closed her eyes and waited.

"Spin, wait," I said as evenly as I could. "We'll do whatever you want." I signed the paper he wanted me to sign. "Here. It's yours."

He took it and looked at me a moment, then lowered the pistol and wiped the sweat off his face with the back of his hand.

"Put them in the box," he said to Puck.

Tacoma looked terrified.

I took her by the hand and for a brief second I thought we might make a break for it, but of course we couldn't. The certainty of instant death trumped the allure of escape.

"Come on, Spin, you've got what you wanted."

"*Get in!*" he said.

I looked at him a moment and realized he was unmovable. Kneeling as slowly as I could, I got in front of the open end of the box and led Tacoma to it by her hand. Still trembling, she knelt next to me and I pulled her into an embrace. "Just do as he says."

I crawled head first into the crate.

She followed.

Puck closed the end of the box, and a few seconds later a nail gun shot nails into the lid, sealing us in.

Tacoma and I rolled toward each other in the dark.

"My God!" she said. "This can't be happening!"

I yelled out as loudly as I could, "What do you want, Spin?"

No answer.

"You've made your point! The money's yours!"

No reply.

I heard the chains on the lowering mechanism being cranked down and the box being jerked earthward.

My God. He was doing it.

WE HIT THE BOTTOM OF THE grave with a jolt, knocking our heads against the floor of the box. I heard the slings pulled out from under it, then silence.

"Max!" Tacoma cried.

I was breathing hard, trying not to panic. I raised my knees toward my chest, pulling up Tacoma's backpack with my feet, and kicked at the top of the box above my knees. "Ahhhhgh!"

It didn't break.

I did it again and again until I heard it crack. I lay still a moment, breathing hard, saturated with adrenaline.

"Spin!" I yelled, but the words bounced back at me off the inside of the box.

Silence. The sound of scraping outside of the box a few inches above my face. *Wham!* The wooden frame shook with the sound of a hammer or a tool hitting the box above my face. Tacoma screamed. *Wham!* Another strike of the hammer—the box splintered above my neck and the smell of fresh wood and metal filled my nose. I touched a hole that had been opened up and felt the end of a crowbar driven through it. Instantly, it was pulled out—I could see the night sky through the hole—then something entered blotting out the light. I grabbed it and felt the softness of rubber—rubber tubing—and pulled as much of it inside as I could.

"What are they doing?" Tacoma said.

"Giving us something to breathe with," I said.

"Oh, my God," she whispered.

We heard the sound of the backhoe engine starting up.

I hit the top of the box with my knees again, but the frame and nails didn't budge. I stopped kicking—I was polluting our space with carbon dioxide—and tried to calm down.

The sound of the backhoe engine revved up as it went to work.

I went berserk and started kicking the end of the box.

The first load of dirt rained down on us inches away from our faces.

Tacoma yelled.

I grabbed her with my good right arm and pulled her face to my neck. She was shaking and her skin was wet with tears and perspiration. Another load of dirt fell on the box, *thud.* The smell of damp earth seeped through the cracks.

We were being buried alive.

SPIN AND PUCK STOOD AT THE side of the grave, their flashlights prowling the bottom for signs of their prisoners.

"I don't see the breathing tube," Spin said.

"It's over there"—Puck shined his light on a small mound at the bottom—"behind that pile of dirt."

"Is everything else set?"

"Everything's back where it was," Puck said.

Taking a moment to consider loose ends, Spin stood at the edge of the grave, unmoving.

Puck stood waiting. "You want to dig 'em up?"

Spin didn't answer, just stood there looking down, wondering, weighing the pros and cons. Yes, he wanted to dig them up. He wanted to run the clock backward and do a lot of things differently. The smell of dirt and grass carried him back to a picnic basket many years before, a quilt under a tree, Audrey's hair blowing in a light summer breeze, their six-year-old daughter, Barbara, watching an ant crawl on her hand, four-year-old Trish asleep in the sun. How did you get it all back? How did you take the road untaken?

He continued staring at the grave, thinking he could let them go and trust their loyalty, or he could play it safe and guarantee his survival. He turned away from the pit and said, "Not yet. Let's go."

They got in the truck. Puck started it slowly, careful not to tear up the grass. Riding in silence, they headed for Spin's Cadillac in the parking area down the road. Halfway there, Spin said, "How could they have done this to me?"

I PULLED TACOMA TO ME, KISSED her forehead, and stroked her hair with my right hand. The space we lived in was full of body heat, compressed air, and death.

"I'm so scared," she whispered.

And claustrophobic. "Try to lie still and think of something calm," I said in the smallest whisper I could speak. In high school chemistry we'd learned that carbon dioxide killed you before a lack of oxygen did. Skiers buried in an avalanche died of carbon dioxide poisoning—not oxygen starvation—in a matter of minutes. If we didn't vent our crypt, we'd be gone. I breathed through the rubber tube and gave it to her to do the same.

It was getting cold.

"Don't fall asleep," I said.

She squeezed my hand, *OK.* We had to keep buddy-breathing and waking each other every minute.

We lay dying at the pace of our fading hopes. The pain in my shoulder was now welcome because it reminded me I was still alive. Tacoma managed to contain her claustrophobia by closing her eyes and counting backward from a hundred to zero, then counting up again.

"Tacoma?" I said when she faltered. "Don't give up."

She said nothing, just kept breathing shallow breaths until the tube was hers.

"He's not going to dig us up, is he?" she said.

"Of course he is. Why else would he give us air?"

"He hasn't made up his mind yet. And he won't until he gets his money back."

"Then he'll decide to come back," I said.

"And do what? Dig us up so we can turn him in?"

I held the tube, took three large breaths, and returned it to her.

"You're the woman he loves and I'm his adopted son. He won't forget."

She finished breathing and said, "Bud Hightower was his father-in-law and Joe Wright was his best friend."

I thought: Maybe Hightower's death really was an accident—Spin's never admitted it wasn't—and maybe Joe Wright was dead before Spin cut him loose. Spin couldn't really, deliberately kill anyone—could he? Even if his freedom and fortune were at stake, he couldn't be that bad, could he? *Go ahead and tell her that . . . but only if you really mean it . . . she can see through you even in the dark.*

"We need to stop talking," I said. "Carbon dioxide."

I breathed three long breaths, gave the tube to her, and the two of us lay there like a pair of twins in a ghoul's womb. She pawed at my side, found my hand, and squeezed it.

God, it felt good.

What a time to find each other.

What a way to lose each other.

UNABLE TO SLEEP, SPIN WENT into the bathroom for a drink of water and an aspirin. As he started back to the bedroom he saw Tacoma's nightgown hanging on a hook on the back of the door. He reached out for it and pulled it to his face. The feel of it, the faint scent of skin and perfume, were pure Tacoma. Lord, he missed her.

How could she have done it? He wanted her back, but how could he trust her?

He lifted the gown off the hook and bunched it up in his hands.

How could he live *without* her?

He carried the nightgown into the bedroom and laid it on the foot of the bed, then walked over to her dresser and turned on a small light. Pawing through her dresser drawers, he pulled out a black bikini, a pair of khaki shorts, and a cotton, ribbed T-shirt—things he thought she'd wear to Mexico if she were really going—things that could be found floating out in the Gulf of Mexico along with her suitcase once the fishing boat she and Max were supposed to be on happened to sink. He had to have an excuse for their disappearance, so he and Puck had worked out the fishing boat story together.

But it was a story for public consumption only if he needed it. Maybe he'd still dig them up. He didn't know.

Reaching for the light, he noticed her jewelry box and opened the lid. Inside, he found a black velvet bag, and inside that, puddled at the bottom, the diamond necklace he'd given her for Christmas. When she'd packed up and left the apartment, she hadn't taken the necklace with her. The thought stung him deeply. She'd given up on him.

He closed the box, turned out the light, and went back to bed. Lightning laid his chin on the nightgown at the foot of the bed and whimpered. He missed her, too.

"I know, boy, I know," Spin said. "What should I do?"

Lightning didn't answer.

TACOMA HAD HER HEAD ON my shoulder. "I'm so tired of breathing through this tube!" she whispered.

"Just stay with it," I said.

"What time is it?"

I looked at the luminescent hands on my watch. "Four twenty." I took my turn on the breathing tube. When it was her turn, I passed it to her and reached for the manicure kit we'd found in her backpack along with a bottle of water, a pair of baby moccasins, her cell phone, and the Indian pipe she'd wrapped in a pair of towels. Her cell phone had no signal but the light on its face was our link to sanity.

I opened the flip cover and lit up the tomb. Tacoma's face was strained, her hair stringy, her skin wet with sweat like my hands and face. I pulled a tiny pair of scissors from her leather kit, turned out the cell phone light to save the battery, and went back to work trying to dig a hole in the wood above my face. I'd already worn out her nail file and clippers, but the cuticle scissors weren't wrecked yet.

"What about the dirt on the other side?" she said.

"If it's not too deep, I'm thinking maybe we can push the pipe stem up through it."

"And do what?"

"Maybe it'll help us hear what's happening out there. If we know when the burial's happening, we can try to make a noise before they lower the casket."

"Think we can make it loud enough to be heard?"

"Try it."

She unwrapped the pipe stem from the towel, brought it to

her lips, and blew on it like a trumpet, but the only sound it made was the sound of air rushing through a small pipe.

"Stop!" I said. "Save your breath."

"Not gonna work anyway," she said.

I kept digging at the wood, one tiny splinter at a time. "Maybe they'll see it poking up through the dirt."

"What if we send up some smoke?" she said.

"How we gonna do that?"

She pawed through her backpack. "Look." I turned on the cell phone and saw a matchbook from the Blue Room.

I kept digging. "Keep 'em handy, but don't count on it. Lighting a fire in here would be incredibly dangerous."

"How could we be worse off than we are?"

"Believe me, it's possible." At least we were breathing. Death by fire would be hideous.

The tip of the scissors broke through the wood siding and a small line of dirt trickled onto my neck.

"I need another tool," I said, "this one's shot."

She felt the contents of the kit and handed me a pair of tweezers. I took them and began scratching at the tiny hole.

"I'm getting sleepy," she said.

"Stay awake," I said, digging. "I'm going to get us out of here."

After another hour or so, I'd widened the diameter of the hole to the size of a nickel. After resting a moment, I gave her the cell phone and asked her to open it, then I took her makeup bag, found a tiny piece of cotton, coated it with lip gloss, and pushed it into the small end of the wooden pipe stem to keep it from getting clogged with dirt. After that, I maneuvered the stem until the tip was at the hole.

"Say a prayer," I whispered, and pushed it upward. It pierced the dirt about four inches—and stopped.

"Hit something," I said.

"Be careful, it'll break," she said.

I withdrew it and pushed again, gently. It stopped again. Should I try to push it through and risk breaking it, or should I dig another hole?

We didn't have time for that. But breaking it now would wreck our only exit strategy and crush our fragile spirits.

It would be a couple of hours, at least, before a sunrise burial brought people to the grave.

I didn't push on the stem. Not yet. "We'll hold what we've got for the time being," I said.

She didn't argue. We were both getting dizzy. We needed the breathing tube.

THE BANK WOULDN'T BE OPEN to the public for another ten minutes but Borden B. Bishop III and Spin Patterson were already in Bishop's office finishing up their business. Spin had presented Bishop with the partnership modification he'd forced Max to sign, and Bishop had read it through. Because Spin had written the document himself, it lacked a certain legal style, but that didn't necessarily make it void, and Bishop wasn't suggesting it did.

Still, given the magnitude of what Spin was requesting—that the entire $325 million in the partnership's account be declared a loan from Spin and return to his personal account—there were the inevitable banking formalities Bishop needed to follow before the transfer could be made.

"How long are we talking about?" Spin said.

"I'll get the bank's lawyers to review the document right away and have the money transferred into your account before three this afternoon," Bishop said. He gathered up the bank's internal authorization documents he'd asked Spin to sign and put them into a manila folder along with the partnership modification.

"So where are you off to?" Bishop said.

"Mexico," Spin said. "I'm speaking at the International Petroleum Association's convention in Tampico."

"You fishing before or after?"

"Max and Tacoma are taking a boat out tonight from Tampico harbor, and I'll helicopter out and join them tomorrow." Spin liked Bishop's curiosity; it gave him the chance to make a record that Max and Tacoma were going fishing together. If he decided not to dig them up, Bishop would support the story that they'd disappeared at sea.

"What do you fish for down there?"

"Marlin, blackfin tuna, sailfish, dolphin. Depends on what's running." Spin looked at his watch. "Listen, Will McLennon's supposed to meet me here at ten, but I'm afraid I can't wait for him. Would you give him this when he gets here?" Spin pulled a white envelope out of his pocket and laid it on Bishop's desk.

"No problem," Bishop said.

"Tell him to come by my office at noon and say hello," Spin said. He'd tell Will that Max and Tacoma were going with him to Mexico, too.

They stood up, shook hands, and both headed for the door.

"Have a great trip, Spin," Bishop said, ushering him out. "And don't worry, the money will be in your account before you know it."

BORDEN B. BISHOP III HADN'T gotten back to his desk before his phone rang with a call from his secretary. "Mr. Bishop," she said, "there's a Mr. Will McLennon here to see you."

"Send him in," Bishop said.

Will came over to Bishop, who was still standing. "Glad to see you, Mr. McLennon," Bishop said, shaking hands. "Have a seat. Did you see Spin on your way in?"

"No. He's supposed to meet me here."

"So he said, but unfortunately he had to run." Bishop picked up the white envelope on his desk and handed it to Will. "He asked me to give you this."

Will opened it and pulled out a check for $250,000 drawn on Spin's account. "Well, thanks, Mr. Bishop, this is what I came for." He stood up to go.

"He asked you to come by his office at noon," Bishop said. He saw a manila folder on his desk, opened it, read the top page, and said, "I wonder if you'd do me a favor, Will."

"Sure, what is it?"

"Spin left this here a few minutes ago. Would you mind giving it to him when you see him?" Bishop handed the folder to Will. "It's the itinerary for his trip to Mexico."

"No problem," Will said. "Maybe I can catch him downstairs."

"Appreciate that," Bishop said, and he shook hands good-bye.

Will left the bank building and walked to the lot next door where he'd parked, but Spin's limousine was nowhere in sight. Maybe it was parked on the street, or maybe he'd already left.

Will left the parking lot, turned the corner of the building, and saw Spin's Cadillac sitting at the curb. Evidently he'd driven himself to the bank instead of taking his limo.

He went up to the car and looked in the driver's-side window, but there was no one inside. Seeing no sign of Spin, he walked into a diner on the corner and took a table by the window where he could see Spin when he returned to his car. Then he ordered breakfast: three eggs over easy, white toast, home fries, sausage, and coffee, black.

Waiting for his food and Spin, he opened the folder Bishop had given him.

The first page was marked ITINERARY—TAMPICO, MEXICO.

He glanced at it and turned to the next page, which was headed PROVISIONS FOR BOAT. A note on top said, *Puck: Here's what Tacoma wants on board.* Below it was a list of things like fresh mango, canned tuna, champagne, red caviar, and a dozen other items.

Halfway down was another note that said, *Here's what Max wants.* The list included frozen waffles, fresh bananas, canned salmon, peanut butter, jelly, and about ten more items.

Will closed the folder and stared out the window, waiting for his food to come and Spin to return to his car.

All at once his knee stopped jiggling and he opened the folder and read it again. He closed it and stared at the place mat on his table. Before his food arrived, he canceled his order and left.

SPIN AND PUCK SAT IN PUCK'S pickup truck with Spin in the passenger seat and Puck behind the wheel. Puck was drinking a Coke through a straw stuck in a plastic cup cover.

"Why'd she do it?" Spin said to Puck, his eyes focused on the windshield. "I've been up all night asking myself, and I still don't have an answer."

Puck drew on the straw.

"I mean, I know why Max did it," Spin said. "But why'd *she* do it?"

"Somebody put a burr under her saddle," Puck said.

"She's always been on my side," Spin said. "She knows we've got a great future, so why'd she give it up? For what?"

Puck tapped his hand on the steering wheel.

"You know her pretty well, Puck. If we take her out of the box, will she rat me out?"

"She tried to take your money, boss."

"But if she's *with* me, she can have all the money she wants."

"What about Max?" Puck said.

Spin put the heels of his hands into his eye sockets and rubbed them with a grimace. "He's been like my son."

"Can you trust him not to go to the DA?"

"I want to, but . . ." Spin hit the dashboard with the palm of his hand. "Dammit!"

Puck drew some Coke into his mouth. "What do you want me to do, boss?"

"You're in this pickle barrel yourself, Puck."

"I'm with you either way, but if you ask me, I don't see how you can trust either one of them."

Spin stared ahead without answering.

"Just my opinion," Puck said.

Spin looked at his watch. His heart ached, his head ached, and his jaw muscles ached from grinding his teeth all night. He'd always managed the tough spots in his life, always talked his way into clubs and out of jams, always come out of the swamp smelling as fresh as a daisy. But never had someone betrayed him like this.

Never.

Puck said, "They may not even still be alive, you know? They're getting no more air than you get through this straw."

"It's enough," Spin said.

"OK. So, what do you want to do?"

Spin looked out the window for a long time, then turned away with his eyes clear and his agony finished. He'd finally made up his mind.

Without saying a word, he reached toward Puck's drink, took hold of the straw, and slowly pulled it out of the cup. Then he gathered the plastic tube into the palm of his hand and crushed it.

Puck looked at him a minute to be sure he had no second thoughts. Spin didn't move. Puck started the truck's engine.

Spin got out and headed for his Cadillac.

"WHAT IS THAT?" TACOMA'S voice was whispery and raw.

"What's what?" I said.

"I heard something."

We stopped breathing through the tube and listened. The sound of my pulse in my ears was deafening.

There were footfalls above our faces. Someone was walking on our grave.

The steps stopped. Was it the gravedigger? Was it Spin?

I grabbed hold of the pipe stem and got ready to push it through.

"Get ready," I said. Tacoma flipped up the cell phone and lit up the coffin. We'd created a cigarette by using the broken cuticle scissors to cut off a lock of her hair and rolling it in the tissue paper of a Tampax. We'd have one chance to do this right—if that.

Tacoma put the cigarette to her lips, pulled a match out of the book, laid the head of it on the scratchpad, and got ready to light it.

"I'm going to push up the pipe stem, blow out the cotton stuffing, and breathe in to see if we've hit air. If we have, you have to light up the cigarette, take a big mouthful of smoke, put your mouth on the stem, and blow as hard as you can. You ready?"

She nodded.

"I'm gonna take one last drag on the breathing tube first. Here goes."

As I put my mouth around the tube and got ready to draw

in a lungful of air, the tube abruptly disappeared from my hand and mouth. Somebody had pulled it out of the box.

Not somebody. Spin or Puck.

Tacoma's face dropped and so did the cigarette.

"It's Spin!" I said. "He's going to suffocate us!"

"Oh, my God!"

"Hold still!" I said.

"We've got no air!"

"I know, I know! Hold still and listen!"

We heard nothing. That was it. He'd done all he needed to do to kill us. He'd pulled out our lifeline and left us there to suffocate.

"What's happening?" Tacoma said.

"I don't know, but we have to wait before we try the smoke ploy."

"We can't wait—we'll pass out!"

"If we do it now, whoever's out there will pull out the pipe, too!"

Tacoma closed her eyes. "I'll count to a hundred and then we do it." She started counting. When she got to ten, she said, "That's enough! We have to try!"

"Nobody's there but Spin!"

"I don't care—we have to try!"

I grabbed hold of the pipe stem and shoved it upward. It moved into the dirt—whether it was broken or not, I couldn't tell. I put my mouth on the end of it and blew as hard as I could. Nothing happened, it was like blowing on a clogged hose. I tried again, and this time the dirt and lip-glossed piece of cotton blew out the other end.

I felt air in my mouth.

"Light up!" I said.

Tacoma stuck the cigarette into her mouth and drew the match head across the striker. Yellow flame erupted and filled our tiny room with light and sulfur.

She lifted her shaking hand to the tip of the cigarette and drew in. The smell of burning hair joined the noxious fumes in our nostrils.

I placed my hand under her head and helped lift her mouth up to the end of the pipe stem. When her lips were firmly around it, she exhaled and fell back, coughing madly.

There was no breathing tube to help her.

Nothing happened above us.

"Give me the cigarette!" I said, but she was coughing too hard to respond. I found it, drew in a mouthful, placed my mouth on the stem, and exhaled. The smoke in my throat erupted in a cough. The insanity of it all was killing us. I crushed out the cigarette and we continued coughing in the blue light of the cell phone.

There was still no sign of anything happening above us.

"Max!" Tacoma yelled. "What are we going to do?"

I held her close, both of us coughing in closed mouths.

"It's over," she said, weeping softly.

This time I had no response.

THERE WAS A SOUND OVER our heads. Or so I thought. But I was getting dizzy, and the light on the cell phone seemed to be fading, although whether it was from a dying battery or lack of oxygen, I couldn't tell.

Another sound. A scraping sound on the other side of the box.

Puck—or Spin—had dug down to the wood with a tool—a trowel, a shovel, something.

There were three taps on the wood.

I took the cell phone and hit the top of the box three times in reply. I thought I'd hit it hard, but the sound was so weak I couldn't tell if the person on the other side could hear it.

Silence.

Silence.

Then the reverberating sound of steel on steel—*wham!—wham!—wham!*

The end of the crowbar came crashing through the box a few inches from my face.

Wham! More pounding. The hole widened with another punch-through. There was the ripping sound of wood being pried away by the crowbar. The hole became big enough for me to feel cool, fresh air on my face.

More silence.

A blinding light—a flashlight beam—in my eyes.

A voice on the other side.

"Are you alive?"

I recognized the voice instantly.

It was Will.

WILL DUG US OUT WITH THE backhoe and a shovel. When he pried off the top of the box, we emerged into a dark, rainy day feeling more dead than alive.

As he helped Tacoma up to the edge of the grave, I saw Puck Tarver lying next to the box with his hands splayed out, unmoving. I couldn't tell if he was dead or unconscious—he looked the way he did the day he collapsed in the crane cab—but I was hoping he was dead. If he was alive, he wouldn't be for long once I got my hands on the crowbar.

I pulled myself up onto the lip of the grave and lay on my back breathing the rain-soaked air. Tacoma rested on her hands and knees, coughing and clearing her lungs.

Will came over to me and looked down. "I followed Puck and clocked him with the crowbar when I saw him pull the rubber tube out of the ground," he said.

"Why'd you follow him?" I said.

"I knew something was wrong when I read the list of things you wanted to eat on the boat."

"What boat?"

"The boat you're supposedly going fishing on in Mexico," he said. "The one he was gonna say you guys fell off of and drowned."

"What was on the list?" I said.

"Peanut butter. Ain't no way in heaven you'd ask for peanut butter, you've hated it since the day you were born."

I rolled over, got onto one knee, and staggered to my feet. Then I grabbed my brother with my hand behind his neck and held on to him.

His head dropped slightly, then his hands rose to me. I let go of his neck and we hugged.

"Sorry for the fuckups," he said.

"That's my line," I said, and we stepped apart.

"The groundkeeper's gonna be here any minute," he said, "we better get moving. Unless you want to talk to the cops."

No, I didn't, not yet. We finally had the goods on Spin—our own attempted murders—but this wasn't the time to make our play.

"I gotta get Tacoma home," I said. "Let's get her to my car."

THE RAINDROPS WERE LIKE small knocks on the door of an addled brain. Each one touched a nerve ending on the man's face and sent small messages to his cerebral cortex: *Wake up. Wake up. No need to sleep now, wake up.*

So that's what he did.

Puck opened his eyes and saw a pile of dirt in front of his nose. At first he couldn't get his bearings, didn't know where he was or how he'd gotten there, but then the neurons in his brain fired up and connected his memory to his consciousness. A few seconds later it all began coming back to him.

He was in the grave. The grave he and Spin had dug for Tacoma and Max. He'd pulled the breathing tube out of the box and was coiling it into a ball when he heard footsteps behind him . . . turned to see who it was . . . and . . . and that's all he could remember.

Someone had followed him and hit him over the head.

Whoever it was, why hadn't they called the police? Or the caretaker?

He struggled to his feet, shaking his head to clear his mind, and climbed out of the hole onto the apron around the grave. After resting a second, he pulled himself to his feet and staggered toward the paved path that rose up the gentle rise.

Follow the yellow brick road. Your truck is at the other end.

IT WAS STILL RAINING WHEN Tacoma and I pulled up to the front of her apartment building. She preferred to skip seeing a doctor and wanted to go home, so I was idling at the curb in front of her building, waiting for the doorman to come and get her. When he did, I told him to give her a hand and make sure a security guard entered her apartment first to be certain there was no one inside. I told her to pack fast and I'd go home and clean up and come back in an hour. We hugged each other and she got out. I waited until I saw her and the doorman safely inside.

I was turning the corner when I saw a car up ahead stop at a traffic light, its brake lights bright red.

Not just a car, a black Cadillac Deville.

I stopped and looked.

It was Spin. He must have just left the apartment building garage.

The traffic light turned green and his car started up.

I followed.

ONLY HOURS BEFORE, SPIN had been wistful about Tacoma, but now he saw things in a more practical light. They were in Spin's Cadillac Deville with Puck behind the wheel, Spin in the passenger seat, and Lightning curled up on the rear seat. Their objective: Hobby International Airport, where Wally was waiting in the cockpit of Spin's Hawker 800XP.

He'd been in survival mode before and knew that it put him at his best. Things were a mess, but not beyond control. If you stayed cool and played your cards right, they never were.

He knew most of what he had to do, and what he didn't know, he'd figure out.

He always did.

MY WINDSHIELD WIPERS WERE beating hard, but I recognised the tail light configuration of Spin's Cadillac and didn't lose sight of it. He was cruising at about seventy—nothing my Z4 couldn't handle.

I fished Tacoma's cell phone out of her backpack on the passenger seat and flipped it open. The light came on, but the battery indicator said Low. We'd used up most of it in the box.

I dialed the apartment number and hit Send. A few seconds later, she answered.

"Hello?"

"It's me," I said. "I'm on the tail of Spin's car."

"Where?"

"Interstate 45 south. Any idea where he's going?"

"That's the way to Hobby! He's going to his plane!"

I pictured him skipping town. "Not if I can help it."

"Don't try to stop him, Max! Puck's carrying a gun!"

I already knew that. I passed a car and slid in behind another between me and Spin.

"Max, listen to me! It's time to call the police!"

"He's exiting Monroe Road."

"That'll take him to a road that goes to the private-aircraft terminal. Listen to me, Max—"

"I'll call you in a minute."

PUCK TURNED TO SPIN, PUT down his cell phone, and said, "The plane's ready to go." He took a turn off I-45 onto Monroe Road. It was noon but it was raining so hard it could have been midnight. They were ten minutes away.

A sign on the road said ROAD WORK AHEAD. Puck was still doing seventy, which was shoulder speed in Texas. He looked in the mirror again. "I think somebody's following us."

Spin looked out the back window. Sensing something afoot, Lightning sat up. It was raining too hard to be sure, but Spin thought the grill on the car had the double-kidney grill of a BMW. Not just any BMW, a Z4.

He knew who it was even before he confirmed it.

"We're in luck!" he said. "It's Max."

I TRIED TO IMAGINE THE POSSIBLE scenarios: We get to a security gate at the airport, Spin goes in, I get stopped, end of chase. Two: We go through the gate, he drives up to the jet, so do I, and I'm out there on a tarmac with no witnesses or protection. End of chase and worse. Three: I call the police, it takes ten minutes to describe what's happening, another ten while they repeat it back to me, twenty minutes for a patrol car to get there, and by that time Spin is off to wherever.

I called Tacoma. "Call the cops," I said, "and try to convince them to keep his plane on the ground." I hung up and was searching for Spin's cell phone number when the phone rang in my hand.

"Hello?"

No answer. I looked in the message window. The caller's number was blocked. I put it back to my ear.

"Hello, Spin," I said. "That you?"

"HELLO, SPIN. THAT YOU?"

Spin heard Max's voice in his ear and hung up without answering. "It's him," he said to Puck. "If Tacoma's with him, we'll do it right this time. I knew we'd have another shot at this."

It was the way the cosmos worked. Even in his worst moments, he had an angel on his shoulder.

Orange construction barrels streaked by. Puck hit his high beams and put the windshield wipers on fast.

"Let's pull over and—"

There was a jolt in the rear of the car—Puck looked in the mirror—Max's Z4 had hit his bumper causing the Cadillac to fishtail to the right. Puck turned into the skid, swung back the other way, and straightened out on the wet road.

"That crazy son of a bitch!" Puck yelled. "He tried to spin me out!" He whipped off his seat belt to free up his chest and pulled out his gun from the shoulder holster beneath his jacket.

"Just stay on the road!" Spin yelled. He reached back and petted Lightning and got him to lie down.

Puck laid his weapon in the console between them and stomped on the accelerator.

THE CADILLAC WAS PULLING away, so I floored it. More orange triangle signs whizzed by in the rain. I saw their shape but not their messages.

Puck hit eighty. So did I. I wanted to put my front bumper up his tailpipes and nudge him again. More orange barrels whizzed by, then a huge reflective arrow pointing to the right.

The Cadillac's brake lights lit up in a visual scream.

I hit my brakes.

Both of us went into a skid to the left.

SPIN FELT THE CAR CRASH through an orange-and-white-striped barrier with warning signs—hit something that jarred his teeth—and launch itself off the ground. He was in a space vehicle that was rolling left in midair.

The silence felt eternal—then a flash—steel on concrete—metal screeching—air bags blowing—sparks showering—the world outside turning upside down. They were skidding along the road on their roof doing sixty miles an hour.

Spin got a glimpse of wooden frames holding freshly poured concrete a brief instant before the front of the car hit them. The Cadillac spun like a teacup on a carnival ride—centrifugal force pushed him against his seat belt—then another enormous crash—a white flash behind his eyes—crumpling sounds—broken glass behind him.

THE REAR END OF MY Z4 hit a wooden, zebra-striped post on the left, spun to the right, hit orange barrels filled with sand, spun back, and came to rest between the remains of a wooden fence that had been taken out by Spin's Cadillac. My front bumper was facing the side of the road. My left shoulder, already wrecked, felt numb. I used my right hand to feel my neck. The taste of blood was in my mouth and warm on my upper lip.

I turned my head to look at the road. Spin's Cadillac was upside down with steam pouring into the rain from the undercarriage. Its horn was blaring.

SPIN FELT NO MOVEMENT. THE car horn was blaring. He felt himself dangling upside down in his seat belt harness, his face pressed hard against the dashboard, the seat behind him jammed forward. He felt the car start to move in a circle, then realized it wasn't the car, it was his head. Everything seemed to be moving slowly now, even the wheel bearings as the spinning tires came to a stop.

He blinked, focused, and saw Puck crumpled between the windshield and the roof, motionless, his neck bent at a bizarre angle to the right, his mouth open, his eyes staring dead ahead. The last time he'd seen Puck look like this was in the crane cab on Wild Stallion.

My God. This time he really was gone.

Lightning—*where's Lightning?*

Spin tried to raise his hands to push himself away from the dash, but he couldn't find anything to push against. Slowly, he worked his right hand up to his side, which meant from the car's roof toward the door, searching for the handle. He found it and pulled, but nothing happened; the door stayed closed.

He was trapped.

I GOT OUT OF MY CAR AND STUMBLED toward a mound of construction sand near wooden forms that had been poured with concrete. I could smell rain and the hot steel of the Cadillac. Its horn was whining higher and higher now, and in a few minutes finally petered out. I sat on the pile of sand watching raindrops dancing in front of the Cadillac's headlights, trying to get my bearings.

I stood up and limped toward Spin's car, then stopped myself with my first rational thought of the day: *Careful—he's got a gun.*

I circled the Cadillac, trying to see through the upside-down windows. The passenger side was covered with a layer of silt. Stooping down to get a better view, I saw the palm of a hand pressing against the window, now moving away, now pressing again, searching for an escape. Coming closer, I saw Spin's upside-down face on the other side. And he saw mine.

He looked frantic. He tried to talk through the glass. I could see his lips moving but couldn't make out the words. But then, I didn't need to: The message was clear. He wanted out.

I made the sign of a gun with my cocked finger.

He shook his head No! and put his hand against the window to show it was empty. His lips formed the words *Open the door!*

I sat back on my haunches. Open the door? The police could do that, not me. It was over now—the sting, Spin's charade, everything. There'd be trouble ahead for all of us, but most of it would be Spin's. It felt OK to be sitting there with nothing to do but wait.

That's when I smelled it.

GASOLINE.

Spin smelled it at the same time. His hands stopped moving and he went quiet like a bird dog sniffing the wind.

Then he lost it.

"Open the door! Open the door!" He was yelling so loudly I could hear him through the glass.

I reached for the door handle with my good right hand and pulled.

It didn't open.

He yelled again, "Open the door, Max! Open the door!"

I tried again. This time, the door gave an inch and stopped.

"Both hands!" he yelled through the crack.

Both might have done the trick, but thanks to his using the lobster claw on me, my left arm and hand were useless. The smell of raw gas mixed with the smell of heat. Then, like a drop of water hitting a hot skillet, a drop of gas hit the engine block. A small *poof* announced fire beneath the hood.

Spin was yelling madly now, pounding the window with his fist.

I pulled at the door again, but there was no more movement, no opening big enough for my foot, nothing to work with.

The fire beneath the hood was getting bigger.

Smoke was beginning to curl from the engine compartment into the car's interior. Spin's eyes were enormous, his mouth open. I pulled on the door again and opened it two more inches.

"Open it!" he yelled. "Keep pulling!"

I stood up and ran to the crashed wooden barrier, found a splintered board, and brought it back to the car. By the time I got there, smoke was billowing out of the crack in the door and Spin was coughing violently.

I jammed the board into the opening, felt it hit his shoulder, and leaned against it with all my weight.

The door opened another few inches.

Fire broke out beneath the steering column.

Spin was yelling incoherently.

The smell of gas was everywhere. The car was about to blow.

I jammed the board in again and leaned on it. The smell of burning flesh—Puck's, Spin's, who knew—mingled with the smell of smoke and gas. I was coughing hard, my eyes watering. The door opened a few more inches.

Spin was still yelling—then he stopped.

I yanked the door open another few inches and kept at it until it was open wide. The heat was intense. I fumbled for the lock on his seat belt, found it, and pressed hard. He fell into a heap on the inside of the car's roof. Smoke was billowing out so hard I couldn't see him, but I found his arm, took hold of it, and pulled. He was limp, unable to help. I pulled again and his head fell through the door. His eyes came open but didn't focus. He mumbled something unintelligible. I kept pulling. He tried to talk again, and this time I got it.

"Lightning," he said in a hoarse grunt.

Lightning?

I coughed, grabbed him by the belt on his pants, and pulled. The flames were engulfing the entire front seat compartment. I dragged him out. His jacket and pants were smoking, and so were his shoes. His hair was mostly gone.

I looked and saw Lightning lying behind the broken backseat, protected from the flames but not the heat, gas, or smoke. I opened the back door, reached in, got a grip on his mane, and pulled. He slid down to the car ceiling and through the door onto the ground.

I caught my breath and dragged Spin away until we were

close to the mound of sand, then I went back for Lightning and carried him over to Spin and set him down. He was breathing hard the way dogs do when they're hurt, licking his chops, squinting and blinking the smoke out of his eyes. But he hadn't been burned.

The car burst into bright orange and settled into a bonfire that burned with a roar.

I sat on the ground next to Lightning to catch my breath. The rain cooled my face. Spin was on his back staring straight up, his eyelids moving, his arms resting at his sides.

"I'm going to call an ambulance!" I yelled.

His right arm rose from the elbow and his fingers opened and closed, begging me to come closer.

I crawled over to him and put my ear close to his lips.

"Lightning . . ."

"He's OK," I said. "He's out of the car and he's OK."

Spin's fingers moved again, bidding me to come closer still. I put my ear near his mouth and heard him quietly gasp for air.

"Don't talk," I said.

". . . bad luck . . . ," he said.

"Don't talk, don't talk!"

". . . need to stay away from . . . burning Cadillacs."

I took his hand in mine and felt him try to squeeze it. His spirit was willing, but the flesh was no longer there. I let go, stood up, and walked to my car to get the cell phone. As I neared it, I could hear a siren down the road and saw cruiser lights flashing in the mist. Tacoma had evidently already called them.

I limped back to Spin. Lightning had crawled over to him and was licking his face and whimpering. Spin's hand was still up in the air and his eyes were open. I yelled at him to hang on, an ambulance was on its way. I thought he understood what I'd said, but it was only my imagination. When I reached him and put my ear near his mouth to hear him whisper his reply, I got nothing.

He was gone.

SIX MONTHS LATER

IT WAS THE GROUNDBREAKING ceremony of the soon-to-be-built College of the Cherokee Nation, an occasion for a reunion of sorts. Tacoma was there, smiling radiantly, and so were Jenny and her two kids, Angela and the guys, various friends from Gulf-Tex, and a crowd of well-wishers. The foundation's chairman, a lawyer from Oklahoma who'd known Spin as a fellow trustee at the Sierra Club, was about to speak.

In order to get to the groundbreaking ceremony, everyone had to cross a muddy patch bridged with boards on cinder blocks. I saw Spin's daughter Trish stranded on a cinder block, the board she was trying to walk on sitting in the mud. Then I saw a young man in a sport coat, slacks, and shiny oxfords replace the board and come to her rescue. She smiled at him as he took her by the hand and led her safely to the other side. After nodding to her politely, he continued on his way.

After the car crash, the police report closed the matter as an accident and we never had to own up to the sting after all. The modification agreement I'd signed under duress at the cemetery didn't hold up when the bank's lawyers reviewed it, so the cash wasn't transferred to Spin's account. Because of Tacoma's sleight of hand on the partnership agreement—and Spin's insistence that the surviving partner inherit all the partnership's assets—I found myself with $325 million in the bank.

My agreement with Audrey was that she'd divide the proceeds as she saw fit, and a deal was a deal. She could have argued that all the money belonged to her, considering the company was her father's before Spin took over, but she knew she wouldn't have seen a penny of it without the sting, and she wanted to split it up fairly. After her out-of-pocket expenses were reimbursed, the roughnecks and their families were made whole on their stock losses, then the college foundation was funded, then the remaining money was split between Audrey and a fund we established for other Gulf-Tex employees who'd taken a bath from Spin's game. When all that was done, Audrey wrote a big check to me out of her portion of the money. Even after taxes, I did very well. And so did Will. A check to him was the first one I wrote.

Spin took the biggest loss, of course, but even he wasn't doing as badly as you might have thought. In his will, he'd bequeathed most of his wealth—if he had any—to his two girls, some to the Sierra Club, some to a nonprofit corporation designed to bring the bounty of Black Eyes to the world, some to Tacoma, and some to me. Unfortunately, because he died broke and in debt, none of his wishes were fulfilled but one. It turned out that he'd sent five million dollars to the Cherokee College Fund before he went into the Black Eyes auction. That made me wonder if he knew he might lose his fortune that day and wanted to make good on his promise to Tacoma. Anyway, that's what I chose to believe.

After Tacoma and a few dignitaries stuck a shovel into the ground and turned some symbolic sod for the new college, the foundation chairman removed a purple velvet cover on a bust of "the man most responsible for this profound occasion, Spin Patterson." Polite applause followed, and the crowd grew quiet. The chairman turned and addressed Spin's likeness on the pedestal.

"Most of the world knew you by your public reputation, Spin, but those of us here today knew you for the man you really were: a loving father, a passionate protector of the environment, and an uncompromising fighter for the welfare of your shareholders and employees."

I could feel the roughnecks' silence roasting the air behind me.

"None of us will ever forget how you risked your fortune to create a technology that would bring peace and prosperity to the world, and none of us will ever forget how you risked your life to try to save your best friend in that noble mission, Joe Wright. How ironic that you survived a brutal hurricane only to fall victim to a gentle rain."

I looked at Tacoma out of the corner of my eye, but her eyes remained straight ahead.

"Even though you succeeded in ways most men can only dream of," the chairman said, "you always gave the world more than you received—your money, your tireless energy, and, most of all, your integrity and extraordinary moral leadership. In an age of personal greed and corporate wrongdoing, your life stands as a beacon in the night."

Now I had to keep my eyes straight ahead.

"Because of you the world truly is a better place, Spin. For that we owe you our eternal gratitude and the thanks of everyone who had the good fortune to know you."

More polite applause and the ceremony ended.

The boss is dead. Long live the boss.

On our way to a reception tent, I found Audrey and gave her a big hug. "Take note," she said into my ear, "that no matter what bad thing you do in life, if you have enough money, you can buy respectability and adoration."

"I refuse to be cynical today," I said.

"Oh, please," she said. "By the way, Trish wants to know who the young man in the sport coat is—the one who helped her across the mud patch."

"His name's Jim Francesca."

"Who's that?"

"He was a roughneck for Gulf-Tex until the crash, then he worked at the country club for a while. Trish met him there last Christmas." Not only met him, tried to have him fired for wearing worn-out shoes.

"Really? She doesn't seem to remember him."

"Oh, I'm sure he remembers her," I said.

Audrey looked at me as if she wasn't going to see me for a

long time. "Come visit me before Christmas, would you?" she said.

"You can count on it."

She turned and left. I found Tacoma and we headed toward the reception and the champagne and cookies.

"They say you can't take it with you," she said, looking around the campus-to-be, "but look at what you can do if you try."

"I say we spend our money on something useful while we're still walking around," I said.

The cinder block in the mud patch was starting to sink, sending rivulets of watery goo across the board toward Tacoma's shoes. I put my arm around her waist and helped her cross it without getting her feet wet, then I slipped and stepped off the side into the muck myself. She laughed, stuck out her hand, and I climbed back onto dry ground.

On the way to the reception tent, I put my arm around her shoulder and she put hers around my waist. At that moment neither of us could have cared less about mud, shoes, or champagne.

A waiter gave us two glasses from a silver tray and moved on. We toasted each other, me with a smile, her with her gorgeous black eyes, and we drank. As the bubbles slid down my throat, I thought, it's great what money can buy, no doubt about it. But money didn't buy this, and never could, and there was something even better about that.

ACKNOWLEDGEMENTS

MELISSE ROSE HELPED ME GET a first draft together faster than I otherwise would have. Thanks for that, M.J.

Sue Fletcher is not only my publisher, but my story editor, line editor, and friend. She is the best.

For their technical help, I want to thank Roger Anderson, Bill Dillon, Art Johnson, Sam Leroy, Bland Lucas, and Roice Nelson. Any detours in the book from oil technology that exists, or might one day, is my doing, not theirs.

Thanks to my lawyer friends who made a big difference in the book, not only on legal matters, but more: Bob Cohen, Bill Feis, Eddy J. Rogers Jr., and Bill Zabel. Bill spent more time helping than he should have, and Eddy showed himself to be not only a legal resource but a fine all-around editor.

Thanks to Michael M. Thomas for his imaginative spitballing at the earliest stage of the book.

Kathleen Friery never gave up trying to make the book easier to read. No doubt she succeeded.

Susan Sosin, a world-class rock climber, explained the sport so well I wanted to try it myself.

Thanks to my early readers for improving the book by commenting on it before it was published: Bill B, Gloria B, Lindsay G, Melissa G, Robert G, Rafa J, Vicki M, Chris P, Katie P, Matt P, Paul P, Donna S, and Fran W.

Finally, I want to thank Elyse Weiner for her excellent reading of the book, her great support, and her willingness to "game" proposed fixes over hamburgers on the Hudson. More than once she pointed out places that needed help that I hadn't seen.

Imagine my horror.